"James writes smart, taut, high-octane thrillers. But be warned—his books are not for the timid. The endings blow me away every time."
—Mitch Galin, producer of Stephen King's *The Stand* and Frank Herbert's *Dune*

Praise for the Novels of Steven James

Opening Moves

"A mesmerizing read. From the first chapter, it sets its hook deep and drags you through a darkly gripping story with relentless power. My conclusion: I need to read more of Steven James."
—Michael Connelly, *New York Times* bestselling author of *The Drop*

"Steven James has created a fast-moving thriller with psychological depth and gripping action. *Opening Moves* is a smart, taut, intense novel of suspense that reads like a cross between Michael Connelly and Thomas Harris. Young detective Patrick Bowers battles his own demons as he uses his intellect and experience to track twisted killers. Full of twists and enjoyable surprise, *Opening Moves* is a blisteringly fast and riveting read."
—Mark Greaney, *New York Times* bestselling author of *Ballistic*

The Bishop

"The novel moves swiftly, with punchy dialogue but gruesome scenes. Readers must be ready to stomach the darkest side of humanity and get into the minds of serial killers to enjoy this master storyteller at the peak of his game." —*Publishers Weekly*

"This novel is fresh and exciting." —*Booklist*

"Absolutely brilliant."
—Jeff Buick, bestselling author of *One Child*

"Steven James's *The Bishop* should come with a warning: Don't start reading unless you're prepared to finish this book in a single sitting. Riveting!"
—Karen Dionne, International Thriller Writers Web site chair; managing editor, The Big Thrill

continued . . .

"*The Bishop*—full of plot twists, nightmarish villains, and family conflicts—kept me turning pages on a red-eye all the way from New York City to Amsterdam. Steven James tells stories that grab you by the collar and don't let go."
—Norb Vonnegut, author of *Top Producer*; editor of Acrimony.com

"Steven James locks you in a thrill ride with no brakes. He sets the new standard in suspense writing."
—*Suspense Magazine*

More Praise for Steven James and His Award-Winning Novels

"Once again, James has given us a rip-snorting thriller with a beating heart."
—*New York Times* bestselling author Eric Wilson

"James delivers . . . caffeinated plot twists and intriguing characterizations. Riveting . . . a gripping plot and brisk pacing will win James some fans eager for his next offering."
—*Publishers Weekly* (starred review)

"[An] exceptional psychological thriller."
—Armchair Interviews

"Brilliant. . . . Steven James gives us a captivating look at the fine line between good and evil in the human heart. Not to be missed."
—Ann Tatlock, Christy Award–winning author

"Exquisite."
—Fiction Fanatics Only!

"Best story of the year—perfectly executed."
—The Suspense Zone (2008 Reviewer's Choice Award)

"In a word, intense."
—Mysterious Reviews

"Steven James writes at a breakneck pace, effortlessly pulling the reader along on this incredible thrill ride."
—Fiction Addict

THE BOWERS FILES

THE KING

THE BOWERS FILES

STEVEN JAMES

A SIGNET SELECT BOOK

SIGNET SELECT
Published by the Penguin Group
Penguin Group (USA) Inc., 375 Hudson Street,
New York, New York 10014, USA

USA | Canada | UK | Ireland | Australia | New Zealand | India | South Africa | China

Penguin Books Ltd., Registered Offices: 80 Strand, London WC2R 0RL, England
For more information about the Penguin Group visit penguin.com.

First published by Signet Select, an imprint of New American Library,
a division of Penguin Group (USA) Inc.

First Printing, July 2013

Copyright © Steven James, 2013
All rights reserved. No part of this book may be reproduced, scanned, or distributed in any printed or electronic form without permission. Please do not
participate in or encourage piracy of copyrighted materials in violation of the
author's rights. Purchase only authorized editions.

SIGNET SELECT and logo are trademarks of Penguin Group (USA) Inc.

ISBN 978-0-451-23978-5

Printed in the United States of America

10 9 8 7 6 5 4 3 2 1

PUBLISHER'S NOTE
This is a work of fiction. Names, characters, places, and incidents either are
the product of the author's imagination or are used fictitiously, and any re-
semblance to actual persons, living or dead, business establishments, events, or
locales is entirely coincidental.
    The publisher does not have any control over and does not assume any re-
sponsibility for author or third-party Web sites or their content.

If you purchased this book without a cover you should be aware that this book
is stolen property. It was reported as "unsold and destroyed" to the publisher
and neither the author nor the publisher has received any payment for this
"stripped book."

ALWAYS LEARNING   PEARSON

To Matt and Shawna

Dum vivimus vivamus.

A Wasp settled on the head of a Snake, and not only stung him several times, but clung obstinately to the head of his victim. Maddened with pain the Snake tried every means he could think of to get rid of the creature, but without success. At last he became desperate, and crying, "Kill you I will, even at the cost of my own life," he laid his head with the Wasp on it under the wheel of a passing wagon, and they both perished together.

—From *Aesop's Fables: A New Translation* by V. S. Vernon Jones, with illustrations by Arthur Rackham (1912)

Prologue

When Corey Wellington woke up at 5:14 a.m., he had no intention of killing himself.

Over the last twenty years the thought of taking his own life had, in fact, crossed his mind many times, but never as clearly, as distinctly, as that first time, when he was a junior in high school and Caitlyn Vaughn stood him up at prom, and everyone knew about it, and it felt like someone had knocked his feet out from under him and hit him with a baseball bat in the gut at the same time.

In retrospect it seemed silly, childish even—feeling so devastated by something so inconsequential—but at the time it'd felt like his entire world had crumbled.

That night he'd gone to his father's den in the basement and taken the key to the gun cabinet from the desk drawer where his dad kept it, where he'd thought it was safely hidden from his two curious children.

Corey had opened the gun case, loaded one of the revolvers, and then sat at the desk for a long time with the handgun cradled in his hands.

It felt cold and heavier than it looked.

Wonder, dreams, hopes, all those things that make life livable seemed to be slipping away like a stream of spent possibilities. There was nothing he could think of that he looked forward to: not summer vacation or his senior year or seeing any movie or listening to any song or playing any video game or being with any girl.

It was as if everything that lay on the horizon of that moment held nothing but the promise of more rejection and despair without any hope of healing.

Yes, a girl can do that to you. Yes, she can rip out your reason for living, just like that, with one glance, one comment, one prom-night giggle when she blows you off and then jokes about it with her friends.

He'd raised the pistol and slid the end of the barrel into his mouth.

Can you ever really know the reason behind an action? Can you ever really tell for sure why you did one thing instead of another? That, yes, this is why you quit your job, bought the Toyota instead of the Ford, ordered spaghetti rather than pizza, didn't pull the trigger when you had the chance.

Maybe it was cowardice, maybe it was some strange breed of courage that kept him from putting a bullet in his brain that night, but at last he'd replaced the revolver and ammunition in the cabinet, and no one had ever known that he'd had a gun barrel clenched between his teeth and his finger pressed against the trigger on prom night.

In the months that followed, thinking about how close he'd come to ending it all had frightened him, and he'd found a persistent heaviness lurking on the edge of his thoughts. Eventually, he'd started taking meds to quiet the depression and keep those thoughts of irreversible solutions away, but still, over the years, it had stolen one marriage, two jobs, and any number of friends from him.

But not since that night in high school two decades earlier had the thought come to him as overpoweringly as it did today: *Kill yourself, Corey. Take your life. This is something you can do right now. This very day.*

5:21 a.m.

He found his way to the kitchen, put on some coffee just like he did every day, drew a hand across his head to calm his tangled mop of slightly graying hair, and ate two doughnuts and an apple whose skin was beginning to wrinkle.

His thoughts chased each other around in an ever-shrinking circle. *I wonder what it would be like to be dead. To finally be free of all the hardships and struggles and disappointments of life.*

Then another series of thoughts: *What disappointments, Corey? Your life is not that bad!*

Things at the law firm were good, his health was fine, he hadn't been diagnosed with cancer or received any other shattering news. But still, for some reason, he found his eyes drifting around the kitchen until they landed on the wooden knife block beside the microwave on the countertop.

Yes, yes, he realized that he really did want to commit suicide, or self-murder, as it used to be so aptly called.

Self.

Murder.

It was true that two weeks ago he'd broken off a relationship with a woman whom he'd been seeing for eight months. Maybe that was causing this. Maybe some form of repressed anger or undealt-with loss was to blame, but he'd realized he wasn't in love with her anymore, and when he told her, he'd found that, apparently, the feeling was mutual.

He'd dealt pretty well with the breakup, and as far as he knew, his ex-girlfriend was doing alright too.

However, now as he thought of it all again, it was as if part of his mind was trying to use that breakup as a justification for letting him think the final, dark things he was considering.

You can't make a relationship work, Corey. It's because of who you are. You can't change who you are.

5:29 a.m.

He eyed that alluring block of knives. They were certainly sharp enough; he knew this because he'd nearly cut his finger to the bone last month while slicing a tomato for his salad.

Yes, a knife was definitely a possibility—wrists, neck, inside of his upper arm. He didn't know what that artery in the arm was called, but it was an important one, he knew that, one that was nearly impossible to quell the bleeding of once it was slit.

Maybe.

Stop it, Corey!

His gaze traveled toward the sink.

There was bleach below it. He guessed that if he swallowed a cupful of that, it would burn through his tongue, his throat, his stomach, kill him from the inside out.

A horrible way to die, to be murdered by yourself, but still he went to the sink, pulled out the bottle, and read the warning: *Harmful or fatal if swallowed! Call a physician or poison control center immediately. Do not induce vomiting. Seek advanced medical care at once!*

Yes, a good long guzzle of that would do it.

What are you even doing here, Corey? This train of thought, you can't let yourself—

But think of it, though. No more breakups or pain, no more heartache or questions or fear, not ever again.

He dialed off the cap to the bleach, but as he brought the bottle to his mouth, the sharp, acrid smell drew him up short. He couldn't imagine that liquid inside of him, that chemical killing him in a way he wouldn't wish on his worst enemy.

But you don't have any enemies, Corey. You don't! You need to get ahold of yourself here, you need to—

He returned the bleach to its home in the cabinet but found himself unable to drive the urge away, that unsettling discomfort, that gathering of terrible thoughts coming together like a convergence of vultures inside his head.

A convergence.

Of.

Vultures.

Self-murder. Yes. You can do this. This is something you can do. Today.

There was still climbing rope in the basement from the times he'd gone out while he was in college. There was a chimney on the roof of his house. He could use that. Tie a good strong knot, loop the other end around his neck, get a running start—

Get control of yourself, Corey!

He rubbed his head, then went to the bathroom, took a shower, tugged on some clothes. He checked his e-mail just to do something normal, to think something normal, to try putting things back into perspective again.

But all the while, it was as if this idea of suicide had lodged in his brain and grown roots. It seemed like a temptation that he could think of fewer and fewer reasons to resist, something he didn't simply want to avoid, but something he consciously wanted to do.

5:44 a.m.

A few years ago his psychiatrist had told him that depression was anger turned inward, but Corey knew that wasn't right. Anger is a symptom of depression, not its cause. Anyone who's dealt with depression can tell you that.

Depression begins with a small disappointment and spirals downward, inward, out of control, like a blackness circling in on itself, pulling in everything else around it, sucking it all in, funneling it out of sight.

Sometimes anger is your only ally, because it gives you something to feel when the rest of your life turns numb. It gives you something to fight against when you feel like giving up. More often than not, it's when the anger dissipates, not when it arrives, that you're in trouble.

And right now, Corey was not feeling angry, but resolute.

It's just the depression. Fight against it.

No, you'll lose. It runs in the family, Corey.

Like mother, like son.

Though she'd been dead nearly three decades, he could still remember the desperation he felt whenever his dad would leave on his truck routes, still hear the sound of his mother's sharp words and the smack of her slapping the face of his older sister, still see her shuffling from the couch to the kitchen to get to a bottle. "Escape in a liquid dream," she called it.

Often she would lock herself in her bedroom. He could hear her crying in there, sometimes for hours. He would knock on the door and call to her, "Mommy, don't cry. It's okay." He was a seven-year-old, too little to know he was doing no good.

Though his older sister tried to reassure him and told him everything was going to be okay, in the end she'd been wrong. His mother didn't find escape in a liquid dream. The nightmares that'd haunted her for so long won on the day she swallowed that handful of pills.

5:51 a.m.

Corey felt his heart race.

An inexplicable sense of urgency swept over him.

You could get a gun like you were going to use in high school. Or use pills like Mom. Or jump from a bridge or a railroad trestle. A cliff. There are plenty of—

Another voice inside of him shouted, *Stop it!*

Drowning? Tying a weight to your feet and jumping into Allatoona Lake? Suffocation? A plastic bag over your head?

He considered those last two options for a moment but realized that to him, the thought of drowning or suffocating was simply too disturbing.

A blade, yes.

A knife really was the best choice.

But not slitting an artery. Something more honorable.

He could stab it into his abdomen—yes, yes—lean forward onto the blade like samurais did long ago. But he would need to make sure the blade was long enough to angle up into his heart. He didn't know much about stab wounds, but he'd heard enough to know that if he ended up stabbing himself just in the abdomen, it would take him a long time to die. And it would not be a pleasant death at all. He would make sure that he didn't—

Why? Why are you even thinking this?!

Because you're a corpse in the making, Corey. Just like everyone. But you have control over the moment when you reach your destiny. And unlike most people, you have the courage to make it happen today. Right here. Right now.

How do people live with the knowledge that they'll be gone so soon? How do they go about their daily lives, watch their movies, sip their cappuccinos, birth their babies, and go to school or work or church with the knowledge that they might stop breathing any second?

Denial.

Constant denial.

It's the only way.

Unless there's something better waiting for you after death, Corey.

Yes, unless.

He returned to the kitchen, went to the knife block, removed the longest one, and walked to the living room.

Not all of us succeed in this life, but there's one thing everyone who's ever been born has succeeded at—dying. And the world simply twirls on, the universe forgetting we were ever here.

Corey went to the living room, where he could have a view of the forest outside, the woods opening wide and full in the spring. There's nothing like spring in Atlanta.

He would die looking at the blossoming trees.

With each moment the question of why he was doing

this felt less and less pertinent, like a blurry memory someone he used to be was having.

Free will.

Free to live, to choose.

Free to die, if we desire it.

Kneeling, he drew his shirt up and positioned the tip of the blade against his stomach just below the sternum.

Like mother, like son.

Get this right. You need to get this right or it's going to be a long and messy, messy death.

When the decision finally came, it was almost a reassurance that finally, now, things could move on, just as they were meant to, a man passing away into his destiny in the grave.

He let out a deep breath to relax the muscles in his abdomen so the blade would slide in easier, then he tightened his grip on the knife's handle so it would go in at the proper angle.

Corey closed his eyes.

And with a swift, smooth motion he drove the blade high into his abdomen aimed at his heart as he leaned forward and then used the force of impact with the floor to bury the knife in up to the handle.

He fell limply to the side.

There was less pain than he expected.

At first.

But based on the position of the handle he guessed the tip had found its mark.

The pain began as a tight circle of warmth unfurling through him, turning hotter and brighter with every passing second until it felt like a strange companion, as if it were something he'd always had close by, but had only now, in this moment, begun to experience fully.

He wasn't certain he'd hit his heart, but it must have been close, because with each heartbeat, the handle quivered slightly, as if it were choreographed to do so, somehow programmed to move in sync with the arrival of his death.

That's when the pain began convulsing through him, and that's when the questions came.

He wondered if hell was real, if that's where he would go for doing this, for taking his own life—for this self-murder—or if heaven awaited him, if he'd ever done enough to deserve it.

A preacher's words came to him from a sermon he'd heard on the radio one time while driving through central Georgia: "It's not about what *you have done for God*, brothers and sisters, but about what *God has done for you*. Amen?"

So, had he believed in that enough to receive it?

Your mother—is she in heaven? Did she go to hell for the things she did to her children on those days when she'd had too much to drink? Will you see her again when you die?

Just seconds after he thought that, he heard the front door click open.

Confused, Corey turned his head toward the hallway, but with no clear view to the front of the house, he saw nothing.

However, he did hear footsteps coming down the hall: two people, he thought, but it was hard to tell, because sound and light were merging with the pain rushing through him, the pain that was engulfing every one of his senses and then blistering apart inside of his chest.

Reality itself was becoming fuzzy around the edges.

All so confusing.

And it hurt. It really, really hurt.

He grasped the handle to draw out the blade, but as soon as he moved it even just slightly, a new shot of pain ripped through him and he had to let go.

He drew in a weak breath and watched the handle quiver as he did.

The footsteps drew closer.

"Who's there?" He tried to speak loudly, but the words were so soft that he was certain no one could have heard them—not even if they'd been in the room with him.

The pain grew tighter and sharper with each breath. Dying wasn't turning out to be at all like they made it seem in the movies. This was no gentle escape into the unknown, this was more like a terrifying descent into a scream you've tried your whole life to hold back inside of you.

"Help me, I . . ." This time the words were even softer, barely louder than a breath—

A voice came from the hallway, strong, masculine: "He's in here!"

A woman and a young man whom Corey didn't recognize entered the living room and strode toward him. He wanted to tell them that he hadn't meant to do this, any of this, that he just hadn't been thinking clearly and had made a terrible mistake, and if they would only help him, he would be okay and—

The man knelt beside him and pressed a pair of fingers gently against the side of Corey's neck to check his pulse. "He's still alive."

The woman watched silently. "Give it a few minutes. It shouldn't be long."

A cold gust of fear swallowed Corey.

The man moved back to his partner's side.

No!

Corey tried to cry out for help but ended up making no sound at all.

And that was the last time he would try to speak, the last time he would try to do anything at all, because after that everything that happened was natural and inevitable and no longer a matter of the will. Nature ran its course, the universe claimed its next life, and at 5:57 a.m. Corey Wellington died in strangled, wet silence as the clock just above him on the wall ticked off the seconds, edging its way into the minutes and hours and years that might have been his to enjoy if only he had not chosen to murder himself.

The couple stood by until his chest was no longer moving. At last the man, who was twenty-five, blond and well built, checked Corey's pulse again. "Okay."

"Okay," the woman said. At thirty-six she was still in stunning shape, had short, stylish light red hair, distinctive green eyes, and a steely, unwavering gaze.

The man stood. "Do you ever wonder what's going through their minds when they do it?"

"I don't think that's something you would really want to find out."

"No. You're right. I . . . I just . . . I wonder sometimes."

She turned from the corpse. "Check the medicine cabinet. I'll look in the kitchen and the bedroom."

"Right."

After they'd retrieved what they'd come here for, as well as the two cameras that had been hidden in the home, the man asked his partner, "So, what now? Up to Boston?"

"No. We won't be visiting there until next Thursday.

First, we need to get back to Chennai—pay a little visit to the people at the production factory."

"Back to India? I thought we were going to go to—"

"The time frame has changed."

"I didn't know that."

"Now you do."

Without another word, she led him outside to the car, and they left for the airport while Corey's still-warm corpse lay on the living room floor soaked in blood, less than an hour after he'd awakened expecting to head to work for another ordinary day at the office after his shower and customary cup of strong, black, morning coffee.

1

"Of all the animals I would rather not be," my eighteen-year-old daughter, Tessa, said reflectively, "I think a bird poop frog is at the top of the list."

I glanced across the picnic basket at her. "A bird poop frog."

"Yes."

"That's not even a real animal."

"Sure it is."

"You're telling me there's a species of amphibian out there that some scientist actually named a 'bird poop frog'?"

"I'm not sure what the official scientific name is, but yeah, it's commonly called a bird poop frog."

"You're being serious?"

"Look it up."

I processed that. "Well, then I'd say being one of those would be almost as unfortunate as being born an albino chameleon."

She gave me a slight head tilt of approval. "Actually, that was not a bad line, Patrick."

"Thank you. I study under a world-class witticist."

She knew I was talking about her and looked pleased. "I wish that actually were a word: witticist. It should be. I like it."

As she took a sip of root beer, a swoop of her midnight-black hair fell across one of her eyes and she gently flicked it back. Today she had on her bloodred fingernail polish and dark eyeliner, and wore canvas sneakers, skinny jeans, and a faded gray T-shirt with an electric guitar splayed across the periodic table with the words METAL IS ELEMEN-TAL imprinted below it.

She was never the pink skirts and hair bow and bubblegum kind of girl. More tattoos and death metal and Kierkegaard. With her pierced nose, eyebrow ring, and the line of straight scars down her right forearm from her cutting days, she'd channeled a little of her inner emo.

However, when you threw in the PETA and Amnesty International buttons she wore, her hemp bracelets and the canvas messenger bag she used as a purse, and the cigarettes she sometimes snuck out, you could see she'd managed to merge it with a Greenwich Village, artsy vibe. She had a paradoxically hard-edged innocence about her, a bristlingly sharp intelligence, and a heart that had already seen too much pain.

"So what made you think of that?" I asked.

"Of what?"

"Bird poop frogs."

"Just what happened to your sandwich a minute ago when you were texting Lien-hua."

I stared at the sandwich on the picnic cloth. It looked clear of bird poop. "You're kidding me."

"Possibly."

I investigated the sandwich carefully to make sure, and it looked fine, but I covered it with one of the plates just to avoid any actual incidents.

Despite the placid clouds and the fresh taste of spring in the air, only a handful of people were in the field on this end of the park—a young woman of Middle Eastern descent, early twenties, slight limp in her left leg, pushing a baby in a stroller on the path west of us; a Caucasian male, medium build, brown hair, mid-thirties, tossing a Frisbee to a border collie; and a college-aged couple about eighty meters away who, over the last few minutes, had become less and less interested in their own picnic than in staring longingly into each other's eyes. Dinner did not appear to be on their minds any longer.

Five kilometers of walking trails wove through the woods beyond them. In February, a woman's body had been found a hundred meters from the trailhead. Metro PD had asked the Bureau for help and I'd worked with them on it, but the case was still open. No suspects yet.

Scavengers had gotten to the corpse before it was discovered. I thought of that now, of seeing the disarticulated remains, and I tried to shake the images loose so I'd still have an appetite for supper.

I glanced at the incoming text on my phone, and Tessa's eyes followed mine. "So, is she on her way?"

"Just parked. Looks like she should be here in a couple minutes."

My fiancée, Special Agent Lien-hua Jiang, was a profiler and one of my coworkers on the Bureau's National Center for the Analysis of Violent Crime, where I split my time between consulting on cases nationwide and my teaching responsibilities at the Academy.

Tessa set down her root beer, touched her hair back again, and quietly studied the cumulus clouds piled soft and high in the sky above us. I knew her well enough to guess that a poem about the sky, perhaps its contradictory qualities of tranquillity and ferocity, was already forming in her head.

We'd met when she was fifteen and living with her mother, Christie Ellis, the woman I was seeing at the time. Christie died tragically and unexpectedly of breast cancer five months after we were married—less than a year after we met. Tessa's dad had never been in the picture, so I ended up with custody of her, and at thirty-five, I'd suddenly become the sole caregiver of a teenage girl I hadn't raised and barely knew.

In the wake of Christie's death, Tessa, who kept her mother's last name of Ellis, had become withdrawn and started cutting. I was clueless as to how to connect with her, and things were really rough between us for a long time. Fortunately over the last year or so they'd improved, and now she wasn't just the girl I'd ended up with when her mom died, but the daughter I fiercely loved, would do anything for, and couldn't imagine living without.

Over time, the "step" part of stepfather and step-daughter had disappeared from our vocabulary, and I wasn't upset about that at all.

She took a deep breath and then steered the conversation in an entirely different direction. "So anyway, our assistant principal, you know, Thacker? He asked me to write something for graduation."

"Write something?"

"Yeah . . ." She hesitated. "Sort of like a speech."

"What does that mean: 'sort of like a speech'?"

"A speech."

"Ah." Earlier this year she'd thrown up in her speech class just getting up in front of a dozen classmates. I couldn't imagine how speaking in front of a thousand people would work out. "And does that mean write one or give one?"

"Well, both. But there's no way I'm gonna give a speech, and there's no way I'm gonna write one that I'm not gonna give."

Over the winter we'd moved here to DC from Denver, and although her stellar GPA had transferred, according to school policy, since she hadn't attended here at least one year, she wasn't in the running for valedictorian. However, her near-perfect SAT score was something the administration couldn't ignore.

She'd found two grammatical errors while taking the test (a missing comma and a misuse of the past tense of "lay") and had purposely gotten those two questions wrong as a way of protesting "having to proofread their stupid test for them."

She could've gotten a free ride at nearly any college in the country, but she still had no idea where she wanted to go and still hadn't applied anywhere. As more application deadlines slipped past, I'd been pressing her to at least send out some applications, but she was procrastinating and it'd become a sore spot for both of us. However, for now, I left all that alone.

"How did that go over, then? When you told Thacker you weren't going to write it?"

"Well, I haven't. Exactly."

"You haven't."

"Not exactly.

"So, not at all."

"Um, yeah." She let out a breath. "Thing is, I was gonna do it on Monday—tell him, you know? But . . ."

She waited a long time, and finally I said, "But?"

"But there's someone who I think . . . well, there's this extenuating circumstance."

"You mean there's a guy."

She looked at me incredulously. "I thought you were supposed to be the one who's always gathering all this evidence before drawing any conclusions? Aren't you the guy who says we're never supposed to assume, but 'hypothesize, evaluate, test, and revise'?"

"So it's not a guy?"

"No, it is, but that's not the . . ." She sighed with her eyeballs. "Never mind."

I wasn't quite sure what the connection was between a boy and her doing the speech, but I took what she'd just said to mean that in some way writing it might impress him. "Is this the guy you were telling me about last week, by any chance? Aiden Ryeson?"

She was quiet.

Normally she went for guys three or four years older than her, and I was actually relieved this boy was in her class. "He's that cute, huh?"

She shrugged. Then suddenly her eyes grew huge. "You *so* better not do a background check on him. I seriously hate it when you do that."

I'd only done a few of those on her potential boyfriends; it wasn't like it was a habit or anything. "You know I have nothing against you dating respectable guys," I told her somewhat evasively.

"Uh-huh. And that must be why you wear your gun when you open the door to let any of 'em in, and why you always happen to offhandedly-on-purpose mention that you track serial killers and sexual offenders for a living and that if you set your sights on someone he's going down."

"I don't think I ever put it quite like that."

That brought an eyebrow raise.

"Just looking out for you."

"Uh-huh." Her attention shifted past my shoulder toward the forest, where I now saw Lien-hua emerging from the woods on the walking trail.

Even from here her Asian poise and athletic grace were striking. For her it couldn't have been one of the milder martial arts; it had to be kickboxing. We spar sometimes, but I try to avoid it as much as possible—even though I'd never admit that to her. Three years younger than I am, she's beautiful, intuitive, cool under pressure, and I'd been attracted to her from the moment our paths first crossed eight months after Christie's death.

Dressed in black jeans and a green button-down shirt, Lien-hua smiled as she approached, and after a quick kiss she took a seat beside me.

Over the last week she'd been in London teaching a class for Scotland Yard on criminal profiling, and apart from Skyping, we hadn't seen each other since last Saturday. After bringing us up to speed on her trip, she asked me, "So, did you finish sending them out?"

"The invitations?"

"Yes." Absentmindedly, she massaged her engagement ring with the thumb and forefinger of her right hand.

"I was going to mail them out yesterday, but when I stopped by the printing place to pick them up I noticed they'd spelled your name wrong: Jang instead of Jiang. They promised to have the new ones printed up by Monday."

She mulled that over. "We should've mailed those out weeks ago, Pat." She politely left out the fact that I'd been the one responsible for getting them out earlier, but we were pretty much behind in everything, and she hadn't even decided on a maid or matron of honor yet, so I didn't feel quite so bad.

"It should be okay," I said. "Everyone who matters already knows when we're getting married. We could just not send the invites out at all. That way we could weed out all the—"

"Careful now, dear. Be nice."

"I'm just saying."

I rummaged through the picnic basket for the rest of our food and overheard Lien-hua ask Tessa quietly, "So, did he ask . . . ?"

I caught sight of Tessa shaking her head.

"Don't worry," Lien-hua had lowered her voice to a whisper. "He will."

Did he ask . . . ?

Ah, prom.

Yes. A week from today.

The puzzle with Aiden wasn't so hard to decipher after all. It annoyed me that I hadn't figured that one out right away.

Only seven days away.

Unfortunately, time was running out on that one.

Tessa, a vegan, used her flatbread to scoop out a dollop of hummus. Even after living with me for three years, she still hadn't gotten used to the idea that I actually ate things that used to have faces, and I noticed her eyeing me unhappily as I took a bite of my bird-poop-free ham sandwich.

I took the opportunity to pour a glimmer of champagne into Lien-hua's glass, and then tipped some into mine as well. Tessa held out her half-finished can of root beer. "You can top this off for me too, Dad."

"Mm-hmm. I don't think so."

"You two are FBI agents. It's not like I'm gonna get in trouble for—"

"Sorry, dear, no champagne. Not today." Then I raised my glass. "A toast. To us. To becoming a family."

Lien-hua lifted her glass, Tessa raised her can of soda and said, "*Dum vivimus vivamus.*"

Both Lien-hua and I looked at her quizzically, and when I asked for a translation she looked suddenly self-conscious that she'd said it. "Umm . . . 'While we live, let us live.'"

"While we live," Lien-hua repeated softly, "let us live. Yes. I like that. That's my kind of toast."

We repeated Tessa's Latin toast and tapped glass against glass and glass against can, then drank, and in that moment, despite the grisly cases I had on my plate at the Bureau, despite all the death and gore I deal with every day, sitting there in the park with the clouds overhead and the cherry trees in full bloom nearby and the two people who mattered most to me in all the world beside me, the moment bordered on perfection in a way that so few moments in my life ever have.

While we live, let us live.

Yes, let us live.

After we'd finished eating and twilight began to descend, we packed up and headed toward the deserted road where Lien-hua and I had left our cars.

"We still on for tomorrow morning?" Lien-hua asked Tessa. "The cake tasting?"

"So you were serious?"

"Of course. I need to decide on the wedding cake and I could really use someone to help me try the samples at the bakeries I'm considering."

Despite Tessa's strongly held beliefs about a plant-based diet, when it came to chocolate cake she had a marked weakness and somehow managed to overlook the fact that animal by-products were used in cake batter. "Are you thinking chocolate?"

"I'm thinking chocolate."

"We just swing by bakeries and sample cake?"

"Pretty much. Is eleven o'clock alright?"

To put it lightly, Tessa was no early riser, and eleven on a Saturday was going to be pushing it. But it sounded like this time around she was properly motivated.

"Sure. Yeah. I can deal with tasting cakes for an hour or two."

"Let's hope we find one we like before two hours of cake tasting or I'll never fit into my wedding dress."

I caught myself picturing how stunning Lien-hua was going to look in her wedding dress—even despite a bit of cake tomorrow—and tried to not let it distract me too much.

It wasn't easy.

We arrived at my Jeep. Tessa told Lien-hua good-bye, then climbed in, and I took both of Lien-hua's hands in mine. "So, cake tasting?"

"It'll give us a little time together. Just us girls. Besides, there's something I need to talk with her about."

"And that is?"

She looked at me wryly. "You'll find out when the time comes."

"Secrets, hmm?"

"Possibly."

I remembered last week when Tessa started riffing on why couples break up, and she told me girls like guys who are dangerous; guys like girls who are mysterious. "It's simple. If you're a guy, stop playing it safe all the time and learn to risk more than you can afford to lose. If you're a girl, stop trying to get a guy by opening up to him. What really drives him mad is when you make him keep wondering about you. Relationships fall apart when the guy turns into a wimp or the girl has no more secrets."

Nicely done for a teenager.

"Well," I said to Lien-hua, "I guess a few secrets are okay." Her deep ebony eyes drew me in and wouldn't let me go, and finally I just whispered to her how much I'd missed her.

"I missed you too."

We were silent for a long time, and when she finally spoke, her voice was soft and delicate and feminine in a way she was not ashamed of, a way that made my heart beat even faster. "I love you so much, Pat."

I wanted to spend time with her tonight, just the two of us, but our schedules weren't making that possible, and I could hardly wait until tomorrow evening, when we were planning a little alone time.

I took her in my arms. "I love you too."

"Just think, next month it'll be official—till death do us part."

"Till death do us part," I said softly, and it was not just a wish, but a promise.

Then we kissed, she left for her car just down the road, and I slid into my Jeep beside Tessa.

During the picnic I'd gotten a couple texts regarding some current cases. I hadn't wanted to interrupt our time together earlier by responding to them, but now I took a few seconds to read them over. As I did, Tessa said, "You two were meant for each other. Really."

"I was meant for your mom, too, Raven." The nickname I'd given her based on her obsession with Poe, her free-spirited nature, and her sweeping black hair, just came out. She'd even gotten a raven tattoo when we were in San Diego last year.

"Yeah," she said, "I know. I didn't mean it in any weird way." She let her voice trail off. "I just . . . I can't believe it's been two years already since she . . . I mean, since she's been gone. Sometimes it seems like forever ago when she died and sometimes it seems like it was just yesterday. That doesn't make any sense, but . . ."

"No." I set down the phone. "It makes perfect sense."

"I'll always love her, Patrick. Like no one else in the world. No one else, ever."

"I know."

"But I'm really glad Lien-hua is here now. She's a good influence on you. You can be a bit impetuous at times, left to yourself."

"Impetuous?"

Her eyes widened in mock surprise. "Um—yeah. Anyway, there's going to be three of us again. You know, a family." Though she didn't often open up to me like this, I knew that she'd always wanted two parents around, and the family I'd formed with her mom had ended way too prematurely.

"There's three of us *now*," I told her. "We don't have to wait for a ceremony to feel like a family."

Tessa looked thoughtfully out the window toward the trees, then back my way. She gave me a tiny, soft smile—something I rarely saw, and I couldn't shake the thought that at least here, now, on this night, everything seemed right in the world.

2

He was in the backseat of her coupe.

That's how he got to her.

He knew this park well and had been watching the picnic from behind a tree on the far side of a small rise near the edge of the forest. Considering what he was about to do, there was something tragic about the scene, about the three of them talking and smiling and raising a toast, so oblivious, so unaware of what this evening was going to bring. How it would change everything.

Their last idyllic moments together.

The small thrill he felt while watching them, the thrill that came from knowing the grief that lay in store, was an aspect of his nature he was neither proud of nor ashamed of. A sadist? Perhaps. Yes, that was the preferred term out there, but he was most definitely not the cartoonish chortling, hand-wringing kind of sadist or the panting torture-porn addict who sits in his basement surfing the Web with a towel in one hand, his mouse in the other.

No, what he felt was just an extension of schadenfreude, that secret, private pleasure everyone feels—but that most people are disinclined to acknowledge—when they see other people fail or suffer.

Philosophers and ethicists have identified the universality of this feeling; he simply allowed himself to feel what was natural to our species. And why should he take pride in that? Or conversely, feel any shame?

In a sense, since he embraced his natural tendencies and instincts so unreservedly, he was more fully, more completely human than those who live in denial of who they would be if only they were to give free rein to their deepest, most primal human desires and fantasies. Or, in other words, if they allowed themselves to truly be what evolution had shaped and intended them to be from the beginning—the planet's most cunning, calculating, ruthless predators.

Now, as Agent Jiang approached the car, he slipped down in the backseat, out of sight. To his advantage, the windows were tinted, which was part of the reason he'd chosen this approach when he decided to go after her.

He had skills, and picking the lock to get inside hadn't been difficult. Neither had it taken him long to disable the horn and the GPS.

Though it was by no means his preference, he was prepared to take care of things here if he needed to. He was very particular about his knives and had his limited-edition Benchmade 42-101 Gold Class Bali-Song butterfly knife with him. Really, however, he was hoping to just get her unconscious, and then transport her back to the apartment, where he could take his time with her.

He was partial to intestines, and he liked them fresh and warm, so he would keep her alive throughout the night—perhaps longer, depending on how everything played out. He figured he would probably enjoy her for at least twelve hours before he let her expire.

He was looking forward to her lungs too.

Those were always a close second.

Tomorrow he would leave her remains on Bowers's doorstep. It would serve as a small recompense for the thirteen years he'd stolen from him. It wasn't by any means a fair trade, but these types of things could never be balanced so metaphysically as that. In any case, he decided that after Agent Jiang was dead, he would call things even and go his own way.

No hard feelings.

But the hunt wouldn't be over. He knew that much. For Bowers, the hunt would never be over.

So there was fun in that too. In the chase.

The driver's door lock beeped as Agent Jiang remotely unlocked it. He tightened his grip on the ends of the leather belt in his hands.

He'd never chosen this method before, never tried to strangle someone into unconsciousness in exactly this manner. It would be a delicate balance between making her pass out and damaging her windpipe so much that she died on the spot. After all his years of lifting weights he knew he needed to be careful so that he didn't kill her too quickly. Then after she blacked out he would administer the drugs that would keep her unconscious while he took her back to his place.

The door opened and she settled into the front seat.

The instant she closed the door he sat up, flipped the belt in a loop around her neck, and slid the free end through the buckle, encircling both her neck and the base of the headrest.

He cinched it tight.

There.

He yanked hard, and with her airway closed off, she

couldn't gasp for breath, let alone call for help, and it was almost remarkable how quietly she was choking.

Yes.

Looking into the rearview mirror, he could see her clutch at the belt with her left hand as she tried desperately to jam her fingers beneath the leather to pull it away far enough to get a breath. She turned her head to the side to try and beat the choke, but he snugged the belt tighter to make sure that wasn't going to happen.

Ten, fifteen seconds and she would be out. Twenty at the most.

In order to free up his hands, he secured the belt by buckling the clasp through one of the holes he'd punched into the leather, then reached past her and tilted the rearview mirror so he could watch her as she passed out.

She really was beautiful. Yes, he was going to enjoy working on her.

Farther up the road, Special Agent Bowers was pulling away in his Jeep, and it lent a touch of sad irony to the moment—as Lien-hua faded into unconsciousness she was actually watching her lover, the only one who could save her, drive away, undoubtedly thinking that she was safe and sound in her car.

Apart from a few parked cars down the way, there were no other vehicles on the road, no one else was going to help her.

As she fought for breath, he leaned forward and gently stroked her perfect cheek with the back of his fingers. "Just relax, Lien-hua." He touched a strand of hair away from her eye. "It'll be over in a few seconds."

He could see that she was growing weaker, still trying futilely to breathe, still grasping at the belt with her left hand, but struggling less against the inevitable.

Yes, she was using her left hand to try to free herself. Her left hand.

But not both hands.

All at once, he realized that something didn't fit. She was right-handed, he knew that already—

Then her right elbow jutted out to the side, almost like a delicate wing, and a split second too late, he knew what she had done.

He was flipping out his butterfly knife to finish her when he heard the gunshot, saw the back of the seat puff open, felt fire slice through both his side and his back where the bullet had entered and then exited his torso.

Positioning the edge of the blade against the front of her neck, he was about to slice her throat, but he didn't need to after all, because her arms dropped to her sides and her head dipped forward as she slipped into unconsciousness.

He retrieved her gun, left the belt in place around her neck, and folded up his knife, then stepped out of the car and gazed up and down the road.

No one. Bowers was gone. The road was empty.

He waited a few more seconds just to make sure Agent Jiang wasn't faking it, then he opened the driver's door and loosened the belt. As he removed it, her body slumped limp and helpless against the steering wheel.

He felt her pulse to make sure he wouldn't need to resuscitate her and found that she was indeed still alive.

Good.

Warm blood was quickly spreading in a widening red stain across his shirt. The bullet had entered just below his ribs. Because of his interests, he knew anatomy quite well and calculated that the wound wouldn't be life-threatening, but it would need to be treated.

Gently, he wrapped the belt around his own abdomen to cover the bullet's entrance and exit wounds and tightened it enough to stem the bleeding until he could get to the apartment and stitch it up.

He produced the hypodermic needle and injected the Propotol into Agent Jiang's neck.

With the gunshot wound in his side, moving her into the passenger seat took longer than he would have liked and it hurt terrifically, but he kept from wincing. Thirteen years in prison had taught him how to handle pain, and he had been hurt worse than this before.

He duct-taped her ankles and her thighs together, then bound her wrists behind her back, just in case she did by some chance awaken before he reached the apartment. He didn't think she was the kind of woman to scream for help or beg for mercy, so he didn't bother to gag her.

Positioning himself behind the wheel, he pulled onto the road and left for the apartment in southeast DC where he would be spending the night with his old friend Patrick Bowers's lovely fiancée.

3

Lien-hua awoke lying on her left side.

She was dizzy, her head thrumming, and it took a few seconds to get her bearings. When she tried to move, she found that her legs were free, but her hands were somehow restrained behind her back. Not handcuffs, though. It felt like some type of packaging tape or duct tape.

For now, at least, whoever had taken her hadn't removed her clothes—thank God.

Dim light in the room. A ball of twisted, discarded duct tape lay on the floor nearby, perhaps from her abductor binding her legs while he brought her here. She couldn't think of many reasons he would free her legs, but she could think of a few.

Her heartbeat began to quicken.

She was on a wooden floor, and by the faint glimmer of neon lights outside the dark window, she knew it was night. No idea how late.

Her holster and gun were missing.

The walls of the living room were sooty—there'd been a fire in here at some point. A tattered couch sat in the corner facing an old television with a crooked floor lamp stationed beside it. A pile of bloody bandages and a spool of black thread lay on the cheap Formica end table.

Still somewhat groggy, she tried to collect her thoughts and remember exactly what had happened before she arrived here.

The picnic.

Saying good-bye to Patrick.

Getting into her car.

Then a strap around her neck, yes, a belt.

The terrible desperate feeling of struggling uselessly to breathe.

Then a calm male voice beside her ear. She hadn't recognized it, and her vision had been blurry, so she hadn't been able to identify whose face it was in the rearview mirror.

He'd called her Lien-hua, though—that, she remembered. So he knew her first name. And he'd had long hair for a man. It might have been a wig.

In those few moments she'd had before blacking out, she'd been transported back to the time last year in San Diego when she'd drowned and Patrick had brought her back to life—literally—with a defibrillator. Both that day and this, as she was losing consciousness, aware that she might never awaken again, she'd thought of him, only of him, and sensed an all-encompassing sadness that she would never be with him, never see him again.

Now, she noticed sounds coming from behind her and she tried to decide what to do. If she moved, if she rolled over, whoever was there might see her do it. On the other hand, she needed to know how many people she was dealing with here.

It sounded like someone was going through some pots and pans, and Lien-hua took the chance that there was only that one person and that, if he was going through the cupboards, he would be facing the other way. Slowly, she eased onto her back and tilted her head toward the sounds.

It was a man.

His back was to her.

The kitchen wasn't separated from the living room, and she could see that he was rooting through a cabinet beside the gas stove.

His face was hidden, but his strongly muscled back and hefty build were evident even when he was kneeling down. With a deepening chill she thought she might know who it was. She couldn't be certain, though, not from this angle.

Evidently, he found what he was looking for, because he stood, holding a frying pan. He laid it on the burner and dialed the gas on, then turned toward the refrigerator and opened the door. And when he did, she caught his profile.

Yes, it was him.

Richard Devin Basque.

He was the man Pat had arrested fourteen years before. He was the man who, during his criminal career, had kidnapped more than two dozen women, kept them alive for hours or even days on end as he slowly sliced out their intestines and lungs and ate them before finally ending their suffering and taking the women's lives. He'd been freed last year after a retrial and had started killing again almost immediately upon his release.

Based on what he'd done to most of his past victims, Lien-hua knew he would be removing her jeans and panties before carving into her.

Get out. You have to—

He retrieved a small jar from the refrigerator. She couldn't tell what was inside it, but she was pretty sure she didn't want to know what it contained.

When he picked up a scalpel from the counter, she knew she'd never have enough time to get to her feet before he'd notice that she was awake. Quickly, quietly, she rolled back into the position he'd left her in, then closed her eyes and lay still.

As he walked toward her, she heard the sound of a slight hitch in each step. He was limping. Taking into account the bloody bandages on the end table, she decided she must have hit him after all when she fired her Glock behind her through the driver's seat.

He's vulnerable. Use that. Capitalize. Attack him where he's weakest. Strike at the wound.

She'd been in situations before when her life was threatened, and she'd found that, rather than being filled with uncontrollable terror or desperation, she was able to think remarkably clearly. It'd happened on a case in Wisconsin a few months earlier, once in Florida, and then that time when she was drowning in San Diego.

That day she'd been able to use sign language to communicate to Pat a way to save her. And today, she hoped that the thing she'd done immediately before firing her gun would save her: tapping in 911 on her phone and tossing it beneath her seat so the call could be traced.

In DC there are a staggering number of hoax 911 calls, and Metro's dispatch didn't always send out a car when they received calls during which no one on the other end of the line spoke. However, she was confident that when her number came up on the system and they realized it was an FBI agent's phone, they would dispatch officers. As long as her phone was still on, they should easily be able to track the GPS location. It might not lead them to this specific apartment, but it would get them close.

Unless Basque had switched cars, or unless he'd found the phone and destroyed it.

You need to buy some time.

By the sound of the footsteps, Basque was about half-way to her.

He was a large man, well trained, a fighter. She knew from the warden that during all of his years in prison Basque had never lost a fight, even when cornered by multiple assailants. They'd never been able to prove that he killed any other prisoners, but he had disabled four and put one gang leader into a coma.

The sound of footsteps grew closer.

Wait, Lien-hua, wait . . .

With her wrists restrained behind her, taking him down wasn't going to be easy at all; her years of sparring and kickboxing needed to come into play. And they needed to do so now.

If she could buy a few seconds, she could jump and swing her arms forward beneath her feet to get her hands in front of her. Then things would be a little more evenly matched. Having her arms in front would at least help her to block any kicks or punches he might throw.

Attack him where he's wounded or take out his knee, then slide backward, put some distance between the two of you, and get to your feet.

Get your hands to the front and go at him.

The footsteps stopped. Basque paused.

Wait . . .

He was right beside her.

Now. Do it.

Lien-hua snapped her eyes open as she rolled onto her back. A flash of surprise crossed Basque's face, but he was too slow to get out of the way. She couldn't immediately identify where he was wounded, so she planted her left foot against the floor for support, twisted her body to get the angle right, and drove a hard, controlled kick with her right foot toward his knee to take him down.

The placement wasn't as ideal as she'd hoped, and at the last moment he pivoted so she ended up kicking the back of his leg rather than the side. It brought him down, but didn't break the knee. As she used her feet to push away from him, he dived at her with the scalpel and buried it into her right thigh just above her knee.

A hot streak of pain shot up her leg.

She tried to pull away, but he shoved the blade in deeper. Using the scalpel to hold her in place and keep her from sliding backward, he drew himself closer.

No, no, you have to—

"Well." With his free hand he flicked out a butterfly knife. "Let's get started then."

The slightest movement hurt viciously, so it wasn't possible to twist away, but she had no choice. She knew that if he brought that second knife down, it would all be over.

She yanked hard, trying to pull her leg free from the scalpel, but the blade was in too deep. When she failed to free herself, Basque drew the butterfly knife back. "This might be a little uncomfortable at first. But by this time tomorrow, you won't feel a thing."

He swung his arm violently forward and stabbed the blade deep into her chest, directly into her right lung, then drew it out again.

Everything splintered apart inside of her. She gasped

for air and did her best to concentrate on something, anything, to keep from passing out, but found it nearly impossible to catch her breath.

She knew enough about knife wounds to know that one this deep in her chest wasn't going to give her much time.

The lung will collapse. The blood will fill it. Especially if you're on the floor.

"I'm not going to lie to you." His voice was calm and even, but his tongue snaked out of his mouth and tapped expectantly at the side of his lip. "What happens next isn't going to feel very pleasant."

He still held her in place securely with the scalpel, but as he leaned closer to gaze into her eyes, she brought her left leg up and scissored it down across his neck, trapping it between her thighs. She squeezed as hard as she could and tried to roll to break his neck, but he punched her near where he'd stabbed her and the pain devastated her, her grip evaporated, and he wrestled free.

However, her move had taken him by surprise and bought her enough time to twist away and roll toward the couch, the scalpel torquing painfully out of her leg as she did.

She climbed unevenly to her feet. Her injured leg felt weak and unsteady, but that wasn't her biggest concern—it was the debilitating stab wound in her chest. She didn't know how many seconds she had before she would pass out, but she guessed it wouldn't be long at all.

She saw her phone on the kitchen counter. The battery beside it.

So, he'd found it after all.

They're not coming. No one is coming.

Her chest wasn't bleeding much externally, but every breath was a struggle. It would hurt too much to try jumping over her arms to bring her hands forward to fight him or defend herself.

But she could use her feet.

Basque was pushing himself to his hands and knees. The smear of emerging blood on his shirt told her where her bullet had hit him earlier.

All he has to do is wait for you to collapse. He doesn't have to fight you, all he has to do is stop you from getting out the door. He'll kill you, Lien-hua. And he will eat you.

After a fraction-of-a-second debate about whether to go for his gunshot wound or his head, she went for both and delivered a fierce double sidekick—one to his wounded side and one to his right temple, sending him crashing against the end table and overturning it next to the couch.

But she was weak, her balance was off, and she almost went down herself.

A deep dizziness began to envelop her.

Do not fall. If you go down it's all over.

If you pass out, you die. It's that simple.

She rushed for the front door and, hands still restrained behind her, turned her back to the doorknob to open it. As she did, Basque rose to his feet holding a Smith & Wesson Sigma that he seemed to produce from nowhere.

Door open, she swiveled backward into the hall as a bullet whizzed past her shoulder and blistered apart the wood across the hallway.

Do not pass out, Lien-hua. Do not fall down!

Her chest and thigh were screaming at her, but she ran as fast as she could for the stairs. Every step sent a fresh burst of pain through her leg, through her chest, but Basque must have made it to the hallway, because another bullet ricocheted off the wall beside her.

She arrived at the stairwell and saw that, fortunately, she was only on the second level. The exit door lay just one flight below her.

Awkwardly, she stumbled down the steps, lost her footing at the bottom, and went reeling against the wall. She coughed up a mouthful of foamy blood.

Behind her she could hear Basque pursuing her, his quick but uneven gait nearing the top of the stairs.

She lunged for the exit door, threw her hip against the pressure bar to open it, and found herself in an alley layered in deep, oppressive shadows.

She staggered toward the street.

Go, Lien-hua. Keep going. You can make it!

A car was rounding the corner in front of her.

Swarms of dark dots crossed her vision and she knew she was about to pass out. The driver wasn't slowing down. She couldn't use her hands to signal to him, and she was too weak to cry out for help.

If he passed her by she would collapse and it would be over. Basque would get her.

There was nothing left to do.

Except one thing.

She rushed toward the car, positioned herself directly in front of it, faced the driver, and time seemed to slow to a crawl.

She saw the reflected glimmer of the streetlights slide across the car's roof.

Heard the squeal of brakes.

Felt the impact that sent her sliding up violently across the hood.

Then time caught up with itself and her shoulder smashed against the windshield, the world went whipping around her in a blur of colors and sounds and bright, consuming pain, and she rolled off the hood and slammed heavily onto the asphalt.

She was vaguely aware of a man approaching her and leaning over her.

And she was aware of spitting out blood and gasping. "Down the alley, second floor, room 212. Tell the police it's . . ." She tried to say "Basque," but nothing came out. The world became a vast, hungry darkness that swallowed everything around her.

And then Special Agent Lien-hua Jiang was aware of nothing at all.

4

11:34 p.m.

I got the call when I was at home on my computer doing some research for my Monday-morning lecture at the Academy.

Lien-hua had been attacked, stabbed in the chest, hit by a car.

Even as I asked the question, I knew it was an absurd one: "Is she okay?"

Of course she wasn't okay, but the words came out just like they do for so many people when they're reeling from news that's too devastating to process.

There was a pause that went on too long, then the officer on the other end of the line said quietly, "From what we know she's in pretty rough shape, Agent Bowers. She's in surgery now."

Ice twisted around my heart.

This wasn't happening. This couldn't be happening.

"How long has she been in surgery?"

"From what I hear, a little over two hours."

"What!"

"She didn't have any ID on her, so they couldn't identify her right away. There was a 911 call earlier that dispatch identified as coming from her phone. Eventually, that, taken with the inscription on her engagement ring, led us to you."

I snatched my keys off the kitchen counter. "Where is she? Which hospital?"

"St. Mary's."

Tessa was in the living room rewatching the movie *The Dead Girl*. As I hurried past her on my way to the garage, I signaled that I was heading out. She must have seen the concern on my face and guessed that something serious had happened, because she gave me a worried look and asked softly, "What is it?"

"We're sending a car to pick you up," the officer told me over the phone.

"I don't need one," I informed him, while quietly trying to wave off Tessa's concern. "I'm on my way."

"What happened?" she pressed me.

I turned from the phone and told her, "Just a sec, Tessa."

He finished by telling me that Lieutenant Doehring would meet me at the hospital.

I knew Doehring. He was a good cop; however, I wasn't about to wait until I got to the hospital before finding out more, so as soon as the officer ended the call, I found Doehring's number on my phone's contact list and called it.

While I waited for him to answer, I hurried to the garage and punched the door opener. As the door rattled upward, Tessa appeared in the doorway to the kitchen. This time palpable fear ran through her words. "It's something bad, isn't it?"

For a second I was tempted to downplay what'd happened, to reassure her that everything was fine, but as she and I had talked about earlier, Lien-hua was about to become part of our family and, in a very real sense, already was.

"It's Lien-hua," I said. "There was an accident." This wasn't the time to get into the specifics of the attack, so I left out the rest, especially the part about her being stabbed.

"What kind of accident?"

"She was hit by a car."

A terrible look fell across her face. "Is she . . . ?"

"It sounds like she's hurt pretty badly." Doehring still hadn't picked up. "She's in surgery."

Tessa must have set her purse just out of sight before coming to the doorway, because now she reached to the side and grabbed it, then joined me in the garage. "I'm coming."

Still no answer from Doehring.

"No, it's late. You need to—"

"I'm coming, Patrick." Her words were unequivocal and she edged past me, making her way toward the passenger door.

The call went to Doehring's voicemail: I told him to send a car to look for Lien-hua's Hyundai Genesis coupe beside the park where we'd had the picnic and—if it wasn't there—to put out an attempt to locate and call me right away if it was found. I left the license plate number, then turned to Tessa. "Really, this is—"

"Look. I lost my mom. I lost my dad. You two are the only . . ." She was obviously struggling with what to say. "You're not the only one who loves her, okay? Now let's go."

I said nothing, just slid into the driver's seat, backed up the Jeep, and the two of us took off for the hospital.

As I saw how worried and afraid she was, I remembered her words from earlier about Lien-hua and how glad she was that we were all together. Tessa would find out about Lien-hua's condition sooner or later, and I realized it would probably be best if she heard it from me now. So, although I was still reluctant to give her specifics, I summarized everything I knew about what had happened.

"What?" Tessa exclaimed. "She was stabbed? Where?"

"In the chest."

A long silence. "Patrick, that's . . ."

"Yes. I know." Though I had no way of knowing if it was true, I told her, "She's going to be okay."

Another pause. "Do they know who did it?"

"No. Not yet."

"But you're going to find him, right?"

"Yes."

"And what?"

"What do you mean?"

"What are you going to do when you find him? You gonna bring him in?"

It didn't surprise me that Tessa was pursuing this line of questioning. She'd been living with me while I worked some of the most brutal cases of my career. The limits and bounds of justice were things we'd talked about a lot over the last year.

In fact, the night her father was killed trying to protect her from a psychopath who'd set his sights on her, she'd been the one to fire the shot that killed the offender just as he was about to murder her. For months she'd barely slept, but she told me on more than one occasion that she was glad she'd done it, that a part of her—a part that frightened her terribly—had actually enjoyed squeezing the trigger that day.

Justice doesn't always have clean hands, and we all have dark desires clawing at our wills. I knew that all too well from my job. Now as we spoke, I sensed where she was going with this. "I'll make sure he pays for what he did," I told her evenly.

"You'd better." Her jaw was set. She let the rest go unsaid, but I could tell we were on the same page. She didn't want me to bring him in. She wanted a different kind of justice.

And so did I.

I merged onto the beltway.

Ten minutes to St. Mary's.

5

We exited onto Pennsylvania, and I was reassuring myself that things were going to be okay when Doehring finally returned my call.

He filled me in: the man who'd struck Lien-hua with his vehicle told the responding officers that she'd mentioned an apartment nearby. "He was distraught," Doehring told me, "said she ran right in front of his car. Her wrists were bound behind her."

I was holding the phone with one hand, the steering wheel with the other. I felt both hands tighten as he said that. "What else?"

"No one was there in the apartment. Lien-hua had ligature marks around her neck. She was strangled, probably with a belt of some type. She was stabbed in the right thigh and the right side of her chest. Punctured her lung." The officer from earlier hadn't mentioned a wound in her leg.

Doehring hesitated and I could sense that there was something he wasn't telling me.

"What did you find in the apartment?" I asked.

"Among other things, a scalpel. And one of the burners on the stove was still on, a frying pan on top of it."

"Basque." The word slipped out before I realized it, and out of the corner of my eye I noticed a wash of fear cross Tessa's face. Over the years I'd been careful to keep the details from her, but the media had been thorough in covering Basque's crimes, and she knew all too well what he did to the women he abducted.

"There were bloody bandages too," Doehring explained. "We tested the DNA right away. It's confirmed. It's him. Apparently, she wounded him."

Over the last twenty years the science of DNA identification has evolved exponentially, and being able to test it on-site and run the results through the system has been one of the great breakthroughs of the last two years for law enforcement. It wasn't available everywhere yet, but it was here in the nation's capital.

I'd caught Basque early in my career while I was still a homicide detective in Milwaukee. He'd been tried, convicted, and then served thirteen years in prison before managing to swing a retrial last year. Based on controversial forensic evidence and conflicting eyewitness testimony, he was found not guilty and released.

Soon after his release, he slaughtered the law professor who'd done the legal work that ended up helping free him. That was last spring. He hadn't slowed down since then, leaving a string of bodies across the Northeast. I fatally shot his partner in January, but even though we'd been close to catching Basque on three separate occasions, he always managed to slip away.

No one knew for sure how many people he'd killed, but based on evidence from unsolved homicides back in the Midwest and here in the DC area, I put the number close to forty.

As far as I knew, Lien-hua was the first woman to ever survive being attacked by him.

If she really does survive after all.

No, she would be okay.

She would.

After I hung up with Doehring, Tessa said to me, "St. Mary's is a teaching hospital."

"Yes."

"So Lien-hua's getting the best medical care in the region, right?"

I could tell she was trying to convince herself of the same thing I was trying to convince myself of.

"That's right."

Then we were both quiet. I sped down the street that led to the hospital and squealed to a stop just outside the emergency room doors.

As Tessa and I entered the building, I told her she needed to stay in the waiting room, but she shook her head. "No, I'm—"

I laid a gentle hand on her shoulder. "I promise I'll come and get you as soon as I find out how she is. But you need to stay here right now."

"Why?"

"Because . . ." *If Lien-hua is as bad off as I think she might be, I don't want you to see her,* I thought, but said, "Because I need to make sure she's in a condition first where she can see visitors."

Tessa opened her mouth as if she were going to reply, then closed it again. I think she caught the deeper gist of what I was saying.

"What am I supposed to do out here?"

"You believe in prayer, you told me that, right?"

She nodded. "Yeah."

"Now would be a good time."

I held her for a moment to try to reassure her, and then I saw Doehring approaching.

"Text me right away." Her eyes went to a sign on the wall prohibiting cell phone use in the hospital, but she ignored it. "As soon as you know anything."

I ignored it as well. "I will."

Lieutenant Cole Doehring stopped in front of us. He'd been a cop for two decades and had the look of a tough, 1930s boxer about him; still, he was a pushover when it came to relating to his two young daughters—a side of him that he tried to keep hidden from other cops. I respected him, even though I didn't always agree with his traditional approach of looking for means, motive, and opportunity when it came to tracking offenders.

Those were not the things I relied on—especially not motives, since they're nebulous, hard to pin down, impossible to identify with any degree of certainty, aren't required to be shown in court, and focusing on them rather than on the timing and location of the crime more often than not slows down or derails investigations.

I hurried with Doehring down the hall toward the operating room. "Who's working the apartment?" I asked him. "Metro PD or the FBI?"

"Our guys are there now. I called the Bureau to get the ERT out there too. Cassidy and Farraday are on the way."

"Good."

The ERT, or Evidence Response Team, is the Bureau's forensics investigation unit. Although the attack on Lienhua was technically under the jurisdiction of the Washington, DC, Metro Police Department, since she was a federal agent, the Bureau's involvement in the investigation went without saying—especially if her assailant was Basque, who was number three on our Ten Most Wanted Fugitives list.

Lien-hua was still in the operating theater when we arrived.

One of the nurses led Doehring and me quietly up a short set of steps to a landing with a wide window allowing a view of the surgeons at work. "They told us they were hoping to have her out within the hour," she explained.

"So that's good news, right?" I said.

She didn't reply right away. "Yes. That's good news. Often thoracic surgery like this can last up to six hours or more."

Just seeing Lien-hua there, the tube in her throat, the doctors bent over her chest, was hard enough, but seeing the blood, so much blood, was almost unbearable.

Blood.

I've seen too much of it in my career. Too much suffering. Too much death.

I didn't want to think about that, but it struck me that in America, death is sanitized. There's a disconnect. To a certain extent Tessa and her vegan friends realized that in a way so many of us don't. We don't think about where meat actually comes from: our beef doesn't have hair on it, our bacon doesn't have hooves, the chicken nuggets we buy at the drive-through don't look anything at all like chickens.

And as far as the death of people is concerned, we prefer to either avoid the topic altogether or speak in euphemisms: "He passed away," "The tumor was inoperable," "We weren't able to resuscitate him," "There was nothing we could do." Those phrases are supposed to make it easier than the stark, honest truth.

I'm not sure they do the trick, but I do know that we all tend to do whatever we can to try to ignore the fact that death is the default setting for the universe, that it's on our heels and gaining on us every moment. In this job, you end up using those euphemisms to try to help others, but you know the game all too well, and they don't work when you tell them to yourself.

I tried my hardest to focus on the fact that Lien-hua was in the hands of the region's best surgeons, of people who were going to save her, but images of death just wouldn't leave me alone.

Too much death.

A few years ago I went to Mumbai, India, to train their police force on principles of environmental criminology. As we were leaving the airport, traffic on our street came to a standstill because of a funeral. Six men were carrying the corpse of a young woman on a funeral pyre that was balanced on their shoulders. Her body lay on a pallet showered in flower petals. The people wailed and wept publicly as they passed. No hiding their grief. Nothing sanitized. No euphemisms.

Definitely not like in America.

Stop thinking about dead bodies, Patrick! Lien-hua's going to be okay.

As I watched the doctors work on her, I wanted so badly to help her, but right now there was really nothing I could do.

Prayer didn't sound like such a bad idea after all, but I figured God didn't need me to fold my hands or close my eyes to know what I was crying out for in my heart. In-

stead, I could do what I was made to do. Maybe that
would be the best kind of prayer of all.

"CSIU is there now?" I said to Doehring. "At the
apartment?"

"Yes."

"Alright." I pulled out my phone. "Good."

"What are you going to do?"

"Help them find Basque."

6

My cell phone was not your typical phone.

It'd been issued to me from a branch of the Department of Defense that I consult with called the National Geospatial-Intelligence Agency. The agency specialized in using geospatial intelligence, or GEOINT, to monitor military hot zones, find terrorist training camps, identify nuclear research facilities in rogue nations, target laser-guided weapons systems, and coordinate troop movements.

Not only did the phone contain the typical array of high-end law enforcement apps (like an infrared camera and a touch screen that could scan fingerprints and pull up names through AFIS), it also had a real-time defense satellite feed and a 3-D hologram projector.

By accessing the world's most advanced geospatial digital mapping program, the Federal Aerospace Locator and Covert Operation Network, or FALCON, I could visually soar through a 3-D landscape of any geographic region on the planet. FALCON contained a degree of detail Google Earth just might reach in ten or fifteen years.

And when I had video footage of the interior of a

building to work with, the phone could project and ma-nipulate a 3-D view of the structure's interior.

That's what I was about to do right now.

Doehring and I found an empty exam room and I reached Tanner Cassidy, one of our ERT agents and a good friend of mine, at the scene.

"I need you to take some video for me, Cassidy. Give me some eyes on what we have there."

"Right."

Normally I would visit the scene myself, ideally at the same time of day as the crime, to gain a better un-derstanding of the spatial relationships between the lo-cation and its surroundings and to identify potential entrance and exit routes. If there was time I'd also in-spect the light conditions at the time of the offense, study the area's road layout, and survey the demo-graphics of the neighborhood and the local land-use and traffic patterns.

It's all part of the deal with environmental criminology and geospatial investigation, my two specialties.

Right now, however, with Lien-hua in surgery, I wasn't about to drive to the apartment. Cassidy and I had done this before at crime scenes and we had a system. If he fed me the video, I could use my phone's hologram projector to re-create a 3-D map of the apartment, and if I had enough video or used the defense satellites, I could get a visual of the surrounding streets and perhaps get an indication of the direction Basque might have fled.

Cassidy went to his phone's video app, and his squar-ish face, studious, careful eyes, and unruly brown hair came into view. He was forty-one, experienced, sharp, and I was glad he was on the case. "How is she, Pat?"

"She's in surgery. They think she'll be out within the hour."

"Any idea if . . . ?"

"It's looking more optimistic than it did at first."

"That's good to hear." But he sounded only slightly relieved.

"Yes. So what do we have?"

"Basque left prints, DNA; the question isn't really who was here, but where did he go?"

"Well, let's figure that out."

Cassidy turned the camera to face the room. I set my phone on the exam bed and turned on the hologram function.

Immediately, a bluish spread of hologram lines appeared two feet above the bed, and as Cassidy turned in a circle, the layout of the apartment and its contents, including the furniture, appeared, and in a matter of seconds the 3-D image of the apartment's interior emerged.

I drew my forefinger and thumb across the phone's screen to zoom out to get more perspective on the apartment, then turned them to rotate the image so I could take in the place's spatial layout. The overturned end table in the living room indicated that there'd been a struggle.

"Is her phone there?"

"Her phone?"

"She had her phone with her, made a 911 call. Is it there; can you see it anywhere?"

He took a few moments to look around and then told me that no, he did not see it.

"If Basque took it and didn't remove the battery, we might be able to trace its location. Can you call that in? Have Angela get on it?"

"Yes."

He spoke to an agent beside him to have her contact Angela Knight in Cybercrime, then he got back on the line with me.

After I had a clear idea of the layout of the apartment I told Cassidy, "Okay, walk down the hall for me, the one Lien-hua took, and then step outside. Let's get a look at the street. Take me around the block."

He did as I requested, and within a few minutes I had a detailed visual of the streets surrounding the apartment building. I noted where Lien-hua had been struck by the car in reference to the room Basque had taken her to.

By overlaying FALCON's satellite imagery of that neighborhood and inputting the location where Lien-hua was found, I was able to identify the three most likely routes Basque might have used to flee the scene.

Environmental criminology studies the nexus of timing and location in a criminal event, the reason the offender might have chosen it (perhaps for seclusion, convenience, familiarity, or expediency), and the spatial and temporal factors that come together when crimes occur. Geospatial investigation analyzes the distribution patterns of serial offenses to try to deduce the offender's most likely anchor point, or home base.

The key to understanding a criminal event isn't trying to guess why the offender might have engaged in it but rather examining why he might have done so in that specific place, at that specific time. It's always about timing and location, not psychological guessing games into motive or intent.

So now, as I considered that, I reminded myself that Basque had gotten her into the apartment building after he abducted her.

Knowing Lien-hua, if she were conscious she would

have fought him off and not allowed him to get her in there. We knew she'd been strangled, so the most likely scenario: he'd knocked her out by strangling either before she left the park or when she arrived at her home.

Cassidy ascertained that no wheelchair had been found in the apartment, so that meant Basque would have most likely carried her inside, or at least supported her, perhaps pretending to anyone who might've seen him that she was drunk.

"We've talked to the neighbors, I assume?" I asked Cassidy. "To see if anyone saw Basque enter or leave the building?"

"No one saw anything." I didn't see his face, but I heard his voice. "But then again, this neighborhood isn't exactly the kind of place where anyone ever sees anything, if you know what I mean."

"I do."

"We found two bullet holes in the hallway, but so far it hasn't led us anywhere."

"And we haven't found Lien-hua's car yet?"

"No. Metro PD searched the whole neighborhood for six blocks out. Parking garages too. Nothing."

Interesting.

Basque would have likely parked close enough to the building so that he wouldn't have had to carry or support Lien-hua very far to get her inside.

Yes, that was interesting.

Also, he would have known that after we found her we would immediately put out an attempt to locate on her car, so I couldn't imagine he would have driven it very far before abandoning it or switching to another vehicle.

Of course, he might have fled on foot, or taken a taxi and risked having the place where he was dropped off identified, but that would mean he carried her more than six blocks. Knowing how he'd avoided capture in the past, I started with the hypothesis that he would have had a vehicle of his own close by so that he could trade it off for Lien-hua's as soon as possible.

"Check with the neighbors, see if anyone's missing a car."

"You're thinking he might have stolen one?"

"It's a possibility we need to eliminate."

But still, what about Lien-hua's car? Where is it?

I couldn't be sure, but considering travel times from her apartment to this location and the length of time she'd been in surgery, Basque would have most likely abducted her at the park rather than where she lived.

Immediately, I thought of checking the Metro stations' security cameras to get a bead on when he might have entered or left any of the stations. Considering Cassidy was on the phone with me, I told Doehring the idea. "We'll want the footage both before and following the abduction. Angela Knight at the Bureau can run it through facial recognition. Depending on the download time, we should have the results within the hour. Tell her it concerns the attack on Lien-hua and it'll move to the top of the stack."

He called it in.

Okay, if they haven't found her car anywhere nearby, where would Basque have left it?

Somewhere close by where no one would see him switching vehicles.

A parking lot?

No, then we would have found it already.

An abandoned warehouse? A garage?

I used FALCON and the hologram to sweep around

the neighborhood and found a garage four blocks away on a side street. I told the address to Doehring and directed him to get a car over there right away. While he radioed dispatch, I kept searching, and found two other potential spots where Basque might have left a vehicle.

That's when we got word from a nurse that they were finishing up surgery and would be taking Lien-hua to post-op. Relief swept over me.

"So she's alright?"

The nurse gave me a slight smile meant to reassure me. "If there were any immediate concerns, they would address them in surgery."

"Can I see her then? In post-op?"

"I'm sorry, we don't allow visitors in there."

"I'm not just a visitor."

"I'm sorry." And she sounded like she was. "It's just not allowed."

I texted Tessa to tell her what I knew, and then, hoping to finish up here while Lien-hua was recovering, I went back to work with a renewed sense of focus.

The first two sites came up empty, and I was thinking I might be on the wrong track entirely when Cassidy informed me that an officer had just located Lien-hua's car at the third location, a mechanic's garage six blocks away.

As soon as Cassidy arrived on-site he relayed the video. There was a fresh oil spot three meters from her car.

Hoping that it might be a unique blend of motor oil or tell us something about the type of vehicle that it was used in, I told him to take a sample and get it to the Lab right away to have them analyze it.

He took footage of the interior of Lien-hua's car, but there was nothing immediately evident that might lead us to Basque. However, there was a large smear of blood across the backseat and a bullet hole through the front and back seats. That explained the bloody bandages at the apartment.

So, she'd shot him.

Yes, Lien-hua. Nice work.

Would Basque chance going somewhere to have the wound treated?

I doubted that he would. Almost certainly he'd know that police are dispatched to the hospital whenever someone comes in with a gunshot wound, but still, checking hospitals couldn't hurt. I had Doehring call it in.

Cassidy took me on a video walk-around of the garage, but I saw nothing else that might indicate where Basque had gone.

Doehring returned from the hallway and told me he'd gone down to the nurses' station to get word on Lien-hua. "After post-op they're taking her to 414 in the ICU. Hopefully within the next fifteen or twenty minutes."

I checked my texts and saw that Tessa hadn't replied.

Considering how quickly she usually responded to texts, and taking into account that she'd told me to contact her right away when I knew anything, I was surprised. The girl was so proficient at texting that she could do it without even looking down at her phone. Maybe she *was* praying and had turned her text notifications off, but why would she do that if she was expecting to hear from me?

I told Doehring, "I'm gonna go touch base with Tessa. I'll meet you in the ICU."

He acknowledged that, I texted her again that I was on my way to the waiting room, then I stepped onto the elevator and punched 1 to get to the first level of the hospital, where I'd left my daughter.

7

Tessa wasn't there.

In fact, only one couple—an elderly man and woman with matching wedding rings—sat in the waiting room. The woman had a bloodied dishrag draped over her arm from some sort of cut, but apparently not one serious enough to get her in right away. When I asked them if they'd seen a teenage girl in here, they told me they'd just arrived and were sorry, but no, they hadn't.

After checking my texts again and finding that Tessa still hadn't replied, I spoke with the receptionist and she told me that she remembered a girl sitting in the corner but couldn't remember her leaving.

"When did you last see her?"

"Just a few minutes ago. I think."

Of course, it was possible that Tessa had turned off her phone, but considering the circumstances, I found that highly unlikely. I tried calling her but she didn't answer and I left her a voicemail to call me.

A few thoughts began to form in my head and none of them were good.

A woman was leaving the restroom just down the hall

and I asked her if there was a girl in there. "Eighteen, about your height, black hair?"

She shook her head. "I didn't see anyone."

"Do you mind checking again? Please?"

It looked like she did mind, but she returned to the bathroom regardless and a moment later reemerged. "Nope. No one."

I walked outside to see if Tessa might've left to get some air or to sneak a cigarette, a habit she'd picked up recently and tended to slip into when she felt stressed or overwhelmed.

Once she'd said to me that smoking is suicide, it just takes longer than a gun, but now that she'd given up cutting, it seemed she still had the need for some self-destructive behavior, though, to me, cutting might actually have been preferable to lighting up. I'd confronted her about the smoking; she told me she was trying to stop.

In any case, she wasn't outside, but a Metro PD officer was. With the attack on Lien-hua it didn't surprise me that Doehring had upped the law enforcement presence here at the hospital. The officer told me he hadn't seen anyone leaving, just going inside. "This older couple. And another officer. Just a little while ago."

"Another officer?"

"Yup."

"Do you know him?"

He shook his head. "No."

I felt a shiver that I couldn't contain.

A disguise? Could Basque have been that second officer?

It was inconceivable that Basque would have come in here, or that he would be able to get to Tessa. She never

would have stepped outside or left by another hallway
with him.

But still . . .

I quelled the thought.

After a quick call to hospital security to have them review the footage of the front entrance, I phoned dispatch
and asked them for the name of the officers at the hospital.
They told me there were two—Langston Honeycutt and
Aleck Kane. Officer Kane was the man beside me.

I told the dispatcher to send some cars to comb the area
near the hospital and gave them a description of Tessa.
Then I called Doehring to see if Honeycutt was with him.

"No. I'll look into it, though. Find out where he is."

"Any word on Lien-hua?"

"I haven't heard anything else."

At the moment there wasn't much more I could do
down here in the lobby. Obviously, Tessa wasn't here and
standing around waiting for her to come back wasn't going to help anything. I texted her again, telling her to call
me right away, then asked the receptionist to keep an eye
out for her.

"Where's post-op?" I asked.

She pointed. "Third floor, halfway down the hall on
the east wing. But they don't allow visitors in with the
patients."

"Okay." I turned to go.

"I said they don't allow visitors."

"Good." I held my creds up to her. "I'll make sure
there aren't any there."

A group of people had gathered in front of the elevators and I shouldered past them, threw open the door to
the stairwell, and took the stairs two at a time toward the
third floor.

8

Four minutes ago Tessa had left the lobby.

Earlier she'd told Patrick that she would pray, and she had. But the whole time she'd been unsure what to say. And even though she was usually pretty good with words, that's not really how her prayer had come out. It was more like a screech in her soul that went beyond language—sort of like fear wrapped in a desperate kind of love, but she hoped that God wouldn't hold her lack of eloquence against her.

Her mom was dead.

Her dad was dead.

All she had was Patrick and Lien-hua.

So, oh yeah, she'd prayed.

And the fact that she hadn't really known what to say bugged her. But then she thought that if it's true what they say, that ninety percent of communication is nonverbal, that most of it comes through in body language, gesture, posture, facial expression, eye contact, and inflection, then why wouldn't our prayers, our communication with God, be the same way? Why should words suddenly matter so much, especially to someone who's so good at reading hearts?

But in the end, praying—the right words or not—hadn't been enough, and Tessa felt like something terrible might happen to Lien-hua while she was stuck out there in the waiting area, and she couldn't bear the thought of that.

So, while the receptionist was looking over some paperwork, Tessa had slipped into the hallway, walked to the nearest nurses' station, and asked what room Special Agent Lien-hua Jiang was in.

The woman looked at her skeptically. "Are you a relative?"

"Yes," she answered.

"And how are you related to Ms. Jiang?"

The words came out before Tessa was really aware of it, and it both surprised her and did not surprise her when she said them: "She's my mom."

9

They'd already left post-op to take Lien-hua to her room, so I headed directly toward 414.

As I was stepping out of the stairwell, I saw Tessa in the hallway in front of me.

"Hey," I called, and she stopped and faced me. "What are you doing up here?" My words were sharper than I intended them to be. "I told you to wait in the lobby."

"I couldn't just sit around doing nothing."

"Tessa, you have to—"

"Let's not do this right now. Okay? I get it. Just . . . how is she?"

Why didn't she text you? She could have done it at any time!

Of course, part of me was relieved to see her, but part of me was angry because she'd made me search for her. "From what I heard, surgery went well. I went looking for you. I was worried." Though I was trying my hardest, my words still had an edge to them, however it was concern, not anger, that lay beneath them.

Tessa said nothing, but gave me a look that made it clear she didn't understand my tone. But she couldn't possibly have known what was going through my head concerning Basque when I'd found that she wasn't in the lobby.

We passed down the hallway toward the room. We were halfway there when a gruff voice rumbled behind me, "Pat."

I turned and saw my friend Special Agent Ralph Hawkins come lumbering our way, his wife, Brineesha, beside him.

Tessa and I paused to let them catch up.

"What do we know?" Ralph asked me.

"They were bringing her up here. She might be in the room already. I'm not sure."

The four of us proceeded and I eased the door open but saw that room 414 was empty. "She should be here any minute. I was just telling Tessa that surgery seemed to go faster than they anticipated."

An ex-Ranger and still a bodybuilder, Ralph seemed to fill the entire hallway. We'd first worked together to solve a series of homicides and mutilations back when I was still a detective in Milwaukee, fourteen years ago. As it turned out, Basque had been the man responsible for the murders we were investigating.

After that case, Ralph encouraged me to join the Bureau, and now, as the head of the National Center for the Analysis of Violent Crime, or NCAVC, he was officially my boss. He was also my best friend.

Brineesha edged around him to peer into the room. A slim, confident African-American woman with a no-nonsense attitude, she worked as a nurse at a hospital across town and called the shots in the family despite the fact that Ralph was the most alpha male guy I'd ever met.

Ralph and Brineesha had one son who was twelve, and they'd just found out that they had a baby girl on the way.

Over the last year Brineesha and Lien-hua had grown close, and I could see deep concern etched across her face.

Tessa gestured down the hallway, and when I followed her gaze I saw a doctor coming our way, walking beside a gurney being pushed by an orderly. A nurse walked beside them. I couldn't tell who might be on the gurney, but guessed it was Lien-hua. The four of us started toward them.

"I heard she was hit by a car," Brineesha said, "and—"

"She was stabbed too," Tessa said soberly.

"Yes. Ralph told me."

"By Basque."

"Yes."

We were close enough now for me to see. It was Lien-hua on the gurney.

She was on oxygen, had a chest tube, and it looked like she was asleep.

Even before I could ask him, the doctor leading the crew assured us, "Surgery went well." He was a studious-looking man, mid-fifties, with white hair that had a wind-blown, Einstein-ian look to it. That, along with his rumpled clothes, made me wonder how long he'd already been on his shift. "We gave her something to help her rest."

It seemed odd that they'd give a sedative to someone right after she awoke from anesthesia, but with a thoracic injury that severe, she probably did need to sleep.

"I'm her fiancé," I told the doctor as I went to Lien-hua's side and took her hand. "Pat Bowers."

While he was introducing himself as Dr. Frasier, the attending surgeon, Ralph got a call and stepped away. Frasier looked at me over the top of his wire-rimmed glasses and gave me a reserved smile. "The good news is, her injuries weren't as extensive as we initially thought. No arteries were nicked in her leg. She has a pneumothorax or—"

"A collapsed lung," Tessa said.

He looked a little surprised that she would know that. "Yes."

I suspected most teenagers wouldn't have any idea what a pneumothorax was, but I would've been surprised if Tessa hadn't known.

As we passed through the hallway back toward the room, Brineesha told the nurse beside me that she was a nurse as well, and they spoke softly about some of the specifics regarding Lien-hua's injuries.

It bothered me that Dr. Frasier had said, "The good news is . . ." And I was waiting for the other shoe to drop—*What's the bad news?*—but just as I was about to ask him, I thought that if Lien-hua wasn't all the way out it was possible she would hear me, and I didn't want her to overhear any bad news, so I held back.

Instead, I told her that I was here and that I loved her and—perhaps somewhat prematurely—that she was going to be fine.

We entered the room, the nurse and the orderly transferred her onto the bed, then tilted it into a slightly inclined position. Ralph returned to my side. "Pat"—his voice was soft, meant only for me—"we might have something."

"Tell me."

He indicated toward the window, and we crossed the room for a little privacy. Ralph kept his voice low. "We have video of Basque leaving the Cleveland Park Metro station earlier, at six."

"That would be when he went to the park to abduct her."

"There's more. Traffic cams caught the license plate of a stolen car eight blocks away from the apartment after the abduction and traveling east."

"Which street?"

"Benning Road."

Basque liked toying with law enforcement, and I could picture him going from one means of transportation to another, one car to another, not just to elude capture, but to lead us on an elaborate chase.

"You said cameras, so we know which direction he headed?" My phone vibrated, and I saw a text from Doehring that he was on his way up and that Honeycutt was at one of the hospital's other entrances.

"Using the shots from the traffic cams," Ralph went on, "Angela tracked the car to a water treatment plant in southeast quadrant of the city. SWAT's on its way over there now."

"He's there? We know he's there?"

He shook his head. "No idea. That's as much as we have."

I felt the twitch, the tightening of my focus and the sharpening of my senses that I always feel when the hunt is on. Even if Basque wasn't there, we might be able to find something either in the car he'd stolen or at the site that could lead us to him.

He might have just gone there to switch vehicles.

"Have them check with the plant employees to see if any other cars were taken."

"Right." Then he added, "I overheard the doc. She's doing okay?"

"It sounds like it. Yes."

"Then I'm heading to the plant."

I gestured for Brineesha to lead Tessa to the hall-way, asked the doctor to join Ralph and me by the window, then asked him softly, "Tell me straight—how's she doing?"

"The stab wound isn't as life-threatening as we first thought it might be. She also has a tib-fib fracture—um, that is—"

"Her tibia and fibula," I interjected somewhat impatiently. I'd been around injured victims all too often, and a long time ago when I still lived in Milwaukee I'd dated a medical student.

"Yes. We'll keep a close eye on the swelling to make sure she doesn't develop compartment syndrome. If it doesn't need to be surgically reduced we'll wait until her chest tube is out before casting her leg."

It's common for pedestrians who are hit by moving vehicles to career up the hood and impact against the windshield with their shoulders. I asked, "Her clavicles—either one broken?"

"No. She impacted with the right one, there's some swelling but it's nothing serious. And it doesn't look like there's going to be any nerve damage in her leg. I'd say, overall, she was lucky. Right now she just needs to rest."

"How long will she be in here?" Ralph said.

"I can't say for sure. For thoracic surgery like this, we're usually looking at four to six days. And then we'll need to put that cast on. After that, she should be able to leave in twenty-four hours or so."

"So, barring any complications, up to a week."

He nodded. "Barring any complications."

Ralph glanced at his watch, and I could tell he was anxious to get going.

"Hang on a sec," I told him.

I was torn. I wanted to be here when Lien-hua woke up, but I also wanted to find Basque.

The nurse had left the bedside and I took Lien-hua's hand again.

"Go get him, Patrick." It was Tessa, who'd reentered the room and had obviously been listening in.

"How did you—"

"You guys suck at whispering." She came to my side. "She'd want you to go. You know that. Brineesha and I will be here. Remember what you said in the car? What we talked about earlier?"

She was referring to our conversation about what I'd do when I caught the guy who'd attacked Lien-hua. I'd told her that I would make sure he paid. "You'd better," she'd replied. And neither one of us had been talking about bringing Basque in.

"Let me think."

"You heard Dr. Frasier; she's recovering. And she just needs to sleep."

After another moment of internal debate, I made my decision and leaned close to Lien-hua. "I'm going after him. Tessa's here. So is Brineesha. I'll be back as soon as I can. I love you."

Then I kissed her cheek, stood, and said to Ralph, "Okay, let's see if he's still at that water treatment plant."

I took one more look at Lien-hua lying there with the chest tube draining blood from where she'd been stabbed, then I left with Ralph to go take down the guy who'd done this to her.

10

We took a police chopper, used the hospital's landing pad. Doehring joined us.

It was possible all this was a ploy, so before we left, we stationed two additional officers outside Lien-hua's door just to make sure there was no way for Basque or any accomplices he might have been working with to gain access to her and finish the job he'd started in that apartment.

As we flew over the city, my hand glanced against the holster of my .357 SIG P229. Most agents these days had moved to Glocks, but the Bureau had also approved SIGs and I was glad. This gun and I went back a long way.

I couldn't help but think back to the one time, the only time, it'd ever jammed on me, that afternoon I arrested Basque in an abandoned slaughterhouse on the outskirts of Milwaukee.

He'd come under suspicion because he frequently flew on business trips to the same cities where young women were disappearing or showing up dead. When I found him in the slaughterhouse, he was bent over his next victim, scalpel in hand. She was still alive, but would bleed to death only minutes later because of her extensive, gruesome injuries.

Basque shot at me, missed, and I tried to return fire, but that's when my gun jammed. He fired again, sending a round through my shoulder. During the fight that ensued, he also stabbed me in the right thigh, just a few inches higher than he'd stabbed Lien-hua's leg earlier tonight—now that I thought about it, it looked like my fiancée and I were going to have matching scars.

After I'd cuffed Basque and gone to help the dying woman, he'd said to me, "I think we may need an ambulance, don't you, Detective?" Then, after I failed to save her, I dragged him to his feet to read him his rights and he said softly, "I guess we won't be needing that ambulance after all."

That's when I lost it.

I punched him in the jaw, sending him smashing to the concrete floor of the slaughterhouse. Then I was on him and punched him again, shattering his jaw—but even with the broken jaw he was able to get out one more sentence: "It feels good, doesn't it, Detective? It feels really good."

A rush of shame swept over me. He was right; it did feel good to dip into the dark, animalistic part of myself, if only for a moment. Violence without restraint or remorse. The truth became clear to me: I was capable of the kind of acts that shocked me most, the ones I assured myself that I could never do.

Shooting that killer had felt good to Tessa in a perverse, savage way, and similarly, physically assaulting Basque, hearing the bones in his jaw crack, had felt good to me.

It wasn't justice, it wasn't self-defense, it was something a lot more primitive than that.

It's unsettling to discover how much we all have in common with the people I hunt.

Afterward, when I filled out my report, I'd stared at the papers for a long time, evaluating exactly what to write. These were the forms that would be used in court.

I faced a dilemma: tell the whole truth about physically assaulting him and risk that he would get off, or tell the truth up to a point and let justice be done.

In the end I simply wrote that there was an altercation and that the suspect's jaw was broken during his apprehension. Later, Basque inexplicably claimed it'd happened when I swung the meat hook at him. I'd done it to distract him. But the meat hook never hit him at all.

Why he said that was still a mystery to me.

In fact, I could come up with only one reason: he knew he was going to be put away and it was a power play, something to hold over me while he was in prison.

But motives are always a mystery.

Especially those of a psychopath.

SWAT was already there when our pilot settled the chopper onto the water treatment plant's parking lot.

While it's true that there's often a sense of rivalry between law enforcement agencies, I'd never had any issues with the DC Metropolitan Police Department, and now Brian Shaw, the SWAT commander, approached us.

Too much time has passed, Pat, Basque's not going to be here.

Yeah. That was probably right.

But maybe it wasn't.

"We're ready to go in," Shaw told us.

So am I.

"Good," I replied.

As he brought us up to speed, I noticed a map of the building's schematics spread out on the hood of a car a few feet away. Two SWAT officers had flashlights out and were leaning over it, studying it. I committed the blueprint to memory.

When I asked Shaw for a vest, Ralph must have realized what I had in mind, because he nodded for him and Doehring to give us a second alone. After they stepped away, Ralph said, "Let SWAT do this, Pat. They'll get—"

"I'm going in with the incursion team."

He shook his head. "No, you're not. We're gonna do this by the book." He put one of his mammoth paws on my shoulder. "I know you're—"

I moved his hand away. "If he attacked Brineesha like he did Lien-hua, what would you do?"

"I'd kill him, but—"

"Alright."

"But I'd also expect you to stop me. You don't need me to tell you that."

From our history working together, I knew Ralph wanted to take Basque down almost as much as I did, but I also understood that in his current position at the Bureau he had to follow protocol.

So do you.

Yeah, well, that's never been my specialty.

"I get it," I told him.

He eyed me squarely. "I'm not gonna say I know what you're going through right now, okay? But you're playing right into his hands."

"How's that?"

"Why do you think he went after Lien-hua? She's never worked his case. He went after her to hurt you, to make you stupid with rage."

"Yes," I acknowledged. But I wasn't really focused on what he was saying. I was busy studying the geography of the land surrounding the treatment plant and comparing it with what I knew of the region's neighboring roads and traffic patterns, trying to form a map of the area in my mind.

"Are you hearing me, Pat?"

Sometimes anger hones my senses, sometimes it blurs my vision. Nothing seemed blurred at the moment. "Okay," I told him.

"Okay?"

"He went after her to hurt me. I get it. I hear you."

"And we do this by the book?"

I tried to lie to him, to tell him that yes, I would do things by the book, that I would follow protocol and trust that the very system that'd let Basque out of prison would do its job this time around, but those weren't the words that came out of my mouth. "If I get him alone, Ralph, I can't promise you that I'll bring him in alive."

He worked his jaw back and forth. "You're not where you need to be right now. We send in SWAT. We let 'em do their job."

Discussing this with him was just wasting precious time and that wasn't helping anything. "Okay. I get it." But I'd already decided what I was going to do.

He evaluated that, then gave me a nod and strode over to talk to Doehring and Shaw. I unholstered my gun and walked directly toward the building's front entrance.

"Get back here, Agent—" someone called, but that's all I heard, because by then I was stepping into the water treatment plant and letting the door swing shut behind me.

11

I leveled my SIG in front of me.

The lights inside the building were off, but I found a switch beside the door, flicked it up, and a string of overhead fluorescents blinked on.

It took my eyes a moment to get used to the sudden, stark light, but based on the blueprints, I already knew where I was—a small reception area with two hallways, one to the right, the other to the left.

If Basque really did come in here, I doubted he was going to hang out in one of the offices. By leaving that car outside in plain sight it sure seemed like he was taunting us. But regardless, I didn't believe he would've come in here unless he had a plan to get away undetected.

I mentally reviewed the building's schematics—the layout of the offices, the orientation of the hallways, the location of the filtration chambers, the labyrinthine network of passageways housing the pipes, ducts, and electrical lines that ran beneath the structure. Actually, that's where I was heading, because that's where I'd be able to access the drainage tunnels that led away from the plant.

From the schematics, I hadn't been able to tell if the tunnels carried waste or water—or nothing at all—but they did radiate away from the building, and if I were Basque, that's where I would have gone to slip past SWAT's perimeter.

Cautiously, I passed through the hallway toward the east stairwell, but when I got there, the lights above the stairs didn't work. I tried them again. Nothing.

I took that as a good sign. At the moment I couldn't think of any other reasonable explanation for why these lights weren't working than that someone flipped a breaker. And if that were true, it meant that a person had passed through here to the breaker boxes on the lower level, precisely where I was heading.

SWAT hadn't pursued me; I wasn't sure why, but I was glad they hadn't moved in yet. If Basque was here, it gave me a chance to be alone with him and that was just what I wanted.

I pulled out my Mini Maglite and the beam slit the darkness in front of me. Using my left hand to steady the flashlight and my right to direct my gun, I descended the stairs.

"Richard?" I didn't know if calling his name would do any good, but considering our history, I figured he just might reply. "I want you to step out and show me your hands." My words echoed eerily through the narrow stairwell but were met only with silence.

I called out for him two more times, but no one replied.

At the bottom of the steps, I turned right and entered the sublevel's maze of narrow winding passages. There were no overhead lights down here, but sporadic bulbs hung from the ceiling, and red warning lights glowed near some of the gauges and electrical control panels, lending a dim, eerie mood to the walkway.

Pipes, thick bundles of cables, and water filtration lines snaked above and beside me through the cramped passage. An electrical panel just to the left of the stairwell had twelve breakers turned off. I flicked them back on, and the stairwell lights came on.

Okay, so someone definitely had been down here.

I wasn't sure how to actually get to the tunnels that ran beneath this level, but from the schematics, I knew where one access point would be—around a bend to the left, about thirty meters ahead of me.

A chug of adrenaline pumped through me, and admittedly, it felt good. I don't mind teaching classes at the Academy or analyzing computer models of the progression of serial crimes, but I'd rather be out here in the field any day, face-to-face with why I do what I do.

And there's no better feeling than bringing someone like Basque in.

Or taking him down.

"You knew those intersections would have traffic cameras, didn't you?" I proceeded around the bend. "Why did you choose that route? So we could track you?"

Nothing.

He'll be long gone, Pat. There's no way he would linger around here, not when he left that car out front. He'd know law enforcement would be all over this place.

Yes. All that was true.

But the breakers were flipped. Someone had come down here.

There was no stairwell to the tunnel system beneath the plant, but I did find a hatch about the size of a manhole cover on the floor.

Beneath it I heard the muffled sound of flowing water, or possibly sewage, passing by, and I realized I might've been completely off-track with what I was thinking—the tunnel below me might be entirely filled with water.

I slipped the Maglite between my teeth so I could use my left hand to tug the hatch's cover free while keeping the SIG aimed down the hole with my right.

The cover was heavy, but manageable, and a moment later I was staring down into the tunnel.

It looked like it was approximately three meters to the bottom, or at least to the water that was rushing past. It was hard to tell how deep the current was, but based on the curvature of the corrugated-metal tunnel, I guessed the water would reach nearly to my knees.

Quite possibly the tunnel served to help channel floodwater away from this low-lying area of the city after storms. However, at the moment I didn't care why this tunnel system was here, as long as it didn't fill up with water while I was inside it.

A rusted ladder led down along the side of the tunnel. The sound of the flowing water was loud enough to make me think it wouldn't do a whole lot of good to call out for Basque, so, still gripping the flashlight in my teeth to free up my left hand, and keeping my SIG in my right, I scrambled down the first few steps, then leapt to the bottom.

I landed with a splash. The water wasn't quite as deep as I'd thought it would be, but it still reached to the middle of my calves. Though the current wasn't strong enough to sweep me off my feet, it was stiff enough to make me realize I'd need to be careful when I moved forward.

Grabbing my light again, I visually swept the tunnel to the right, saw nothing, then directed both the beam and my SIG down the tunnel to my left.

And I saw a man about thirty meters away, just on the edge of the flashlight's beam.

He was facing me, but turned and disappeared down a side tunnel before I could identify for certain that it was Basque. I yelled for him to stop and the words reverberated off the metal walls with a coarse, hollow sound before being quickly overcome by the noise of the rushing water.

I sprinted after him as fast as I could through the rapidly flowing current.

12

A dot of light bobbed in front of me, indicating where the man was running.

I didn't want to jump to any conclusions, but obviously all the evidence pointed to this guy being Basque. If it really was him, I didn't need to see him to picture him: Caucasian, six-two, athletic build, dark hair, striking features, piercing aquamarine eyes. He could have stepped off the cover of *GQ* magazine, but beneath his impressive exterior was one of the vilest hearts of anyone I'd ever encountered.

Lien-hua shot him. He's injured. You can catch him.

The damp smell of mold and decay filled the tunnel, while the sound of the splash and flow of water echoed off the tunnel's metal walls, slightly disorienting me.

I'd been running for maybe sixty or seventy meters when the light ahead of me went out. I turned off my flashlight as well, hoping to pick up movement of the light again, but all I saw was uninterrupted blackness before me. Light back on, I pushed forward, and a few moments later I arrived at an intersection.

Alternating my Maglite back and forth between the two tunnels, I saw nothing to indicate which direction the man I was pursuing might have fled.

No sign of anyone.

The building's schematics hadn't included the tunnels this far from the structure itself, and even taking into account the geography of the surrounding area, there was no way to know which of the two tunnels might lead the most directly to the outside world.

Two tunnels.

One veering left, the other right.

The tunnel to the left leveled off, allowing less water to pass by.

My first thought: *That water dissipates eventually; you'd be able to hear him running. He would take the one that would hide the sound of his footfalls—he'll stay in deeper water.*

But then a second thought: *No, Pat, he would know you'd think that.*

I equivocated.

Go. Hurry. Decide!

The water rushing past me had to go somewhere or else it wouldn't be able to have such a strong current. At some point it had to empty into a drainage ditch or the Anacostia River. Taking a moment to orient myself, I guessed it might lead toward the grove of trees I'd seen earlier, east of the plant.

Knowing he would have to exit the tunnel system somewhere, I chose the tunnel carrying the swifter current and flew down it.

The musty air down here reminded me of that day when I first caught him in the slaughterhouse.

He abducts women, he eats them, he kills them. That's what he was going to do to Lien-hua.

Anger flared inside me.

Ralph had said that Basque was trying to make me

stupid with rage. Well, maybe that was true. And maybe that wasn't such a bad thing. I recalled my words to Ralph: "If I get him alone, I can't promise you that I'll bring him in alive."

No.

No, I couldn't make a promise like that to Ralph or to myself.

After two more bends I still hadn't seen any flicker of light or any indication that the man had come this direction, and I was beginning to think I'd probably chosen the wrong passage when I saw the water disappearing down a metal grate in front of me.

Sticks, waterlogged garbage, and half a dozen dead rats lay compressed in a pile above the two-meter-wide grate, forced there by the current. I could only guess that the water pouring out of sight probably channeled into an underground stream leading to the Anacostia.

If the man I was chasing had pushed that grate aside and dropped in there to escape, this debris would've been disturbed and the grate wouldn't have been pushed back into place.

If he came this direction, he would have had to pass by it.

I inspected the floor of the tunnel beyond the place where the water went down the drain and I saw what I was looking for—wet sole impressions.

I dashed forward until the sound of the water draining through the grate behind me began to fade, but when I paused to listen, I heard no footsteps, just that faint echo of churning water and my own ragged breathing.

Pressing on, I cornered a bend in the tunnel and nearly smacked into a locked metal gate that reached from the bottom of the tunnel to the top.

The tunnel terminated a few meters beyond the rusted

steel bars, opening up into the night, and from the looks of it, the tunnel ended halfway up an embankment. I guessed that during storms it would feed overflow water into a streambed or drainage ditch below.

A light snapped on outside the tunnel on the left side of the embankment and a voice of someone out of sight called to me, "Did she survive?"

I recognized the speaker right away.

Yes, without a doubt, it was Richard Basque, and he had made it past the gate.

13

I grabbed the bars to get to him, but the gate only rattled harshly against its chain when I did. Not even Ralph could've wrenched it free. The lock looked new, which made me think that Basque must have been prepared for this—chaining and locking the gate behind him as he fled.

It was a keyed lock rather than a combination one, and that might actually play to my favor.

I'm pretty good with locks, and although I didn't have my lock pick set with me, I did have a pen. And it had a spring inside.

"From where I was standing, Pat," Basque said, "it looked like that car hit her pretty hard."

He was around the corner; I still couldn't see him. Still had no shot.

I slipped the pen out.

He used your name. He knows it's you back here.

But my light had been in his eyes when I first got into the tunnel. How did he know I was the one who'd followed him? *He heard you calling? Or maybe he was watching through a window in the front of the building and saw you enter?*

Right now it didn't matter. All that mattered was getting to him.

Since he was standing to the side of the tunnel, he wouldn't be able to see me work on the lock. Transferring my gun to my left hand, I jammed the flashlight under my armpit to free up my right hand so I could pick the lock. It was a little awkward, but there was no way I was going to holster my weapon right now.

"So, did she survive?"

"Richard"—I was not going to talk with him about Lien-hua—"if you turn yourself in, I'll see what I can do to get you the death penalty." I unscrewed the pen's top and pulled out the spring, straightened it, and set to work.

"Is that your idea of reverse psychology?" There was disconcerting familiarity in his voice.

"Back to solitary confinement? Spending the rest of your life in a cell the size of a walk-in closet? Just one hour a day alone in the yard to exercise?" I was working on the lock the whole time I spoke. "Is that what you want? And there aren't even any good ways to kill yourself in there—except maybe chewing through your wrists to the arteries. I wonder, even being the way you are, would you have the nerve to do that?"

He went on unfazed, "That stab wound was pretty deep, Pat. There must have been a lot of internal bleeding. It would have made her lungs quite moist. I prefer them that way."

Rage cut through me, and I tried my best to keep it out of my voice. Mentally reviewing the footage from the apartment, I said, "I saw the overturned end table."

I focused, focused, focused, keeping my fingers steady, but it didn't seem like I was making any progress. "There was a scuffle, wasn't there? You couldn't even stop her when her hands were restrained behind her? That must be a little humbling."

A slight pause. "Aesop," he said. "'The Hare and the Hound.' Do you know the story?"

"Remind me."

This lock was just not cooperating.

Come on!

"A hound was chasing a hare. All afternoon he tried to catch him but he couldn't. A shepherd was watching the whole time, and when the dog finally gave up and went home without the rabbit, the shepherd laughed and said, 'I used to think you were faster than the hare. But now I know the truth—the hare's faster than you are.' But the hound replied, 'No, you don't understand. It's one thing to run for your dinner; it's another to run for your life.'"

"So you have the advantage? That's your point? That you're more motivated to get away than I am to catch you?"

"You work a lot of cases, Patrick. I'm just another meal to you."

"You don't know me as well as you think."

There was another beat of silence. "Well, in that case, I guess the chase is on."

Yes, it is.

Oh, yeah, it's rabbit season.

His light flicked off and there was a soft swish of movement through the underbrush.

Working as fast as I could on the lock, I called, "I'm coming for you, Richard."

"I'm counting on it." His voice was fainter now; he was getting away.

I jiggled the thin wire futilely in the lock. Every second I wasted here he was getting farther—

The mechanism clicked.

The lock opened.

Unthreading the chain, I threw my weight against the gate. It flew open and, flashlight in one hand, SIG in the other, I dashed to the tunnel's terminus and swept my gun to the side where Basque had been. No one. The bank above me angled up steeply into the night. He must have scrambled down to the streambed to flee.

I leapt off the lip of the tunnel and made my way down the embankment.

Using the Maglite, I scanned the woods all around me.

No sign of him.

I pushed my way into the underbrush, looking for footprints or snapped twigs that might have indicated which direction he'd fled, but found nothing.

A strip of woods stretched before me. I took a second to replay the twists and turns I'd made through the building, through the passageway beneath it, and through the drainage tunnels. I calculated that I was about a quarter mile southeast of the perimeter SWAT had set up.

I whipped out my cell and speed-dialed Ralph.

He answered, blurted out a string of expletives. "Pat, I told you not to—"

"Later. Listen: he was here. He's close. We can still catch him."

"Where are you?"

I relayed my location. "We need to get choppers in the air, and I want a team over here. Now. Get this whole area cordoned off. There's a residential neighborhood about half a kilometer east of me." I caught myself— Ralph always gave me a hard time about using the metric system, so I translated for him: "About three-tenths of a mile east of here. He might have another car waiting. He would have thought of a way out of here."

Thankfully, at least for the time being, Ralph didn't hassle me for pursuing Basque. I knew that as my supervisor, he might be obligated to write me up, but we could both deal with that later.

End call.

Why was Basque still in that tunnel when I arrived? Surely he'd had enough time to get away.

He was facing you when you first shone the light at him, Pat. He was monitoring that tunnel.

Yes, he was. He was waiting down there for someone to pursue him.

There were twelve north-facing windows in the water treatment facility that would have afforded someone inside the building a view of the entrance I'd used. He must have been watching, waiting for someone to come in, just to lure that person to follow him. Really, since radio and cell communication would have been impossible in the tunnel, it was a perfect escape route.

Maybe it was about the chase to him after all.

A game of cat and mouse.

Or, in this case, dog and hare.

Actually, come to think of it, dogs were not a bad idea.

I put a call through to Shaw to get a K-9 unit out here to track Basque. "Have them get his scent from the driver's seat of the car." Metro PD used Belgian Malinois, and they were some of the best-trained ones I'd seen.

"Roger that."

I pocketed my phone and scrutinized the forest again.

The residential area lay to the east. A deepening cove

of woods loomed before me. To the west, a broad field eventually met up with a sprawling industrial district.

It would make sense for Basque to disappear into the forest, but I was more concerned that he might go toward the homes to the east. With civilians potentially at risk, protecting the people who lived here took precedent over tromping through the woods trying to find him in the dark.

As I ran toward the neighborhood, I called Shaw again to confirm we were getting roadblocks set up. "And I don't care how late it is, I want officers to go door-to-door to interview and warn residents."

Let's see how fast you can run after all, Richard.

As sirens cycled through the night, I bolted toward the nearby neighborhood to search for the hare.

14

It was really hard for Tessa to be here in this hospital room.

Even though gothic horror was her favorite genre of literature, and thrasher metal her favorite type of music, and even though she was a cutter, blood in real life made her seriously queasy, graveyards freaked her out, and hospitals made her think of the long days sitting beside her mom as she weakened, slipped into a coma, and died.

No, hospitals were definitely not on Tessa's top-ten list of favorite places to be.

And now, here, tonight, she was terrified that Lienhua might die. She'd already seen her mother and her father die—her mother from cancer, her father from a bullet meant for a killer.

After their deaths, it seemed like pain had become permanently etched across the surface of her life—almost as if it were engraved indelibly on her heart. Over the last six months things had improved a little, but the pain was still there, and time didn't seem to quiet it but only served to bring the ridges of it more distinctly to the surface.

So now Tessa sat quietly with Mrs. Hawkins beside the bed.

Lien-hua lay asleep, her heartbeat monitor pulsing evenly, a chest tube that Tessa kept trying not to look at, but found herself eyeing nevertheless, trailing out of her torso to a machine that drained blood from her lungs to keep them from filling with fluid.

The doctors had assured them that Lien-hua was on her way to recovery, but seeing her lying there like that, it was hard to believe.

Over the last couple years Tessa had taken to calling Agent Hawkins and his wife by their first names and now she said, "Brineesha, I was praying for her, but I'm not sure God was listening."

She expected Brineesha to reassure her that of course God was listening, of course he was, but she didn't do that at all. "Tessa, I'm not sure if you know this, but Tony was three months premature."

Okay, not the reply she was expecting.

"No, I didn't."

"Honey, that boy weighed only two pounds and two ounces when he was born. We didn't think he was going to make it a week."

Ah. The point of the story became clear. "And you prayed for him, and he recovered, is that it?"

She shook her head. "The more I prayed, the worse he got. Only when I stopped praying, only then did he get better."

Tessa looked at her curiously. "Are you saying prayer didn't help?"

"I'm saying it didn't help when I wanted it to."

Tessa didn't reply, and in the silent wake of Brineesha's words their attention shifted back to Lien-hua. It seemed to Tessa that she'd never seen anyone who was alive lie so still.

The point of Brineesha's story seemed to be: hang in there, God will help Lien-hua eventually, in his own time. But Tessa knew enough about life to know that things didn't always work out like that. They definitely hadn't worked out like that two years ago for her mom.

Maybe God had his reasons, but look at the world closely enough and you can't help but come away wondering why he seems so random in the prayers he does answer, and so, well, capricious in the ones he does not.

As Tessa tried to sort all that through, she watched Lien-hua lie there so still. Apart from her chest rising and falling, she didn't move at all. Didn't even stir.

+++

We didn't find him.

Not in the neighborhood, not in the industrial district or the woods. We didn't find any sole impressions in the mud near the stream or any broken twigs that might have indicated his path through the forest. Even the dogs came up empty.

I had the thought that Basque might have slipped back through the steel gate after I exited, so we searched the network of tunnels but found nothing. If he had doubled back, he must have found another way out. The dogs couldn't track any scent through the flowing water, and a detailed search of the water treatment facility came up empty.

He was like a poltergeist from a horror movie, a phantom that leaves traces of its presence only when it wants to and then dematerializes again into thin air. But Basque wasn't a ghost. He was a real person of flesh and blood who'd slipped past us. Again.

During the search, I texted Tessa half a dozen times to

find out about Lien-hua's condition, but her only reply was that she still hadn't awakened.

More often than not, working with the media backfires, but tonight we put out word for them to inform the public that Basque was at large and in the vicinity. I honestly wasn't sure how much good it would do, but right now the team thought it was the best chance we had of finding Basque. And, reluctantly, I had to agree with them.

Ralph and I touched base, and I recounted the search through the tunnels beneath the water treatment plant, outlining the specific course I'd taken while pursuing Basque. Shaw was standing nearby. "That's a lot of tunnels to remember," he said. "You sure you didn't get turned around down there?"

"I'm sure."

A pause. "Okay."

"Trust me," Ralph said, "Pat's good with directions."

Latex gloves on, I took some time to inspect the car Basque had driven to the facility. Inside, I found two empty water bottles, a number of crumpled-up napkins and discarded fast-food wrappers, three fashion magazines from last year, and a beat-up mass-market version of a crime novel.

And that's what caught my attention.

The novel, *On My Way to Dying*, was written by Saundra Weathers, a mystery writer who'd grown up in my hometown of Horicon, Wisconsin.

She was a year older than I was, but besides being from the same town, we were linked in another way, a macabre connection that not too many people knew about.

When I was a junior in high school, an eleven-year-old

girl who'd recently moved to town with her parents disappeared while walking home from school. The next day, I was the one who found her body in an old tree house on the edge of the vast marsh just outside of Horicon. The girl had been raped and then killed by a man I tracked down nearly a decade later while I was a homicide detective in Milwaukee.

Saundra's parents owned the land that bordered the marsh.

And now, here was one of her books in the car Basque had stolen.

It might have been a coincidence that this specific book just happened to be in this specific car at this specific time, but I don't believe in coincidences.

I flipped through the novel to see if there were any underlined words, highlighted passages, or dog-eared pages that might have been clues left intentionally or unintentionally by Basque about where his burrow really was, but I didn't find anything.

The Lab could analyze the book and the rest of the items in the car. Maybe they'd be able to pull something up. I put a call through to FBI Headquarters to find out where Saundra Weathers lived. "Basque has worked with partners in the past. I want some agents to check on her and then watch her house tonight. I'll be in touch with her in the morning."

"Yes, sir."

Finally, after more than an hour of searching the area and finding no clues whatsoever about which direction Basque might have gone, Ralph told me to get my butt back to the hospital, that they could finish the search out here.

"It's dark, we're not coming up with anything, and you need to be there with your fiancée."

Even though I was more than ready to change out of my wet clothes, I wanted to see Lien-hua a lot more than I wanted to switch outfits.

And truthfully, she wasn't the only one I was concerned about. Tessa was used to staying up late, but I'm sure she was stressed. It was almost two o'clock, and she'd be useless unless I got her home to bed.

The chopper pilot needed to stay on hand in case Ralph and the rest of the team came up with anything, but one of the SWAT guys who wasn't involved in the search lived near the hospital and offered to give me a ride.

"I'll catch up with you later," Ralph told me. But before I left, he pulled me aside. "Pat, you can be headstrong, I get that, but the next time I make it clear to you that I don't want you accessing a potential crime scene, you don't access it. Period. End of story." Then he sighed. "As if you're gonna listen to that anyway."

"You would have done the same thing, Ralph."

He scoffed, and I took that as a form of agreement.

"Just don't do anything stupid that would screw up our case against this guy," he said.

"You have my word on that."

As I was walking to the car, I received a text message from Tessa that Lien-hua was waking up.

15

Back at the hospital I hurried to Lien-hua's room and found Brineesha, Tessa, and the white-haired doctor, who was checking Lien-hua's charts, gathered around the bed. My fiancée was awake and looked weak, but remarkably alert, considering all that she'd been through.

Before I could ask her how she was doing she said, "Did you get him?" Her voice was scratchy and soft but she spoke with just as much quiet intensity and resolve as ever.

"No." I went to her side, took her hand. It seemed like whatever I said at the moment would be inadequate, but I managed to get out what was in the forefront of my mind. "Lien-hua, I love you so much. I was . . . I knew you were going to be okay."

"Yes." She coughed slightly and cringed, and it was clear that despite the pain medication she was still having a rough time.

I kissed her, then asked the obligatory question: "How are you feeling?"

"Like I was strangled, stabbed twice, and then hit by a car." She gave a faint smile.

Brineesha glanced at Tessa. "Well, at least the woman still has her sense of humor."

Lien-hua said to us, "The doctor here tells me no sparring for a while."

"Too bad," I replied. "I practiced my spinning side kicks while you were in London."

"You're not falling over anymore every time you do them?"

"Only about half the time."

"We'll work on that as soon as this leg starts feeling better."

The doctor finished up and left the four of us alone.

I wasn't sure what to do. I wanted to spend the rest of the night here in the room with Lien-hua, but with Basque out there I didn't like the idea of Tessa being at home alone—even if we assigned a team of officers to guard the house.

It was almost as if Brineesha read my thoughts, because she suggested that Tessa spend the night at their place. In their basement they had a spare bedroom—actually more of a mini apartment—where Brineesha's mom had lived until last August when she died. "Tessa can stay downstairs," Brineesha offered. "There's plenty of room."

Considering Ralph would be at the house with them, it seemed like a good plan to me.

"I guess we'll have to postpone that cake-sampling trip tomorrow," Lien-hua told Tessa.

"Maybe I should give it a trial run on my own. Test the waters, you know?"

"Not without me you don't." Lien-hua scolded her lightly with her finger, but then coughed again, and I could see on her face how much the coughing hurt.

"Shh. You don't have to talk. Just relax."

"I feel better than I look," she said, but I wasn't sure I believed that.

As Tessa and Brineesha were getting ready to leave, Brineesha called Ralph to tell him the plan and he said he'd meet them at the house. I phoned dispatch to have them send a squad to escort Brineesha and Tessa on the trip home, and then stay there with them until Ralph arrived.

After they were gone, I wanted Lien-hua to rest, but it seemed important to her to tell me about what had happened when she was attacked. She was one of the toughest women I knew, but going through an encounter like that would be terrifying for anyone, and that fear came through clearly in her voice as she recounted the story.

She said, "You know how they talk about your whole life flashing before your eyes right before you die?"

"Yes."

"Well, it wasn't as if my whole life flashed before my eyes, it was more like one moment appeared, then time, well . . ." She struggled for how to phrase things. "You've faced death before, Pat."

"Yeah."

"It's like time stretches out and . . . and you see how, well, I'm not sure of the right phrase."

"How unfathomable it is. And how brief."

"Yes. How unfathomable life is—how unfathomable every moment is. And how fleeting they are." She shook her head. "I really thought I was going to die, Pat. And all I could think of was how I'd never see you again."

Shame stung me, regret for not looking back at her car as I drove away from her at the park. "I should have made sure you were safe. Before Tessa and I left."

"No, that's ridiculous. I'm not a child. There was no way you could have known I'd be attacked."

That might have been true, but it didn't really make me feel any better. The whole situation still seemed surreal to me. "You thought to call 911 and then shoot him while you were being strangled." I shook my head. "You're amazing."

"I just wish I had better aim."

When she pressed me, I summarized the chase at the water treatment plant and related the fable Basque had told me about the dog and the hare.

She reflected for a moment, then, always the profiler, said, "Think about it—he's a cannibal and he tells you a story about one animal trying to capture and eat another."

"But in this case I would be the one chasing him."

Maybe he was telling you that you're not all that different.

No, I slid that thought aside. It was just a story. Just a fable.

"There's no way he thought of that off the top of his head. He had it prepared. All of it, everything, was a way of taunting you," Lien-hua said, then coughed harshly and winced again.

"Shh," I said. "Just rest."

But she went on. "That's why he waited outside the metal gate. He could have fled, but it's become more than that to him now. It's all about the chase."

"The hunt."

"Yes."

That reminded me of the crime novel I'd found in the car. Lien-hua already knew about me finding Mindy's body in the tree house back when I was a teenager, but I'd never mentioned the family that lived beside the marsh. It'd just never come up. So now I told her I'd found the novel, and then I explained who Saundra Weathers was.

She repositioned herself slightly on the bed. "The Lab is looking over the book?"

"The ERT guys were there at the scene. I'm assuming they have everything back to the Lab by now." I patted her arm. "Really, I think you should rest."

"When was the last time you saw her, Saundra Weathers, I mean?"

"It's been over twenty years. Now, Lien-hua—"

"We should find out where she lives and get a car over there."

"I did that while I was at the plant."

"Great minds." She yawned, although it was clear she was trying to stifle it.

"Great minds."

"It's possible he chose to leave the book behind to do more than show a connection to your past. It's possible he also left it there to show you a connection to the future." She yawned again.

"Miss Weathers is safe. We can talk about all this tomorrow. You need to sleep, Lien-hua."

"Yeah," she said wearily. "I think I agree."

I shed my wet socks and damp pants, hung them up to dry, pulled up one of the hospital chairs so I could sleep by her side, and tucked my legs under a blanket. Thankfully, the chair reclined, but I'm over six feet tall and I found it impossible to position myself comfortably on it. However I was mentally and physically exhausted and hoped that, as awkward as sleeping like this was going to be, I'd at least be able to get a little rest.

"I love you, Lien-hua."

"I love you, too." It sounded like she was already half asleep.

As soon as I closed my eyes, thoughts of Basque and his tale of the dog and the hare invaded my thoughts. I tried to clear my head, to relax, but failed.

And so as I lay there, I mentally reviewed the case—what we knew, what we didn't know, what Basque had done, and if there was anything I was missing. And I tried to figure out what our next step in tracking him down needed to be.

16

Keith Tyree and Vanessa Juliusson landed at the Chennai International Airport just seven kilometers south of the city.

Though they'd been planning to get there earlier in the day, a canceled connection out of Frankfurt had set them back, and now they were already behind schedule.

Ever since watching Corey Wellington bleed to death in his living room in Atlanta the other day, they'd been on the move, and they still had one more leg of their journey to complete. This wasn't their first assignment together and it was no coincidence that their employer had chosen Corey, just like it was no coincidence that he'd chosen that specific woman in Montana two weeks earlier.

And now, although Keith was weary of traveling, he said nothing to Vanessa, who never seemed to sleep, thinking that it might appear to her as a sign of weakness.

He needed to focus, to stay alert. It might end up being a long night.

Especially if he had to use the handheld pruning shears he'd brought along.

Admittedly, that part of his job was unpleasant, but he wasn't about to take chances; he would do what he needed to do to see this project through to the end.

After all, the man whom he and Vanessa worked for did not like loose ends, did not like it when people disappointed him, did not make allowances for even the smallest degree of incompetence. More than once they'd seen what he did to the people who let him down, and to say the least, it would not be an enjoyable way to go.

Keith was not about to let that happen to him.

He knew that running or trying to hide would be useless, would only make things worse in the end. So he'd decided long ago that he would rather eat a bullet—or take the drug himself—than fall into the man's hands.

Now he directed his attention to the reason they were here.

First order of business: get to the facility in Kadapa and do a little quality control.

Then make sure the shipment and paperwork were all in order. Finally, get back to Boston by the end of the week to visit the inspector.

Whenever he and Vanessa were in India, they didn't rent a car but rather hired a driver. Today the man was supposed to meet them in Chennai, so they would need to take a taxi that far.

Normally, beggars were not allowed on the premises of India's international airports, but for some reason today they were congregated outside the terminal, and Keith and Vanessa had to push their way past them.

As they passed an elderly woman with an outstretched, leprous hand, Keith reached into his pocket and pulled out a coin, but Vanessa stopped him before he could hand it over, clutched his arm, and led him to the street corner. "If you give money to one of them, they'll all gather around you expecting handouts. I've told you this before."

"Yes."

"So don't do it."

A pause. "Okay."

Even though the caste system was officially banned, it wasn't culturally banned—and millions of people still treated cows with more respect than they treated human beings from the lowest caste. Streets all throughout India's major cities were cluttered with invalids and outcasts.

On an earlier trip to India, Keith had realized that this was a natural result of the country's prevailing belief in reincarnation. After all, if these people were being punished for deeds done in a previous life, why would you want to get in the way of the natural order of things and relieve their afflictions? It would serve both your best interests and theirs if you let them suffer now so they could be purified and appear in a better form, or as a member of a higher caste, in a future life on their journey toward nirvana.

Love of outcasts and a belief in reincarnation simply do not go hand in hand.

Keith did not believe in reincarnation; he believed that one time around was all you got, but despite what he did for a living, he felt a twinge of guilt whenever he passed these suffering, dying people who were so categorically ignored and scorned by their culture.

Once they were in Chennai, buses, trucks, oxen, cars, taxis, and the ever-present motorcycles whipped past and jockeyed for position on the frenetically busy street, in some cases leaving only inches between the vehicles. In India, people flip their car's side-view mirrors back so they don't stick out because otherwise they'd almost certainly be ripped off or end up taking out a pedestrian.

Five people were killed every day in traffic accidents in Chennai, mostly from being struck by the three-wheeled taxis. Taking into account the number of motorcycles with a husband driving, his wife behind him, their baby on her lap, Keith found it astounding that there weren't more fatalities.

Their taxi driver dropped them off, and Keith and Vanessa found their man, Baahir, waiting for them across the street, parked at an angle in front of a small storefront. Indian music and the smell of musky incense drifted out the front door. Two men sat outside the shop smoking languidly, eyeing the two Caucasians as they climbed into the vehicle.

Baahir was a rotund man full of energy who was always talking about how he needed to "reduce," which was the Indian way of saying "lose weight." But despite his outgoing personality, he knew how to keep secrets, and they knew he would never admit to anyone where he had driven his two American passengers. They paid him well for this confidentiality and had also made it clear to him what would happen to his two children if he ever failed them at all in this regard.

Fear can be just as effective a motivator as money. In Baahir's case, they decided to go for both approaches.

In many places in India it's considered an insult to the driver to wear a seat belt: a way of telling him, "I don't think you're a good enough driver to keep me safe. I don't trust you with my life." Keith and Vanessa saw no need today to insult Baahir, so they didn't buckle up.

After a cordial greeting, Baahir asked them in his clipped English, "To the facility?"

"Yes," Vanessa replied. "As quickly as possible."

"Two hundred seventy-five kilometers . . ." Both Keith and Vanessa had been there numerous times before and knew the distance already, but clearly Baahir was calculating in his head. "On these roads, with this traffic, that may take four hours. Perhaps longer."

"Let's just get going," Vanessa said.

Baahir edged the car into the stream of traffic, nearly taking out a helmetless couple whipping past on a motorcycle, and then he directed the car north, toward Kadapa.

17

There is terror, sometimes, in dreams.

Though you know they aren't real, couldn't possibly be real, they seem real. And while there's an ontological difference between what seems real and what is real, what, at its core, is the *experiential* difference?

People with hallucinations, or those playing virtual reality video games, or even people dreaming, all experience thought, emotion, exert will, and create memories. The same parts of the brain light up in "virtual" experiences as they do in "real-life" ones.

Although dreams and hallucinations might not happen per se, to your mind it's as if they did. And so, if your mind experiences something, who's to say it's not an actual experience?

Because of all that, in my dream my terror is real.

I'm in my car again at the park just after our picnic. Lien-hua is climbing into her coupe.

But this time, rather than drive away from her, I glance at my rearview mirror and see her slip into the driver's seat.

It strikes me that I haven't told her I love her. I'm on my way to her car to do so when I see Basque attack her.

I sprint toward her car and throw open the door and grab Basque and beat him in the face, beat him like I did when I first arrested him back when I was a homicide detective. But now I do more. I drag him from the car and slam his head against the pavement again and again until he's no longer moving.

Then I turn to the car and check on Lien-hua.

But I am too late.

Her head is lolling forward, her neck still strapped to the headrest. In desperation, I work the belt loose and pull her from the car and yell her name and start chest compressions and rescue breaths to get her breathing again.

And then, because it's a dream, logic evaporates and Christie, my dead wife, is standing beside me, and I hear her say, "You waited too long, Pat."

And as I watch, Lien-hua's skin turns to bluish gray. Before my eyes, her moldering flesh becomes mottled with the color of death, her eyes stare unblinkingly at the sky, and her jaw drops open.

I stumble backward.

"No, Lien-hua, no!" I hear myself cry.

It's too late, Pat. You waited too long!

Then Basque rises from the pavement, his face a mess of blood and jutting bones, and he brushes himself off and smiles. Then he shrinks, morphing into the form of a rabbit, and scampers away.

"Pat," a voice calls. Christie. It must be Christie, because Lien-hua is dead.

They're both dead! They're—

"Pat?"

When I open my eyes, I'm in the hospital room and early morning light is seeping through the window. My heart is slamming hard against the inside of my chest, and shivers run through me as the dream world that seemed so real—that was so real—slowly fades into a memory that succeeds in already scarring my day.

"Pat, are you okay?" Lien-hua is staring at me concernedly. "You were shaking. In your sleep. I was calling for you."

"Yes." The dream still hovers around me. I try to calm my quick and tense breaths.

"You sure you're alright?"

I flexed my fingers so she wouldn't notice that they were shaking, then I laid them on my legs and repositioned myself so I could look at her. For her sake, I made myself smile.

"I'm okay."

"You're a terrible liar, Pat."

"So Tessa tells me."

Lien-hua knew I was a restless sleeper, that nightmares all too often chased me from real life into my dreams. "What happened in your dream?"

With her background in psychology and her expertise in profiling, she often asked me this question. Though I tended to view dreams as merely a way that my subconscious was sorting through my experiences from the day, she always seemed to pull something deeper from the images in them.

However, today I wasn't about to tell her that I'd dreamt that she was dead and that it was my fault because I'd been too busy beating Basque to death.

"It's okay," I explained. "It was mostly about the things that happened last night."

"They wouldn't let you go."

"No." I took a deep breath and changed the subject. "How are you feeling today?"

"Pretty sore. So, tell me about your dream."

"Lien-hua—"

"You cried out my name while you were sleeping. You said, 'No! Lien-hua, no!' What was happening, do you remember?"

I really did not want to do this. "Let's just not worry about—"

"Humor me."

After a moment's hesitation, I said, "I dreamed you died."

"I see."

"And it was my fault—because I was preoccupied with Basque. But it means nothing. It was just a dream."

A pause. "Yes. It was. So don't worry about me, okay? I'm going to be alright."

"I know. It's just that—"

There was a knock at the door and a waifish Hispanic nurse pressed it open slightly but paused politely before entering. I made sure the blanket was covering my bare legs. She had a grin that was just way too broad for this time of day, and I whispered to Lien-hua, "Okay, I'm a little frightened."

"Why's that?"

"She's got 'I'm a Morning Person' written all over her."

"You stole that line from Tessa, I can tell."

"That is possible, yes."

Lien-hua invited the nurse in, she entered, greeted us enthusiastically, spent a few minutes checking Lien-hua's vitals, then informed us that this was the day that the Lord had made. "Let us rejoice and be glad in it!" she chimed.

Admittedly, a little rejoicing and thanksgiving couldn't hurt anything, but maybe not with this woman's degree of chipperness.

Lien-hua asked her if they could up her pain meds, and the nurse agreed to see what she could do. "Would you like breakfast in the meantime?"

"I don't really have an appetite right now."

"Just call down when you're ready."

"Thanks."

She gently patted Lien-hua's shoulder. "Get some rest."

"I will. Thanks."

After Nurse Perky had excused herself and left the room whistling, Lien-hua and I were silent for a few moments.

"So, the pain," I said, "it's worse than it was yesterday?"

"Yes," she told me. "It is."

"Is there anything I can do?"

She shook her head. "No. But, just . . . thanks for being here."

I wanted to help her, but felt inadequate, powerless. "Of course."

She put her hand on mine. "By the way, I like you with the scruffy, five-o'clock-shadow look."

I rubbed my hand across my face. Definitely some stubble there. "It's been a couple five o'clocks by now."

She saw me uneasily eyeing the IV needle in her arm. To put it mildly, needles are not my thing. Ever since I was a kid, they've made me more than a little squeamish.

"Don't look at it, Pat. It'll just make it worse."

I shifted my gaze. "Right."

"You're not going to pass out on me now, are you?"

Well . . .

"Course not." I brushed a strand of hair from her eye. "What about you? The pain?"

"I'll be alright. It was a bit of a rough night, but I think I'll feel better if I can get some more sleep."

I'd had my phone on vibrate while I slept, and now I noticed a text from Angela Knight asking me to call her. Angela's face was on the screen beside the text, and Lien-hua noticed. "Go ahead," she said. "She usually gets off work at seven."

Angela worked in the Bureau's Cybercrime division and was one of the first people I always contacted when I needed some intel fast. Despite the fact that she was perpetually overworked and behind, she somehow always found a way to get me the information I needed when I needed it.

She was a bit of a character, though. She'd named her computer Lacey and referred to her as if she were a colleague rather than a machine. It made conversations a little awkward sometimes, and neither Lien-hua nor I had ever quite gotten used to it, but we'd learned it was best to just work with it.

I speed-dialed Angela's number, and the phone rang eight times before she picked up. "This is Angela." She sounded as weary as Lien-hua looked.

"Angela, it's Pat. How's Lacey?"

"Tired. How's Lien-hua?"

"Recovering. I'm with her right now."

"Can I talk with her?"

"Sure. I think so."

I handed the phone to Lien-hua, and after she'd convinced Angela that—considering everything—she was doing well, I accepted the phone again and Angela said, "You wanted Saundra Weathers's number. There's no landline, but Lacey found an unlisted cell number." She told it to me. "She lives in Chesapeake Beach, Maryland."

That was about thirty-five miles southeast of DC, plenty close enough for Basque to have traveled to last night. He could have made it over there after he fled the water treatment plant. "We still have some agents watching her house?"

"As far as I know, but I've been a little swamped here." I heard her yawn. "Oh, I analyzed the audio of the 911 call Lien-hua made last night. When I enhanced it, I could hear a male voice—I'm not sure if it's Basque or not. Listen."

She tapped at Lacey's keyboard and a moment later the audio began. It was a little faint and staticky but I could make out a voice: "Just relax, Lien-hua. It'll be over in a few seconds."

"Yeah." I felt a slice of fresh anger cut through me. "That's Basque. What else?"

"That's all I have for you right now."

"Can you have Lacey send me that audio file, as well as the traffic camera and Metro station footage you reviewed last night? I want to see if there's anything in them that might lead us to Basque."

"Sure."

After we'd ended the call, Lien-hua shook her head. "It just sounds so weird when you refer to Lacey as if she were a real person."

"Angela gets offended if I don't."

"I know, but sometimes I think we're feeding her delusion."

"I don't think it's a delusion. Just a quirk."

"Well," she acknowledged, "I suppose we all have our share of those."

It was nice, steering away from the case for a moment. "What are mine?"

"Your quirks?"

"Yeah."

"Well, you love your little Mini Maglite, you like to say, 'Everything matters,' whenever you're working a case, and you're a coffee snob."

"Snob is a little strong."

"Uh-huh, so are your views about Starbucks. So what about me?"

"Let's see . . . You always set your alarm clock to a prime number, you're very peculiar about your flower arrangements, and you have a weakness for watching nineties romance movies while overindulging on Fritos."

"They're yummy."

"Yes, they are."

The conversation fell into a lull, and I thought back to last night, when I first heard the news that she'd been attacked. I'd rushed out of the house right away. Now I realized that I'd left my laptop both on and plugged in. I wished I had it with me, but at least I could access my files remotely with my phone.

I went to the bathroom to get dressed. Maybe when Tessa came by later she could bring my computer and a dry set of clothes. Though mine were drier this morning, they still carried the damp, rangy smell of the water from the drainage tunnels I'd traversed through last night.

Lien-hua did her best to get comfortable, then closed her eyes and told me she was going to try to get some rest. Actually, I was glad she needed to sleep, because it gave me a chance to make some calls.

So that I wouldn't disturb her while I was talking on

the phone, I slipped into an empty room just down the hall. I confirmed that there were still agents outside Saundra's house, then contacted the Lab to find out if they'd lifted anything from the novel or the other items in the car Basque had stolen. Finally, I phoned Doehring to get an update on the case from his end.

Here's what we knew:

(1) Yes, the agents were in place at Saundra's house as I'd requested, but she wasn't home and hadn't been last night when they arrived. Neighbors said she'd taken her daughter camping in West Virginia for the weekend. No one had been able to reach her on her cell phone.

The neighbors had seen her packing the car yesterday afternoon to leave for their trip, which didn't completely quell my suspicions that Basque might have gotten to her and her daughter, but it did quiet them a little bit. Regardless, if Basque had a connection with Saundra, it was possible she might know something about his whereabouts. I called FBI Headquarters to get an agent assigned to put some calls through to her family and friends to find out where she might have taken her daughter.

(2) The Lab found prints on the novel, but they didn't match Basque's or those of the woman who owned the car he'd stolen from a parking garage. Interestingly enough, they didn't match any of the prints we had on file.

(3) There was no evidence in the apartment that Basque had taken any other women there. I decided

to proceed with the working hypothesis that it was not the anchor point for his crimes.

(4) Doehring informed me that despite a careful inspection of Lien-hua's car, the other car Basque had used, the mechanic's garage, the water treatment plant, and the apartment where he'd taken her, the team didn't find anything that gave us a clue as to where he might have gone after he left the drainage tunnels beneath the facility.

(5) Officers had been combing the woods since dusk and hadn't come up with anything that indicated where Basque had gone.

Back in Lien-hua's room again, I used my phone to remotely log into my computer, then I pulled up the case files on Basque's previous crimes.

No criminal thinks of everything. Nobody can plan for every contingency, and eventually it'll catch up with you and you'll leave something behind. You'll overlook one little detail, and it'll haunt you the rest of your life as you sit in your prison cell and think about what you did: *If only I'd thought of that one thing. If only I'd planned a little better, thought things through a little more.*

My job was to find out what Basque had overlooked.

All people form cognitive maps of the areas they frequent. These mental maps skew toward the places we're familiar with. By studying the travel patterns of the victims of serial crimes and analyzing the places where their lives intersected with the offender's, I'm able to use algorithms developed by my mentor, Dr. Werjonic, to work backward to locate the most likely home base, or anchor point for the offender's crime spree.

The more locations I have to work with, the more accurate the geographic profile can be.

This analysis is what lies at the heart of my specialty, geospatial investigation.

Over the last year I'd worked on a geoprofile of the most likely anchor points for Basque's crimes and the previous homicides in our region that we suspected him of, but so far that hadn't led us anywhere. However, now, with the crimes he'd committed last night, I had a number of new locations to input into my geospatial analysis: the park, the apartment, the water treatment plant, the Metro stations, the site where we'd found Lien-hua's car.

I plugged in the numbers and set to work.

18

Nothing.

I kept coming up empty and two hours later I still hadn't found anything helpful. I closed my eyes and rubbed them in frustration.

An hour ago Dr. Frasier had come in and given Lien-hua some more pain medication and since then she'd remained asleep.

Thankfully.

And I'd been able to keep my eyes off the needle in her arm.

Thankfully.

My stomach had been grumbling for a while, so after giving the analysis a few more minutes and failing to come up with anything significant, I took the opportunity to trek down to the cafeteria and grab some oatmeal, a banana, and a bagel for breakfast.

I passed on the coffee, though. I'm brave enough to lead climb in Yosemite, go mano a mano with serial killers, and navigate a teenage girl's mood swings, but I'm nowhere near brave enough to drink hospital cafeteria coffee.

Returning to the empty room down the hall from

Lien-hua, I tried Saundra Weathers's cell number but no one picked up. I left my name and number and requested that she return my call as soon as she could.

I decided it might not be best to leave a voicemail that I was the one who'd found Mindy Wells's body in the tree house all those years ago, so I avoided that topic and just told her I was with the FBI and that this concerned an ongoing investigation.

When I called Ralph, he informed me that Tessa was still in bed, which I was thankful for. After last night, she definitely needed the sleep.

I said to Ralph, "We have a few things to look into."

"What are you thinking?"

"I want someone to talk with the owners of the car Basque drove to the plant, the apartment he used, and the garage where he left her car, as well as the people who work at the water treatment plant to see if anyone has seen him around there before. Find out aliases he might have used, forwarding addresses, phone numbers, the whole nine."

"Right." There was a pause and I assumed he was jotting down a few notes. "Hey, let me ask you something. Were you afraid of going in there after Basque last night? Heading into that plant alone?"

"Yes."

"But it wasn't Basque, was it." It sounded more like a conclusion than a question. "Facing him wasn't what you were afraid of."

"Not primarily, no."

"It was what you were going to do to him if you got him alone."

That was partially true too. "You know, mostly I was afraid I wouldn't catch him, that I wouldn't stop him before he could escape to kill again." Since I'd failed, we both processed the implications for a moment. "What about you?" I asked. "Would you have been afraid to go in there?"

"I eat the smell of fear for breakfast."

"You eat the . . . ? That doesn't even make sense."

"Maybe not, but it'd be a great line for a movie."

Ralph was a huge fan of summer blockbuster films where guys his size pound aliens to a pulp, unleash wicked weapons at terrorists, and blow up secret hideouts to save the world, so his observation didn't exactly surprise me.

"Let's put this stuff into play," I said, "see where it leads us."

Returning to the awkwardly uncomfortable chair that I'd done my best to sleep in last night, I pulled up the video footage Angela had sent me. While Lien-hua rested, I traced the path Basque took yesterday to see if I could notice anything at all that might lead us to him.

19

Baahir had been right.

With traffic and road conditions that were—to say the least—less than ideal, the drive to Kadapa took nearly four and a half hours.

When they arrived, Keith was definitely ready to be done traveling.

Vanessa ordered Baahir to park on the edge of town, just down the road from the slum where Keith and Vanessa had first tested the drugs to make sure they were effective. She told Baahir to keep his mobile on—that she would call him when she needed him—then she led Keith through the narrow, winding alley to the building.

The guard beside the door immediately recognized them and swung open the gate with a deferential nod.

Vanessa did not acknowledge him.

Keith proceeded with her inside.

The factory, if you could call it that, was small, but ever since his first time there, he'd been impressed with what they were able to accomplish.

It doesn't take a lot of space or an elaborate setup to

manufacture impressive quantities of counterfeit pharmaceuticals. As Keith had found out when all this got started, everywhere around the world people are producing pills by the millions in squalid apartments, warehouses, and back rooms.

You just need enough of the ingredients of the actual drug to avoid immediate detection (actually, with some cheaper drugs you don't even need that), a few other ingredients to create the right consistency, a packaging machine, silk screens to imprint the logo of the namebrand pharmaceutical on the foil blister packs, and you're ready to go into business.

Here, there were a dozen tables holding containers of pills and chemicals. Other tables held bottles, labeling equipment, and blister packs to produce the packaging. There were two ultra-high-end printers in the corner that could produce the imprinted 3-D holograms necessary for the packages for Calydrole, PTPharmaceuticals' hallmark depression medication, to make them appear authentic.

Boxes containing tens of thousands of caplets and pills were piled against the wall to Keith's left, waiting to be shipped.

Nobody produces a single counterfeit pill; the typical batch size is about fifty thousand. Despite this facility's size, the workers were quite proficient and could produce nearly forty thousand pills each week. Not all were counterfeit Calydrole pills, but there were seventy thousand or so of them from the last couple months boxed up along the walls, ready for their blister packs.

Over the last decade, counterfeit pharmaceuticals had become one of the most lucrative commodities in the world. Produce a pill for less than fifty cents and sell it for, in the case of some cancer and HIV drugs, over forty-five dollars, and it was clear why.

That profit margin, along with the low risk of being caught, the slap-on-the-wrist sentences if you were, and the ease of distribution—just mail the pills to people who ordered them through Web sites that were designed to look like legitimate pharmacies—and it was no mystery why it was an eighty-billion-dollar-a-year industry, or why it was growing by twenty percent every year.

Because of the low-risk/high-reward ratio, many Asian gangs, the Russian Mafia, and some of the drug cartels in South America were switching from producing, selling, and distributing illegal drugs and controlled substances, to counterfeit pharmaceuticals.

Looking at the bottom line, there wasn't much of a question about which choice made more financial sense.

Most Americans have no idea that eighty percent of the active ingredient in the drugs they buy comes from overseas and more than forty percent of the drugs are manufactured abroad. Only a fraction of those factories are ever inspected by the FDA, and the pharmaceutical supply chain in North America isn't secure. At least five percent of the drugs used by U.S. consumers are counterfeit.

Which meant that at any given time, eight million U.S. citizens were unknowingly taking counterfeit drugs.

Unsuspecting consumers order off the Internet thinking they're just saving money, never realizing that they might very well be purchasing drugs containing sawdust, floor wax, insect parts, chalk, industrial lubricants, brick dust from cement mixtures, paint, heavy metals, boric acid, or safrole—which is used to make Ecstasy.

Keith tended to overestimate people, but still he found

it hard to believe that anyone would be foolish enough to order lifesaving medication from Web sites that don't require a prescription or a doctor's visit, or from sites that offer name-brand drugs at seventy percent off. If an offer is too good to be true, it almost always is. And yet Americans still used those pills. By the millions.

It was ironic to him, in a tragic sort of way: people in America will complain vociferously to their maître d' if there's a human hair touching their pasta, but will ingest hundreds of pills a year that were produced using water polluted with human waste without ever giving their legitimacy a second thought.

So far, counterfeit versions of more than four hundred different drugs had been found in more than a hundred different countries, including twenty of the world's top-twenty-five bestselling drugs—two of which were produced in this very room.

Now, at this time of day, only two people were here—Eashan and Jagjeevan. Keith had never been able to pronounce—or remember—their last names, so he didn't even try. Actually, it was confusing, because in India people sometimes told you their surnames first and sometimes they didn't, so he just stuck to the names he knew.

Eashan, a slim, twitchy man who made Keith think of a fox, was in charge of the facility. Jagjeevan, who was husky, quiet, and wore a dark, bushy mustache, stood nearby, printing out labels that the women who worked here would be using in the morning when they came in.

The women had all been told that the drugs being produced here were authentic, but almost certainly they knew the truth. However, with the scarcity of jobs in the area—especially for women—Keith and Vanessa were confident that they wouldn't say anything to anyone. Career choices for women were pretty much limited to being a seamstress or working at a factory that produced goods for Westerners. Although some women, of course, had been forced into becoming street workers—that is, prostitutes—by family members.

The women who worked here were paid well to keep quiet about the specifics of their jobs.

But Keith and Vanessa had also paid off the local police, just in case.

Vanessa was a lawyer, but ever since Keith had known her, she'd only shown interest in circumventing the law, not operating inside it. The situation begged for a punch line about lawyers, but Vanessa was not a woman with a robust sense of humor and Keith had never been tempted to joke around with her about it.

When the two of them entered the room, Keith noticed Eashan gulp, and he took that to be a bad sign—perhaps the drugs weren't ready to be shipped. But of course, that was primarily the reason they were here.

Primarily.

The products' readiness to be shipped to America.

Eashan approached them and gave them a polite, albeit reserved, greeting. Jagjeevan nodded heavily to them but said nothing.

Vanessa didn't waste any time. "We have a problem and we've come here to address it."

"A problem?" Eashan said. "No. There is no—"

"Yes"—she produced two boxes and laid them on the table—"there is. See if you can tell me which is legitimate."

"That's not my specialty. I'm not an expert at—"

"Look at the holograms, Eashan."

After a moment, he picked up the two boxes and inspected them. Even as he continued to object, claiming that he couldn't tell, it didn't take him long to identify which of the two boxes was the counterfeit one.

"The detail?" he said nervously. "Is that it?"

"Good for you. You have gifts you weren't even aware of. The name of the drug company in the foreground of the hologram isn't as well-defined."

"I—"

"This will never pass an inspection by either PTPharmaceuticals or the FDA, not even a cursory one. Even pharmacists and doctors will be able to tell them apart. I thought we had this fixed?"

"I . . . I mean, we did. We do. Maybe this box is an earlier attempt."

"It is not."

Keith noticed Eashan's fingers tremble as he asked, "What would you like me to do?"

"It needs to be fixed and it needs to be fixed now. The shipment is supposed to be on the plane that leaves on Tuesday." She nodded toward the boxes containing the counterfeit Calydrole. "Those drugs enter the supply chain on Friday."

"Yes, I know."

"Don't tell me you know. If you knew, you wouldn't have been so careless as to print these labels." She threw the box against his chest. "And our employer would not have sent us here to assure that you fix things."

"Miss Juliusson, that is not enough time to recalibrate the machine and print all the—"

"I'm afraid it is going to be enough time."

"But those labels were designed in Hyderabad." He

indicated the printing press in the corner. "We don't have the technology here to redesign it. All we do is print them."

"I am well aware. Of the process. We go through. To print the labels."

Almost imperceptibly, Eashan swallowed. "Yes, of course." But then he paused. He had something more to say. "You could have called, perhaps, saved yourself the trip. And . . ."

"And?"

"And . . . forgive me for saying so, but did you come all this way just to tell me to fix this?"

"No." She walked to the door, closed it, and locked it. Keith removed the pruning shears from his pocket. Both Eashan and Jagjeevan froze. Vanessa said, "We came all this way to punish you if you do not."

Eashan cast a look toward Jagjeevan and the big man reached for his jacket pocket, but Keith was too quick for him. He was on him in an instant. He grabbed the man's wrist, twisted it backward to control him, and had him on his knees before he could get the gun out.

Setting down the pruning shears for a moment, Keith retrieved the gun, tossed it to Vanessa, then took the shears and positioned them carefully around the base of Jagjeevan's left ear, encircling the place where it attached to the side of his head.

He began to cry out for Keith to stop, not to do it, that he was sorry.

"Be quiet now, Jagjeevan," Keith said to him. "Or your ear is going to end up on the floor."

Properly motivated, the man managed to stifle his cries.

Vanessa directed the gun at Eashan's right kneecap.

"No!" he cried.

She didn't fire, but instead gestured toward Keith. "You do know what my associate did to Caleb three weeks ago? How things turned out for his wife and children?"

Eashan was stone silent. Jagjeevan begged again, this time reverting to Hindi, and Keith told him once more to hush, then squeezed the shears just enough to convince him to obey.

"It's after office hours, ma'am." Eashan was shaking. "We'll have to wait until morning to make the calls and get started."

She handed him her mobile phone. "Get started now. Either that, or we'll get started with the pruning shears. On both of you."

20

The morning passed and Lien-hua slept.

Saundra Weathers did not return my call, which worried me somewhat, but if she and her daughter had gone camping, it did make sense that she wouldn't be checking her messages.

The team didn't find any clue as to Basque's whereabouts. However, inputting the sites from the video footage and using FALCON and my geographic profiling algorithms, I did come up with three possible hot zones Basque might be working out of.

One was in southeast DC; the second, about five miles north of the city; the third, twelve miles east of us past Joint Base Andrews Naval Air Facility, which most people around here still refer to as Andrews Air Force Base, or simply Andrews.

Distance decay refers to the diminishing likelihood of someone committing a crime as the distance from his anchor point and his awareness space surrounding it increases. Depending on the distance decay values I used for the calculations, the three areas came up with differing degrees of probability.

Just before noon, Lien-hua woke up and we made a few necessary phone calls to members of our families.

Last night I hadn't taken the time to notify our relatives about what had happened, but I found out that Brineesha had sent out e-mails this morning. Fortunately, she hadn't Facebooked about it or else I could only imagine how much we would have been inundated with messages.

As it was, I had received e-mail messages from Lien-hua's two brothers, my parents, and my brother, all urgently asking how she was.

I'd sent them brief replies, but now Lien-hua suggested it would be best to talk with them.

Both of Lien-hua's parents were dead—her mother from a car accident four years ago, her father from a heart attack a year before that. Her two brothers—Nianzu, who worked as a software designer in Beijing, and Huang-fu, a veterinarian who lived in the Houston area—both e-mailed that they would be glad to fly over here to be with her.

She wasn't keen on the idea and arranged a three-way video chat on my phone—which was necessary, since Huang-fu had been born deaf.

Using both verbal communication and sign language she tried to convince her brothers that she was going to be okay, and that since they were both coming to her wedding next month, they didn't need to come now. "Really, I'm going to be alright," she signed. "There's no need for you to fly in."

Huang-fu's wife had recently left him, and he had sole custody of their young daughter. He was easier to convince than Nianzu, who definitely had the money to make two separate trips to the States, but at last Lien-hua was able to fend off his rebuttals and persuade him that she would be okay.

My parents, who lived in Denver, also offered to come to DC if there was anything we needed. I told them honestly that I would let them know if anything specific came up, but that for the time being we were fine.

Then it was time to contact Sean and Amber.

My brother, Sean, is an avid outdoorsman, doesn't like to be disturbed when he's in the woods—or really, anytime—and doesn't own a cell phone, so I dialed his wife, Amber, to tell her what was going on and waited somewhat anxiously for her to pick up.

My conversations with her were always a little bit stilted and awkward. Back when she and Sean were engaged—before I'd ever met Christie or Lien-hua—Amber and I had gotten a little too close. Nothing physical, but sometimes emotional affairs are harder to break off than physical ones.

Even after her marriage to Sean, our feelings for each other hadn't evaporated immediately, and I'd had to categorically break things off with her for everyone's sake.

At the time Sean never knew about it, and it seemed like telling him would've only hurt him, so neither Amber nor I had ever brought it up.

However, everything came out in the open last winter. At first it looked like the truth might rip their marriage apart, but in the end Sean accepted Amber's apology and mine—after landing a fist that I deserved against my jaw—and providentially he and I were closer now than we'd been in years.

There wasn't anything between Amber and me anymore, but still, we were both careful to keep a little distance between us so that no one got the wrong impression.

She picked up, I told her what was going on, and after she'd spoken with Lien-hua, I asked if Sean was there.

"He just got back from the shooting range. He's out in the garage cleaning his gun. Do you want me to fill him in?"

"No, I'll talk to him. If you can get him that'd be great."

A couple moments later Sean was on the line, and after I'd summarized Lien-hua's condition, he told me how relieved he was that she was recovering, then said softly, "I found him, Pat."

"You found him?"

"Derek Everson."

When he told me the name, I felt a chill.

Back when we were teenagers, Sean, who's two years older than I am, was driving me home after a New Year's Eve party when he swerved, hit a patch of ice, and struck another vehicle. The driver of the other car was killed. Her name was Nancy Everson and she had a twenty-two-year-old son named Derek.

Sean had some drinks at the party—that much I'd known—but exactly how much, I didn't.

He told the responding officers that he'd swerved to miss a deer. It seemed almost certain that the officers would have given him a sobriety test of some sort, but I couldn't remember them doing so. If they did, it didn't lead them to disbelieve his story.

Only last winter did I learn that there was no deer, that for two decades Sean had been living with the guilt of losing control of the car while he was intoxicated and striking Nancy Everson's car and fatally wounding her.

In Wisconsin there's no statute of limitations on first-degree reckless vehicular homicide. However, in January, after Sean told me the truth about the accident, he also told me he'd decided to tell the woman's son, Derek, the truth as well.

The man could have pressed charges, and based on Sean's confession, my brother might realistically have gone to prison for up to twenty years.

At the time, Sean had thought Derek lived in Green Bay, Wisconsin, but it turned out he'd moved.

Sean had been looking for him ever since.

And now, apparently, he'd found him.

"Did you talk to him?"

"Yes."

My anxiety level was rising quickly. "And?"

"When I told him, he just sat for a long time without saying anything. Then he looked at me and I honestly didn't know what he was going to say, didn't know if I might be facing prison time or not. I thought he might hit me, threaten me, whatever, but he didn't do any of those things. He just stared at me and asked me point-blank why I'd waited so long before telling him."

"What did you say?"

"I told him I was afraid. Simple as that. I just told him straight out that I was scared. And he asked me if I wanted to hear him say that he forgave me. I didn't know which direction he was going with that—if that's what he was planning to say or not. I just told him, 'Only if you do.'"

Sean paused, I waited, and finally he said, "He told me his mother was a good woman, that she died long before she should have. And then he told me he could see by looking in my eyes that I'd already served enough time for what had happened. It was his way of saying he forgave me."

"That took a lot of courage," I said, "for both of you."

"Well, I know it did for him. I'm just glad it's finally in the past. I'm not sure if it belongs there, but I'm glad that's where it is."

Christie used to say that forgiveness is the first step toward peace, and now, hearing what Sean said, I couldn't help but agree with the sentiment.

We closed up the conversation and I promised to keep him informed about Lien-hua's progress.

After my fiancée and I had processed what Sean had said, she mentioned that she was finally hungry, and I used the room's phone to request lunch for her.

A few minutes after the food arrived, so did Ralph and Tessa.

21

My daughter carried a vase of elaborately arranged flowers. "These are from Brineesha and me." Tessa knew about Lien-hua's penchant for flower arranging and sounded a little worried that she wouldn't be satisfied with the arrangement. "I hope you like 'em."

There were lotuses and chrysanthemums in the vase, and I knew it was no accident. Lien-hua's name meant "lotus," and her twin sister Chu-hua's name meant "chrysanthemum." Chu-hua had been murdered when she and Lien-hua were twenty-three, and Tessa knew how much chrysanthemums meant to my fiancée.

"They're exquisite." Lien-hua accepted the flowers from Tessa. "Really. They're beautiful."

Ralph laid my laptop down and flopped a set of clean clothes onto the chair. "I had to get these for you. Tessa refused to go in your room. Said she was scared of what might crawl out from under the bed."

"It's not that bad in there."

Ralph scoffed. "Depends on your definition of 'bad.'"

"I thought you were supposed to be so brave? I thought you ate the smell of fear for breakfast?"

"It's lunchtime."

Tessa snickered, and I noticed Lien-hua look away from me and smile.

I cleared my throat slightly. "Just give me a sec to change."

Using Lien-hua's bathroom, I cleaned up, put on the dry clothes, and when I returned to the room I saw that the television was on. A commercial for this afternoon's opening-day matchup between the Nationals and the Cubs promised to be "an epic opening to an exciting season."

Despite their dismal reputation, Ralph was a faithful Nationals fan and was eyeing the screen intently. He off-handedly commented about how much he wished he could have been at the game.

Tessa cringed.

"What?" he said.

"Baseball."

"Baseball?"

"Yeah. Ew."

He furrowed his eyebrows. "What do you have against baseball?"

"Oh," I cautioned, "don't even get her started."

"What? How did I not know this?" He turned toward Tessa. "Seriously, you don't like baseball?"

"Ralph," I said, "I'm telling you, you don't want to—"

"Who doesn't like baseball?"

Tessa raised a finger into the air.

Oh, boy. Here we go.

"Think of it like this," she said. "Let's say no one in America ever heard of it before, right? And you're trying to sell them on the idea: 'Oh, this'll be great. We'll have these eight guys dress up in dorky-looking knee pants and stand around a field and scratch their crotches while two other guys play catch. We'll give those two clever names: the catcher and the pitcher.'"

"Um . . ." Ralph began.

"'Then we'll have someone swing a stick at the ball. Half the time he'll miss, but once in a while he'll hit it. Then the game of catch turns into a game of tag. We'll go back and forth taking turns and after seven rounds of this we'll just acknowledge how brain-numbing it all is and have a sing-along.' I mean, are you kidding me?"

"It's not that bad." He sounded a bit like a boy who'd gotten caught with his hand in the cookie jar. "I mean, it's not as good as football, but . . ."

"And"—she was just getting warmed up—"unlike most sports, where you have to actually be successful to be considered great, in baseball you get to be an all-star if you manage to hit the ball just one-third of the time. Not like in school, where a thirty-three percent will buy you another year in fourth grade. Nope. We wouldn't want to raise the bar too high or anything, considering we're only paying the guys ten mil a year. I mean, can you imagine a surgeon who's successful a third of the time getting that kind of a salary? Or how about a pilot who manages to land on the runway one out of every three attempts? Wow. Give that guy a raise, he's an *all-star*!"

She took a breath, but didn't pause long enough for Ralph to get a word in edgewise. "And if watching some guy miss the ball isn't exciting enough for your television audience, every few minutes we'll cut to shots of a bald, middle-aged guy chewing bubble gum. He gets paid hundreds of thousands of dollars—or probably more—to make the monumental decision about which of the guys in the knee pants gets to throw the ball next."

"It's not always easy to know which pitcher to send in," Ralph countered.

"Uh-huh. It's the only sport where one of the main goals is to have nearly everyone fail. The announcers actually sound excited when no one is able to accomplish anything. I mean, every batter is missing the ball and the announcers are all: 'It's a great pitcher's duel!' Really? That's what you call it when everyone sucks except the pitchers? And if things get really bad, they'll exult, 'We might have a no-hitter on our hands!' Only sport where people get so worked up over so much failure."

"Did you just say 'exult'?" Ralph asked.

"Sorry." Suddenly, she looked self-conscious. "It means to feel, show, or exclaim jubilation, usually over an accomplishment of some kind."

"Yeah, no, I know that. It's just—I've never heard anyone actually use it in a sentence before."

"It sorta just came out."

"So what sport do you like?"

"Reading."

"Reading's not a sport."

"It oughtta be. It's more exciting to watch than baseball."

Ralph opened his mouth as if he were going to reply, but then he must have thought better of it, because he said nothing, just walked over and, looking somewhat defeated, plopped onto the chair by the window.

That afternoon we did not watch the baseball game.

Tessa's school was in the process of transitioning to e-books, but her class still used printed texts and she'd brought four of them along and spent her time studying. To put it mildly, she did a good job of remembering what her teachers said in class, but I was proud of her for not sloughing off her work like she must certainly have been tempted to do this late in her senior year, especially now that she'd handed in her senior project for her AP Lit class, which was half of the semester grade for her least-favorite teacher, Mr. Tilson.

Ralph and I used my laptop to review the case files, analyzing the revised geoprofile and looking carefully at the relationships between the travel route Basque had taken and the locations of his previous crimes.

Time slipped away; evening approached. When Lien-hua wasn't resting, she was offering Ralph and me a profiler's perspective on the investigation. Officially, profilers don't solve cases—they help eliminate suspects—but Lien-hua hadn't gotten that memo and had helped solve any number of them in her time in the NCAVC.

"It's not going to end for Basque," she said. "He'll feel irritated that he wasn't able to kill me. That won't be acceptable to him. He'll be more determined than ever."

"He'll try to hurt Pat some other way?" Ralph said.

"Yes."

"The author of the novel?" I asked, but thought, *Tessa?*

Lien-hua shook her head. "That's impossible to say."

Tessa had her earbuds plugged in her ears but even from across the room I could hear the coarse sounds of one of her screamer bands scratching harshly out of them.

I made a decision that either I would be watching her or she'd be under police protection until we could bring Basque in.

Considering the circumstances, it didn't take me long to clear it with Ralph. He assured me that he'd work things out with the Bureau and with Doehring and I thanked him. He didn't bring up the mounds of paperwork he would face or the budgetary issues he would need to iron out and I wasn't surprised one bit.

When Brineesha got off work, she joined us.

It wasn't something I really wanted to get into, especially with Tessa here, but somehow we got to talking about how clever criminals are, how they can be a lot more imaginative than investigators.

"How so?" Tessa, who had set her iPod aside, asked.

Experienced criminals know you use whatever you have on hand as a weapon. Before they were banned, forks were one of the most popular weapons in prisons. I'd seen firsthand what kind of damage the tines of a fork could do when they were jammed into someone's eye, or through his cheek, or into his chest. Not pretty.

I decided not to bring up the fork incidents and moved on to something harmless. "Well, for example, to get cell phones, prisoners have a partner wrap padding around it, sew it into a football, and then cover the football with artificial turf so it'll match the grass in the yard. They just throw it over the wall, the guy inside retrieves it from the yard, and voilà."

"Huh," Brineesha said, "that is clever."

"Last year I interviewed Lester Berring, a serial arsonist who operated mainly in New York State."

"I remember hearing about that," Tessa said. "When was that? Maybe . . ."

With her memory it didn't shock me that she recalled the case. "He was caught eight years ago," I said. "He used everything from fingernail polish to cough syrup to nondairy coffee creamer as accelerants."

"Coffee creamer?"

"Nondairy. It's surprisingly flammable. Rip a packet open, flick the powder into the air as you light a match beneath it, and watch what happens. People in prison sometimes light other guys on fire with it. Forget nondairy, stick to the real stuff. Trust me."

Just a little friendly conversation here. About how to burn people alive.

Perfect.

Brineesha leaned forward. "I once heard that prisoners put fruit in fire extinguishers and let it ferment to make booze. They use grapes, peaches, apples, anything they can sneak out of the mess hall. That true?"

"That's true," Ralph answered. "And then there's the weapons they make in prison. Of course, they always try to get into the kitchen—knives, stirring spoons, all that kind of stuff. Guys have been beaten to death with soup ladles. Remember that time you got called in, Pat, to investigate that guy who'd apparently been stabbed by his cell mate, but there was no murder weapon found?"

"Um, I'm not sure we need to talk about that one."

But that didn't deter him. "Man, they had nothing. Then you noticed that white powder on the floor of his cell."

"Ralph, we really don't need to—"

"What was it?" Tessa asked. "Cocaine? An OD?"

"Nope," Ralph said proudly on my behalf. "Mashed potatoes."

"Mashed potatoes?"

"Actually, powdered mashed potatoes. After Pat learned that the guy had checked out a magazine from the prison library and hadn't returned it, you had him, didn't you, Pat?"

I was getting nowhere here. "I guess so. Yes."

Brineesha looked at us curiously. "You lost me some-where between the mashed potatoes and the library."

Lien-hua was still just lying there propped in her bed, listening quietly.

"Well"—Ralph was enjoying this a little too much—"the guy mixed the mashed potatoes in his sink while his roommate was asleep. Then he twisted the magazine to a point, dipped it into the mashed potatoes, and let it dry under his cot. The starch in the mashed potatoes acted as a hardening agent."

Tessa muttered, "He made a paper shiv."

"In a sense, yes." Ralph just wasn't going to give this up. "He stabbed his cell mate in the throat so he couldn't cry out, then in the abdomen so he'd bleed out more quickly. And then to hide the evidence—"

"Okay, okay. We can—"

"Let me guess," Tessa said reflectively. "After the mur-der he what? Soaked the magazine in the toilet and, once it was soggy enough, ripped it to pieces and flushed it down piece by piece?"

"Yes," I said, "and I have to say it frightens me a little that you figured that out so quickly."

"Anyway"—it was Ralph again—"the point is, nearly anything can become a weapon in the wrong hands. A pocket Bible soaked in water and then slipped into a sock can make a pretty effective bludgeon. Screwdrivers, ma-chine parts, sharpened toothbrushes, they all work well." He pointed to his neck. "A pencil in the throat, right here."

"Ralph. Thanks, I'm sure we—"

But he twisted his finger to show the action of stabbing someone right where the wound would need to be. "Med-ical personnel can stop the bleeding on the outside, but not on the inside. The person drowns in his own blood."

I held up both hands. "Let's change the subject."

"By the way," Tessa said to Ralph, "I'm glad I'm not locked up with you."

He grinned slightly, accepting that as a compliment.

"Tessa," Brineesha told her, "I hope you weren't taking notes."

"I promise not to make a dagger out of mashed potatoes or burn someone alive with nondairy coffee creamer."

"Well," I said in a very responsible, fatherly way, "I'm glad to hear that."

Before Ralph and Brineesha left, he set up a two-o'clock meeting tomorrow afternoon at the NCAVC headquarters, which was about ten minutes from Quantico. Yes, the briefing would be on a Sunday, but in this job you work when you need to and grab time off when you can.

After dinner, Lien-hua told me to head home. At this point her condition wasn't really life-threatening, and when she pointed out that I'd gotten less than four hours of sleep last night, I had to agree that I needed to give it a go in my own bed rather than trying to sleep here again on the chair in her room.

I made certain an officer was assigned to guard Lien-hua's room, and then Tessa and I left for home.

22

I threw my dirty clothes in the wash, and when I met up with Tessa again she was in the kitchen pulling off a strip of Saran wrap to cover a plate of leftover spaghetti and meatless marinara sauce so she could microwave it without the sauce splattering all over.

The plastic wrap twisted into a useless mess. She sighed, ripped it off, and tried again with the same result. "Okay, so we can build a computer the size of your fingernail that can pilot a probe to Neptune, but we can't design a Saran wrap box cutter-blade-thing that actually rips this stuff off in a straight line?"

"I'll get it for you."

"No," she said firmly. "I got it."

I could tell she was frustrated, but it seemed like more than just the plastic wrap was bothering her.

She finally managed to cover the plate and slide it into the microwave. "Patrick"—she punched the start button—"how come you never take me to church?"

"To church?"

"Yeah."

"I didn't know you wanted to go to church."

"I don't."

"You don't."

"No. I think it'd be boring."

"Then why would you ask me to take you?"

"I didn't ask you to take me, I just asked why you don't take me."

"Okay," I acknowledged. "That's true."

"Mom would've wanted you to. I think."

I felt a twitch of guilt. Tessa was right—Christie would've wanted me to take her, but in the months following her death, it was a hard time for me to believe in God at all, and I would've felt like a hypocrite walking into a church. Over time I'd just gotten out of the habit. "Well, I guess I was hoping I could let you decide what faith to follow rather than imposing my beliefs on you."

"Oh, how very PC of you. No, really. I'm impressed."

"Okay, I sense a touch of sarcasm there."

"Not much gets past you, does it?"

I stared at her. "What are we talking about here, Tessa? What is this all about?"

The plate of spaghetti and sauce was beginning to pop and sizzle and it was a little annoying.

"C'mon, if there was a room with twenty bottles in it and, say, nineteen of 'em were poisonous and one was okay to drink and I was thirsty, would you just tell me to go in there and choose a bottle and drink from it?"

"No, of course, I— Oh, I see. Some belief systems are dangerous and why would I let you sample those? But what if none of them were poisonous? What if they're all safe?"

"Are you actually saying beliefs like Nazism or sexism or fascism or speciism are safe?"

"Speciism?"

"Thinking we're better than other species."

"I'm not sure about that last one, but yeah, okay, I get your point. Yes, there are destructive ideas and worldviews out there that I don't want you adopting. But let's say most of the bottles are good for you. That only a small percentage of beliefs are destructive. Let's say maybe nineteen are healthy and only one has poison in it."

She looked at me, aghast. "You'd let me go in? If even one of them was poisonous and I was thirsty, you'd still let me go into the room without telling me which one it was?"

"No, I didn't mean it like that, it's just . . ."

She shook her head and started for her bedroom.

"Hey, okay, I'll take you to church."

"I already told you"—her voice was sharp—"I don't want to go to church."

Okay, starting to get exasperated here. "Then what do you want?"

Silence.

I followed her down the hallway. Behind me, in the kitchen, the microwave cut off.

"What it is you want, Tessa?"

She turned to face me. "Just the truth. Okay? Alright?"

"Well . . . Good. I'm glad to hear that."

"Yeah," she said ambiguously. Then she disappeared into her room, leaving me standing there staring at her closed door.

She didn't slam it. If she had, I might've thought she was just pouting and I could have discounted, at least somewhat, her little outburst. But she didn't, and I realized that somewhere deep inside she really was searching for answers and all I'd managed to give her was more frustration.

Obviously she was upset, and trying to talk to her more was certainly an option, but over the last few years I've learned that there are times when it's best to leave her alone—and often those are the times when I feel the most like I want to go and help her out. I had the sense that this was one of those times when I needed to give her some space.

I called to her that the spaghetti was done and she thanked me from the other side of the door, but when I waited for her to come out, she did not.

Finally, I put the plate in the fridge and returned to the hall. I paused when I came to her door, tried to sort out what I might say to her if I actually did knock on it, but in the end I passed by and simply went to my room instead.

Before going to bed I reviewed my schedule for tomorrow: in the morning I planned to look over the case files early, then visit Lien-hua before driving to NCAVC headquarters for the afternoon briefing.

In the meantime, more than anything I needed some sleep.

Even though it wasn't quite nine thirty, I was exhausted, but now, with the case on my mind, as well as this little, somewhat disconcerting exchange with Tessa scratching away at my conscience, I wasn't confident at all that I'd be able to quiet my mind enough to get the rest I really needed.

23

Keith did not enjoy what Vanessa had directed him to do to Eashan and Jagjeevan over the course of the last twelve hours.

Eashan had cried too much, which had annoyed Vanessa and caused her to instruct Keith to do more work on him than he would have liked. Jagjeevan had struggled too much for his own good and ended up worse off than he should have.

Both men were alive. But neither was fully intact.

Honestly, since she'd threatened to hurt them only if they didn't get their job done, Keith wasn't sure all of that was necessary. But he knew better than to second-guess Vanessa, and once she decided she wanted to make an example of someone—or simply to punish a person for her own private enjoyment—he knew there would be no changing her mind.

And, for fear of what their employer would do to him if he didn't obey her, he didn't have much of a choice in the matter and had followed her instructions to the letter.

Her aggressive attitude last night might have been her way of impressing the man who'd hired them and whom Keith had gotten the sense she had a relationship with— or at least wanted to have one with.

Regardless, in the end, Keith and Vanessa had accomplished what they'd come to India to do. The hologram had been redesigned. The women who were now coming in to work were already sending the boxes through the two printing machines.

Each of the printers could imprint one box every fifteen seconds, so, given forty-eight hours, that was more than enough time to package the ten thousand packets that were going to be shipped to America.

Keith and Vanessa's flight wasn't scheduled to leave until tomorrow evening.

"So what's the plan?" he asked her. "Back to Chennai? Check on the paperwork for the shipment?"

"We'll stay here for today, oversee things, then Baahir can take us back tomorrow morning. Maybe I'll see if we can get on an earlier flight. Either way we should arrive in Boston with plenty of time to get ready for Thursday. We'll need to be prudent about our steps from here on out. You know how he is if everything isn't in order."

Keith nodded soberly, realizing that what he had done to Eashan and Jagjeevan last night would be nothing compared to what would happen to him if he and Vanessa let down their employer, Alexei Chekov. "Yes."

Chekov, who was better known under the alias "Valkyrie," had worked as an assassin for Russia's foreign military intelligence directorate, the GRU, before launching out on his own last spring.

It seemed that since then he'd found his real calling and had worked tirelessly to refine his skills.

He was wanted not only by Interpol for international terrorism and numerous assassinations, but also appeared on the FBI's most-wanted-terrorists list with a five-million-dollar reward.

Keith had heard that Alexei used to have his own private code of ethics and never harmed women or children, but somewhere along the line he'd given that up and these days he was as ruthless with them as he was with the grown men who crossed him or let him down.

To call the Russian Mafia "ruthless" is like calling a sharks' feeding frenzy a "meal." And the Mafia was afraid of Alexei. To put it bluntly, when Alexei wanted something, he got it, and he wanted these drugs in the American pharmaceutical supply chain by this coming weekend. It was Keith and Vanessa's job to make sure that happened.

The drug they were so concerned with was the same one Corey Wellington had taken for the seven days preceding his suicide.

As Keith remembered him, he thought about pressing his fingers against a dead person's neck and feeling no pulse.

The cool skin. The unblinking eyes. The tongue that lolls to the side.

Every time Keith had felt for someone's pulse, both in the States and in the slums of India where they'd done their initial trials, had been difficult for him.

From the tests he and Vanessa had done, a week, just like it had been for Corey, was the average time frame. It was almost always six to eight days, depending on the dosage, body size, and degree of depression that the test subject was suffering from.

With Corey, it'd happened abruptly. That was unusual, but it wasn't unheard-of. Most people had gradual mental disorientation beforehand, but there were always those who simply woke up one day and decided on the spot to end it all.

Keith and Vanessa had watched Corey for nine days prior to his death. That's why they'd copied his house key and placed the two hidden cameras in his house—to monitor his progress.

And it was why they'd switched his prescription medication packets with ones from the facility here in Kadapa, the ones with their own lot numbers on them, so they could better track and monitor their use by the test subjects.

During Corey's last three days of life, they'd watched him every morning and evening on the video feed in the apartment they'd rented just down the street.

As far as Keith could tell, Vanessa hadn't slept the whole time.

It was amazing. And a little unnerving.

Calydrole was prescribed only to people who had suicidal tendencies. In clinical studies it showed a remarkable ability to help steer depressed individuals away from those kinds of thoughts.

Taking an inert pill would have increased the likelihood of those thoughts recurring, simply because the person's condition wasn't being treated. But the drug that Dr. Kurvetek, a neuropathologist with an above-average sadistic streak, had helped Alexei develop, did more than just allow the thoughts to return. It activated the parts of the brain that facilitated self-destructive behavior in depressed individuals.

Now, within a week, the drugs would be distributed to ten thousand moderately to severely depressed patients around North America, all of whom had seriously contemplated killing themselves.

And then, within six to eight days of those people taking their meds, the suicides would begin.

24

Considering all that I had on my mind, I slept well. No nightmares haunted me, and I felt refreshed and ready to go at it today.

After breakfast, I spent some time examining the forensics reports from the apartment where Basque had taken Lien-hua.

For security reasons, members of the National Center for the Analysis of Violent Crime didn't meet at FBI Headquarters or at the Academy.

Our offices were located in a warehouse that the Bureau had purchased ten years earlier near Quantico. The sign for Tarry Lawnmower Supply still hung out front, the lobby still had posters of lawnmowers on the walls, and when you called in, the receptionist cheerfully told you that you'd reached Tarry Lawnmower Supply.

Every week, semis drove to the back of the warehouse and loaded and unloaded the mowers alternately. All of these precautions were necessary, because the building didn't just house the NCAVC, but also all the records and computers that made up ViCAP.

I shared the official definition with our students so I had it memorized: "ViCAP maintains the largest investigative repository of major violent-crime cases in the U.S. It is designed to collect and analyze information about homicides, sexual assaults, missing persons, and other violent crimes involving unidentified human remains."

And the location of that was worth keeping a secret.

Even if Tessa chose not to come along with me to the hospital this morning to see Lien-hua, I figured I should let her know that I was heading over and wouldn't be back until later this afternoon, when the briefing was over.

It would probably also be a good idea to inform her that there would be police protection for her if she decided to stay at the house.

Going to her room, I knocked lightly on the door to see if she was awake. "Tessa?" I heard her gerbil, Rune, running on his gerbil-wheel-thing, but Tessa didn't reply.

I eased the door slightly open and caught a glimpse of her still lying in bed, eyes closed, her teddy bear, Francesca, snuggled up tightly in her arms.

Christie had given her the bear on her fifth birthday, and as far as I knew Tessa had slept with that stuffed animal every night since then. Yes, a girl whose walls were covered with posters of death-metal bands like Boomerang Puppy, Death by Suzie, and Trevor Asylum had a pet gerbil and slept with a teddy bear.

A quirk? Yeah, I guess that would definitely count.

I remembered when Tessa first told me she wanted a

gerbil. "I figured you for a snake person," I'd told her. "Maybe a rock python or something."

"I like gerbils."

"But they're cute and furry and they don't really go with the death motif here in the room."

"It's not a death motif. It's just posters of the bands I like."

"Find one without a skull on it."

She pointed.

"The name of that band is House of Blood."

"Well," she countered, "there's no skull. Besides, gerbils don't eat meat . . ." She caught herself. "Well, I suppose locusts and grubs—but only if there's no other food around. Anyway, I couldn't deal with a constrictor. I could never watch it kill mice like that every week. Totally disturbing."

In the end, I'd thought it might be good for her to have a pet to take care of and I'd told her that it was fine with me if she got a gerbil. She'd named him Rune, which came from an Old English word that meant "mystery," or "secret."

"Because I'll never know what he's thinking," she explained, "and I'm always going to wonder about that. What would it be like to think what a gerbil thinks, from a gerbil's point of view? Kind of like Thomas Nigel's 1974 paper 'What Is It Like to Be a Bat?' There's a subjective character of experience that's never captured in reductive accounts. Know what I mean?"

"Um . . . Sure."

Now I called to her again, a little louder than before, using her nickname: "Raven?"

Finally she groaned and rolled over, turning her back to me.

"I'm going to leave for the hospital in half an hour."

She groaned again in acknowledgment.

"Would you like to come along or are you going to stay here? I won't be back until later this afternoon."

"Yeah," she said feebly.

"Does that mean stay here or come along?"

"I'll come," she mumbled. "I wanna come."

"You sure?"

She gave another groan and I took that as a yes.

Twenty minutes later she staggered blearily into the kitchen in her pajamas and without a word poured herself a mug of coffee, mixed four heaping tablespoons of sugar into it, and flumped onto the chair across the table from me. "So what are we drinking today?" she asked sleepily.

"Tanzanian Peaberry."

She nodded, cupped the mug in her hands, and took a sip. "So you're really leaving in ten minutes?"

"I was planning to."

She sipped some more coffee. I had the sense that she'd gotten up about fifteen seconds before entering the room.

I added a little honey and cream to my cup.

"Yeah," she said, "okay—ten minutes."

She rummaged through the cupboard for some granola, dumped it into a bowl, and poured soy milk over it. "I'm gonna change. I'll meet you in the car." She turned toward the hallway and I wasn't sure if she was being morning-brain-distracted or if she was going to bring her breakfast with her to eat on the way.

Before she left the kitchen I cleared my throat. "Hey, listen. I was thinking about last night, when you were talking to me about going to church."

"Never mind." She brushed a hand across the air as if

she were erasing something. "It's all good. It doesn't matter."

"No, it does. I didn't want you to think I was blowing you off."

"Okay."

"I mean—"

"I get it. Okay." She yawned, started for her room, but then stopped suddenly, leaned against the wall, and rubbed some sleep out of her eyes. "I don't think I ever told you, but when I was little I was always scared of the dark, scared of monsters in my closet. You know, like what happens with kids."

"Sure."

"Anyway, Mom told me there was no such thing as monsters." She scratched uneasily at the back of her neck. "But there are, aren't there?"

The transition from church to monsters wasn't immediately clear to me. "I'm not sure I know what you mean."

"Don't you ever wonder about vampires and werewolves? Where all the stories come from?"

"Actually, I've got a theory on that."

"Let me guess, it has to do with serial killers?"

"Well"—she'd taken a little air out of my balloon—"yes, actually."

"That villagers maybe . . . what? Found bodies, mutilated or something, and didn't think a human being could ever be capable of doing that to someone?"

I nodded. "The term 'serial killer' is fairly recent. They used to be called ghouls or fiends and were often attributed superhuman powers—often they weren't even considered human. After all, it's a lot easier to believe a monster could do those things to another person than to accept that it was someone who lived in your same village, maybe next door, maybe even in your own home."

"Those who should know killers best, often know them the least."

"Yes."

"And those around them suspect nothing at all."

"That's right, all too often they suspect nothing at all."

"But," she said, "it's worse this way, that's my point. With monsters, I mean."

"What do you mean?"

"I mean if you had real monsters they'd be easy to identify, you know? Werewolves and vampires only look like the rest of us some of the time, sometimes they look like what they really are."

Now I saw where she was going with this and concluded her thought for her. "But serial killers always look like the rest of us. They never really look like what they are."

"Or maybe they always do."

That was a troubling thought.

She looked at me intently. "I've been thinking about it since we talked about how clever criminals can be in prison—how they could ever act so inhuman to each other. Do you know how to turn someone into a monster?"

"I'm not sure. No."

"Let him be himself without restraint."

Then she went to her room and left me to sort through what she'd just said.

We'd had discussions on this subject before, and she'd quoted to me the words of Dr. Werjonic: "The road to the unthinkable is not paved by slight departures from your heart, but by tentative forays into it."

Being yourself without restraint.

Taking deeper forays into your own heart.

Two ways of saying the same thing.

She reemerged, brought her cereal and a copy of Michael D. O'Brien's novel *Island of the World* with her to the car, and we drove to see Lien-hua.

As I picked my way through the morning DC traffic, I reflected on what Tessa had just said about people turning into monsters.

I think it was Plato who first recorded asking people what they would do if they weren't visible—if they could do anything without consequence or chance of discovery. Almost no one answered the question by listing all the good things they would do for other people. Instead, they fantasized about all the things they could get away with, all the things that society and culture and their own consciences constrained them from doing on a day-to-day basis—a *Lord of the Flies* sort of thing.

Inadvertently, both Plato and Tessa had identified one of the premises of environmental criminology: crimes almost never occur in the presence of an authority figure.

Are students better behaved when the teacher steps out of the room? Are gang members more law-abiding when the police stop patrolling their neighborhoods? Is genocide less frequent when the UN stops imposing sanctions?

No, we don't become kinder, gentler, and more virtuous in the absence of authority figures, we become more violent and ruthless. The unrest and genocide in Africa over the last thirty years hasn't been because of closely guarded, fair laws, but in large part because of the absence of anyone to enforce them. The true nature of man left to himself without restraint is not nobility but savagery.

What an encouraging thought to start the day off with.

Lien-hua was asleep when we arrived.

I figured that, more than anything else, resting would help her recover, so rather than wake her, I lost myself in reviewing online case files from the previous Basque crimes while Tessa read her novel.

The morning became the afternoon.

At twelve thirty my daughter and I had a quiet lunch in the cafeteria, and at twenty after one Lien-hua was still asleep when I left to attend the briefing south of the city at NCAVC headquarters.

To try to catch a monster who looked just like the rest of us.

25

Ralph and I passed through security at Tarry Lawnmower Supply and met up with the rest of the team in conference room 2B.

Cassidy was there, as well as Doehring, SWAT Commander Shaw, and two other NCAVC agents, one of whom was the agent who'd been following up with Saundra Weathers's friends and family to try to locate which campground she'd taken her daughter to. His name was Gavin Syssic and he was a slim, studious man close to retirement who knew how to get things done.

The other agent, a platinum blond woman in her late twenties named Sara Hammet, had been working with Doehring and his officers to interview the water treatment plant employees.

"Alright," Ralph said. "We all know how much Pat loves briefings, so let's make this one brief."

"I appreciate that," I replied.

I filled everyone in on Lien-hua's progress, then Ralph nodded toward Sara. "What do we know about the people at the treatment facilities?"

"Not much. No one recognized Basque or remembered seeing him around. Neither did the woman who owns the car he stole, or the man who owns the garage where he stowed Lien-hua's car."

"And we still don't know whose prints those were on the novel?"

"No."

Doehring spoke up. "We talked with the owner of the apartment building Basque took Lien-hua to. The guy says that the man who rented the apartment called himself Loudon Caribes, paid six months' rent in advance. Cash. He rented the place two weeks ago."

"Six months?" Gavin shook his head soberly. "I guess Basque was definitely planning to use that place again."

"Could have just been the normal lease time," Doehring pointed out. "Anyway, wanna know what Caribes means?" He didn't wait for a response. "It's the root word for 'cannibal.'"

Well, that was appropriate.

"Gavin," I said, "go ahead and do a background on that name—Loudon Caribes—see if anything comes up. Also, look up other iterations of 'caribes' or 'cannibal' and the root words for 'anthropophagy' and 'maneater.' Add those to the mix."

Anthropophagy was an antiquated word that meant "cannibal" and was really only used today by law enforcement agencies.

"Got it." He typed a few notes into his laptop.

"Did you reach anyone who knows where Saundra Weathers is?" I asked him.

"No. Not yet."

I spent some time detailing the geoprofile I'd come up with, and Doehring agreed to get some officers looking into possible sightings of Basque in the three hot zones I'd identified as likely anchor points for the crimes.

"And," I said, "let's follow up on apartments, condos, and homes in those regions, see if any have been rented under this Caribes alias."

Understanding the travel patterns of the victims of a crime spree reveals information about the travel patterns of the offender, so when I develop a geoprofile, I always consider not just the primary and secondary crime scene locations, but also the victimology. What are their preferred routes to and from work? Where were they going, and what were they doing when they encountered the offender? Where are their favorite places to hang out or eat at? I'm really interested in why and where the offender first met up with that victim, how his life intersected with hers.

Basque had been implicated in five murders in the DC area over the last year. "Let's take a closer look at the places where the victims' lives intersected. Maybe they all shopped at the same grocery store on their way home from work or bought life insurance through the same agent. I'm thinking the key to finding Basque is finding him through them." I didn't want to admit it, but I did anyway: "It's possible he's been taunting us with these other attacks and we haven't noticed. And let's see if any of the previous victims have any connections with me. Sara, I can do the online work, but with Lien-hua laid up, I—"

"Sure, I'm glad to make the calls."

"Great."

So, the process: We would establish the typical travel routes by interviewing family, friends, and coworkers to find out about the habits and known routine routes of the victims. Some of this we already had; some of it we needed to get.

That was time-consuming, and thankfully, Sara would be heading up that part of the process.

Meanwhile, I could log into the Federal Digital Database and review phone records to study the GPS locations, where calls were made and received, and comb through credit card receipts to find where the victims shopped, ate out, bought gas, and so on to identify their travel patterns.

From working the Basque case over the last ten months, I'd done some of this already, but it was time to take it to the next level.

Cassidy offered to follow up on the lock I'd picked in the tunnel beneath the water treatment plant to see if he could figure out where it might have been purchased. "Maybe we can dig up something on Basque—a credit card, a check—who knows. I'll see what I can do."

We spent the rest of the briefing analyzing what we knew, then split up job responsibilities and Ralph brought the meeting to a close.

Traffic was not kind to me and I didn't get back to the hospital until six.

26

When I entered Lien-hua's room, I noticed that the pile of cards and the number of flowers had continued to grow. She told me that Tessa had stepped outside for a minute. "Don't worry, the officer from the hallway joined her."

"Did she say she was going to get some fresh air by any chance?" It was the euphemism Tessa used when she was really heading out to grab a smoke.

"Yes. That's how she put it. Smoking, huh?"

"Yup."

Well, I could address that later.

Lien-hua shifted in the bed. "Remember when I was in the hospital in San Diego last year and Margaret brought me a card?"

"Yes." FBI Director Margaret Wellington had been the head of the NCAVC at the time. "And then she suspended you for some ridiculous little—"

"Well . . ." Lien-hua pointed to an impressive bouquet in the corner of the room. It looked almost as nice as the one Brineesha and Tessa had brought by earlier.

"You're kidding me."

"Nope. The note said she knew I liked flower arrang-

ing and that she hoped this was done well enough for me
to enjoy. And it is."

Margaret was not exactly known for her sentimental-
ity, and a gesture like that from her was nothing short of
extraordinary.

The two of us had a long and patchy history together.
Six years ago, when I'd brought up some missing evidence in a case to the Bureau's Office of Professional
Responsibility, things had pointed back to her. As it
ended up, she wasn't censured but was shuffled off to
serve a stint at the Resident Agency in Asheville, North
Carolina—an assignment she definitely did not consider
to be an upwardly mobile one.

However, her fortunes had turned and over the last
few years she'd moved steadily up the ranks. Last year,
after Director Rodale resigned, the Senate approved Margaret as the Bureau's Director, and now she was enjoying
the office she'd been aspiring to ever since I first met her.

Over the years I've noticed that to a lot of people,
power is as addictive as any drug is. Once they've snorted
it, once it gets into their system, it's the hardest habit of
all to kick. Lately, it appeared that being FBI Director
wasn't even enough power for Margaret. It was no secret
that she was eyeing politics, and I had a feeling I knew
who would be running in next year's congressional elec-
tion for Virginia's first-district seat.

"So," I said, referring back to the flowers, "word has
definitely gotten around about your quirk."

"I suppose it has. And I'm starting to think that there's
more to Margaret than meets the eye."

I said, "Did I ever tell you that she mentioned to me
one time that she volunteers at a shelter for battered
women on the weekends?"

Lien-hua was quiet. "That's something I didn't know."

Last summer a serial killer had left a DVD in the trunk of Margaret's car that contained footage of seven of his victims—some in the process of being killed. But that wasn't all it contained. There was also footage someone had filmed of her asleep in her own bed—video that was taken from inside her bedroom.

That night, the man who'd murdered those other women had been killed and we never found out for certain if he was the one who'd invaded her privacy, snuck into her bedroom, and filmed her as she slept.

Most people didn't know about it, how much it had affected her.

While Tessa was out of the room, I took the opportunity to recap the NCAVC meeting to Lien-hua. She listened intently and then suggested I add her own home and travel patterns to the geographic mix. "Remember? Victimology? I'm one of those now. Let's see if we can find out where Basque's life might have intersected with mine, or mine with any of the other known victims'."

It made me feel a little uncomfortable talking about her in these terms, but she was right—she was a victim.

"I'll add the data when I get home."

A moment passed. "Pat, I have to ask you something."

"Yes?"

"Catching him, putting him away, are you trying to find Basque for revenge or for justice?"

It wasn't an easy question to answer. "Sometimes those two reasons converge, you know that."

"You need to be objective about this, Pat, or Ralph might remove you from this case."

Many times on television shows as soon as a killer

threatens a detective, he's removed from the case so things don't get "personal." It might be a useful screenwriter's device, but it's not the reality of life on the streets. If it were, criminals could evade capture by simply intimidating the people investigating them so that different officers or agents would have to be continually assigned to their case, and it would slow down the investigation.

"Ralph wouldn't do that."

"He could. If you're not approaching things impartially."

"That's the last thing I would want to do."

"Why on earth would you say that?"

"Anger sharpens my focus."

"No"—she was drifting into profiler mode—"if you get too emotionally involved in a case, it'll skew your judgment."

"There's a saying in India," I said. " 'A mind that is all logic is like a knife that is all blade.' "

She looked at me quizzically. "Talk me through that."

"The harder you grip a blade, the tighter you squeeze it, the more you'll bleed. You need something other than the blade to hold on to or you'll never be able to wield the knife properly."

"So you're saying you need emotion."

"I think so, yes. And passion. You need to care. And I care about you enough to pursue both justice and revenge. Whichever one, whatever it takes, I want it to be personal. That'll make me angry enough to catch him."

"Catch him."

"Yes."

"Or kill him?"

I was quiet.

"So the fable isn't true," she said. "About the hare

being faster because it's running for its life. You're saying the hound can be more motivated when he has enough anger to drive him."

I didn't correct her.

Her eyes showed a mixture of understanding and concern.

Tessa returned to the room smelling of cigarette smoke and carrying takeout from a vegetarian Indian restaurant across the street from the hospital. "I figured we could use some real food."

"Did you get enough fresh air?" I asked her somewhat pointedly.

"Um . . ." The look on her face told me she knew she was busted.

"No more of that."

"Right."

She must have known just as well as I did that this would come up again, but for now it was a step in the right direction, and at least that was something.

As we were finishing our rather late dinner, Brineesha swung by and, after about twenty minutes, took Tessa home so she could get to her homework. I planned to return home soon myself, but just as a precaution I had an undercover car follow them.

After they were gone Lien-hua said, "Pat, how's your lecture coming for tomorrow morning?"

"I called Dr. Neubauer. He's going to cover for me."

"The pollen guy? From the Lab?"

"Yeah. The lecture is about forensic palynology and its relationship to geospatial investigation."

"Sounds scintillating."

"Oh, it would have been, but I figured Neubauer

could cover the palynology portion better in his sleep than I ever could. Anyway, that way I can be here."

"I think you should go teach. If you lurk around here all week it's going to make me feel guilty."

"I'm not lurking."

"What are you doing?"

"Lingering."

"Ah. Well, if you linger around here too much I'll feel guilty that you're not out there doing what you need to be doing. I really just need to rest anyway. If I'm lucky, I might be able to get released Wednesday or Thursday."

"The doctor said it might be six days," I said protectively. "Plus one more after they cast your leg."

"I'm a quick recoverer. Teach your class in the morning and then you can linger here in the afternoon."

"I don't know, I—"

"Pat, stop being stubborn."

"I'm not stubborn. I'm strong-willed."

"I see."

I took a breath and considered her antilingering request. "You sure?"

"Yes. Maybe you can bring me something for lunch from that burger place you like so much. That one near the Academy. I always forget the name of it."

I doubted that was true; I figured she just wanted me to say it. "Billy Bongo's Burger Hut?"

"That's the one. I'll take a grilled chicken salad."

"You don't go to Billy Bongo's for a salad."

"I have to watch my figure."

"I can take care of that for you."

"Mm-hmm."

I took her hand in mine.

I already knew what I would get from Billy Bongo's,

and undoubtedly so did Lien-hua: an Ultimate Deluxe Classic Cheeseyburg Extreme, curly fries, and a medium Cherry Coke. I have a weakness for cheeseburgers—I guess that can count as a quirk too. Either way, it definitely isn't an ideal food choice, living with a vegan animal rights activist daughter.

At last I gave in. "Okay. It's a deal."

After making her promise that she would call me right away if she needed me—if she needed anything—I got in touch with Dr. Neubauer, told him about the change of plans, then I gave Lien-hua a kiss and left the hospital.

I'd just slipped into my car and was starting the engine when Saundra Weathers returned the call I'd put through to her yesterday morning.

27

"I was gone for the weekend, just got the message you left me," she said. "You mentioned your name, Patrick Bowers. Are you the same Patrick Bowers I'm thinking you are?"

"From Horicon."

"So that is you. And you're an FBI agent now?"

"I've been with the Bureau for ten years."

"The last I heard you were a homicide detective in Milwaukee."

"I was on the force there for six years before joining the FBI."

"And you sent those two agents here? The ones who are outside my house parked at the curb right now?"

"Yes." I assumed they must have introduced themselves when she arrived home, told her only what they were supposed to—that her name had come up in an investigation and they were there "as standard operating procedure."

To help transition to the reason I'd asked her to call, I said, "I saw that two of your books have hit the *New York Times* bestseller list. Congratulations."

"Thank you." She quickly brushed the compliment aside. "So you're the same Patrick Bowers who found . . .

Well, who found that girl. Back when we were in high school."

"Yes, I am. Miss Weathers, I would—"

"Saundra. Please."

"Saundra, have you ever heard of Richard Basque?"

"The serial killer? Doesn't he eat the people he kills?" Since she lived in the region, and considering the media coverage of his crimes, I wasn't surprised she was familiar with who he was.

"He does."

"Is that what this is about? That's the investigation my name came up in?"

"Last night a copy of one of your books, *On My Way to Dying*, was found in a car he'd stolen."

She didn't say anything. "And?"

"And I have reason to believe that he left it there for me to find. Since your family owned the land bordering the marsh, you and I are connected—in a way—through the death of Mindy Wells. I don't believe it was a coincidence."

"That book has sold over five hundred thousand copies, Patrick. Are you sure it didn't just belong to the person who owned the car?"

"We contacted her. It isn't hers."

A moment passed. "Saundra, I'm wondering if you've noticed anything unusual lately. Any strange phone calls, anyone you didn't recognize watching you or coming by your house? Anything at all?"

"No. Nothing like that. You think he might be coming after me?" Surprisingly, she didn't sound either shocked or afraid, more curious than anything.

"I'm not saying that at all."

"Then why are the agents outside my house?"

"As a precaution."

"A precaution against what?"

"Basque is an extremely dangerous man. Anyone he's had contact with could be in danger."

"So I'm in danger?" Again she sounded more intrigued than afraid.

"There's no evidence to suggest that you are, but I'm going to ask you to call me if you see or hear anything out of the ordinary. And I'd like to keep those agents assigned to you."

"As a precaution."

"Yes. Will that be acceptable to you?"

"For how long?"

"That'll depend on how our investigation progresses. But I think it's better to—"

"What? Be safe than sorry?"

"To cover all our bases."

She didn't reply right away and I sensed that she was gearing up to argue with me, but in the end she didn't. "They can stay."

"Thank you."

Then she abruptly returned the conversation to what had happened in Horicon. "Do you ever think about that day? About that girl in the tree house?"

Yes. All the time.

"Yes. Do you?"

"Yes. I guess that's what led me to become a crime writer. After being there, you know, in town when it happened. Maybe writing has been my way of trying to sort all that out. Is that why you got into law enforcement?"

"I'm really not sure," I told her truthfully.

We were both silent for a moment and then she said, "I'll contact you if I hear or see anything. But I'd like to ask you something in return."

"What's that?"

"That you'll call me if you find out anything more. I have a little girl. You understand."

"I won't be able to give you specifics concerning the investigation, I hope you can understand that, but if we find out anything more regarding the novel or if we find out Basque has taken any kind of special interest in you, I'll call you right away."

"Alright. Thank you."

We ended the call and as I drove home, Saundra's question plagued me: "Is that why you got into law enforcement?"

Yes, maybe it was.

At home, I looked up the info the team had gathered on Saundra Weathers and her soon-to-be-six-year-old adopted daughter. Someone had tracked down press photos from Saundra's last book-release party.

Just like I remembered her from high school, Saundra had a slim, pretty face and an earnest gaze. Noni was a slight Ethiopian girl with a cute smile that was made even more endearing because she was missing one of her front teeth.

I worked late, entering information corresponding to Lien-hua's cognitive map of DC into the geoprofile to see if I could identify anywhere her life might have intersected with that of the other victims or with the regions we were looking at for Basque. It seemed pretty clear that he hadn't chosen her because of expediency or opportunity but because of her connection with me, but I didn't want to discount anything, so I took a careful look at her data.

It didn't lead anywhere, but while I was going through

the files again, I was reminded of a connection two of the victims had.

One of them worked at a sporting goods store where another had bought fishing tackle. It was a small, privately owned store and didn't have any security cameras on-site—I'd looked into that months ago. But this location seemed to be the only one where these two women's lives intersected. I reviewed the interviews with the store owner again, but didn't come up with anything.

Offenders who are peripatetic—in other words, who commit crimes while traveling through an area—skew the results of geoprofiles. However, in the case of Basque, he had committed enough other crimes in the DC area that it was highly unlikely he was just traveling through.

Also, as I'd promised to do at our briefing, I studied the cognitive maps of the previous victims in relationship to my own. The travel pattern data from my life and from Lien-hua's helped narrow down the places where Basque's anchor point might be and moved the hot zone on the east of the city farther out, past Joint Base Andrews, and a few miles south.

After uploading the information to the online case files for the rest of the team to access, I reviewed my notes for tomorrow's eight-o'clock forensic palynology lecture at the Academy, until exhaustion finally overtook me and I fell asleep.

28

Monday, April 8
7:02 a.m.

Richard Basque awakened to the sound of his two pit bulls snarling restlessly, agitated, in the yard near the edge of the Jug Bay Wetlands Sanctuary where he lived.

' He peered out the window and saw that one of them had killed a rabbit and the two dogs were tearing it apart. Beyond them, the languorous wetlands stretched back more than a mile before dissipating and merging with the Patuxent River.

He'd chosen this location carefully. The flowage gave him a place to dispose of bones after he and his dogs had each had their fill of the meat he brought back to the house.

He went into the kitchen and put on some coffee.

Richard had read both of Patrick's books on geospatial investigation and knew all about his specialty of tracking the locations of the home bases of serial offenders. Bowers had a PhD in environmental criminology and put it to good use.

Because of that, Richard had been careful not to leave

any discernible pattern for him to track. He made sure to take the people he abducted to random locations—or he brought them back here, where he could dispose of their remains in the marsh in places where they would never be discovered.

No, the apartment he'd taken Lien-hua to was not one he'd used before, and not one he'd planned to use again.

He cracked an egg, tipped it into a bowl, and whisked it lightly.

Sausage was also on the menu. A special recipe he'd come up with himself.

There was nothing in Richard's childhood that would lead you to believe he would grow up to become what he was.

No abuse.

No absentee father or overbearing mother.

No warning signs. As a child he'd never started fires, tortured animals, or had problems with bed-wetting—the triad of characteristics that so many serial killers, for whatever reason, share.

He grew up in a modest home with nurturing parents and a younger sister whom he had always loved—and still did. He did well in school, found success in the workplace, and then somewhere along the line developed a liking for human flesh.

People want to find something essentially different about serial killers—that they were abused, or are genetically predisposed to act the way they do, or perhaps had a brain injury or something along those lines.

Some people believe spiritual forces are at play—demonic possession and the like—because then, if the behavior was caused by the environment or predestined in their genes or could be blamed on the devil, then other people—normal people—wouldn't have to be afraid that they might one day become like those who torture and kill and rape and cannibalize their victims.

In a way, Richard was thankful for the teachers he'd had during his formative years, thankful that they'd been so nonjudgmental and hadn't tried to impose their values on him, but just taught him that every culture has its own norms and mores and that we should accept all of them as equal. And they emphasized how important it was that he clarify his own "personal values."

And, of course, they'd told him over and over to feel good about himself. That seemed to be very important to them.

So now he had a healthy self-esteem—he wasn't proud of who he was, nor was he ashamed of it. He simply felt good about himself just as his teachers had encouraged him to do all those years.

And Richard's values had become quite clarified.

Quite clarified indeed.

Yes, he was grateful for an educational system that had helped steer him away from feeling shame over the personal values he felt so strongly drawn to. He had taken those experts' advice to heart.

Certainly, when it comes to genetic makeup, the deck was stacked against some people, but Richard had always known the truth: people like him choose to become what they are. It's an act of the will, pure and simple. Jeffrey Dahmer, Albert Fish, Andrei Chikatilo, they might have felt a compulsion to do as they did, but ultimately they all made the decision to act on it. To blame genes or upbringing or the devil was to shift responsibility and diminish the accountability of the people making the choices, committing the crimes.

After all, as philosophers throughout the ages have noted, the definition of freedom is the ability to do otherwise. If you have no choice in a situation, you aren't free. So if there is such a thing as free will, killers choose their path and deserve to be held responsible. On the other hand, if there isn't such a thing as free will, why would anyone be held accountable or punished for anything, since he wouldn't have had a choice in the matter and had no power to resist the temptation?

Richard knew these things, knew that everyone has, within himself, both the potential for evil and the potential for good. We are, each of us, free to follow socially constructed moral tenets. And we are free to do otherwise.

Everyone is.

Maybe the most frightening thing about killers is not what they have done, but that, given the right circumstances and stressors, everyone is capable of doing the very same things.

Richard turned on the burner, got out the frying pan, and thought back to his encounter with Patrick at the water treatment plant Friday night.

After Lien-hua escaped, he'd left bread crumbs for Bowers to follow—her car in that garage, going through intersections with traffic cameras, parking outside the water treatment facility.

Bowers had followed the trail faithfully, determinedly, just like the hound in the fable.

Richard had known all along that he was not just another meal to Bowers, but to hear him say it, yes, that was encouraging: to hear Patrick vow to take him down just reaffirmed their symbiotic relationship—the pursuer and the pursued, the chaser and the chased.

Each derived meaning from the pursuit: the hare escapes, but then ventures back into the hound's territory. The hound returns home disappointed, not just that he did not catch the hare, but that the chase is over for the day.

And yes, in this case the hare was going to venture into the hound's realm once again.

Richard wondered if the Bureau was following up on the novel he'd left in the car at the plant. He assumed that Patrick would make the connection, but he couldn't be sure. Sometimes little things like that slipped through the cracks.

Well, either way, it was not the time to be careless.

Yes, he would visit the mystery writer tomorrow night, would attend her daughter's six-year-old birthday party. Even if the Bureau decided to assign protection to her, he had in mind a way to get to her and to the girl.

Richard had never eaten a child before.

But there's a first time for everything.

He would leave the girl's remains in a tree house. That would have special meaning to Patrick.

So.

Tomorrow at five.

To get ready for it he needed to do a little shopping, and then he could spend some time practicing a few new tricks.

He finished cooking the sausages and ate them slowly, savoring every bite. After taking some antibiotics and changing the dressing on his gunshot wound, he went online, looked up the location of the store he would be visiting later in the day, and entered the address into his phone. When he was done, he glanced out the window and saw his two dogs, snouts bloody from their kill, stalking along the edge of the marsh looking for more game.

29

The New Agents gathered in my room on the second floor of the classroom building at the Academy.

The class of fifty, all dressed in their required attire of dark blue polo shirts and khakis, was unusually quiet as they filed in.

I figured they'd heard about what had happened with Lien-hua and were trying to figure out the best way to ask me about her condition, so I started class by giving them a quick update. "The surgery went well and Agent Jiang is recovering." I told them about her injuries. "The doctors are hoping she'll be released by the end of the week."

One young woman in the back row flagged her hand in the air.

"Yes?"

"I heard it was Richard Basque—that he's the one who did it."

"It was."

New Agents aren't allowed to work on any cases until after they graduate, but the assistant director in charge of the Academy encouraged us to read them in as much as possible on ongoing cases, as long as they didn't discuss them outside the classroom. "Think of them as residents in surgery," he told us. "The only way they'll learn is if they actually pick up a scalpel."

Not the image I wanted in mind as I talked about Basque, but I slid it aside and took the opportunity to fill in the class on what we knew regarding the case, and on the investigative procedures we'd followed Friday night in tracking Basque to the water treatment plant.

It was a natural lead-in to today's lecture. "Rather than trying to understand criminal events from a sociological perspective, I think the most effective framework for understanding them is to approach them from a geographical one instead."

This wasn't necessarily a popular view at the Academy, or at NCAVC, but I figured it's only fair to let your students know where you're coming from.

"Different types of serial offenses have different spatial clusters. Generally, the closer the crimes are to each other, the closer they are to the offender's anchor point— basically the location from which he bases his criminal activity."

"His home," a young man in the front row offered.

"Yes, often, but it might be his place of work or a relative's, friend's, or lover's house where he spends a significant amount of time."

He looked slightly confused. "But that's assuming people have stable travel and movement patterns. Right?"

"Back in 2008, Northwestern University tracked the movement of more than a hundred thousand Europeans for six months through their cell phones—Europe, because it would have been illegal in the U.S. Privacy issues. In any case, they confirmed all the major premises of environmental criminology. People's habits and patterns are relatively stable. We consistently travel the same routes through the same cities and frequent the same stores, clubs, gas stations, pharmacies, and, at least to a limited extent, vacation spots."

I thought of the case again, the victimology information I'd studied.

The three potential anchor points I'd come up with for Basque seemed to hover before me, as if they were etched there in midair.

The sporting goods store had no video camera . . .

That might be why he chose it. So that he wouldn't appear on any footage.

I tried to stay focused but I found myself distracted as I went on.

"Which leads us to the implications this study has on investigative theory. Rather than ask why the offender committed this crime, we accept that, for whatever reason—even perhaps a reason that's unclear to him—he was motivated to act in that way. We ask, 'Why then?' 'Why there?' 'What is the balance of rewards versus risks that led that offender to make the choice to commit this crime in this specific place at this specific time?'"

I pulled out my laptop, which was wirelessly connected to the video screen in the front of the room.

"And one of the ways we can place an offender at the scene of a crime at a specific place and time is through forensic palynology." I tapped at the keyboard and projected a slide of an enlarged pollen grain.

"Palynology is the study of the distribution patterns of pollen and spores. The characteristics of the pollen can reveal the genus and species of the plants they come from."

Slide number two.

"Plants produce millions of pollen grains that are carried by the wind, on people's clothing, on everything. In fact, pollen can be lifted by the wind up to forty thousand feet in the air and can even cross oceans. Those are the smaller ones; the bigger spores will just drop to the ground. The more ornamentation they have, the more likely they are to be carried by the biotic vector of insects and birds."

Before clicking to slide three, I warned the New Agents to prepare themselves. "It's a crime scene. And it's not pleasant."

I went to the slide: the unsolved homicide of college student Brandi Giddens, who'd been found in February at the park where Tessa, Lien-hua, and I had picnicked on Friday.

The slide contained the graphic, grisly image of Brandi's disarticulated corpse.

Even after all these years, seeing images like this wasn't easy for me. Whether that was a strength or a weakness, I've never been able to figure out.

A mind that is all logic is like a knife that is all blade.

There wasn't any chance of that at the moment.

Some of the New Agents looked troubled. Others looked intrigued. From my experience, the first group would make the best agents.

"By looking at the sediment on the bottom of this woman's shoes we could tell she had been near wetlands or a marsh sometime during the last day of her life. The pollen told us it was here in the DC area. Clothes act as a pollen trap and people are walking pollen collectors. One square centimeter on your clothes could have twelve hundred or more pollen grains, depending on the season. They're also trapped in your hair and nostrils. Taken together, studying the pollen collected on—and in—an individual, gives us the floristic signature for the day, where that person has been the last twenty-four hours."

I went through what we'd deduced about the woman's last twenty-four hours based on the pollen and spores we'd collected from her corpse.

Next slide: an air filter from a 1991 Dodge conversion van. I explained that the first time I worked with Dr. Neubauer was five years ago, when I was consulting with local law enforcement in North Carolina, trying to work out the timing and location of a kidnapping near Durham.

"When Dr. Neubauer found out the kidnapping was in the spring he was thrilled. He e-mailed me, asking if I'd thought about pollen. I called him and asked how pollen was going to help find the kidnapper. Then he asked me if I had any air filters."

Now I recounted the conversation as best I could remember it:

"Air filters?"

"Yes. Any vehicles involved with the crime?"

"We have a van the kidnapper used."

"Perfect. I'll need the air filter."

"I'm not sure I'm really following you here."

"Pollen gets caught up in vehicles' air filters. Since the van was used during the spring—when plants are flowering—we can study the pollen in the air filter and work backward to figure out the region the vehicle was in and possibly even the route the vehicle took—"

"Based on the pollen trapped in the filter."

"Yes. Well, I say we can use that air filter, I haven't done that type of work yet. But theoretically, I can."

"And," I told the New Agents, "he did. It helped us solve the case."

Afterward, though I was no expert, I fielded their questions about palynology as best I could. Then they asked me again about Basque, about how to catch him. Obviously, they were more interested in the hunt for one of the best-known and highest-profile fugitives in the country than in pollen and spores.

I pointed out that, despite our best efforts, criminals always have the advantage in at least three ways. "First, they have more to lose. We keep our jobs, they keep their freedom or, in some cases, their lives."

In a sense, the fable Basque had told me was right—they are just another meal to us.

At least, to most of us.

"Second, criminals don't play by the rules. We have to follow protocol, conscience, regulations, policies, procedures, ethics, all those things. It's like trying to win a basketball game in which you have to follow the rules, but your opponent can carry the ball, run out of bounds, and never foul out. That's what it's like on the streets, every day. Can anyone think of number three?"

I was encouraged when the woman who'd first asked about Basque responded. "Criminals can choose the time and location for their crimes, but the investigator has to follow around after they've occurred."

"That's right. Until we catch them, they're always one step ahead. Predicting when and where a crime is going to occur is terribly difficult, and despite what you might see in the movies, it's extremely rare."

"So with the odds stacked against us like that," she asked, "how can we win?"

We declare that it's rabbit season.

"We let it matter enough to make sure we don't lose."

Lien-hua's words came back to me: "You're saying the

hound can be more motivated when he has enough anger to drive him."

Yes, enough anger.

To drive.

Me.

Although it didn't take us into new territory, I gave them the chance to pull out their scalpels on Basque's case, so to speak. Afterward, we took a short break. I wanted to find out how Lien-hua was, but I couldn't text her because her cell was still missing—taken somewhere by Basque—and I didn't want to call her hospital room phone in case she was sleeping, so I texted Brin instead and almost instantly she replied that Lien-hua was fine and was asleep.

I checked in with Ralph to see if the team had come up with anything since yesterday afternoon's meeting. The call went to voicemail, I left a message, and then waited for the New Agents to return from their break.

But the map of the hot zones continued to hover in the air in front of me, mocking me, challenging me to decipher it.

And, despite my best efforts, I couldn't seem to do it.

Maybe I just needed a little more anger to drive me toward the hare.

30

Tessa had a ton on her mind.

Not only was there Lien-hua's recovery, but also just the fact that Richard Basque had attacked someone so close to Patrick and her. It was all terribly disquieting.

There was also the awkward conversation she'd had with Patrick the other night about going to church. It'd started out just as a question she had, but had turned into something where she basically said he didn't care what she ended up believing in, which she knew was not the case.

Of course she knew he wanted her to believe the right things, the true things.

And then there was the whole deal with this stupid graduation speech. It made her physically ill just to think about it, about getting up in front of all those people.

Yes, definitely bail on the speech.

What about Aiden?

Yeah, what about Aiden?

Prom was Friday. He'd broken up with Tymber Dotson a month ago, and Tessa had heard he wanted to ask her instead, but so far—nothing. Nada. Not even any serious flirting. Time was not on her side, and she had just about the worst history in the world getting asked out by guys who were not total losers.

If she ended up getting asked out at all.

She'd dated guys throughout high school but had never been to prom before and she hated that it bothered her, but it did. Despite how self-assured she felt in other areas of life, when it came to guys she felt so needy and unsure of herself. It was weird and it annoyed her. She'd done everything she could think of to get over it, but nothing worked and that just made it bug her worse.

And now it was looking like she would go all the way through high school without ever getting asked out to prom.

She didn't know why she'd gotten the vibe that Aiden wanted her to give this speech, but it had definitely been there ever since he'd found out she'd been asked to write it.

Deal with that later. Just get out of the speech first.

She decided that right after AP Lit with Tilson she would tell Assistant Principal Thacker that she wasn't going to do it.

Oh, joy.

AP Lit with Tilson.

That was just plain brutal.

He was always trying to impress the students, embarrassing those he didn't like or who weren't as dialed into his version of what English Lit was supposed to be all about.

His version.

Normally she held back from mixing things up with him, but there were a few times when she couldn't help it and ended up disputing him.

Last week, for example. After he'd had Shaleigha

Gage, the valedictorian, explain a poem that no one else in the class really seemed to get, he'd said, "Thank you for unpacking the meaning of that poem for us."

And Tessa had said, "Excuse me."

"Yes?"

"It's not a poem. Not anymore. Not to us."

"And what do you mean by that, Miss Ellis?"

"As soon as you can explain a poem, it stops being a poem and becomes nothing more than a lesson. After you cut out its heart to get a good look at it, you kill the mystery. All you have left is a corpse of words. Poems are meant to be experienced, not explained."

Oh, Tilson really loved that.

But she didn't regret saying it at all. Sometimes you need to speak up when you come face-to-face with sciolism.

She headed for Trig. After that, lunch, then Tilson, then meeting with Thacker to tell him she wasn't going to do that speech.

An afternoon chock-full of things to look forward to.

+++

I was at the drive-through window of Billy Bongo's Burger Hut when Ralph called to bring me up to speed.

I handed over my credit card and waited for the food while he filled me in: "The background checks on people named Loudon or Caribes didn't give us anything. It doesn't look like Basque has used that alias before—at least not in renting or buying any apartments, condos, homes within a hundred miles of here. Nothing on the other iterations of 'cannibal' either. Cassidy did find where Basque purchased the lock, however. I'll send you the location so you can add it to your geoprofile."

"Anything else?"

"Nothing major. I'll e-mail you everything we have."

"Ralph"—I had a thought—"I'd like us to take a closer look at the location where that car was when Basque stole it. Maybe there's a video camera from a nearby business that might have caught someone walking toward that parking garage or frequenting the area."

"It might be in his awareness space."

"Spoken like a true geographic profiler."

"I've been hanging around you way too long."

"There could be worse fates."

"Name one," he said.

"Having to watch baseball with Tessa."

"Good point."

We ended the call, I picked up the food and aimed the car for the hospital.

31

Saundra Weathers went to the basement and unlocked the trunk where she kept the newspaper articles.

The conversation with Patrick Bowers last night had gotten her thinking about when she was a senior in high school and that eleven-year-old girl had been murdered.

She never allowed Noni to see what was inside this trunk, so thankfully her daughter was in kindergarten for the day.

Saundra tipped the lid open.

When Mindy Wells was killed, Saundra had followed the story in the papers every day and had clipped all of the newspaper articles about it.

Now she paged through them.

There weren't any crime scene photos or anything like that, but there were several pictures of Mindy—reproductions of the school photographs taken at the beginning of the year, one of the tree house where her body had been found, one of the school, one of the girl's mother at the courthouse, and one of the tire impressions in the muddy road that led along the edge of the marsh.

That was the road the killer had used to get to the tree house when he took Mindy Wells out there so that he could be alone with her.

The man did unspeakable things to her before he killed her. Things that had seared the consciousness of that small town for years.

Last Christmas, Saundra had been back to visit her parents and she'd found out that, for a lot of people in Horicon, the memory of Mindy's death still hadn't healed.

A little girl with her whole life ahead of her.

Patrick Bowers's name was mentioned in the articles, but there wasn't much about him.

Saundra remembered him, though, since he was the starting quarterback of the football team and Mindy had disappeared during the week leading up to the state semifinals.

She was a senior, he was a junior, but everyone at the school knew Patrick Bowers.

Based on how well he played that year, he probably could have played college ball, but he didn't go out for the team his senior year.

No one knew why, but back then people speculated that it was because of finding that girl's corpse right before the state semifinal game, that it had been too much of a shock and had turned him away from football.

Saundra let her finger graze across the photo of Mindy Wells.

Someone's daughter.

She shuddered to think what the girl's parents went through.

Eight years ago her husband had left her after she found out she was pregnant. He'd said he wasn't ready to become a dad; however, she'd pointed out that since she was pregnant he was already a dad and by leaving, he was just showing that he wasn't man enough to face the responsibilities of being one.

When she miscarried her baby girl, it almost destroyed her.

Two years later, while adopting Noni, she'd learned a lot about all the hoops people have to jump through for overseas adoptions. In fact, it took nearly a year and two trips to Ethiopia before she got approval and was finally able to bring Noni home.

Since her second book had just hit the *New York Times* bestseller list, money hadn't been a big hurdle for her, but being a single mom and battling depression had been.

But the journey to adoption wasn't as rocky for her as it was for most adoptive parents.

The wait time for getting your child was typically twice as long as her wait and for most families who wanted to adopt, it was cost-prohibitive. That's why Saundra had started her foundation—to provide money for parents who wanted to do overseas adoptions from Africa.

But lately Saundra's books hadn't been doing as well—with the emergence of online booksellers and e-publishing, publishing houses weren't giving big advances anymore, even to authors like her who had a track record. Money might have been down, but the need for would-be parents hadn't gone away, and neither had her passion to help them adopt orphans from Africa—kids who would likely starve to death if they weren't adopted.

It broke her heart to think about the fact that in Africa more than ten million children were growing up without parents. It was almost as if the future had been ripped out of an entire continent by war and disease.

No, admittedly, she wasn't able to make a big dent in the problem, but every adoption was one more life saved.

One.

More.

Life.

A plan began to form in her mind.

She carefully placed the newspapers back in the trunk.

Now there was another killer on the loose, one even more twisted than the one who'd taken Mindy Wells's life.

And Saundra realized that it was very possible that he had taken a special interest in her.

It was strange, really, the thoughts she was having, about the children who needed to be adopted and how expensive it is to get started, how it's so hard to afford your dream of raising a child, about what her foundation did in giving grants to prospective parents to bring adoption into reach, and in the process, rescue children just like Noni.

One more life.

Despite how ridiculous it sounded, Saundra found herself hoping that this man, Richard Basque, would somehow try to contact her. If he did, and the news media caught hold of the story that a serial killer was stalking a crime novelist, it would be a national story.

The exposure would give her a natural platform to talk about protecting her daughter from the man. And here was the thought that was unfolding in her mind: she was good enough at interviews to bridge the conversation to her foundation to help other children who were in danger of losing their lives.

It wouldn't be easy financially, but maybe she could donate the proceeds from her book sales from her next royalty check to the foundation. If she could get on the right talk shows, that could mean hundreds of thousands of dollars for the foundation. And that could mean saving the lives of thousands and thousands of children.

Yes, literally saving their lives.

Agent Bowers had intimated that Basque might try to contact her somehow.

If that happened, it would set everything in motion.

How could you even think this?

But she was and she couldn't put the thoughts aside.

Maybe, if there was some way, she could contact him.

That's ridiculous!

Her mind was spinning, sorting through the possibilities, and she realized that first, before she did anything else, she needed to find out more about this man, Richard Basque.

An Internet search was helpful, but the details on different Web sites of what he'd done were contradictory and incomplete. She really needed to get the facts straight.

She searched for true crime books that had been written about him.

No, don't go to this dance, Saundra. Leave this alone. Her instincts tugged her in two different directions— self-preservation and the protection of children just like her daughter.

But she and Noni were safe—one agent was outside her house, the other had gone to the school where Noni was in kindergarten.

Regardless of what she decided about communicating with Basque, finding out more about him was the smart thing to do. It would help her understand him better and equip her to better protect her daughter.

After finding the titles of four books online, she grabbed her keys and drove to the bookstore in the mall.

The agent in the black sedan followed her as she did.

32

As Lien-hua slowly worked her way through her salad, she told me that the doctor had been in to check on her and was pleased with her progress, although it was clear to me that she was still weak and tired.

"They're planning on moving me out of the ICU this afternoon and hoping to put the cast on my leg tomorrow. That means I should get out on Wednesday."

My phone vibrated from an incoming text message.

"Let's just make sure you're okay before we decide any of that." I normally don't like to check texts while I'm talking to someone, but with so much going on right now, I wanted to make sure it wasn't Ralph with something important regarding the case, so I unpocketed my phone. "The most important thing—" I began, but when I saw who the text was from, I cut myself off midsentence.

"What is it?" she asked.

I turned the phone so she could see the photo of the sender that had come up on the screen. "It's from you."

"Basque has my phone." Her voice was nearly a whisper.

"Yes, he does."

I read the text aloud:

A fable:

> A farmer's wife was bitten by a poisonous snake and died. The grief-stricken man took an ax out to kill the snake. When the snake was on its way to its hole, the farmer swung at it; however, he was too slow, managing only to chop off its tail.
>
> From then on, the snake went about biting the farmer's sheep until the farmer tried to coax it out, offering a truce. But the snake said, "There can never be peace between us, because you will never be able to forget the loss of your wife and I will never be able to forget the loss of my tail."

Immediately, I called Cybercrime to see if they could trace the text. While I waited for word, I asked my profiler fiancée what she thought.

"Well, clearly you're the farmer," she said. "I'm the wife. Basque is the snake. Thankfully, he didn't actually manage to kill me, but he did wound me."

Angela wasn't in, but I got through to her department. They started a trace and said they'd call me back momentarily. After hanging up, I uploaded the text message onto the online case files. "How did I cut off his tail?"

"You did that when you first caught him, when you sent him to prison. He'll never forget those thirteen years."

"And I'll never forget his attack against you."

"Yes."

"And in the story the snake goes after the farmer's sheep."

Lien-hua's eyes got large. "Tessa."

My heart clenched in my chest and I speed-dialed her number, but it was school hours and she was actually obeying the rule not to take calls.

Either that or . . .

I texted her to go to the office, then called the school to have their public safety officer find her and let me know as soon as he had—and I left word that I wanted him to shadow her for the rest of the day.

It could be that Basque's going after Saundra Weathers. He might think of her and her daughter as your lambs.

I wasn't going to take any chances. After hanging up with the school, I confirmed that the agents were still watching Miss Weathers and her daughter—one was with Saundra at the mall, the other was with Noni at her school.

A call from Headquarters told me they weren't able to trace the location of Lien-hua's phone, which didn't really surprise me. Basque would certainly have known we'd try to track it and he would have removed the battery or destroyed the phone as soon as he sent the text.

Just moments after I set down my cell, it rang again. I looked at the number, and saw it was from FBI Director Wellington's office.

Well, that was quick.

I picked up. "This is Agent Bowers."

"Sir, this is Alicia Becerra, I'm calling on behalf of Director Wellington. She would like to see you this afternoon."

This meeting might be in regard to our current progress in the Basque case, or it might have to do with the incident at the water treatment plant.

Margaret was uncompromising when it came to agents following standard operating procedures and I'd defied

Ralph's orders and gone into that facility alone after Basque.

I doubted Ralph would have brought that up to her, but the grapevine is alive and well at the Bureau and it wasn't hard to imagine that Margaret had heard the details from someone else about what'd happened at the plant.

So I probably had an official reprimand waiting—hopefully not a suspension. That would not be good with the Basque case heating up right now.

"The Director has a meeting at three," her receptionist told me. "She would like to meet with you before then. Can you be here by two fifteen?"

"Does this concern Saturday night? The search for Basque?"

"I'm sorry, sir, she hasn't informed me what it concerns. So, two fifteen, then?"

Getting across town by then would not be easy, but if I left right away I could probably make it.

"Alright. Two fifteen. I'll be there."

33

Tessa quietly watched things unfold.

Mr. Tilson steepled his fingers and stared down at Melody Carver, who was sitting in the chair just across the aisle. From where Tessa sat, she could smell Tilson's body odor.

"So," he repeated, "can you tell us the difference between fiction and nonfiction, or not?"

Melody looked dumbfounded, embarrassed. "Um, well . . ."

Everyone knew her gift was glee club and not English Lit. Tessa had no idea how she'd ended up in the AP class, but she had and she'd struggled all semester and this wasn't the first time Tilson had made a point to put her on the spot in front of the rest of the class. It was pretty infuriating.

Now Melody was really struggling. "I mean, some nonfiction stuff is made up, right?" she fumbled. "And, like, fiction is novels? Or . . . Is that . . . ?"

"We covered all of this last week," Tilson said condescendingly. He had critical eyes, a sharp nose, and a single eyebrow that diminished only slightly in thickness as it crossed the bridge of his nose. "Really, Miss Carver, you should know this by now."

Tessa could feel her temperature rising.

"Fiction," he stated, "refers to what is made up. Non-fiction refers to what is true. The first is a product of imagination, the second is always based on facts. Do you remember last week's discussion at all, Miss Carver?"

Tessa scoffed loudly enough for him to hear.

He directed his attention to her and said somewhat curtly, "Do you have something to add, Miss Ellis?"

"I might."

"And that is?"

"Melody is right."

Arms folded now. "Really?"

"Yes."

"That 'some nonfiction is made up'?" When he went on he mocked the way Melody had said the words. "And, *like* 'fiction is novels'?"

Okay, that was it.

"That's right."

"Well, I'm afraid both you and Miss Carver haven't been paying close enough attention in class."

Tessa saw Melody gaze down at her textbook, more embarrassed than before.

"Are you sure you want to do this?" Tessa asked her teacher.

"Do what?"

"This? You and me, here in front of the whole class?"

Stillness invaded the classroom. Every student who'd been shuffling in his seat or doodling or sneaking out his cell phone to text stopped and stared at Tessa.

Fire rose in Mr. Tilson's eyes.

He walked briskly to his desk and picked up the

English textbook he'd chosen to use for the year and flipped through it, then said, "Page two twenty-five: 'Fiction refers to stories that come from the imagination of the author; nonfiction refers to the record of facts.'" He closed the book authoritatively, placed it on his desk.

"That's not the only place that textbook is wrong," Tessa said.

"Well, perhaps you can enlighten us then." He spread out his hands. "About how Baldric and Grisham are wrong."

"Do you know Latin, Mr. Tilson?"

"Do I know Latin?"

"Yes. It's the language Baldric and Grisham refer to as 'dead,' even though it's not."

"Latin isn't spoken anywhere anymore, Miss Ellis. Thus it is referred to as a dead language."

"It's spoken at the Vatican. It's not dead. So do you know it?"

His jaw tightened. "What does Latin have to do with the distinction between fiction and nonfiction?"

"The word 'fact' comes from the Latin *facere*—to make or do. The word 'fiction' comes from the Latin *fingere*—to make or shape, more specifically referring to the way a potter would shape his clay."

"Well, then, it still remains that 'fact' means 'a thing that is done' and 'fiction' means 'a thing that is made up.'"

"But that's not true anymore."

"What are you talking about?"

"Is poetry made up?"

"Yes, of course."

"At every library and on every bestseller list in the country, poetry is classified as nonfiction."

"Well, perhaps that's because it's based on the poet's observations of real life."

Even he had to know how lame an answer that was, but Tessa wasn't going to be finical.

"And plays are nonfiction. So if I were to write a novel, it would be fiction, but if I were to leave out the passages of narration and the descriptions and simply include the dialogue and some stage directions, the story would be categorized as nonfiction."

"I don't believe that's the case."

"It is. And graphic novels are nonfiction, too. So novels without pictures are fiction; novels with pictures are nonfiction."

"No, they're not."

"If you'd like, we could take a field trip down the hall to the library, find out for sure. Comic books are also classified as nonfiction. So are humor and joke books. That's why Dave Barry won a Pulitzer prize—for writing a humor column. So here's my question: are you really telling us that poetry, plays, jokes, humor, graphic novels, and comic books are all *factual?* That none of them are made up? Melody was precisely correct: novels are fiction and some nonfiction is made up. You, Baldric, and Grisham are wrong."

The bell rang but no one in the class moved.

"Miss Ellis, I would like you to stay for a moment after class."

"Not a problem."

"The rest of you are dismissed."

No one moved.

"Dismissed."

At last the students shuffled out of the room. Tessa picked up her book bag, slung its strap over her shoulder, and stood unmoving beside her desk. Mr. Tilson was glaring at her from the front of the room but she didn't care and she didn't look away.

As the last few students were leaving, Tessa crossed the room to his desk.

When he spoke to her, she sensed that he was trying to slap her in the face with his words. "You haven't graduated yet, Miss Ellis. Don't burn bridges that you haven't crossed. The final grade for your senior project has not been submitted yet."

"Are you threatening me?"

"Hardly. I would never threaten a student. I'm simply exhorting you to focus on your work."

"Ah. Well, I'll exhort you to stop putting Melody on the spot or else I'll point out other places where your precious Baldric and Grisham—and you—are wrong."

She exited the room and didn't turn around, even when he called her to come back, even when he warned her not to walk away from him like that.

This was not the day to threaten her. Not when her mom-to-be was in the hospital and there was a serial killer out there targeting the people she loved.

Just down the hallway, she found Melody waiting beside the drinking fountain near Aiden's locker—oh, yeah, Tessa definitely knew where that was.

"Tess." Melody had a breezy smile and was one of the Beautiful People. She wore a gentle pink sweater that looked like it was made out of Muppet hair, but she somehow managed to make it look cute.

"Yeah?"

"Thanks."

Aiden materialized from a clutch of students and went to put his books away. Blond hair that was a little too long, a little unkempt. An infectiously impetuous smile. *Oh, man.* Tessa tried to focus on her conversation with Melody, but it was not easy.

"Okay."

"No," Melody said. "Seriously, I mean it. I don't know why he does that, it's just . . . Anyway. Thanks."

Aiden glanced Tessa's way, and she pretended not to notice.

"You had the right answer, Melody. All I did was agree with you."

It looked like putting his books away was taking Aiden longer than it needed to.

"You're awesome."

Tessa looked at Melody again. No one except Patrick had ever told her that she was awesome. "Thanks."

"Yeah."

Then Melody thanked her again, said they should hang out more. "There are a bunch of us going out for supper before prom Friday night. You should join us." She winked good-naturedly. "You got a date, right?"

"Oh. Sure. Of course."

"Text me."

"Yeah, I'll let you know." They exchanged numbers.

Tessa appreciated the offer but knew she wouldn't take Melody up on it—even if she actually did have a date. Melody's crowd was definitely not into fringers like her.

Then Melody flitted away and merged with the stream of students walking past them—the stream that was not swallowing Aiden.

Tessa tried to hide from looking at him and checked her texts to see if there was anything from Patrick about Lien-hua and saw that he wanted her to go to the office and talk to the public safety officer ASAP.

When she looked up Aiden was right beside her. "Hey," he said.

She flushed. She couldn't help it. "Hey."

"I heard about what happened in there. In Tilson's class."

Already?!

"Oh."

"That was cool. What you did. I mean, standing up to him. He can be a real . . . Well . . ."

"Yeah, no kidding."

Awkward silence.

Awkward, awkward silence.

He's talking to you. He's actually talking to you!

"Um . . ." she stuttered. "I heard you got third in the hundred-ten-meter hurdles the other day. At the meet."

"The other schools weren't really that good."

"But third, I mean, it's still pretty good, right?"

He shrugged. "I guess."

More silence.

Oh, man.

"So, how's your speech coming along for graduation?"

"Good," she lied.

"Good."

"It's not, I mean, you know, it's not that big of a deal."

"From what I hear you'd be valedictorian, if you'd come at the beginning of the year."

He was so, so different from most of the guys who showed any interest in her. He seemed to actually value intelligence, rather than just, well, wanting to get into a girl's pants.

"I don't know. Maybe."

She found herself lowering her gaze as if her shoes were suddenly the most interesting thing in the universe.

"If you need to practice it, the speech, I mean maybe, um . . . Well, I could listen to it."

What?!

"Um . . ."

Do not do this! You're on your way to tell Thacker that you're not gonna write the stupid thing anyway!

Her hesitancy to agree seemed to cause Aiden to back-pedal. "Not that you need someone to—"

"No, I mean, that'd be great."

"Yeah?"

Tessa, shut up!

"Yeah." She saw the school's public safety officer walking her way.

"So you have my number?"

Seeing the cop distracted her. "What?"

"My number. So you can text me, you know. To get together."

"Oh, right. Yeah. Um, no, I don't."

The officer was just down the hall and had obviously singled her out, because he made eye contact and then angled through the crowd directly toward her. The kids between them started to filter back into their classrooms.

Aiden pulled out his phone. "What's your number? I'll text you, then you'll have mine."

She told him, barely getting out the words. He tapped at the buttons of his phone and then she saw his number come up on hers.

He wants to see you, at least. That's something. That's a start.

Over the years she'd had a few run-ins with the police

and she definitely did not want to have the public safety officer start talking to her with Aiden here. "Hey, I gotta go. Thanks. So, I'll text you."

He looked a little confused by her sudden urgency to leave. "Sure."

Then another thought: *Patrick wanted you to go to the office. Something's going on. Something's up.*

She hurried down the hallway, figuring she'd double back again after Aiden had left for class.

She made it around the corner and, when she glanced back, saw the school cop rounding it right behind her.

"Miss Ellis."

"Is it Agent Jiang? Did something happen?"

"No." He looked confused. "Are you alright?"

"Sure. Of course. What's going on?"

"Your father wanted me to check on you."

"Why?"

"Don't worry, it's just as a precaution."

She knew what that phrase meant. It was Patrick's way of saying he was worried about someone.

"Is it Basque?"

"All I know is that I was asked to stay close until he could meet up with you after school."

"Oh."

Fortunately, the halls were almost completely empty of students now. "I'll only remain near your room," he said. "Don't worry, I'll keep my distance. I won't embarrass you or anything."

"Wonderful." Just what she needed, a cop tagging along behind her for the rest of the day. "How thoughtful."

The tardy bell rang and she shook her head. "Listen, okay, whatever."

And instead of aiming for the assistant principal's office to bail on the speech, she went to her study-hour classroom.

Thinking about Aiden. About having his number.

And about the speech that she was now going to have to give.

And about the fact that Patrick was concerned enough about her to send a cop to watch her while she was still at school.

She wasn't stupid. Basque must have done something or Patrick wouldn't have taken a step like this.

Maybe her dad was closing in on him.

Or maybe Basque was branching out.

34

I got a call from the office at Tessa's school telling me she was fine.

Good.

As I was pocketing my phone, the receptionist motioned toward Director Wellington's office. "She's ready."

"Thanks."

I tossed my coffee cup in the trash can in the corner. I'd finished it outside but had to carry it in here, since there were no garbage cans on the block encircling the Hoover Building. It would just be too easy to drop an explosive device in one and walk away. So, after 9/11 they were all removed. A little piece of trivia not too many people know.

I gave the office door a small knock and received a prompt reply from Margaret: "Come in."

Entering, I found everything just as I remembered it. The books on the bookshelf were arranged according to the Dewey decimal system. Her desk contained two photos: one of her dog, a purebred golden retriever named Lewis, another of a family with two children standing next to a merry-go-round. The clothing suggested it was taken maybe thirty or thirty-five years ago.

Beside the pictures lay her laptop computer, an in-box with one sheet of paper in it, a matching pencil holder that held four pens, one highlighter, one black Sharpie, and five pencils, tip up so that she could evaluate how sharp each one was before using it.

Her Italian leather briefcase leaned against the side of the desk.

She was standing beside the window when I entered. Mid-forties, tightly clipped dun-colored hair, a professional pantsuit, narrow but intelligent and attentive eyes.

"Agent Bowers."

"Director Wellington."

I prepared myself for her to berate me, write me up, or suspend me for entering the treatment plant before SWAT was able to go in, but she didn't bring any of that up yet. She didn't ask about the Basque case either, but inquired about Lien-hua's condition. I told her she was recovering. "She really appreciated the flowers you sent."

"The prognosis?"

"It looks like they're taking her out of ICU today and they're hoping to cast her leg tomorrow. She's already planning on going home Wednesday morning."

A dubious look. "Even after a stab wound to the chest?"

"She's a rather resilient woman. As she put it, she's 'a good recoverer.'"

A small nod, then she gestured toward the chair facing her desk. I took a seat. She positioned herself in the office chair behind her desk and after having me give her a quick update on the team's search for Basque, she got right to the point. "This concerns my brother."

In all the time I'd known Margaret, she'd never mentioned that she had a brother. In fact, now that I thought about it, I couldn't think of a time when she'd ever mentioned anyone from her family.

"What is it?"

"Corey took his own life." Before I could respond, she went on, trying to keep her voice even. "Decomposition tells us it happened sometime late last week. He didn't show up for work on Thursday. His body was only found this morning."

The words stunned me. "Margaret, I'm so sorry."

She gave me a small, perfunctory nod of acknowledgment. "Thank you." I could tell she was doing her best to remain detached, objective, professional, but it wasn't working. Honestly, that made it even harder to hear her news. "He stabbed himself, so it seems, in the abdomen. Bled out on the floor of his living room."

"I don't know what to say." I almost asked her how she was doing, but I could already tell by the look on her face.

"There's very little to say."

It surprised me that she was bringing any of this up to me, but I realized almost immediately that there must be a professional reason rather than just a personal one. "You said 'so it seems.' Were there any unusual circumstances surrounding his death?"

It took her a moment to reply, and when she did, she didn't address my question. "My brother is eight years younger than I am. When I was a freshman in high school our mother overdosed and died. We're not sure if it was intentional or not. She was an alcoholic. You see, depression runs in our family. So, my brother—Corey—he takes medication for it; has been since he was in college. We aren't as close as . . . well, as we could be, but . . . Well, frankly, we aren't very close at all."

"So you think it was the depression, perhaps? That's what led him to do it?"

"I'm looking into the possibility that his medication might influence people who take it to have suicidal thoughts. You've seen ads on television warning about that sort of thing? Yes?"

"Where they list all the potential side effects of the drugs."

"That's right."

"Did he ever attempt suicide before?"

"Not that I know of." She rose and walked toward the window where I'd found her when I first came in. "As I'm sure you're aware, stabbing yourself in the abdomen is a more common way of committing suicide in certain Asian countries than it is in North America. It's possible, of course, that Corey took his own life, but the method he chose is so culturally atypical that I would like to have someone with more experience in homicide investigations than the local authorities take a look at the police reports. That's why I called you in."

"What do we know about the scene?"

"The knife he used was from a matching set in his kitchen. I asked the Atlanta Police Department to look for prints there, as well as on the doorknobs, the light switches, the usual."

"Anything?"

She shook her head. "Nothing so far, and there was no sign of forced entry. He's a large man and would have been difficult to overpower. There was no sign of a struggle."

I processed that. "What did Corey do for a living? As far as you're aware, was he involved in anything illegal? Anyone out there who might want to harm him?"

"He works for a small law firm, lives alone, no children, no spouse, no criminal record." She kept referring to him in the present tense, something so many family members do subconsciously in the days after they lose someone close. It was hard hearing it coming from Margaret. Not surprisingly, it didn't appear that she was aware she was doing it.

"But," she said, "as I mentioned earlier, we aren't very close. I have no idea if he's involved in anything illegal or if he's made any enemies."

"What exactly would you like me to look for?"

"Review the autopsy reports, the police report, find out . . . well, whatever you can."

I didn't want this to come out wrong, but the answer might help me if I was really going to do this. "Of course, I'll do whatever I can, but—"

"But you're wondering why I'm asking you to do this. Why you." She left off saying anything about our working relationship in the past.

"Yes."

"Especially with Lien-hua in the hospital and with the Basque case landing in your lap."

"Yes."

"Quite simply, because I don't know anyone who's better at noticing when things don't fit together than you are. I can have the New Agents Unit Chief assign another instructor to take over your classes for the rest of the week. But I'll leave this up to you."

Everything about this conversation was starkly different from our normal, somewhat forced exchanges, and that told me how important all of this was for her.

"Yes. I'd like to help. I'll do it."

A nod. "I'll have the Atlanta PD send you their files."

In this line of work you never really have the luxury of working only one case at a time. It's almost like having three or four pots on the stove. You have the burners turned on higher in the front and the water in those pots is at a high boil, but there are always other pots there, simmering in the background.

As you wrap up one case and get moving on others, it's as if you're shifting the pots around, sliding off the ones in front and bringing up others from the back to take their place.

And right now it looked like the two cases that were on the front burners were the investigation into locating Basque and unraveling what had happened to Corey Wellington.

I took Margaret up on her offer to have someone else teach my classes for the next couple days. She gave me her private cell number, thanked me, then abruptly told me she needed to go. She shook my hand and insisted that I have Lien-hua contact her personally if she needed anything.

This was a different Margaret from the one I knew, and I hoped the change hadn't come just as a result of Corey's death. To me, that seemed too tragic and sad.

It was close to three o'clock, and, still wanting to keep a close eye on Tessa, I headed to the school to meet up with her. The whole way I tried to wrap my mind around what Margaret had told me.

Was it really possible that the brother of the FBI's Director had been murdered in a way made to look like a suicide? Or was it just the medication or depression?

She'd said that she had entrusted me with this because I was better than anyone else she knew at noticing when things didn't fit together.

Well, let's see if I could live up to her expectations.

35

"It's because of Basque, right?" Tessa asked me as we walked toward her car. "That's what all this is about—the school cop showing up? That's why you want to drive me home?"

It seemed like the time to be candid and straightforward. "Basque sent me a message."

"A threat against me?"

"An apparent threat against the people I know. Those under my care. Until we catch him I'm going to do whatever's necessary to protect you."

A look that I wasn't able to read crossed her face. "You know what? That annoys me and also makes me feel safe at the same time."

"I appreciate that." We crossed the street. "So did you tell Thacker you aren't going to do that graduation speech?"

She was quiet. "Actually, let's not go there right now."

She gestured toward her car, the black VW Beetle she'd bought—or at least, I'd helped her buy—when we moved to DC in January. "I've got something I want to do for Lien-hua. I guess we could take two cars, but it'll save gas if we left one here, picked it up later."

"What is it you want to do?"

"Something to tide us over until supper. I'll explain on the way."

We took my car. For some reason I'm just not into being seen in a Beetle.

+++

All afternoon Richard had been thinking about the fable he'd sent to Patrick. In the story, the snake continues to attack the farmer's sheep.

And in just over twenty-four hours, he was planning to do precisely that.

As he considered everything, he came up with a number of ways to gain a child's trust, but he had definitely ruled one out.

Dressing up as a clown.

No, he couldn't figure out why anyone hoping to work with children would do that.

When he was doing research on John Gacy, the question had really intrigued him.

John Wayne Gacy was the serial killer from Chicago back in the 1970s who would dress up like a clown and volunteer at hospitals and perform at children's birthday parties.

In fact, when Basque was reading about Gacy, he stumbled across an article in a 2008 *Nursing Standard* magazine in which Dr. Penny Curtis, a researcher at the University of Sheffield, had found that children were universally frightened of clowns.

Not some, not most, but all of the children in her study were scared of clowns. Stephen King capitalized on the fear people have of clowns in his book *It*.

So, if you wanted to gain the trust of a child, becoming a clown was not exactly the ideal way to go about it.

And although clowns were frightening to children, one of the things they do actually did serve to engender trust.

And in this case, that's what Richard was interested in.

He parked, dropped a few coins in the meter, and crossed the sidewalk toward one of the last locally owned magic shops anywhere along the East Coast.

For a number of years he'd been quite close to a federal agent who, unfortunately, was no longer among the breathing, and Richard was well aware of how sophisticated the Bureau's online tracking capabilities are.

He'd often thought that if people knew how much information the government collects on their online activity, they would probably never surf the Web again. Certainly never to child porn sites.

So Richard made no Internet orders.

Used no credit cards or checks.

Only cash transactions at small businesses that didn't use video surveillance.

He entered Ryan's Magic Emporium.

"Can I help you?" The stringy-haired twenty-something kid behind the counter looked bored, but was expertly vanishing and reappearing a coin in his hand even as he stared at Richard.

"Yes, I'm looking to learn a few tricks." He swept his arm around the store. "I used to do this—sleight of hand, that sort of thing—when I was young. I always wanted to be a magician."

"Didn't we all." The young man sighed lightly, held the quarter out, closed his fist, blew on it, and when he opened his hand the quarter was gone.

"Nice," Richard said.

The guy closed his fist again, turned his hand over, and, with a flourish, flattened his palm against the counter. When he lifted his hand, five nickels were lying there.

"Very nice."

"Thanks." The kid yawned. "So, what? You want to do walk-around gigs? Birthday parties? Not too many people do the big effects anymore, the escapes, you know. Except for *that* guy." He gestured toward a poster of a magician stepping through a wall with four words stamped across the bottom of the poster: THE JEVIN BANKS EXPERIENCE.

The kid continued, "That dude, man. He's the real deal. Apart from him, the stuff he does—you can find out how to do almost any of the big effects—the walk-around ones too, for that matter—on YouTube. Everything's posted these days. Some magicians thought it would be cool to break the magicians' code and reveal all the tricks. Problem is—"

"It takes the fun out. For the kids."

"For everyone." The boy gathered up the five nickels. "See, the thing is, we say we want to be in on the trick, but as soon as the audience is—"

"It's like guessing the end of a book—readers want to guess how it will end, or how it will get to the end, but secretly they want to be wrong. They're disappointed if they're right."

The boy looked impressed. "Yeah, exactly. So it's a game we play with the audience, right? A game of deceit."

"So where is the quarter?"

He got a small gleam in his eye. "Where do you think?"

"In your right jeans pocket," Richard said, though he knew it was the left one.

The boy smiled. "No, I saw your eyes. You were watching closely. You saw, didn't you?"

"No," Richard lied.

He pocketed the nickels. "Anyway, what kind of tricks you looking for?"

"Rope tricks."

"Oh. Cut and restore, make the knot move down the rope, close-up effects, street magic, that sort of thing?"

"That sort of thing. And I'd like some that are reasonably easy to learn. I only have twenty-four hours before the big performance."

"Hmm . . . which is?"

Richard smiled. "You hit the nail on the head earlier. I'll be performing at a little girl's birthday party."

"Well, I've got a few you can buy, and really, you shouldn't have to worry, most of 'em are easy to learn."

"I'd rather learn them from someone who knows what he's doing. What would you charge for a little lesson?"

The boy scoffed lightly and looked around. "It's not like people are knocking down the door to get in here." He went to the wall, ripped open a plastic bag with a rope in it. "Okay, so, how much time do you have?"

"As much as I need."

"Tell you what, we're supposed to close at five, but go ahead and flip the sign on the door."

"To closed?"

"Yeah. That way no one will interrupt us."

"Perfect."

Richard took care of the sign.

"Well," the kid said, "like I mentioned before—deceit. It's all about deception and misdirection." He looked at Richard good-naturedly. "Think you can handle that?"

"I think so."

Richard felt a mixture of emotions. Before this night would be over, this young man was going to be dead and he had no idea how short his life span had become. If he knew, what would he do? What phone calls would he make? Would he cry or pray or go outside to look up at the sky and enjoy its majesty one last time? To Richard it was always a fascinating question.

Sometimes he told people exactly when they were going to die, just to see their reaction.

Usually, it was denial at first, but eventually it turned to fear, then desperation. And then, in a few cases, to peace. Mostly though, to unassailable terror.

However, Richard decided he wasn't going to tell this young man. He would let him die while innocently, obliviously, teaching his tricks, which was something that he seemed to like doing. How many people get to exit this life really enjoying themselves?

In a way, it was a small recompense for the favor he was doing of giving this private lesson.

Richard decided to use the rope. After he'd learned a few tricks from the boy, he would show the boy a few of his own.

36

Lien-hua was out of the ICU and in a new room on the second floor when Tessa and I arrived at the hospital.

I carried the wedding invitations I'd picked up on the way, the ones with her last name finally spelled correctly. I also had a candle that I now set down out of sight. On the way over here I'd decided to give it to Lien-hua a little later, when we were alone.

Tessa brought the rather formidable cardboard box containing the fifteen desserts we'd purchased. She laid it on the chair beside the bed.

Lien-hua looked at her quizzically. "What's that?"

"Something I think you're going to like." She gestured for Lien-hua to go ahead and open the box, which she did.

Inside were pieces of chocolate cake, three each from five different bakeries, all nestled in recycled cardboard containers—that little detail had been very important to Tessa.

"Friday night you promised me we were going to go cake tasting," Tessa explained. "I've been waiting to do it ever since."

"And," I interjected, "as long as I was going to be here I figured I'd pitch in."

"Well, you two just made my day."

The next twenty minutes brought a nice respite from the case. We celebrated Lien-hua's move from the ICU and the fact that she was a good recoverer, and in the end, she chose the double chocolate cake with white cream cheese frosting and yellow frosting chrysanthemums from Weber's Bakery.

Tessa and I concurred.

The two women didn't finish their five pieces of cake, but I looked at it as my duty to thoroughly taste-test each of mine.

After the impromptu cake tasting, I asked Tessa if I could borrow her lighter, which she somewhat embarrassedly handed over, then I requested that she give Lien-hua and me a few minutes alone.

I didn't know if she had a backup lighter. "No fresh air," I told her.

"Gotcha."

She stepped out of the room.

"What do you need the lighter for?" Lien-hua asked me.

"In a sec. First, I need to tell you about my meeting with Margaret."

When I'd finished summarizing the situation concerning Margaret's brother, Lien-hua said, "Clear it with her. Maybe I can help with the profile—if you do end up suspecting foul play."

"Good idea."

I put the call through to Margaret right away, and she approved the idea as long as it wasn't "too taxing on Agent Jiang." I handed the phone to Lien-hua, who reassured her that she was ready to get back to work.

After we'd hung up, Lien-hua said, "Now, what about that lighter?"

Weddings in America tend to have a lot of white, but in China red is a much more prevalent color. Now I palmed the red candle I'd brought in and tried to make it appear magically in my hand.

"You need a little more work at that," Lien-hua said good-naturedly.

"I'm better at picking pockets than sleight of hand."

"Not a skill you should probably be advertising."

"In any case . . ." I held the candle up. "We spoke about getting one of these for the wedding. A unity candle."

"I remember."

"And remember in the park when we were talking? Till death do us part?"

"Yes."

"And then later in the hospital you said that when Basque attacked you it was like time stretched out and you saw how—"

"How unfathomable it is." She was not quite whispering. "Yes. And how brief."

For a moment we were both silent.

I laid the candle in her hand and gently curled her fingers around it. "Most people just light these at their weddings. I'd like us to light this one whenever we want to remember that we're one, that we have a lifetime of unfathomable moments together."

"Every time?" she asked.

"Every time."

We probably weren't supposed to be doing this in a hospital, but following protocol has never exactly been my specialty. I flicked out the lighter's flame and Lien-hua held up the candle, and then said softly, "I have a feeling we're going to go through a lot of candles." There was a delicate intimacy to her words that held the promise of forever.

"Sounds like my kind of life."

And there, in the candlelight of our unity, I kissed her.

And the moment welcomed me into it and stretched into one that I planned to hold on to forever.

Tessa returned a few minutes later, saw the burning candle, and didn't ask, but she smiled a little and that was nice to see.

After all that cake sampling, Lien-hua and Tessa didn't have any appetite left for supper, but I managed to eat the meal the hospital staff brought up for Lien-hua so it wouldn't go to waste.

Before Tessa and I left, I told Lien-hua I'd look over the police reports regarding Corey Wellington's death and let her know if there was anything suspicious.

On the way to the car, I returned Tessa's lighter to her. "I really don't want you smoking."

"I know."

"So, are we cool?"

A pause. "Do you want me to lie and tell you I'll never smoke again?"

"I don't want it to be a lie."

She said nothing and I said nothing as we drove to pick up her car and head home.

+++

Saundra Weathers had spent the day reading through the two true crime books about Richard Basque that she'd purchased at the mall.

And, honestly, after finding out what the man had done to his victims, she was having second thoughts about her comfort level should the killer actually try to contact her.

However, she reassured herself that the two agents outside her home wouldn't let anything happen to her.

Or to her daughter, Noni.

+++

Richard finished up with the young man from the magic store.

It'd turned out to be messier than he thought it would be. He'd started out with the rope, but in the end, had moved on to the blade he carried. However, he'd been careful to keep the blood off his clothes. So, no harm done.

He found a DVD that taught how to escape from handcuffs, both metal handcuffs and plastic flex cuffs. It was a skill he'd always wanted to have and he figured it might come in handy if things didn't go according to plan tomorrow.

Then, so that he could practice at home, he helped himself to a few pairs of different types of handcuffs and shackles that were stocked on the shelf.

Before leaving the magic shop, he scrawled four words in the man's blood on the floor in the back room, then he straightened his shirt and went home to his dogs to practice his tricks for tomorrow night.

37

The files from the Atlanta Police Department concerning Corey Wellington's death were waiting for me in my e-mail in-box when I arrived home.

After checking the online reports to see if Agent Hammet had posted any updates on the calls she'd been making to the people close to Basque's previous victims, and finding that she had not, I turned to Corey's files.

Even though I'd never met him, as I looked over the police reports I couldn't help but feel a sense of grief and loss.

Mostly I work homicides, but I've been called in to look over all too many suicide cases over the years and I've never gotten used to them. Seeing the corpse, knowing that the person did this to himself in whatever manner he'd chosen—a self-inflicted gunshot wound, an overdose, hanging, or, as in this case, a stab wound up into the chest—makes me feel a visceral sweep of sadness.

You can't help but wonder what drove the person to such an extreme act, to actually end his own life. You can't help but wonder those things.

If this one is even a suicide at all.

Many times it's depression, just as Corey evidently suffered from. Sometimes it's disappointment or grief. I've worked suicides in which someone lost a job and killed himself, or lost a loved one and couldn't stand the thought of living without her.

I consulted on one case in which a teenage girl slit her wrists and bled to death in her bathtub because she saw that her boyfriend had changed his status on Facebook from "in a relationship" to "single." One of the most tragic suicides I've ever run into was a father who took his own life when none of his children wished him a happy Father's Day. He left them a note telling how disappointed he was in them, how it was their fault. But he had the date wrong. Father's Day wasn't for another week.

It's deeply disturbing to think about how many people in the world are dying inside, screaming for someone, anyone, to care, reaching out again and again, sometimes to the hand that slaps them, because, all too often, without that hand they have nothing at all.

And eventually they stop reaching out altogether.

I directed my attention to the fatal knife wound.

It looked like it was consistent with a self-inflicted one that would be caused by leaning forward and thrusting the blade up into your abdomen toward your heart.

Based on the position of the body and the blood patterns on the carpet it certainly appeared that Corey had killed himself.

I spent the rest of the evening studying the files, taking notes, deciding what aspects of the enigmatic suicide warranted further investigation. In the end, I decided that in the morning I would begin by taking a more careful look at the same thing Margaret had mentioned: the medication Corey was taking, specifically, the type, dosage, and potential side effects.

+++

Tessa stared at her phone.

At Aiden's number.

All she had to do was hit "reply."

But what was she supposed to tell him?

Nothing.

Nothing yet.

But she needed to see him.

She needed to . . .

It would've been a lot easier if he'd been the one to offer to text her.

She flipped the phone over and plunked it facedown on her desk.

Everything that was going on this week seemed to press in on her, tightening around her, causing this suffocating pressure on her heart. It made it hard to think.

Lien-hua was recovering, so that was one bit of good news. But Basque was on the loose, apparently somewhere nearby. Plus, all the questions she'd talked about with Brineesha concerning unanswered prayer, and with Patrick about, well, poisoned beliefs, and now her own personal issues with Aiden and trying to come up with a speech and the nerve to speak in front of a thousand people—all of it was overwhelming.

A graduation speech?

They're always about how to have a successful life.

What did she know about being a success?

Well, basically, nothing.

But she was an expert at the opposite.

Just tell people not to be like you and you'll be all set.

She jammed in her earbuds and disappeared into the lyrics of Boomerang Puppy's song "Eclipse." It was pretty hard to make out the words, but if you could, they were actually not that bad, and she knew them by heart:

> A dark ache clutched at me
> tearing apart the tower of hope that
> looked so shiny, so permanent, so true.
> Tremors run deep
> beneath the confidence that
> I'd hoped would carry me through
> the night.

A nice encouraging sentiment there to really lift her spirits.

She retrieved her pack of cigarettes from where she kept them hidden in her closet and fished her lighter out of her purse.

Stared at it for a long time.

Man, she hated, hated, *hated* that she'd gotten into this. Cancer, whatever, she knew all that, of course, she did, but still . . .

And the worst part of the whole deal: whenever she smoked she felt like she was letting Patrick down.

Still, it did something for her, helped calm her in some weird way and she understood why people got hooked on it.

But at least she wasn't cutting anymore. At least there was that.

She told herself the mantra of all addicts: that she could always quit tomorrow.

She slipped outside and went to the small hedgerow on the edge of their property where she usually went to smoke. Crickets chirped at her from the dark folds of the night. Somewhere, a dog barked.

Lighting up, she closed her eyes and took a long drag.

She wanted the cigarette to comfort her, wanted the cool, damp night to wrap around her and just help her to *relax*, but it didn't take long at all for her to realize that none of it was helping.

Praying? Yeah, well, she wasn't even sure she believed in that.

Over the last couple months she'd been reading her Bible a little—which was one of the reasons she'd brought up the whole church thing with Patrick—and now she remembered the opening lines of Ecclesiastes: "'Meaningless! Meaningless!' says the Teacher. 'Utterly meaningless! Everything is meaningless.'"

More encouragement for her.

Maybe she could give a speech on that.

Yeah, that would totally fly.

Right now, she just needed a way to sort out the questions and see if any answers lay beneath, as the lyrics of "Eclipse" referred to it, the confidence that she'd hoped would carry her through the night.

38

From his hotel balcony Valkyrie stared out across the nighttime DC skyline, with the Washington Monument rising into prominence against the dark sky. The city's building height restrictions made the skyline not nearly as magnificent as New York City's, but still, with all the symbols of freedom, it was just as memorable.

At one time, Valkyries were worshipped as goddesses in Norse mythology. They were the ones who chose who would live and who would die on the battlefields. Eventually, the stories morphed, as myths do, and Valkyries became known as seductive spirits who lived in Valhalla and served fallen battle heroes.

No, he did not think of himself as a deity or as some type of alluring or servile spirit. However, since the day he'd emerged, he had thought of himself as the one who had the duty to determine who would live and who would enter eternity.

Tomorrow evening Keith and Vanessa would be arriving from India. They didn't yet know that he was in the States, but they would find out. He had a meeting planned with them before the drugs entered the country's secure supply chain.

Well, the supply chain that was supposed to be secure. So now, DC.

The Washington Monument rising regally into the night.

Here was the center of democracy in the world, the beacon of freedom, the convergence of all that he had fought against while he was still working for the GRU. The Cold War was long over, but Russia's network of spies, and his homeland's interest in the politics and policies of Washington, had remained the same.

However, over this last year his heart had turned against Mother Russia. Her concerns were no longer his. In fact, these days he had no master directing his life. None, that is, except his past, which, in a way, dictated everything, shaped who he was and how he had become the determiner of life and death.

His past, his choices, had transformed him.

The day last May when his wife, Tatiana, died.

No, not died. Was murdered.

Before he'd ever identified himself as Valkyrie, he'd been known by his given name, Alexei Chekov, and had been in the business of cleaning up messes no one else wanted to dirty their hands with. Sometimes that involved taking the life of another person, a job he had never enjoyed, but one that he did, out of duty to his homeland, when called upon to act.

And he did his job well.

But then something happened that changed things forever.

Last May he'd argued with Tatiana, told her words he would always regret, words that would always ring like a terrible death knell through his mind, the sharp, most painful lie of all: telling her that he did not love her and never wanted to see her again.

Then, later that same day, he found her body, with a single bullet hole in her forehead staring at him like a dark, unblinking third eye.

She'd only just been killed and the blood wasn't done seeping from the back of her head across the sheets of the bed.

He'd searched for her murderer, vowing to punish him.

But he never had the chance, because she hadn't been killed by another assassin, as he'd first thought.

He had blocked out the truth. It took him a long time to come to terms with what had actually happened, but last winter an FBI agent named Patrick Bowers had confronted him and made him realize the truth: that day when Alexei was with Tatiana, in a moment of terrible loss of self-control, he had done the unthinkable—he had killed the woman he loved.

Bowers had apprehended him, but, under the supervision of a law enforcement officer who was not nearly as astute as Bowers, Valkyrie had escaped. Still, Bowers was the one who'd deduced what Alexei had done to Tatiana, and nothing had been the same since.

A palpable, sweeping darkness had crept into his heart, a new personality that relished pain, that sought to make others suffer, that took him to places he never would have allowed himself to go before the metamorphosis in his soul took place.

And now, finally, he would avenge Tatiana's death.

It had to do with the drug shipment, yes, but it went a lot deeper than that.

The suicides would only be the beginning.

Ultimately, it had to do with striking back at Mother Russia for training, honing, creating the man who had killed his wife.

The Valkyrie.

The harbinger, the courier of death.

He returned to his suite, drew the shades shut, and used his encrypted, untraceable cell to reach his contact from the Chechen Republic to tell him the drugs were ready to be shipped to the States.

39

For reasons she didn't tell me, Lien-hua asked me not to come by until after the doctors had put the cast on her leg at eleven, so after dropping Tessa off at school and making sure the public safety officer had her schedule for the day, I'd gone to my office in the classroom building at Quantico and set to work.

With notes from Agent Hammet's recently posted interviews with the people who were friends and family with Basque's previous victims in the DC area, and my own investigation into their travel patterns, I was able to refine the representations of their cognitive maps.

I compared the background checks that the team had done yesterday with what I already knew, adding the location where Basque had purchased the lock and taking a more careful look at Lien-hua's awareness space.

I'd hoped the location from which Basque had stolen the car might shed some light on what we were looking at, but it didn't do much, other than give me one more location to add to the geoprofile.

After updating the online case files with what I had, I turned to the other front burner.

Corey Wellington's suicide.

Obviously, I couldn't visit the scene myself today, so I called the Atlanta Police Department and convinced them to send an officer there to be my eyes. Thankfully, they sent the man who'd been the first one to arrive yesterday when Corey's body was discovered.

While I waited for him to get there, I ran through what we knew.

Corey hadn't shown up for work on Thursday or Friday and didn't call in sick. When he didn't answer texts over the weekend or come to the office yesterday, one of his friends went to his house, found it locked, and went around back. He saw Corey's body through the living room window.

Margaret's brother hadn't left a suicide note, hadn't texted or e-mailed anyone telling them what he was going to do.

He hadn't updated his will or, as far as we could tell, set his affairs in order. There was no sign of forced entry.

Now, when the officer, a somewhat impatient man in his early twenties named Dustin Wilhoit, arrived at the scene, we started a video chat. I asked him about something that hadn't appeared in the police report: if there were any pills found near the body.

"No, sir. We checked."

Based on what Margaret had told me, Corey was taking depression medicine and I wanted to know what it was. "Corey was taking prescription meds. Look through the rest of the house. The bathroom medicine cabinet, the kitchen cupboards maybe, find the pills."

While he searched, I contacted Angela Knight, who was at home when I reached her. I asked her to do some checking through Corey's credit card records to see what pharmacy he used. "I'm not at work," she objected.

"You can remotely log into Lacey, can't you? It should only take a few minutes."

It took three.

Putting through a call to the pharmacy, I learned that Corey took Calydrole, which was prescribed to people who'd attempted or contemplated suicide. Then I phoned the waste management company to find out when they picked up the garbage and recyclables, just in case my gut instincts, which I don't put much faith in, happened to be right.

Wilhoit returned my call and told me that he hadn't found anything.

"No prescription meds in the whole house?"

"No, sir." He sounded ready to be done with this.

"I want you to check the garbage cans for me."

A pause. "Sir?"

"Look for any empty bottles or blister packs."

"Really, are you sure that's necessary?"

"I'm not sure what's necessary, apart from being thorough. Take a look for me."

He didn't agree right away. "Alright."

It took him a few minutes, but then he got back to me. "There's an empty foil packet in the trash can in his bathroom."

"Is the name of the drug imprinted on it?"

"Yeah. Calydrole." He told me the lot number printed on the back of the packet.

"How many pills did it contain?"

"Fourteen."

So, likely two weeks' worth, or perhaps one, depending on how many Corey took each day.

A thought began to form in my mind.

"In the crime scene reports, the photo of the bathroom shows the medicine cabinet door open. Was it open when you arrived?"

"It must have been."

"Don't tell me it must have been. Tell me if it was."

A pause. "It was."

"Yes?"

"Yes. I closed it myself. Look, what does it matter if it was open or closed?"

"Everything matters. Get it dusted for prints."

"This was a suicide, Agent Bowers."

"Then there shouldn't be any anomalous prints there to slow things down when you run them through the system."

He didn't try to hide his sigh. "Alright. Sir. We'll dust for prints."

I ended the call, contacted the pharmacy again, and the pharmacist told me that Corey was prescribed four hundred milligrams per day of the drug. "The ones in the packets he bought were two-hundred-milligram pills."

"Did you just say packets?"

"Yeah, he bought a month's worth when he came in here on . . ." He paused and I pictured him pulling up the records. "It looks like March twenty-seventh. Right at five o'clock. Got here just before we closed."

"At what time of day do people take Calydrole?"

"In the morning."

I did the math in my head. "Thanks."

One more call, this one to PTPharmaceuticals, the makers of Calydrole, to have them run the lot number on the back of the blister pack. They told me they'd call me back.

Margaret had been concerned about the meds, so I thought at this point I should probably fill her in. Rather than go through the Bureau's switchboard I tried her cell.

She jumped right in. "What do we know?"

"The drugs Corey was taking for depression are used to reduce or quell suicidal thoughts, but they weren't there."

"What do you mean, they weren't there?"

"There was an empty packet that held a week's worth of meds, but no prescription pills were in the house. And, by all indications, the medicine cabinet was open when the police arrived."

"What does that mean?"

"It's hard to say, exactly. The garbage is picked up every Friday and he hadn't taken his out yet. I contacted his pharmacy and they told me he'd purchased enough for the next month on Wednesday, March twenty-seventh."

She thought that through. "So if he took one the next day after he bought them and had the last one on the day before he died, then he took a week's worth."

"Yes."

"But he bought a month's worth."

"Yes."

"And so, where are the rest of the pills?"

"That is the question."

A moment passed. "You mentioned that the medicine cabinet was open. What are you thinking? That someone removed them from his house?"

"We'll have to do some checking—his car, at work, maybe at any gyms he had memberships at to see if he kept any meds there. But yes: who removed them from the house. I'm having the pharmaceutical firm verify the lot number. I want to see if there were any other reported suicides from people taking this medication, specifically this lot number of it."

"You said reported suicides."

"Yes. Because if someone did remove the rest of the pills from Corey's house before the police arrived—"

"His death might not have been a suicide. And there might be other victims out there just like him."

"For now, that's the line of inquiry I want to pursue. Yes."

"Hypothesize, evaluate, test, and revise."

She knew me pretty well after all.

"Exactly."

I checked the time and saw that Lien-hua should have her cast on by now, so after ending the call with Margaret I left to meet her, fill her in and let her know we were ready to have her do a little profiling on the case of Corey Wellington's death.

+++

Keith stared out the window of the Boeing 757 at the ocean far below him.

Vanessa sat beside him with the law brief from one of her clients laid open on the tray table in front of her. However, rather than review the papers, she was taking a break and was coolly observing the flight attendants as they served the people ahead of them, studying them one at a time as if they were specimens and not fellow human beings.

Keith still hadn't seen her sleep at all on this trip.

She was a woman who seemed to want nothing more

than to please their employer, Valkyrie. The longer she worked for him, the more it seemed to become her obsession.

Not a woman Keith wanted to get on the bad side of.

He had not enjoyed this trip to India, and he was glad to be on his way back to America. At last it was all coming together. And by the weekend this assignment would be over.

The shipment should be arriving in just under forty-eight hours, but in the meantime he and Vanessa had a few people to visit to make sure the drugs would enter the supply chain and be shipped to the pharmacies.

Their plane would be landing tonight at Logan International Airport in Boston at 9:39 p.m. local time. Then they could get a hotel room, lie low, and, at least in Keith's case, catch up on some sleep.

He imagined that Vanessa might rest for an hour at the most before being ready to go out and do Valkyrie's bidding again.

And although Keith said nothing to her, he hoped that whatever that might be, this time it would not involve the pruning shears he had in his checked luggage.

40

12:34 p.m.
9 hours until the drowning

Because of the electronic trail it might leave, Valkyrie avoided online trading and instead made all his financial transactions through a certain very reliable broker in Dubai.

It was after office hours there, but that wouldn't make any difference to the woman who managed his investments. She was a discreet lady from whom he had kept his identity hidden and whom he had paid well not to ask any questions that either of them would end up finding awkward. A recent law in Dubai allowed for the nondisclosure of the client's name in some financial transactions, and Valkyrie had taken advantage of the somewhat expedient legislation.

When she picked up, he greeted her, then said, "I would like to buy some put options in PTPharmaceuticals."

A pause as she typed, no doubt checking the company's recent performance. "I'm not sure this is the time for that, they've been performing well lately."

"Regardless, I'm not confident that they'll trend in this direction for long."

A put option is the right but not the obligation to sell the underlying share at a fixed price. An option, whether that's a put option or a call option, is essentially a bet, and he was betting that the stock value of the company was going to drop. Locking in a price now that was below the current market value, one that he could then sell the options at when the stock dropped below that price, he would be able to sell at a profit. In this case, a substantial profit.

It was the same strategy Al Qaeda had used to raise millions for their cause on 9/11.

And he would use it to raise money for his cause as well.

"How much?" his broker asked him. "How many options?"

"One million struck at a hundred."

A beat of silence. "One million. I'm not sure that's possible."

"It is. I looked into it."

"What price are you suggesting?"

"Half of what it's trading at. And I want a three-month expiry."

"Half?"

"Yes."

"As your broker, I have to say I would suggest you rethink this investment."

"Of course, and that is one of the things I respect about you. In this case, my mind is made up."

"So you're certain about this?"

"I am."

"And you know what this will cost you on this premium if the stock price remains the same, or continues to rise?"

"Yes."

When he exercised the option at expiry, he planned to cash settle rather than physically settle. It would be harder to track, since, in essence, no one would be buying or selling the shares, and the transaction would be completed without his actually owning the underlying shares. He was confident he wouldn't have to let the option expire worthless. Confident enough to bet millions on it.

"Alright, then. I'll send you an e-mail confirming the specifics."

"Thank you."

They ended the call and Valkyrie set down the phone.

Some people confused short selling with buying put options, but they were entirely different kinds of transactions, and in this case, put options were definitely the more prudent choice.

After everything went through, after the counterfeit Calydrole was shipped and the suicides began, he would make known who had already taken the medication. That would help even more with the investment he'd just made and with the expected returns, which he estimated to be upward of sixty million dollars.

Money he was going to put to good use.

He received a message from Alhazur Daudov, his Chechen contact, that he would be arriving in DC on Friday night.

That was unexpected, but undoubtedly Alhazur was interested in the progress of the shipment, and it did make sense that he would want to meet with Valkyrie.

Alhazur never traveled alone, so Valkyrie knew that he would be accompanied by at least one or two of his soldiers. Freedom fighters. Suicide bombers dedicated wholeheartedly to the cause.

Valkyrie also knew that they always traveled with explosives when they were overseas, but he wondered if they would be so bold as to smuggle suicide vests into the States—particularly DC. Though he didn't want to rule it out, he considered it most likely that they would not.

In either case, he didn't anticipate any problems, but he was willing to deal with enhanced negotiation procedures if necessary.

41

1:34 p.m.
8 hours until the drowning

Lien-hua felt optimistic.

The chest tube had been removed, she was out of ICU, her leg was in a cast, and if all went as planned, she would be leaving the hospital tomorrow.

Yes, she was still in a lot of pain and it would take her weeks or perhaps months to fully recover, but she was feeling markedly better than she had a couple of days ago. Already she was anxious to get out of the hospital and start on the path back to her typical routine.

Pat, who'd been waiting for her when she returned to her room after the doctors were done with her leg, had told her what he'd discovered about the missing drugs at Corey Wellington's house.

Working together—Pat making calls while she surfed on his laptop—they found out that Corey had no memberships at any gyms where he might have kept the drugs. Pat had officers comb through Corey's desk at work and his car and they found no sign of the rest of the blister packs of drugs. His ex-girlfriend did not have any packets of his Calydrole.

Another relationship we don't know about?

A secret place where he kept his meds hidden?

Lien-hua had to acknowledge that those were possibilities, but it seemed to be looking more and more like someone had removed the medication from Corey's house after his suicide and before the police arrived.

But still, she didn't have nearly enough information to work on even a preliminary profile, so together, she and Pat focused on pursuing the investigative leads that they actually did have.

The fingerprints from the medicine cabinet came back with four results: Corey's, those of Officer Dustin Wilhoit, who evidently hadn't worn gloves at the scene, the woman whom Corey had been seeing, and a former Marine: Corporal Keith Tyree.

A background told them that Corporal Tyree had served with distinction and had disappeared off the grid after he left the military a year and a half ago.

When they dug deeper, they found that there were no credit cards, e-mail accounts, addresses, phone numbers, or insurance polices in his name. Someone had wiped him off the electronic map, and in today's world that was not something that was easily done.

It pointed to a major player, maybe a nation-state.

Considering how thorough the wipe was, Pat noted that it was surprising that Tyree's prints were still in the system.

"I agree," Lien-hua said. "Somebody went to a lot of trouble to turn him into a ghost and now he leaves identifiable prints at a scene that was supposed to be a suicide? Something isn't clicking here."

"First, I think we need to find out everything there is to know about Corporal Tyree. Also, we should see if there's any way that Corey's life might have intersected with his."

"I'd say we have enough to get Margaret to assign a couple more agents to delve into the possibility that there are other apparent suicides related to the use of this lot number of Calydrole."

"Especially those where Tyree might have left his prints."

"Yes."

He put in the request, but Margaret was currently in a meeting and her secretary said she would relay it as soon as the Director was available.

He also contacted the pharmaceutical firm to find out more about this drug's known side effects and about any class-action lawsuits that might be pending regarding the product. The analysts at the firm were going to e-mail him their data. Also, they were still looking into the lot number and promised to get back to him with details of the side effects of the drug.

"PTPharmaceuticals," he mumbled. "I can't believe it's those guys."

During the first case she'd worked with him in North Carolina, they'd had a run-in with the man who used to own the company.

Actually, it was more than a run-in. The guy, who, as it turned out, was sociopathic, had tried to kill Patrick and a group of dignitaries and media representatives.

It was a complex investigation that had tendrils running all the way back to the Jonestown massacre in the seventies. Lien-hua considered that briefly, but since the former owner hadn't had any real connection with the firm for years, at least for the time being, she set those thoughts aside.

It didn't take much research to find out that PTPharmaceuticals imported most of its products from India, where the FDA inspected only a small percentage of the plants to assure that the supplies weren't tainted or substandard.

"So," Pat said, "if there was tampering, it might have been done before the drugs were shipped rather than after they entered the supply chain here in America." Lienhua had done more interagency work than he had, and now he asked her, "Who do you think we should call? Homeland Security or FDA?"

"Well, if we're going in the direction of the supply chain, let's start with FDA. I know that some of their Office of Criminal Investigation agents pose as pharmaceutical wholesalers and distributors of counterfeit drugs to record conversations and confessions of wrongdoing, that sort of thing. Maybe there's someone from the OCI who's worked in India who can help us."

He contacted the FDA's Counterfeit Alert Network, but that proved to be a dead end. The FDA has only two hundred investigators total, but U.S. Immigration and Customs Enforcement, or ICE, has more than three thousand who work to stop illegal trafficking of guns, humans, drugs, and intellectual property. It took Pat a little while, but he finally set up a meeting with an ICE agent named Jason Kantsos who'd worked in India. He agreed to meet tomorrow morning at ten o'clock at Pat's office at the Academy.

After they ended the call, Lien-hua shook her head. "If there are counterfeit pharmaceuticals involved here, this is going to be a jurisdictional nightmare."

"It shouldn't be that bad."

"Really? Are you serious?"

"Well, sure, there's some overlap between us and the DEA . . ." While he contemplated that, she thought about that overlap.

Most people don't know this, but the FBI has over three hundred different types of crimes it investigates, and one of them is drug trafficking. In fact, back in 1999 there was going to be a merger between the DEA and the FBI to take care of the overlap, but nothing ever came of it. Lien-hua hadn't been with the Bureau at the time, but she'd heard about it all, yet to this day no one had ever been able to give her a satisfactory explanation for why the merger hadn't happened.

"And," Pat continued, drawing her out of her thoughts, "the OCI and ICE."

"And U.S. Customs and Border Protection, and the U.S. Postal Inspection Service, if they were shipped to someone here in the States."

"Hmm . . ." he reflected. "So, hypothetically, let's say someone living in India produces a counterfeit version of Calydrole."

"Okay."

"He ships it to a U.S. port and then has an associate mail it to a customer in another state. That crime would be investigated by local and state law enforcement agencies, as well as CBP, because it crosses our borders; US-PIS, because it was mailed; OCI, because it's a counterfeit drug; DEA, because it contains a controlled substance; ICE, because it's a form of illegally trafficked intellectual property; and the FBI, because it involves interstate crime?"

"And that's not to mention working with Interpol, the World Health Organization's Anti-Counterfeiting Task Force, and . . ." She tapped at the laptop's keyboard for a few seconds. "The Permanent Forum on International Pharmaceutical Crime, and testing agencies like the Centers for Disease Control and Prevention."

"Okay, you win. A jurisdictional nightmare."

She scootched into a different position in the bed, trying unsuccessfully to get comfortable. "Reporting procedures vary from jurisdiction to jurisdiction, but unless there's an overdose, I'm thinking that most law enforcement personnel wouldn't search for fingerprints at the scene of a suicide."

"We're going to have to do a national search for reports of suicides of people taking Calydrole."

She didn't even want to think about how long that could take. "Let's start with people who have fatal stab wounds in the abdomen like Corey did. If there's foul play involved here, it's possible others who were taking the drug might have died from similar types of wounds."

A call came through and when Pat answered, from listening to his side of the conversation, Lien-hua could tell it was from the Director.

When he hung up, he announced that Margaret had agreed to assign two other agents to the case.

"Great."

But he seemed distracted. She sensed that he was doing his best to be present, but his attention was split—which only made sense, with everything that was going on this week.

"I had a thought," he said. "We should also do a metasearch to see if there are any suicides in which Calydrole should have been found at the scene but wasn't." Then he admitted, "I know that's a long shot, but let's throw it in the mix."

She typed a note to herself. "There's one other thing we've been overlooking. The most obvious one of all."

"And that is?"

"Corey was the brother of the FBI Director. If there was someone tampering with his medication, do you really think that could be a coincidence?"

"So you're thinking we look into suicides of relatives of other FBI staff or agents?"

"Yes. Especially high-ranking ones."

He shook his head. "This is going to take some time." His focus seemed to drift into another place again.

"Is it Basque?" she asked him.

"What?"

"Basque. You're here with me, but for the last fifteen minutes you haven't quite been here with me. I'm wondering if it's Basque."

"You're pretty good at reading minds."

"Occupational hazard."

He sighed. "Honestly, I am having a hard time putting him on the back burner."

"Listen, ever since Friday night you've been almost as cooped up as I've been. You need to get out. Go visit the neighborhoods of the hot spots you identified. You haven't even had a chance to orient yourself to the locations yet."

"You're even better than I thought."

"At reading minds?"

"See? That just proves my point."

Typically, profiles were drawn up before the apprehension of a suspect and were used to narrow the search. But in some instances, such as in the case of Basque, the NCAVC had detailed profiles of the people they'd already identified and were actively searching for. And though Lien-hua hadn't worked on Basque's case personally, because of Pat's close involvement with it, she was familiar with the files.

Of course, she was aware of how excited Pat was about using profiles—a point of mostly friendly contention they'd had since their relationship began—but she went ahead and gave him her take on it anyway.

"He'll want privacy," she said, "anonymity, control. He's brash but definitely not stupid and would have a home base where he could work without the fear of discovery."

"So, no normal life in suburbia."

"Sometimes the suburbs can be as anonymous as the city, but I think in this case it's more likely he'll seek a greater degree of isolation."

"So, outside of town."

"But not too far from an interstate or highway that would give him quick access to the city, or away from it if he needed to flee."

"You're thinking a farm, maybe? Somewhere on the outskirts?"

"Maybe. And there'd be some way of warning him that people are approaching—security or infrared cameras, a dog, motion detectors, maybe something that would trigger a silent alarm in the house, I'm not sure. And he'll have an escape plan if law enforcement should arrive."

"Like he did in the water treatment plant."

"Yes. His face has been all over the news for months, so it's likely he'll avoid too much exposure to the public, or at least to people who might identify and report him. A disguise is a definite possibility." She thought again of the long hair he had.

He might be using a wig.

In either case, that wouldn't really help Pat nail down a location, but it might help if he spoke with someone or reviewed video of Basque leaving or entering a place of business in one of the hot zones. She brought it up and he nodded. "Good thought."

"Brineesha said she'd stop by," she told him. "Don't worry about me. No more lingering today. I'll work on bringing the two new agents Margaret is assigning to this thing up to speed. You take some time to go and look for Basque."

"Sounds like a plan." He leaned in for a kiss. "Thanks."

"Be careful."

"I always am."

"I mean it."

"Okay."

After she'd told him how much she loved him and he'd replied in kind, he took off.

She tracked down the two newly assigned agents and invited them to her hospital room for a briefing.

The agenda: get them started pulling up more background information on a former Marine who'd disappeared from the system, exploring his possible connection with Corey Wellington, looking for victims of fatal, self-inflicted stab wounds, and searching for suicides of the relatives of FBI agents or staff—especially those scenes that might be missing packets of Calydrole.

This promised to be an interesting afternoon.

42

Over the years, despite my reticence to trust profiling, I had to admit that more often than not Lien-hua's insights were right on target. It was somewhat disconcerting and a little exasperating, but it was what it was.

Before I left the hospital parking lot, I called Ralph to tell him I'd be in the field investigating the hot zones.

"Man, I need to get out of this freakin' office too. I'll come with you. We can catch up on the case and you can tell me about this meeting you had with the Director. I heard about her brother. That's terrible what happened."

"Yeah, it looks like he killed himself, but we're starting to suspect he was murdered too."

"That, you're going to have to explain to me."

"I'll do my best."

Actually, it really would be beneficial to connect with Ralph and bounce some ideas off each other. With my teaching responsibilities and the time I'd been spending with Lien-hua, we had a lot of catching up to do.

We agreed to meet one block from the Capitol, and I left to pick him up.

+++

Richard Basque had practiced his tricks all morning and into the early afternoon.

Getting out of steel handcuffs wasn't as difficult as he'd thought it would be, and using hairpins, a barrette, and even paper clips, he'd been able to decrease his time from two minutes to forty-five seconds.

The plastic flex cuffs were a different story.

It was possible to use a wire to saw through the plastic, also possible to wedge a pin into the locking point to release it, but it was difficult, especially if your hands were cuffed behind your back.

Richard decided to give himself another two hours or so of practice with the plastic cuffs before heading to Chesapeake Beach for Noni's birthday party, where he would go after some little sheep.

+++

Based on Lien-hua's ideas, Ralph and I didn't bother with the first hot zone, the one in southeast DC. It didn't afford the kind of isolated opportunities that the potential zones north and east of the city would provide.

Instead, he drove my car north while I used my phone's 3-D hologram app and FALCON to identify isolated homes in the geographic area I'd come up with that might be worth looking into. As I worked, I gave him a recap of what Lien-hua and I had uncovered about Corey Wellington's death.

Ralph listened reflectively. "Did we hear back about the side effects of this drug yet?"

Checking my e-mail, I found that PTPharmaceuticals hadn't sent the data on their studies regarding Calydrole's side effects, but they had finally e-mailed the results of their probe into the lot number and explained that "there is no evidence that this lot exists, but it is only two digits off from a shipment that is produced in Hyderabad, India." There were no class-action lawsuits against them for this drug.

Thinking aloud, Ralph said, "Pat, if you were going to come up with a fake lot number, don't you think you'd make it close to a legitimate one? That way it'd be easier to slip into the supply chain."

"Quite possibly, yes."

"Maybe by analyzing the locations in India where similar lot numbers are produced, we can zero in on the facility that's producing the ones in question."

"I like the way you think."

"I've been working with you for a decade. 'Bout time you took note of that."

"Funny how it just occurred to me."

"Uh-huh."

Lien-hua didn't have a cell, but I phoned her room to tell her to have the two new team members look into the location of the facilities that produced closely related, legitimate lot numbers from India, specifically that plant in Hyderabad.

FALCON brought up forty-two homes for Ralph and me to check out—isolated residences in the area north of DC that fit the geoprofile.

I couldn't imagine we'd have time to look into that many. We needed a way to cut the number in half—at least.

"Call Doehring," Ralph suggested. "Have him check

the home owners and see if any red flags come up. Also, maybe run vehicle registrations from the residents of those addresses."

"Good. And let's focus on the homes with the easiest access to the highway, as Lien-hua suggested."

After a few phone calls and a little calculating, we were able to decrease the number of likely homes to twenty, which was at least manageable.

Going door-to-door asking questions was old-school and tedious, but more often than not that's how cases are untangled. One question, one person at a time.

And besides, it felt good to be doing something tangible to eliminate possibilities rather than just looking at the case from one side of a computer screen.

With traffic, I figured visiting the homes might take two or three hours.

Unless, of course, we found Basque at one of the houses first.

43

As Tessa was walking to her car, she saw Aiden approaching her and she couldn't help but feel an immediate swallow of nervousness. She wanted to talk to him, of course she did—but since she still had nothing to share about her graduation talk, she had no idea what to say.

"So"—he was smiling in that totally disarming, melting way—"any ideas?"

"Ideas?"

"About the speech."

"Oh. Right . . . No. Not really."

"I was thinking about it. Maybe you should tell people to be true to themselves, you know, follow their hearts, pursue their dreams. That sort of thing."

"Don't you think that's a little clichéd?" The words just came out and she wished right away she could have taken them back.

He shrugged. "I don't know."

"I just . . ." She remembered a discussion she'd had

with Patrick last year. "Aren't there times when you need to be true to something bigger than yourself?"

"What do you mean?"

"Well, let's say pedophiles. They follow their hearts, they definitely pursue their dreams. I don't know for sure, but I'll bet if you asked them they'd say they're being true to themselves, that they were born the way they are."

"You mean like gay people are?"

What? Where did that come from?

"I'm not saying gay people are or aren't born that way."

"But pedophiles are?"

"I'm just saying that they would claim to just naturally be attracted to—"

"Kids."

Okay, this conversation was definitely not one she'd been expecting to have. "Yeah. To kids."

He looked at her a little strangely and she could only guess it was because she'd sort of refuted what he'd suggested by bringing up pedophiles pursuing their dreams.

Oh, that was just stellar, Tessa. That's really going to move things along with this guy!

"Um . . ." she began, "I was just . . . that was a bad example."

He was quiet. "Well, I guess you might need to go in a little different direction then."

"No, no, no. I think you might have it. Dreams. You know, pursuing your dreams, telling people to pursue their dreams."

Yeah, right. That is so lame.

"Okay."

She bit her lip.

Say something!

But she didn't. She couldn't think of any way to climb out of this.

"Let me know, okay?" Aiden said. "If you want to catch up, throw some ideas around."

His words were spoken respectfully enough, but his body language was all wrong. Everything about his tone of voice and his posture said, "This whole offering-to-help-you thing was probably not such a good idea, now that I think about it."

"Yeah," she replied feebly. "Okay. I'll let you know."

And, of course, after all that, he said nothing about prom.

Pedophiles pursuing their dreams?! What is wrong with you!

He left, and the officer who was supposed to follow her home watched her from his supposedly undercover car nearby.

She strode toward him and he opened his window. "Enough already!" she shouted. "I'm fine!"

Okay, maybe not the best way to talk to a cop, but thankfully he let it pass and didn't hassle her. Maybe Patrick had warned him about her. Who knows.

Who cares.

She got into her car and took off to see Lien-hua.

Let the cop follow if he wanted to, whatever.

Pedophiles? Really?!

She let out a deep breath, and then smacked the steering wheel.

Truthfully, though, despite how annoyed she was by what she'd said to Aiden, she was having a hard time discounting it. And it wasn't just pedophiles, after all. She'd talked with Patrick about this stuff before: serial killers follow their hearts, rapists pursue their dreams, the Nazis were true to themselves.

So there you go.

People left to themselves without restraint.

Becoming monsters.

Okay, here's a great speech: The Three Ultimate Keys to Success. (1) Don't pursue your dreams; (2) stop following your heart; and (3) be careful not to be true to yourself. And, oh, yeah, P.S.—All is meaningless.

The most antigraduation speech in the history of graduation speeches.

That would go over brilliantly.

44

Ralph and I had been knocking on doors for nearly two hours and hadn't found anything that might lead us closer to Basque. Now we were leaving the last house that looked like a candidate in the hot zone north of DC, and both of us were feeling a little frustrated.

He hated battling rush-hour traffic, so he went to the passenger side, tossed me the keys, and told me, "You drive. My gift is patience."

"Your gift is patience?"

"Yeah. I just haven't gotten around to opening it yet. Take the wheel."

In the car again, I said, "So, you ready to head east? The hot zone out past Andrews?"

"Hmm . . . What about retracing Basque's route? The one he drove the other night on the way to the water treatment plant?"

Not a bad idea. We were deliberating which direction to take things when Doehring radioed with an update.

Tips had been coming in ever since we put out word to the media that Basque had fled from the water treatment facility, and all afternoon Doehring and the team had been following up on them. Just minutes ago they'd found an apartment rented under the name Anthropos Phagein by someone who fit Basque's description. Gavin had been looking into the etymology of words related to "cannibal," as I'd suggested at the NCAVC meeting, and had found that "anthropos" meant "human" and "phagein" meant "to eat." Together they were the root words for "anthropophagy."

Another word for cannibalism.

"Where is it?" I asked.

"Southwest DC." He told me the address; he didn't have to tell me it wasn't anywhere near any of the hot zones I'd come up with. "We have officers there now, but the place is empty—not even any furniture."

Ralph said, "Why's Basque using names that are traceable?"

"Because," I answered, "he wants me to chase him. It's all about the hunt."

All.

About.

The hunt.

Think, Pat. Pull this together.

The algorithms I was using might identify where someone currently lived or where he used to reside, but there was no guarantee that Basque would still be using that apartment right now. Taking into account this newly discovered apartment and the one he'd taken Lien-hua to, it seemed that he was moving around the city to elude capture.

Or maybe to give you more sites to chase him.

So, go and visit the empty apartment or hit the third hot zone?

I quickly evaluated things.

"You say the place is empty?" I asked Doehring.

"Yeah. We'll get the forensics guys out here, but other than that, I'm not sure what to tell you."

As much as I wanted to get a visual on the third hot zone, any way you cut it, finding this apartment was a break in the case and I wasn't going to let that pass us by.

"We're on our way over," I told him. "We'll be there as soon as we can."

+++

Richard became reasonably proficient at freeing himself from the plastic flex cuffs.

Good.

Because it was time to go.

After putting in brown contact lenses and using a fake mustache and some latex face makeup to alter his features, he fitted a suppressor onto the modified, threaded barrel of his Sigma. With the subsonic ammo he was using, he would be able to fire the gun in the residential area without any worry of being heard.

Leaving his pickup in the garage, he chose his anonymous-looking Mazda sedan and left for Saundra Weathers's home in Chesapeake Beach.

He had the rope from the magic store with him. He also had his butterfly knife in his pocket.

Although he was going to play things by ear, he was planning to show up and explain that Saundra's literary agent had hired him as a surprise to perform for the children.

As he drove, he ran through what he would do if he

found that Saundra's house was under surveillance. He might need to abandon the idea of doing the rope tricks until he got Noni and her mother back to his place.

But he was flexible. He was willing to adapt. Whatever it took to see this through to the end.

45

5:34 p.m.
4 hours until the drowning

The apartment reminded me of the one Basque had taken Lien-hua to last Friday—dingy, cramped, and cheap. However, this place was devoid of furniture and didn't look like it had ever been used.

By the time Ralph and I had gotten here, the crime scene guys had already confirmed Basque's prints on two of the doorknobs, but were still dusting for other prints to see if they could identify any victims he might have brought here or coconspirators he might have worked with in his crimes.

In the movies, killers always leave behind an orgy of evidence when they abandon their secret lairs—photos, newspaper clippings, bundles of receipts that have their credit card information on them, and so on. I've only seen that happen in real life three times in my entire career. And it wasn't happening today.

No photos.
No clippings.
No receipts.

No computer with a recent browsing history prominently displayed for us to use.

Nothing like the movies.

I pulled out my laptop and plugged this location in to the geoprofile.

What are you missing? What clue are you overlooking here?

As I perused the case information, that sporting goods store I'd thought of while teaching my class came to mind once again. It was a point of connection, but we had no surveillance footage from it, no video.

Video . . .

I remembered what I'd spoken with Ralph about earlier—getting CCTV security footage of businesses near the parking garage where Basque stole the car from that he drove to the water treatment facility.

Maybe we could do that with the places of business near Erikson's Sporting Goods too. The store was in a minimall across the street from a gas station that had been the site of two robberies over the last year. I wondered if one of their cameras might be directed east, where the sporting goods store's parking lot was.

I phoned Angela and told her what I was thinking.

"I'll get Lacey on it," she said. "Do you have a specific day you want me to check first?"

"Let's start with the days preceding the disappearance of the woman who worked there."

"This could take a while, Pat—if they've even kept footage that far back."

"Yeah," I acknowledged. "I know."

About twenty minutes later, one of the rookie officers brought over a stack of fast-food burritos and we met outside the apartment to attack our dinner. We must have all been hungry, because no one really spoke until we were nearly finished.

"Well?" Ralph checked the time on his cell. "There isn't much more we can do here, Pat. What are you thinking? Stay and keep running the numbers, or do it on the road? I'll even offer to drive; you can analyze."

"Good. We're close to the route Basque took to the water treatment plant. Let's retrace it like you suggested earlier, then go to the last hot zone."

Clouds were starting to move in and rain was predicted, but I figured we would have plenty of daylight to finish up before it got dark.

"Right." He crumpled up his burrito wrapper and landed it in a trash can four meters away. "Let's move."

+++

Richard arrived at Saundra Weathers's home in Chesapeake Beach, the house with the red and pink balloons on the mailbox to make it immediately apparent to the parents of the children who were invited to the party which house it was being held at.

Two men in a nondescript black sedan were parked across the street.

Richard had been around law enforcement officers enough to know an undercover, unmarked car when he saw one. But just to be sure, he cruised past and glanced toward it. The man in the driver's seat was sipping from a truck stop coffee cup; the passenger was speaking into a radio.

That was enough for Richard.

So, Patrick must have made the connection to Saundra after all.

Well-done, old friend.

It looked like Richard needed to take care of the two men here before crashing Noni's party.

And he had just the way to do that.

But he needed to get pulled over by another officer first.

46

We finished retracing the route and parked at the water treatment plant.

It hadn't started to rain yet, but seeing the clouds swirling and mounting above us, I was reminded of Tessa staring at the sky when we had our picnic Friday at the park where Basque attacked Lien-hua. A thought hit me: most likely Richard wouldn't have made a move on her there unless he had some familiarity with the park, the sight lines, the road layout.

Which would mean Rock Creek Park was in his awareness space, too.

If he knew that area, then—

I recalled my lecture, the slide of the woman's body that had been found near the trailhead there in February. That crime didn't fit Basque's MO, but neither did strangling his victims like he'd done with Lien-hua. Studies on serial rapists have found that there's a stronger correlation between the locations of the crimes than to the similarity of the MO of the crimes. The jury was still out, but some indications pointed toward it being true of serial killers too.

I sat on the bumper and flipped open my laptop.

"Pat, you've got that look in your eye," Ralph said.

"That's because I think I may know where our hare's been running."

There was a set of unidentified prints on the novel.

He weaves everything together.

He's been taunting you from the beginning with the other attacks.

It's all about the chase.

No, I don't believe in coincidences.

I looked up Brandi Giddens's case files to get the address of the Upper Marlboro, Maryland, apartment she'd lived in, then I radioed Doehring. "Cole, see if you can pull up a set of prints from Brandi Giddens, the college girl we found last February over in Rock Creek Park."

"Prints?"

"I want to know if they match the ones on the novel from the car at the water treatment plant."

It took him a second to process that. "You really think Basque has been playing us all this time?"

"I think it's possible. Let's find out."

In the shadow of the water treatment plant where Basque had slipped away Friday night, Ralph and I began to review the Giddens murder case files, looking for clues regarding Brandi's travel patterns and Basque's previous crimes to see if we could find a place where they intersected.

47

What's the one type of car you can steal and then drive with little or no risk of being pulled over?

A police car.

And that's what Richard Basque was going to acquire.

But as it turned out, he didn't need to get pulled over himself first, because he found a Maryland State Police officer who'd set up a speed trap and lay in wait, nearly hidden in a pull-off on the highway.

Richard slowed to a stop behind the squad. Rather than get out and approach the cruiser and perhaps arouse suspicion, he waited for the officer to leave the squad to come to him.

As the man did so, Richard eyed him carefully.

Yes, he looked just about the right size.

His uniform would work just fine.

+++

The first dots of rain fell just as we got word from Doehring that the prints matched.

"Okay," I said to Ralph. "Brandi had marsh biota on the bottom of her shoes. She'd been near a marshland within twelve hours of her death." I had my laptop out and was scrolling over a map of the DC area. "Joint Base Andrews would create a mental barrier in someone's cognitive map of this area."

"Make it seem farther to get to the city?"

"Yes, if the offender lived on the east side of the base . . ." I was studying the exits off Pennsylvania Ave/ Maryland 4 near the Patuxent River Park. "Basque knows how I think. He would try to hide his home base by scattering his crimes as randomly throughout the region as he could, but—"

"Nothing's random."

"No, not when it comes to choosing the sites of your victims' homes or their travel patterns."

We called Angela and found that she'd received the video footage from the gas station's archives and Lacey was still analyzing it.

With cloud cover, I couldn't use FALCON to evaluate the prospective homes in the hot zone east of Andrews, specifically those near the rivers and neighboring marshlands.

So, as Ralph and I took off, I used the next-best thing. Google Earth.

+++

Richard eased the patrol car around the corner and onto Spring Street, where Saundra Weathers lived with her young daughter.

The body of the officer whom he'd just killed lay safely stashed in the trunk. Richard had been quick about dispatching him, careful to keep blood off the uniform.

Now he confirmed that the two UC agents—or perhaps police officers—were still parked across the street in Saundra's relatively vacant, placid neighborhood.

He pulled alongside the curb behind the undercover car.

Richard decided not to use his butterfly knife, but rather to shoot both men in the head with the suppressed Sigma.

When you see a squad drive up behind you, it's natural to think that a police officer rather than a fugitive serial killer is going to step out of the driver's seat. Richard was banking on the fact that these two men would be blinded by their preconceptions and wouldn't see him for who he truly was. He didn't need much time, just a second or two, and then it would all be over.

Perception determines expectation.

He still had on his perfunctory disguise, but since law enforcement officers almost always have short hair, he tucked his hair up beneath the dead officer's hat.

Being approached by an officer of the law, the two men wouldn't unholster their weapons, since it could create an immediate misunderstanding.

His plan: have the driver roll down his window, lean into the car, fire two shots, and be done with it.

That quick. That simple.

Most likely they would have their IDs out before he could even tell them the lie that there'd been a report of two suspicious men sitting in a black sedan near a little girl's house.

The driver rolled down the window as Richard neared his door, and, just as he'd anticipated, both men had their creds out when he bent to speak with them.

"Officer," the driver began, "we're federal—"

But that's all he got out.

The bullet did its job well and Richard shot the other agent in the face before he could even reach for his weapon.

With the suppressor, the sound of the shots was barely a whisper—not nearly loud enough for any neighbors to hear. None of the dogs on the block began to bark.

The two dead agents slumped forward and Richard positioned them so they wouldn't be visible from Saundra Weathers's porch.

Yes, there was some blood spatter on the passenger-side window, but most of the mess was on the seat and he figured he would be fine.

After a moment of consideration, he tipped the head of the driver back and licked off the blood that was oozing from the bullet wound in his forehead.

He savored the moment, then reminded himself that there would be plenty more in store tonight once he got the woman and her daughter back to his place.

Richard leaned the corpse's head forward again, then walked past the mailbox with the red and pink balloons tied to it and strode up the driveway toward the front door.

Though he was wearing a fake mustache and dressed as a police officer, he ducked his head slightly as he neared the house so that if Saundra was looking out the window she wouldn't be able to identify him—if she even knew what he looked like.

Things had gotten later than he had originally planned, and he guessed that the other children at the party would've been close to the age of Saundra's daughter, probably in kindergarten too. And by this time on a school night, they would almost certainly all be gone.

But he had his Sigma and butterfly knife and he would take care of a few extra little lambs if he needed to.

He knocked and a moment later Saundra opened the door. "Yes?"

Looking past her, he saw wrapping paper on the floor, Dixie cups and paper plates covered with cake crumbs lay on the end table and footrest in front of the couch. No other children were present, just Noni, playing by herself with a Barbie doll next to a newly opened dollhouse.

"Ma'am," he said to Saundra, "we have reason to believe Richard Basque is in the area. Agent Bowers has requested that we bring you and your daughter over to the station until we can ascertain that the neighborhood is safe."

She glanced past him toward the car containing the corpses of the two dead agents. Richard didn't have to turn around to realize that she was almost certainly noting that it looked empty.

"They're sweeping the neighborhood," he told her.

Saundra nodded nervously.

"Why don't you go ahead and get your daughter. I'll bring my car up to the house."

Another nod; then she went to get Noni.

+++

The rain started.

We passed the Air Force base. Using Google Earth I chose Wrighton Road as the first place to investigate. It led toward the marshlands and yet was close to the highway and we knew Brandi had a cousin in the neighborhood.

48

Richard started the engine and eased onto the street.

Saundra Weathers and her daughter were tucked in the back of the squad behind the police cage partition.

He wasn't sure if either of them suspected anything yet, but in the rearview mirror he noticed Saundra studying his face, and then drawing her daughter close and wrapping an arm around her. "Which station are you taking us to?" she asked him.

"It's safest if we head over to DC."

"DC?"

"Yes. Don't worry. I'll take care of you."

She said nothing, but he saw the change in her eyes.

Oh, yes. She knew.

Now she knew for sure.

He took off his hat and let his hair fall free.

+++

Saundra felt terror tighten like a thick fist in her gut.

Oh, dear God, what have you done!

This man was Richard Basque, the cannibal, the killer, and he hadn't just gotten her, he'd gotten her daughter too.

The two agents must be dead. He must have killed them. He must have—

Just like he's going to kill you.

And Noni.

A deep chill corkscrewed through her.

The squad's doors didn't open from the inside. She was trapped.

She debated whether she should try to talk to him now, try to negotiate with him, but she couldn't stand the thought of saying anything that might frighten her daughter.

Instead, she decided she would bide her time, and then, when he'd taken them to wherever they were going, she would quietly offer to let him do whatever he liked to her—whatever he liked—if he would only let Noni go free.

It might accomplish nothing, might not do any good at all, but it was the only thing she could think of to save her daughter.

It was as if she'd stepped into one of her own novels. And she knew, if she were writing the narrative of this night, how it would inevitably turn out, even if she pleaded with her captor.

And she prayed that, in this case, life would not imitate art.

+++

We didn't even have a chance to stop at any of the homes I had in mind.

Angela called and told us that Lacey had found Basque

on the CCTV footage from the gas station. "I'm sending you the file now, but I'll stay on the line, talk you through what we know."

A moment later the video arrived and I tapped the space bar to start it.

The footage was from an exterior camera and showed the gas station's pumps in the foreground. The sporting goods store's parking lot lay across the street.

An older-model blue Chevy pickup drove up to Erikson's Sporting Goods and Richard Basque stepped out. He turned briefly as he locked the car and that's when his face was visible.

"That's what Lacey caught," Angela said. "Facial rec. So, he goes inside and returns to the car six minutes later, climbs in and drives away. For now I edited out the part while he's inside. I'll send you the complete file too, though."

Just as she told me that, the video flickered briefly and then showed Richard exiting the store carrying a small paper bag. He slipped into the truck and left the parking lot.

"You ran the plates?" I asked her.

"Yes. Registered to Armin Meiwes."

I just shook my head. Meiwes was a killer and cannibal from Germany who'd put out an ad on the Internet looking for "a well-built 18- to 30-year-old to be slaughtered and then consumed." Astonishingly, a man named Bernd Jürgen Brandes answered the ad and Meiwes filmed himself killing and eating Brandes. Why didn't it surprise me that Basque had chosen Meiwes's name as another of his aliases.

"An address?"

"One that doesn't exist in Alexandria."

I replayed the footage.

The truck had a hitch and brake light wires for pulling a trailer.

"Have Lacey see if anyone has bought a fishing license or registered a boat under Meiwes's name. Maybe we'll get lucky and get an actual address."

I scrutinized the video and saw a sticker in the pickup's rear window. Zooming in on it, I said, "That sticker in the window. What is that? A parking sticker from a college?"

"I'm not sure . . ." A moment passed as she studied it herself. "It looks like it might be."

With the angle of the vehicle and the glare from the sunlight, it was impossible to read the writing, but it appeared to contain an image of a fish leaping out of the water.

"A state park sticker?"

"Maybe. I'll have Lacey do an image-based search online, see what we can pull up. Anything else?"

"See if you can find out what Basque bought when he went inside that store."

After the call, Ralph asked me, "What do you want to do?"

"Pull over. I want you to watch this too."

49

Over the last twenty minutes we went through the complete footage twice and the edited version close to a dozen times and didn't see anything that seemed significant. I was about to suggest we move on when Ralph reached over and paused the video. "Hold it. What is that?"

"Where?"

"On the hood."

I zoomed in.

"Man," he said, "that is one big streak of bird poop."

I couldn't help but think of the picnic with Tessa and Lien-hua, when Tessa had joked about a bird pooping on my sandwich.

"You grew up right next to Horicon Marsh," Ralph said half jokingly. "You gotta be an expert on goose poop, see if you can identify the bird, maybe lead us to—"

"That isn't from a goose." I thought back to all of my years fishing with my dad and my brother in Wisconsin. "It's from a heron. Taking off. At least, that's my best guess."

He eyed me dubiously. "Okay, so you're a sharp guy, but how could you possibly know that?"

I pointed. "Just like blood spatter. If the bird was stationary, then the excrement would be in a—"

"Ah. I get it. In one spot, a circle, something like that. Sure. But since this is a streak, the bird had to be flying."

"Anyone who's been around blue herons enough can tell you that they often leave a white trail behind when they're taking off. It's distinctive. This vehicle was parked near a river, lake, or marsh where a heron would be taking off."

"The Patuxent River?"

"Maybe . . ."

Blue herons. A sticker of a fish leaping out of the water. Wrighton Road. Marsh biota on Brandi's shoes. A hitch and brake light wires, perfect for pulling a fishing boat.

Nothing solid, just clues. But arrows that were all pointing in one direction: a wetlands.

As I was studying the map more carefully, Angela called back. "The sticker, it's from a private boat landing near the Jug Bay Wetlands Sanctuary."

"You said a private boat landing?"

"Just for people in that residential area."

"That's it. Give me the neighborhood and get me a list of names. Now."

+++

Richard turned onto Blue Shirt Road toward his home on the eastern fringes of the sanctuary and let his thoughts scamper ahead of him to all that the evening held in store.

+++

Angela found the list, but no names popped out to us and there was nothing yet on what Basque might have purchased in the sporting goods store.

But we had the neighborhood and everything pointed to it as a potential anchor point for Basque.

Basque would want isolation, a place to take his victims, dispose of bodies.

One street wove back into the very edge of the wetlands.

Blue Shirt Road.

I hung up and punched my finger against my laptop screen and said to Ralph, "We start there, at the end of the road, and then move through the area house by house."

+++

Richard pulled into his driveway.

He removed the fake mustache, contacts, and peeled off the latex from his cheeks.

As he exited the squad, he shielded his face from the driving rain, and was welcomed by his two pit bulls. They were kill dogs and he called them off so they wouldn't attack either of the two prizes now in the backseat as he moved them into the house.

When he opened the squad's door and brought Saundra out, she offered herself to him, told him she'd do anything he wanted if only he would let Noni go.

With a straight face he told her convincingly that if she cooperated he wouldn't harm her daughter in any way. After that, it was not difficult to get her into the house.

Once he had her in the living room, the rope around her wrists and ankles made sure she wasn't going to go anywhere. He tied her in such a way that she would never be able to fight back as Agent Jiang had done on Friday.

Then he went back to the car to get the girl.

He would do her first.

Let her mother watch as he did.

+++

8 minutes

I parked beneath the dark tunnel of branches arching over the road. The embankment led down to the marsh on the right side, a thick tangle of trees rose on the left.

A torrent of rain was slashing down all around us, most likely obscuring, to anyone in the house, the sound of our approach up the road.

A Maryland State Police car was parked in front of the garage. Ralph put in a call to Headquarters to find out the name of the officer who lived here.

A jon boat on a rusted trailer sat beside the woodshed.

+++

Richard left the girl tied up beside her mother in the living room, and went to the kitchen to heat up the frying pan.

+++

There were no law enforcement officers living at this address.

Quickly, we ran the plates: they belonged to a Maryland State Police officer who hadn't been in touch with dispatch in over ninety minutes. I tried to reach the two agents guarding Saundra's house but they didn't pick up. Neither did Saundra when Ralph phoned her.

"He's here," I said. "He's got her here."

Headlights off, Ralph angled the car to block the road while I called for backup. Then he turned off the engine.

I wondered how many women Basque might have brought here, how many corpses might lie at the bottom of the dark water of that marsh.

Anger and revulsion rose inside me.

And the anger was just what I needed.

"Don't tell me to wait around until backup gets here," I said.

Ralph was already unholstering his weapon. "Last thing on my mind."

Guns out, we stepped into the rain.

The night was filled with the damp, pungent smell of the stagnant water of the wetlands.

Ralph gestured for me to go around to the back of the house, that he would take the front. Both of us had our flashlights off, using the dim porch light oozing through the rain to guide our way.

We were halfway to the house when, somewhere above the sound of the rain pelting the ground, I heard attack dogs—at least two of them, barking viciously, rushing toward us through the night.

50

5 minutes

Pit bulls.

The porch light illuminated part of the lawn and we were still pretty much hidden in the darkness, but I could make out one of the dogs cornering the house and coming my way. I heard another somewhere in the dark near Ralph.

Pit bulls can be trained not to bite, not to kill, but they're not naturally docile animals. Once they latch onto you, they do not let go.

And they go for the throat.

I doubted Basque would have pit bulls that were friendly, and the way these dogs were snarling they didn't sound tame at all.

The dog sprinted toward me.

Instinctively, I raised my weapon.

I shouted, tried to call it off, but that did nothing to slow it down. I fired and the bullet grazed its flank as it leapt into the air. Shielding my neck with my left forearm, I was about to fire again when the dog jerked to the side in midflight as the dampened echo of a gunshot reverberated through the rain.

In the bleary light, I could see the dog lying dead at my feet, its head a mess of splintered bone and dark blood rinsing off into the mud.

I pivoted toward Ralph.

He stood stoically, gun raised, still aiming at the place where his bullet had met the dog in midair.

Twenty meters away. Quite a shot.

Then I saw it.

"Ralph, behind you!"

He whipped around as the pit bull sprang at him and latched onto his right forearm. He raised his arm to lift the dog off the ground where he could control it and grabbed its collar with his free hand. The porch light flicked off before I could squeeze off a shot.

"I got it!" he hollered. "Go!"

I trusted him and, flashlight on, dashed toward the house.

My heart was churning in my chest, the adrenaline taking me to another plane, an elemental high, as I threw open the front door and swept through the entryway and into the living room. In my flashlight's beam the room came into view. Couch. Recliners. Lamps. Magazines on the end table.

A woman and a girl lay bound on the floor. From the photos in the case files, I identified them immediately as Saundra and Noni Weathers.

Secure the scene.

I quickly checked the adjoining rooms, saw no one, and rushed back to Saundra and Noni, removed their gags, and slit the ropes with the automatic knife I carry. "Are you hurt?" I asked Saundra.

"No, we're okay."

"How many people?"

"Just one, I think. Basque. I don't know if there's anyone else here."

He's worked with partners in the past.

"Where did he go?"

Even as she spoke, I heard the engine of a car firing up.

"That's him." She pointed toward the window where the taillights of the squad outside were visible.

I rushed toward the front door, snapping on the living room and porch lights as I flung it open. "Don't leave the house."

Outside, Ralph had made it to the porch and was facing the police cruiser that was careening away from us through the mud. He fired three times but the squad's windows were bulletproof.

His right forearm was bloody, chunks of meat gouged out from where the pit bull had attacked him. The dog lay dead in the yard.

"Saundra and her daughter are inside. Stay with them." I sprinted past him. "Clear the house. He might not have been alone. I'll get Basque."

With my car blocking the road, there wasn't enough room for Basque to get by on either side, but in the slick mud, if he had enough speed and hit the side panel just right he might be able to nudge it out of the way and get past it.

As I bolted through the rain toward the squad, Basque backed up to gain enough speed to ram my car.

I closed the space between us as he gunned the engine, and, fishtailing in the mud, roared forward and slammed into the front passenger side of my car. The vehicle moved, but not enough for him to get past. It looked like the squad's driver's door might have banged open for a moment.

His tires spun determinedly and started sinking in the soft earth. Both cars were sliding slowly toward the embankment.

I skidded in the mud on the way to the driver's side, almost slipping down the bank into the marsh stretching away from me into the darkness. I stood back from the door so I'd have a clean shot. From this angle I couldn't see inside the driver's seat. The headlights from the car cut a glowing swath of light through the rain.

"Hands out the window!"

Nothing.

"Hands out! Now!"

The squad's tires were spinning in the mud. With the loose embankment giving way, my car was starting to tilt off the road, and I realized Basque might just get past it.

Whipping my gun forward, I threw open his door and saw that he wasn't inside.

There was a metal accelerator bar pressed against the gas pedal, the other end Velcroed to the steering wheel.

Lien-hua had said he'd have an escape plan. He was ready for this, he was—

I spun to search the night, but even as I did, he emerged from the shadows and was on me.

The impact of his fist against my jaw threw me backward and I smacked into the car. A burst of pain shot through my face, and then I was raising my arm to fire when he grabbed my forearm and twisted my wrist backward to go for my weapon.

51

Basque's grip was like steel, and when he cranked my wrist sideways he was able to wrench the gun free. My SIG dropped to the mud.

Don't let him get it, Pat. Do not let him get it!

Hurtling forward, I threw my arms around him and drove him toward the marsh. His legs smeared out from under him and we tumbled backward, landing together in the mud and rolling down the embankment toward the water. The Mini Maglite that I'd somehow managed to hold on to sent light spinning and flickering through the rain-drenched darkness until I lost hold of it.

When we hit the water he was on top of me.

I snatched in as much air as I could before my head went under.

Struggling to get free, I tried to disentangle myself from him but he squeezed my neck with both hands to hold me under, then repositioned himself to straddle my chest.

Grabbing at his hands I tried to pull them off my throat, but he had the leverage and I couldn't peel his fingers away.

I thought of Tessa and of Lien-hua, of the picnic we'd

had, the hope of a future together, then of getting the news that Lien-hua had been attacked, of seeing the look on Tessa's face when I told her.

Every moment.

So brief.

So unfathomable.

He was choking me just as he'd done with Lien-hua with the belt. She shot him in the right side when he did. She had—

Yes.

I didn't know exactly where the wound was, but I went for it and landed a series of fierce blows against his side; it only served to weaken his grip a little.

The world was growing dim, and what little air I had left in my lungs escaped in one sharp, final burst of bubbles.

While we live.

Let us live.

My SIG was still by the car and all I had for a weapon was that automatic knife in my pocket, but the way I was positioned I wasn't sure I could get to it. Desperate for air, I dug my right hand into my pocket while I tried to peel his fingers off my neck with my left.

The world was becoming a splintered hungry darkness and as I was starting to fade out for good, I managed to pull the knife free. I flicked out the blade, pictured where his neck would be, and then, with all the strength I had left, I stabbed it fiercely at his throat.

I missed, but hit the side of his face.

My hand slammed into his jaw, the blade sliced through his cheek and into his mouth, probably also smashing through his teeth.

His grip loosened and I pushed him back. I wrestled

free from his weight, scrambled against the mire that tried to hold me down, and managed to get my head above water.

I gulped in a mouthful of air.

Stood to fight him.

The headlights from the squad on the road above us gave me enough light to see Basque. The knife was still protruding from his jaw, dark blood draining in thick streaks from his mouth. Off to my right, more clumps of loose soil were cascading down the embankment and my car was teetering on the lip of the bank.

Basque grabbed the knife and drew it out of his jaw without even flinching, then spit out a mouthful of blood and fragmented teeth. He looked more savage than ever, like some kind of primal beast moving through the marsh toward me in the driving rain.

As he swiped the knife at me, I dodged to the side and then threw a punch at his bloody mouth and connected hard. His head snapped backward. Before he could turn toward me again, I tugged my feet free of the mud, grabbed him, and threw him under the water.

He went into the marsh face-first, and I scrambled on top of him and, pressing him down, grabbed his arms, got the knife from him, and cuffed his wrists behind him.

I didn't pull him out of the water, but held him there, kneeling on his back, forcing his face into the muddy bottom of the marsh.

There is a dark side to justice.

And it calls to us all.

This man deserved to die.

And he was going to.

Sirens whined faintly in the night. Backup. They were

on their way, but they weren't close enough to save Basque.

Beneath me, I could feel his body start convulsing.

End this.

For all the times you've wanted to stop him, vowed to stop him.

End this.

Lien-hua's question about whether I wanted to catch Basque because of justice or revenge wedged itself like a thorn in my mind, and Tessa's query about what I would do when I found him—if I was actually going to bring him in—came crawling back to me.

Basque's body stopped spasming.

A few more seconds just to make sure.

It can end right here, right now.

Justice doesn't always have clean hands.

All I had to do was let go of him and he would never rise, never breathe again. That was justice on behalf of all the people he'd killed, all the lives he'd destroyed.

I stepped back and caught my breath.

Apart from the ripples from my movement and the unrest caused by the fearsome rain, the water in front of me began to become calm.

Basque did not rise.

You did it. You stopped him. You killed him.

I tried to catch my breath.

The shift in the headlights caught my attention as the bank gave way. My car came rolling toward me in a landslide of mud and uprooted marsh grass. Instinctively, I grabbed Basque's body and lurched backward in the mud, dragging him to the side as the car sluiced down the bank and landed with a thick, heavy splash in the marsh almost exactly where we'd been wrestling with each other.

Basque was a big man, and it wasn't easy getting him to shore. At last, I flopped him onto the bank and stood peering down at his motionless body.

The squad remained at the top of the embankment, but the headlights had stopped moving and I assumed the cruiser must have become lodged against one of the trees bordering the road.

There was just enough light to see the outline of Basque lying at my feet.

The sirens drew closer.

I could remove the cuffs. No one needed to know exactly how this had all played out. My report could simply state that we struggled, that as we fought he tried to drown me and though I was able to free myself, he was killed in the process.

When I'd first captured him fourteen years ago, I'd told the truth but not the whole truth about what had happened in that abandoned slaughterhouse. I'd let my most basic instincts of violence and fury take over and found pleasure in giving them free rein.

The battle I'd been fighting inside of myself ever since that day raged inside me still.

Revenge isn't your duty, justice is.

I knew that, yes, I knew it but—

I stared at Basque, lying dead at my feet.

And, as much as I wanted to, as much as the shadows called to me, I realized I couldn't do it, not again. I couldn't let the truth get blurred, not like it was the first time when I caught him.

Not again.

Justice doesn't always have clean hands.

But it should.

So, in the mud and in the rain, I knelt, and I shoved at his abdomen until the water spewed from his mouth, and I did chest compressions and resuscitation breaths against his shattered, bloody mouth—made even harder by the wound in his jaw—and after about thirty seconds, I brought him back, turned him onto his side so he could cough up the marsh water and blood without aspirating on them, and I brought Richard Basque, the man I'd wanted for so many years to kill, back to life.

To prove to myself that I wasn't like him.

Or at least, to attempt to.

52

Over the last couple minutes, half a dozen police cars and two ambulances had arrived. Basque had been loaded onto one of them, his wrists and ankles strapped down securely. Two officers sat beside him to make sure he didn't somehow pull free and escape. The stab wound in his jaw was not life-threatening, but was undoubtedly painful. The gunshot wound in his side was bleeding heavily, having ripped open during our struggle.

Well, too bad.

After confirming that they weren't going to take him to St. Mary's, the hospital where Lien-hua was, I retrieved my SIG from where it'd fallen on the road when I was fighting Basque, then I went back to the house and found Ralph sitting on the porch with a paramedic kneeling beside him inspecting the jagged, gaping bite wound on his right forearm.

Through the living room window I could see Saundra and her daughter sitting on the couch, a female officer with them, no doubt asking the kinds of questions it would have been awkward for a male officer to ask.

While the paramedic tried to convince Ralph to ride back to the hospital with him, I watched the taillights of the police escort and the ambulance carrying Basque rumble away in the rain, down the road that led alongside the marsh.

We had him, finally had him, the man who'd taken the lives of so many, the man who'd tried to kill Lien-hua. And even though we'd managed to get here in time to save Saundra and her daughter, sadness still weighed down on me.

We'd discovered the body of the missing Maryland State Police officer in the trunk of the squad. And we received word from the Chesapeake Beach Police Department that the two agents who'd been stationed outside Saundra's house were both dead.

In just the last few hours, Basque had taken the lives of those three men and he had been about to cannibalize and kill a mother and her little girl.

I tried to hold myself back from asking the obvious question—"Why?"—but it was hard. Motives are so indecipherable, so elusive. And yet, it's human nature to try to figure out what they are.

And despite myself, I found that I was doing that now. I kept coming back to the fact that we were dealing with an elaborate chase reaching back at least to February, to Brandi Giddens's death.

Her prints were on the novel in the car.

Her body was left in the park where Basque tried to kill Lien-hua.

It was a long, convoluted trail that ended here tonight.

A chase through time and space.

The hound and the hare.

Tessa was always trying to get me to learn investigative techniques by studying Edgar Allan Poe's fictional detective Auguste Dupin, and now I thought of something Dupin had said in one of Poe's stories.

In "The Purloined Letter," when faced with an inexplicable crime that had completely baffled the police, Dupin noted that the most frightening criminal of all is "an unprincipled man of genius."

That was Basque: a man of sweeping intelligence, but with no conscience, possessed only by the insatiable desire to kill.

An unprincipled man of genius.

"I'm fine," Ralph was telling the paramedic. "My wife's a nurse. She can look at this when I get home. I'm not gonna go to the hospital."

"Agent Hawkins," the EMT argued futilely, "I really think—"

But Ralph raised a hand to cut him off. "Just clean it out and wrap it up so it doesn't bleed so much. It's just a scratch." A ragged chunk of meat was missing from his arm. It was not just a scratch.

I figured this argument might go on for a while.

"I'm going inside for a minute," I told him.

The lights in the house were on, and the entryway felt almost cozy and inviting—until I remembered whose house I was standing in.

In contrast to the squalid apartment where he'd taken Lien-hua, Basque's home here on the edge of the wetlands was clean, neat, and rustic, with handmade cherrywood furniture that matched the log cabin–esque feel of the place. The soft smell of pine and a hint of fireplace smoke gently permeated the air.

I stepped into the hall.

Thinking about the vile things Basque had done over

the years, what he was capable of, sent a shiver running through me. He was a psychopath, or a sociopath, or whatever term you preferred, yes, he was that, but he was not some kind of fairy-tale monster, he was just as human as anyone.

And that was the most troubling part of all.

At times each one of us pokes around the rubble of our dark desires, seeing how far we can wander into the nightmare and still remain who we are.

Like I had in the marsh not more than ten minutes ago.

It would be easy, so easy, to get lost there in the shadowlands that lie inside of me.

When you spend as much time as I have tracking people through the territory of the damned, you can never entirely shake off the shadows—they become part of you. And sometimes it's hard to find your way back home again.

The thought troubled me deeply.

I told myself once again that I wasn't like Basque, that no one was.

But, in a sense, I am, we all are.

Saundra and Noni were still seated on the couch, the female officer speaking softly with them.

Miss Weathers looked shaky and had one arm around her daughter, who was leaning against her side staring wide-eyed around the room.

The officer, a slim woman with deeply concerned eyes, looked my way. Her name tag read T. Kayne.

I indicated toward Saundra and Noni. "Can I speak with them for a moment, Officer Kayne?"

She hesitated at first but then nodded and went to join two officers who were standing in the kitchen, staring uneasily at the refrigerator, waiting for the crime scene investigators to get here to process the house.

When I was in high school I'd known Saundra only in passing. Earlier I'd seen her photo in the case files— gentle features, auburn hair, that serious but thoughtful face. Russet eyes. She hadn't changed much.

"Agent Bowers. Thank you. For catching him."

"You're alright?"

A nod.

I knelt beside her daughter. "You're a very brave girl."

"My name is Noni."

"Hi, Noni." I extended my hand. "I'm Pat."

She looked to her mother as if for permission to shake my hand, received it, and her grip was gentle but firm. "It's my birthday."

I seriously hoped this was one birthday she'd be able to forget. "Happy birthday."

"I'm six."

"Well, you're a big girl."

A small pause, then she gave me a smile. "I got a lot of presents at my party."

The girl had been through an incredibly traumatic experience and yet it didn't seem to be on her mind at all. She might be in denial or possibly experiencing a child's version of shock.

"I'll bet you did."

Through the kitchen door I saw Officer Kayne glance my way.

I wished there was something I could say that would make this night disappear from Saundra and Noni's minds, but there wasn't. Time might help, but it was also possible that the nightmares might never go away.

Standing again, I asked Saundra, "Is there anything at all I can do for you or your daughter?"

She put an arm around Noni. "I think we'll be okay."

Then she sighed. "It's like we became characters from one of my books."

"Well, if you ever write about a crime victim again you'll know firsthand what it's like."

A thoughtful look. "Yes, I will."

The sound of raindrops splattering against the roof was growing more sporadic as the storm moved on.

My gaze landed on a photograph on the fireplace mantel. From the case files I recognized the thirty-something woman as Basque's sister, the only person I'd ever known him to care about. "Did he say anything to you about any other victims? Anyone else he might have hurt?"

Saundra shook her head, then Officer Kayne came back in and the paramedics led Saundra and Noni to the second ambulance so they could transport them to the hospital for observation. Surreptitiously, I told the paramedics to make sure they took them to a different hospital from Basque.

Then I had a look around.

No sign of Lien-hua's phone. Quite possibly destroyed by now.

In Basque's study, I found a copy of a 1912 collection of Aesop's fables written by V. S. Vernon Jones. When I flipped to a dog-eared page in the middle of the book I found a fable that'd been circled with a neat red line:

"Prometheus and the Making of Man"

    At the bidding of Jupiter, Prometheus set about the creation of Man and the other animals. Jupiter, seeing that Mankind, the only rational creatures, were far outnumbered by the irrational beasts, bade him redress the bal-

ance by turning some of the latter into men.
Prometheus did as he was bidden, and this is
the reason why some people have the forms of
men but the souls of beasts.

The forms of men but the souls of beasts.
Basque's essence summed up in one succinct phrase.
Monsters.
That look just like the rest of us.
A fable that was all too true.
Before heading outside I did a walk-through of the
rest of the house.

Nothing seemed out of the ordinary. There were no
bodies or body parts, no instruments of death or bloody
knives or photos of victims pinned to the walls. The fishing hat and vest with lures hanging from it stowed by the
door only added to the impression that we were in the
innocuous, normal house of a loner outdoorsman who
liked to go fishing on the nearby river and wetlands.

But looks can be so very deceiving.

Back outside, I met up with Ralph. With the rain dissipating, the night was damp and cool and the air tasted like
early spring but was also soaked with the lingering mud-
rich smell of the marsh stretching away from us into the
night.

Some type of bird let out a screech and the lonely
marshlands swirled to life nearby—something heavy moving through the water. A few deep-throated frogs croaked
hoarsely from the edge of the bank.

The paramedic had bandaged Ralph's arm, but even as
tough as my buddy was, he couldn't conceal a grimace
when he moved it.

I wondered how severe that dog bite really was.

We were silent, and all the events of the night were cycling around inside my head as we walked through the drizzle toward the row of police cars: the grip of concern when I found out Saundra and her daughter were missing from the house in Chesapeake Beach, the adrenaline from the dark thrill of the chase, the desperation of trying to breathe while I was underwater, the lack of clarity about letting Basque stay dead or trying to bring him back, the sick feeling that gripped my stomach when I heard that two agents and a state patrol officer were down.

Ralph and I came to the dead pit bull that had attacked him. It still looked fearsome and intimidating even though it was no longer alive.

"I didn't hear a shot," I said.

"I didn't use my gun. Twisted the collar, choked it out." He didn't sound happy at all about what he'd had to do. He patted its head as if it was a way of saying he was sorry, then he stood again. "So, you brought him back."

"Basque."

"Yes."

"First, I drowned him."

Silence.

"What did it feel like?"

"Killing him or bringing him back?"

"Both."

"The first felt good; the second, not so good."

"Why did you do it? Why'd you save him?"

"Honestly, Ralph, I'm not sure."

"Well, I'm proud of you."

"What, for killing him or for bringing him back?"

"Both."

The Evidence Response Team arrived, and Cassidy, Farraday, and their crew started the arduous task of processing Basque's house.

I would have work myself: forms, paperwork, completing the case files—but right now there wasn't anything else for Ralph or me to do here.

"Let's get you to a doctor to stitch up that dog bite," I told him. "You really do need some antibiotics. A rabies shot too, probably."

"Naw, I'm okay."

"Buddy, having biceps as big as my thigh isn't going to help you fight off an infection."

He scoffed.

"Do you really want to face Brineesha with an untreated bite wound like that?"

That made him think. "She *can* be a determined woman."

"Yes, she can. We'll get your car, swing by St. Mary's, I can say hi to Lien-hua, and you can have someone look at your arm."

He wasn't thrilled about the idea, but when I reminded him how many nights he'd spent on the couch last year when he didn't get the wound from a knife fight stitched up, he finally gave in.

My car lay mired in the mud at the base of the embankment, but an officer nearby offered to give us a ride to pick up Ralph's car.

Only when I'd mentioned Lien-hua's name a few moments ago did it hit me that I hadn't called her yet to tell her the news about Basque.

After I retrieved my laptop from my car and we were on our way to DC in the cruiser, I caught Lien-hua in her

room saying good-bye to Dr. Frasier, who'd been checking her charts. "Still scheduled for release tomorrow."
She sounded satisfied and relieved.

"Excellent. Listen, we caught Basque."

"He's in custody?"

"Yes."

I summarized the fight in the marsh.

"And Miss Weathers and her daughter are okay?"

"It looks like they are. Yes. Ralph got bitten by a
dog—"

"I'm fine," he grumbled loud enough for her to hear
on the other end of the phone.

"So he says," I told her.

Now for the news I hadn't really wanted to share: I
related what Basque did to the two agents and the Maryland State Police officer.

There was a long stretch of silence and at last Lien-hua
said, "At least it's finally over."

"Yeah. It's over."

Another moment passed. "I'm not sure this is the
right time to bring this up, but Margaret assigned Agents
Davenport and Perry to look into the possibility of other
Calydrole-related suicides. A few minutes ago Davenport stumbled across a suicide in Montana that looks
related."

"What did he find?"

"A woman named Natalie Germaine took her life
about two weeks ago. The mechanism of death was different from Corey Wellington's—she overdosed rather
than stabbing herself—but she was taking Calydrole, and
here's the clincher: she was the sister of Congressman
Welker."

"Siblings of two important public figures—the FBI

Director and a congressman—both commit suicide and both are taking the same medication for depression?"

"It could have been a coincidence," she said unconvincingly.

"Yeah, I don't think so."

"In this case, I'd have to agree with you."

"Was any Calydrole found at the scene?"

"No. But Natalie had been spending a few nights each week at her boyfriend's house and left a blister pack of pills over there—and yes, it's the same lot number as the empty pack found in Corey Wellington's house. Perry just confirmed the lot number not five minutes before you called."

"So we have samples of the pills?"

"There are ten left."

"Alright, tomorrow morning have them next-day-air the pills here to DC—some to the FDA and PTPharmaceuticals for testing, and let's have a couple sent to the FBI Lab for analysis."

"Already packaged and ready to go. Davenport and Perry are going to broaden this thing, look more carefully into other government officials and members of Congress who've had family members commit suicide recently."

"Good. And have the police out in Montana look for Tyree's prints at the scene. Especially on the medicine cabinet."

"I'll have Davenport put the request through." Then she added, "And, Pat. I'm glad you got Basque. And that you're okay. Good work."

"I'm glad we got him too."

It seemed like there might be more to say, but neither of us came up with anything and we ended the call.

We had Basque.

Saundra and Noni were safe.

Lien-hua was scheduled to be released tomorrow morning.

We were moving in the right direction to decipher the Calydrole riddle.

Despite all the tragedy that had happened tonight, starting tomorrow, maybe things would finally settle down and begin to get back to normal again.

53

Keith closed the hotel room door and set his suitcase beside the bed closest to the bathroom.

"I may be up for a while," Vanessa told him. "I have a brief I'm preparing."

"I understand."

"You did a fine job in India. With Eashan and Jagjeevan."

It wasn't really something he wanted to talk about. "Thank you."

"We get paid this weekend. Maybe you can retire those pruning shears." But she gave him a half grin that spoke for itself: *Or not.*

Honestly, there was nothing Keith wanted more than to be done with those shears for good. However, fear of Valkyrie had kept him involved in this so far and, although he hated to admit it, would keep him involved as long as Valkyrie wanted.

"Good night, Corporal," Vanessa said. "I'll try not to keep you up too late."

"Alright, good night."

When pharmaceutical products are shipped to the U.S. from overseas, as long as they're part of the legitimate supply chain, they're not inspected. They arrive at a dock or an airport, the paperwork is verified, the packaging is checked for tampering, and then, rather unceremoniously, they're loaded onto semis and shipped to distribution centers.

Tomorrow, he and Vanessa would be taking the steps necessary to ensure that this process went by without a hitch for the seventy thousand pills that were on their way to Logan International Airport.

+++

Valkyrie reviewed his plan.

Keith and Vanessa had untangled the snags at the facility in Kadapa; the shipment would be ready for distribution Friday evening. The packets of medication would be sent out and the irreversible effects would ripple through the pharmaceutical industry.

PTPharmaceuticals' shares would plummet, he would cash-settle his options, and the transaction would be complete.

It would provide him with enough funds to take revenge, not on the person who'd taken Tatiana's life, but on the people who had trained her killer to do so.

Valkyrie unlashed the tarp covering the deck of the thirty-five-foot cruising yacht he had acquired yesterday. The boat was still docked at Seaboard Marina on the Potomac River, but it was going to provide him a way to leave the city if circumstances called for it.

Airports and roads would be out of the question.

The river would work.

Last winter, after dealing with a misunderstanding in Pakistan involving a terrorist sympathizer named Abdul Razzaq Muhammad, Valkyrie had been able to funnel a substantial amount of money into the hands of the Chechens to help fund an upcoming attack against Moscow. Now he would get the amount they would need to complete their mission.

In September of 2004, they'd taken over a middle school in Beslan and 335 people were killed when Russian troops entered the building and failed to stop the rebels.

That was one school.

And although the Chechens hadn't been nearly as proactive over the last few years in contending for their independence, a small group of determined freedom fighters had been putting some rather elaborate plans together to strike at the heart of Moscow, at twenty-two schools where the majority of the children and grandchildren of the ruling party attended.

Valkyrie recalled something he'd read long ago: "Vengeance will never bring you peace, only a new kind of prison."

Well, over the years he had learned that it was true.

After all, there is a beast that lives within each of us, a beast that screams out for its own kind of justice and will be restless and enraged and sometimes all-consuming until it gets what it wants.

Even if it destroys you.

Or seals you in your own personal prison.

He'd taken the life of the person he loved the most. Now he would punish the people who had created the beast that he was.

Not justice, perhaps, but at least fulfilling the role of the Valkyrie in deciding who will live and who will die on the battlefield of life.

He finished rolling up the tarp.

According to the message Alhazur Daudov, the Chechen paramilitary commander he was working with, had sent him, the meeting to iron out all the details was scheduled to happen on Friday night at 7:30 p.m. here on the yacht. From there, if necessary, they would travel together to the distribution center here in DC where the drugs would be waiting, to ascertain that everything was in place for the shipment to go out the following morning.

54

Graham Webb, president of Yorke & Webb Import Services, reminded his eight-year-old daughter, Abigail, not to go too close to the water.

"I know, Daddy," she grumped at him.

"Okay."

Then, after offering him a smile, she ran out of the house to play on the narrow stretch of sand encircling his home on Lake Beulah.

His living room window afforded him a clear view of the lake, although woods on each side of the property did restrict the visibility to a stretch of beach a few hundred feet wide. Abigail knew better than to wander out of sight of the house. Graham had made that clear to her and kept reminding her whenever she came to stay with him.

Now he watched her through the window to make sure she obeyed him, which she did. The early evening was too cool to swim, and apart from a woman walking her dog along the shore, the beach was empty.

Satisfied that Abigail was playing safely, Graham grabbed a martini from his home bar and then scrolled through the latest earnings reports on his tablet computer.

His company, an import and distribution service that worked with all the major players in the pharmaceutical industry, continued to fare well in the current rocky economic landscape.

He glanced outside again. The day was calm, the lake still. He took a satisfying sip from his drink and then went into the sunroom, the place in the house that gave him the clearest view of the lake. He peered out the window one more time to make sure Abigail was safe.

The woman with the dog had stopped beside his daughter, and Abigail was kneeling beside the terrier, gently petting him. The dog looked well enough behaved, sitting obediently at the woman's feet, and Graham's attention went back to his tablet.

After checking the day's stock market report, he started evaluating if he should sell some of the shares he had in the tech giant ChipEvolution. He was finishing up when his cell phone rang and he glanced at the screen.

His ex-wife's number.

Oh, she'd better not be calling to try and take Abigail home early. They had joint custody, alternating weeks, but Erin had pulled this stunt before, demanding that she pick up Abigail early, trying to get an extra weekend with her.

The phone rang again.

As he tapped the cell's screen to answer the call, he glanced out the window once more and saw that the beach was empty. No woman. No dog. No Abigail.

As he brought the phone to his ear, he headed to the

door to check on his daughter. "Erin, I told you not to—"

"Stay in the house." A man's voice cut him off.

"What? Who is this?"

"Stay in the house, Graham. I want to talk to you and I want your undivided attention. Believe me when I tell you that you would not want to step outside right now."

The words hit him like a slap in the face and sent a terrifying chill worming through him. "Who is this?"

"This is the man who can get to your ex-wife's phone. This is the man who can get to your daughter whenever he wants to."

Abigail!

Graham rushed toward the door but as he grabbed the handle, the man commanded him again not to do it: "Stay in the house. We have your daughter and believe me, if you step out that door you will never see her again. And you would not want to."

"You have my daughter?"

"We do and—"

"I swear to God, if you touch her, if you hurt her—"

"It would be best at this point not to threaten me, Graham. She's safe. For now."

Graham went to the kitchen window to try to see the strip of beach from another angle, but his daughter was nowhere to be seen. "Let me talk to her!"

The man ignored him. "Listen carefully. Tomorrow morning a shipment of pharmaceutical products is going to arrive at Logan International Airport. You're going to approve the paperwork personally and oversee the loading process onto the semis for distribution. I know that you aren't always involved in signing off on arrivals like this, but in this case I would like you to expedite the order. If you call the police or contact the authorities we will know. And we will harm your daughter in ways that I would rather not like to describe."

Graham peered out the window at the vacant beach. "I don't understand what any of this has to do with my daughter. Let me talk to Abigail!"

"Just take care of things tomorrow and we will never bother you or your daughter again."

"So you'll let her go? Tonight? Right now?"

"We'll do what we deem necessary to encourage your cooperation."

"I'll do it, I . . ." His thoughts shifted for a second from Abigail to his ex-wife. He might not like her, might not like how much she'd gotten in their settlement, but she was Abigail's mother, and if anything happened to her it would shatter their daughter.

This guy has Erin's phone.

"Erin. Is she alright?"

"She is. But if you don't do as I asked, we will make use of her to hurt Abigail. We'll make the girl watch and the things we'll do would not be ones that—"

"Okay, okay. Stop. I'll do it. I swear."

"Alright, we're counting on you being a man of your word. You are a man of your word, aren't you, Graham?"

"Yes, I'll do it. Don't hurt them, please."

And then the line went dead and Graham bolted from the house toward the beach.

"Abigail!" He rushed across the lawn toward the water's edge. "Where are you?"

He was almost to the sand when he saw her walking his way along the shore from his right.

"Abigail!" There was both anger and worry in his voice, the tone a parent can't keep from using when a child has wandered away and then been found again. "Are you okay?"

"Yeah." She sounded a little frightened. "I was just petting the dog."

Beyond her the beach was vacant.

"You're sure you're okay?"

"Of course, Daddy."

"You know better than to wander off. To go out of sight."

"I'm sorry." She lowered her head. "It's just . . . She told me I could come and see her other dog too."

"Where did she go?"

Abigail turned, looked behind her, and saw the empty beach. "I don't know. When we got over there she got a phone call and told me she needed to go and that I'd better head back home so you wouldn't worry about me. I'm sorry, I didn't mean to—"

"She didn't touch you, did she? Did she touch you?"

Abigail shook her head and brushed away a tear. "Don't be mad, Daddy, I didn't mean to."

"Come here. I'm not mad, baby." He encircled her in his arms. "I'm not mad."

On the way to the house she told him that the woman was nice and that she was "normal-looking" and had red hair and that she'd said she would see her again soon, "if your daddy decides that's what he wants."

Whoever these people were, Graham was not going to gamble with his daughter's life. And as harsh as his feelings toward Erin were, he wasn't going to take any chances that she would be hurt in the ways he was imagining. All these people were asking him to do was oversee the transfer of a shipment. There was nothing illegal or unethical about that.

He took Abigail inside and locked all the doors, although he had a feeling that if the people who were behind this wanted to get in, locking a door wasn't going to make any difference.

And, for fear of what they would do to his daughter and his estranged ex-wife, he decided that tomorrow morning he would do exactly as the man on the phone had demanded.

55

The last forty-eight hours had passed in a blur.

The rain returned yesterday and settled drearily over the nation's capital. It was a gray, somber rain that made it seem like the sun couldn't possibly exist beyond the thick slabs of clouds hanging so heavily in the sky.

Between yesterday afternoon and this evening, there'd been four funerals for the men who'd lost their lives on Tuesday in Basque's killing spree: the Maryland State Police officer, the two federal agents, and a young man who was working at a magic shop on the coast. At first we didn't know that homicide was related to the others, but when I saw on the news that there'd been a message written in blood in the back room of the store and I heard what the words were, I knew the killer was Basque.

The message read: *I remember my tail.*

The snake in the fable would never forget, and neither would Basque.

And neither would I.

I had made it to three of the funerals—the ones for the two agents and the slain officer.

There are many times when second thoughts become chains on your soul. You scour the past, looking for that small decision you could have made, that tiny choice that would have turned out to be monumental. "If only" becomes the catchphrase that echoes through every moment, every hour. Was there something I could have done to save those men?

You could have found Basque sooner.

But we had him now. Since he was such a high-profile criminal we were holding him at the undisclosed detention facility below FBI Headquarters on the Federal Triangle in downtown DC. It was only recently built and was located beneath the three underground levels of parking. The area was so classified that even most of the people in the building didn't know what that newly added lower level of the building contained.

Doctors had treated the gunshot wound Basque had sustained in his right side when Lien-hua shot back through the seat of her car at him. His stabbed jaw and shattered teeth hadn't posed any real threat, just cosmetic damage. From what I heard, he was recovering fine. I wasn't sure if I was happy to hear that or not.

So far he'd refused to talk to anyone, including his court-appointed legal counsel.

Corey Wellington's funeral was also held yesterday in Atlanta. Margaret flew down for it. Though the cable news networks were clamoring for an interview, she hadn't granted any. It was still officially considered a suicide. The last time I spoke with her was this morning, and I had nothing substantial to report.

The bright spot yesterday was Lien-hua's release from the hospital—minor compared to everything else that was going on, but it was at least one thing to be thankful for.

For the time being at least, instead of going back home, she'd moved into the one-bedroom apartment in the basement of Ralph and Brineesha's house. With her injuries and crutches, she wasn't able to navigate any stairs and there was a lower-level entry, unlike at her place. We'd discussed her staying at my house, but this way she would also have a resident nurse in Brineesha in case there were any health concerns that came up regarding her recovery.

Both of our families—her brothers and my relatives—were excited, relieved, thrilled that she was on her way to recovery.

Earlier today, I visited the sites of the two apartments Basque had used. I spent more than an hour at each location but didn't take anything away from them clue-wise, just a reminder of how thankful I was that he was finally in custody.

Regarding the investigation into the suicides, the Calydrole pills that had been found at the apartment of Natalie Germaine's boyfriend had arrived in DC this morning and both FDA and PTPharmaceuticals were studying their chemical composition. The team at the FBI Lab was also working on their own inspection, as well as a forensic analysis of the packaging—prints, DNA, and so on.

This morning we'd reviewed the information about the side effects of Calydrole. The FDA requires every antidepressant medication to carry a warning that some adolescents and children may be at increased risk of suicide while taking the medication. The official disclaimer on Calydrole warned: *This drug may lower your immunity to certain diseases, cause impotency, abdominal bleeding, dizziness, and nausea. Sometimes fatal events can occur. It may increase the risk of suicide in certain people.*

Talk about covering your bases, that about did it.

To put it bluntly, our team hadn't made much progress at all in unraveling the suspicious circumstances related to Corey Wellington's death.

Even with Angela's and Lacey's help, we came up short in finding any other suicides that might have been related to the two we knew about. Missing packets of depression medication at the sites of suicides was just not the kind of information that was typically recorded on police reports.

Killing yourself doesn't usually initiate as much investigation or scrutiny as cases in which someone else murders you. Generally, in cases judged to be suicides, police investigations are brief, the reports are succinct and more often than not, rather incomplete.

We had, however, pulled up a more detailed background on Corporal Keith Tyree. I'd managed to locate one photo of him in Moscow with Nikolai Demidenko, a known associate of one of the world's most infamous terrorists—an assassin named Alexei Chekov, but better known throughout the international counterterrorism community by the code name Valkyrie.

I'd encountered Chekov last winter during an ecoterrorist plot to take over a Navy communication base in the Midwest. As it turned out, Alexei had actually helped us thwart that attack, but since then he'd been responsible for the deaths of scores of innocent people, having masterminded, among other things, a bombing at an elementary school in Kenya, at least half a dozen suicide bombings throughout the Middle East, and the assassination of Olivia Tonneson, the U.S. ambassador to Egypt.

I'm no expert on split-personality disorders, but after Chekov killed his wife he suffered some sort of mental break. In the end, the darker side of who he was had emerged and taken over.

I wasn't sure who scared me more, Chekov or Basque. Chekov probably knew more ways to kill you, but Basque knew how to keep you alive while he slowly ate your internal organs, and I couldn't think of many things more disturbing than that.

Chekov spoke four languages, had any number of false identities, was an experienced hacker, and was one person who had the resources and contacts to wipe Tyree off the grid.

We didn't have enough yet to know anything definitive, but cases are built on threads of evidence. You weave them together until you can see the broader context, and right now the threads were starting to wind into a strand that led back to Chekov.

So, while the search into Tyree's background went on, in light of all that'd happened, we'd rescheduled my meeting with the Immigration and Customs Enforcement agent Jason Kantsos for tomorrow at one o'clock.

My insurance company was working on getting me a new car, for now I had a rental.

Ralph bought me a new Maglite, since mine was lost in the marsh.

We replaced Lien-hua's missing cell phone. And the

two of us burned the unity candle more than a few times to celebrate our moments together.

We'd all had a chance to process what'd happened on Tuesday, and though there was by no means any closure, life, as it has to, was starting to move forward, one slow, unsteady step at a time.

56

Hoping to clear my head, I went for an early morning swim at the YMCA ten minutes from our house.

When I was in college, I'd worked as a wilderness guide and had become pretty proficient at rock climbing and raft guiding. I'd tried to stay in shape over the years so I could still play on those days when I'm able to pull away from my job. Running, climbing, swimming—whatever I could find time to do. If I wasn't in shape, I wasn't sure how I'd deal with the stress of this job.

After about an hour I returned home.

By then the sky was sharp and bright summer-blue, as if it were finally washed clean of the dark deeds that had marked the first couple days of the week.

At the house, I found Tessa sleepily finishing her breakfast of rice cakes, grape juice, and an orange. She didn't always wear the black tourmaline necklace I'd given her on her seventeenth birthday, but today she did and it dangled prominently on the outside of her shirt. The necklace looked at home on her and it seemed to signify, to both of us, the day we started to mend the rift caused when her mother died.

Tessa had on fresh makeup and fingernail polish, and I found myself wondering if all this had anything to do with looking nice for the guy she'd fallen for, the one who she was going to see tonight, Aiden Ryeson.

Back on Wednesday, when he still hadn't asked her out, I'd broached the topic with her. "I don't understand. If you like him so much, why don't you just ask him out?"

"I'm a girl. It doesn't work that way."

"This is the twenty-first century. You're pretty independent. I mean, you're not someone who's normally intimidated by—"

"I'm not intimidated. I just think that if a guy likes you he should be the one to ask you out. It shows he's serious about it."

"So what happens if he doesn't know you like him?"

"Oh, he knows."

"How?"

She stared at me. "You are so clueless when it comes to women. No offense."

"None taken. So you're telling me that you made it clear to him, flirting, that sort of thing?"

She shook her head in exasperation to reiterate how clueless I was. "Whatever."

"But still, I mean, you could just pick up the phone and—"

"If he knows I like him and he doesn't want to ask me out, then he's not worth it. If he likes me and he's too much of a chicken to call me, then I don't want to go out with him anyway. I want a guy who's got the— well—"

"Sure. I know what you meant."

But as it turned out, she didn't need to call Aiden, because yesterday he'd done it: he'd asked her to tonight's prom.

In a text message.

I wasn't sure how kids did things these days, but from my perspective, he'd definitely waited long enough. And he asked her to prom by texting her? To me, it sure seemed like that at least bordered on being too chicken to call.

However, she was excited about it and I was glad to see that. In fact, despite how much she hated shopping, she was planning on going out this afternoon after school to buy a dress, just hours before heading out to the dance.

It was certainly last-minute, but knowing her, I wasn't so sure she would have gone dress shopping earlier even if Aiden had asked her weeks ago.

When Lien-hua had been looking for her wedding dress, she must have been anticipating that Tessa would need a prom dress, because last night after Tessa received her text from Aiden, Lien-hua had informed us that she'd seen the perfect one at a shop in Arlington.

Of course, she didn't know if it would still be in stock, but she'd offered to go look for it with Tessa this afternoon. I wasn't thrilled about Lien-hua trekking out of bed, but she told me she would be fine for an hour, Brineesha agreed, and to avoid an argument, I'd backed down.

So, it was shaping up to be a big day for everyone.

Tessa got to go to prom with the boy she had a crush on, Lien-hua was ready to start venturing out into the world again, and, with Basque out of the way, I could start focusing more on the case involving Corey Wellington's and Natalie Germaine's suicides.

As I walked into the kitchen I saw Tessa texting with one hand without looking at her phone. She was lifting a rice cake to her mouth with the other hand.

"I'll never understand how you do that," I said, referring to her texting. "I can barely hit those keys when I'm staring at them."

She swallowed her bite full of rice cake. "My fingers are smaller. Plus I text a couple hundred more times a day than you do."

"True."

She yawned. "Besides, you're good at pickpocketing."

"Well, that came out of nowhere."

"No, I mean it. You could snag someone's wallet, check his ID, slip it back into his pocket, and he'd never know."

I recalled trying to conceal and reveal the unity candle to Lien-hua, which hadn't exactly been a stellar performance. "Yeah, well, I'm not sure I'm that good." I got some grape juice for myself. "Anyway, you learn that stuff, you know, at the Academy, mainly so you can spot it."

"It's cool, though."

It didn't exactly thrill me that my teenage daughter thought pickpocketing was cool.

I pointed to the package of rice cakes. "How do you eat those things anyway?"

"They're good." She rose and shuffled toward her room, then paused and must have realized she'd forgotten to put them away in their plastic bag. I offered to do it for her.

"Yeah," she said, "if we leave 'em out they might get stale."

"They're rice cakes, how could you possibly tell?"

"Don't try to be clever." She yawned. "It's way too early for that."

"Ah."

She went to get her things while I bagged them, downed a quick breakfast, and then mentally prepared to spend the day trying to untangle what might well be a string of suspicious suicides somehow related to one of the world's most wanted terrorists.

57

Tessa was glad that she didn't know any of the people Basque had killed this week. It made hearing the news a little easier, but it was another stark reminder to her of how diaphanous the fabric of life is.

It was something no one liked to talk about, but it was something that lay there, like a carpet beneath every passing moment. A carpet everyone tried to step over but no one actually succeeded at doing.

She cleared her textbooks off her desk, stuffed them into her backpack.

Ever since Aiden had asked her to the prom, she'd been thinking about her speech. And maybe it had to do with all the murders lately, but death was on her mind and what she had so far in regard to her graduation talk was not exactly what you would call inspiring.

Life in a nutshell: we're born, we suffer, and then we die.

Heartache and grief and loneliness chase us every day, the kind of love we long for is never quite within our reach, justice eludes us, and in the end, meaning is nothing but an illusion.

After all, life is an anomaly, the exception, not the norm. Death is the natural state of affairs both here and everywhere else we know of in the universe—and it's on its way to reasserting itself.

All the evidence from evolutionary biology, astrophysics, astronomy, all the theorizing in statistics and probability make it clear there's no possible way intelligent life exists anywhere else other than on earth. Any other view is either wishful thinking or a carefully cultivated blindness. Death is the default setting of the universe. The end of life on this planet would be the end of life everywhere.

And that day is coming.

Because our planet is dying. The second law of thermodynamics is unrelentingly exerting itself. Entropy will win. Human extinction is inevitable. One day all the stars will grow cold and bleak darkness will be the final destiny of all that there is. The final result of all of our efforts, all of our advances, all of our accomplishments, technology, our hopes, our dreams, will be nothing but evanescent memories disappearing into a vast dead expanse.

In the end, all is for naught.

We are tiny specks on a tiny speck in an immense, barren, lifeless universe. And if there is no God, then there is no heaven and no hope; there is only futility.

So live for today.

Go ahead and make the best of it. Eat, drink, and be merry and all of that, because, really, what's the alternative?

Try to scrape out enough hope to make it through the day without screaming. Use denial. Tell yourself the comforting lie that your life has some sort of ultimate purpose, some degree of lasting significance. Bury yourself in busyness, distract yourself with pleasures, delude yourself with naive optimism, because the alternative is unthinkable.

Hoping that there is hope is the most necessary sedative of all. Without that, suicide is the only reasonable response. Religion is not the opiate of the masses, distraction is.

There.

How was that for a graduation speech?

Unless.

Unless there really was something more, unless eternity is a reality and the physical universe we see is only a shadow of another deeper entelechy breathing out love all around us.

Unless that.

Then, nothing.

But no, she didn't dare mention any of that—God, heaven, eternity, ultimate meaning—because it was a public school speech and that was just not acceptable. In government schools freedom of speech—which *is* in the Constitution—must always bow to the almighty dictum of the separation of Church and state—which is *not*.

She glanced at her phone and saw a text from the school's administration office—the number they used to reach the students in case there was a snow day, that sort of thing.

Okay, weird.

She tapped the screen and found out that she was supposed to meet with Assistant Principal Thacker right after sixth hour.

Oh, great.

He probably wanted to see how her speech was coming.

Well, if she told him about what she had so far, that would be interesting, to say the least.

She found her thoughts splitting off in two

directions—a touch of concern about meeting with Thacker, and excitement about tonight, about prom with Aiden.

She texted back that she'd be there and promised herself this meeting with Thacker was not going to ruin her day.

+++

7:48 a.m.

Graham Webb watched the men unload the boxes from the belly of the cargo plane.

The rather unintimidating private security guard with the clipboard looked at him quizzically. "Mr. Graham? I didn't expect you to be here. Not at this time of day."

"It's good to get out of the office once in a while." He nodded toward the boxes. "That's the shipment from Chennai?"

"Yeah. Got a lot of pills in those boxes."

"Yes."

"Lots of sick people out there."

"Yes, there are."

All Graham had to do was route the drugs into the pharmaceutical supply chain and they would be shipped to pharmacies and hospitals nationwide.

That was it.

Then his family would be safe.

He accepted the clipboard from the man.

All he had to do was sign these forms.

Once the drugs were in the system, unless someone checked the lot numbers of all the individual packages one at a time, they would be distributed to the public, starting this weekend.

And nobody did that. No pharmacies, no doctors, no hospitals would. It just wasn't worth the time.

However, despite all the reassurances he tried giving himself, Graham knew that the man on the phone last night would not have threatened him and his family unless there was something outside of the law going on with these drugs.

He let the tip of his pen rest against the top form on the clipboard.

After the moment had stretched out uncomfortably long, the man beside him said, "I got a lot of work to do here, Mr. Graham. I wonder if you could—"

"One second."

The security guard was quiet.

Graham thought of Abigail again, of that woman getting to her, of the man threatening to hurt his little girl and his ex-wife—hurt them in ways that, from what the man had said, they would very likely never recover from.

If they even let 'em live.

Graham signed his name, then flipped through the stack and scribbled his signature on every page that required authorization.

The security guard already had his hand out, waiting for the clipboard. "Thanks." Once he had it, he immediately signaled for the workers to transfer the boxes onto the waiting semi.

Graham waited until they were done.

There.

He'd fulfilled his role in all this—whatever *this* was—and his daughter, his ex-wife, would be safe.

As long as the people who'd threatened him kept their word.

And there was no guarantee of that.

Telling himself that everything was going to work out alright, he went to his office to make sure all the details were in place for the shipment to arrive tonight at just after six o'clock at the distribution center in the nation's capital.

+++

One last flight, this time to DC.

Keith had never threatened a child before his phone call to Graham Webb last night. He would have preferred being the one with the dog, the one talking with the little girl on the beach, but Vanessa had thought that both the girl and her father would be less suspicious if it was a woman who was walking the dog, and honestly, Keith had had to agree.

After they'd left the beach, Vanessa had ordered him to slit the dog's throat, but this time he'd finally refused her, and after a brief argument, she'd done it and left the carcass at the end of a dead-end road about a mile from Graham's house.

Keith had watched silently.

He wanted this to be over.

Wanted so badly for this to be over.

They confirmed that Graham had kept his end of the bargain this morning, and then made it to the airport just in time for their flight to DC, where they would land at 10:33 a.m.

58

Ever since coming into my office I'd been trying to find out more about Corporal Tyree, but in the end, all I could locate was a photo that appeared in a regional newspaper in southwest Virginia of him returning from the Middle East. In the photo, he stood next to an unidentified, attractive red-haired woman who was apparently welcoming him to the States.

I contacted Cybercrime to have them run the photo through facial recognition, but nothing came up. She was more of a ghost than Tyree was.

Frustrated, I turned my attention to the two things right now that mattered most: (1) unraveling the relationship of Calydrole to the suicides of Corey Wellington and Natalie Germaine, and (2) stopping more of them from occurring.

+++

11:05 a.m.

Over the last couple days Valkyrie had been following the story of the apprehension of Richard Basque by Special Agent Patrick Bowers.

It brought to mind his own clash with Bowers in January.

According to the news, a week ago Basque had tried to kill Special Agent Lien-hua Jiang—another FBI agent Valkyrie had met in Wisconsin.

He remembered her well. She was a fighter. She had skills.

And she'd escaped from Basque.

Interesting.

In Wisconsin, while Valkyrie was still living out his life as Alexei Chekov, Bowers had vowed to catch him again.

And he was the kind of agent who seemed smart enough, tenacious enough, to stick with a case as long as necessary to see it through to the end.

The angel of death had an idea.

It would take a little work, he would have to call in a few favors, pull a few strings, but if he could arrange it he was certain it would be interesting to watch how things would all play out.

Yes, to get things rolling, Richard Basque would be needing a good lawyer, and Valkyrie knew just the person. He phoned and caught her as she was getting in line to rent a car from Avis at Dulles International Airport.

"This is Vanessa."

"Yes, dear," he said, keeping up the facade that she meant something to him. "There's something I would like you to take care of for me."

+++

11:32 a.m.

Ever since we caught Basque back on Tuesday, I'd spent whatever free time I could scrounge up researching counterfeit pharmaceuticals, and now I collected my thoughts in preparation for my one-o'clock meeting with U.S. Immigration and Customs Enforcement Special Agent Jason Kantsos.

I reviewed a few notes from the documents I'd assembled:

- Thousands of Web sites sell substandard, tainted, counterfeit, misbranded, unapproved, contaminated, and adulterated pharmaceutical products. Half of the drugs sold by rogue Internet pharmacies are counterfeit.

- According to World Health Organization estimates, one out of three drugs for sale worldwide is counterfeit.

- Nearly every type of prescription pharmaceutical is available as a counterfeit: antibiotics, psychotropic meds, seizure medication, and drugs to treat cancer, hypertension, and diabetes. Some of the most common are weight-loss drugs and those meant to control high blood pressure.

- FDA doesn't test drugs per se, at least not for consumption, but it can do tests on drugs to determine if they're counterfeit or not, as its analysts were doing this week with the Calydrole pills that'd been found in Montana.

- The authenticity of a drug can be established by superimposing the imprint on the pill (the symbol, number, or name) in question with one known to be genuine, also by studying its chemical composition and biological effects. Sometimes analysts use forensic light sources to compare the ink on the packaging or on the bottles.

- Back in 2008 when the CEO of the company that produces heparin testified before Congress, he said the counterfeit version "was able to evade the quality control systems and regulatory oversight of more than a dozen companies and nearly a dozen countries." A dozen agencies in close to a dozen countries. That didn't bode well for my hopes of determining if the Calydrole we'd found was counterfeit.

Last year, one pharmaceutical company tried to circumvent the infiltration of counterfeit copies of their drugs by printing alphanumeric codes on their packages. Before consumers used the drugs, they were told to enter the code on the company's Web site and verify that it was legitimate. Then, if it wasn't, to return the product to the pharmacy where they'd purchased it. Or, if it'd been ordered through the Internet, to contact the FDA and the pharmaceutical company to report the product as counterfeit.

But there were ways around that as well. Counterfeiters had hired hackers to get into the firm's authentication Web site and enter in codes of their own that would come up as legitimate when customers entered them.

Move.

Countermove.

The never-ending dance of law enforcement and crime.

Reviewing the different ways of determining whether or not a product was legitimate gave me an idea.

I called to leave a message for Dr. Neubauer at the FBI Lab, and since he was almost always in his laboratory instead of his office, I was a little surprised to catch him at his desk.

"Doc, this is Pat. I'm wondering if you can look into something for me."

"The pills?"

"You heard about them? The ones from Montana?"

"The boys down the hall are working on them as we speak."

"Well, I was thinking: pollen is everywhere, right?"

"Pretty much, yes."

"So, would it get on pills? I mean, while they were being produced?"

He contemplated that. "You're thinking a palynological analysis of the drugs?"

"We have FDA and PTPharmaceuticals studying their composition, but I'm not interested just in what the pills contain, but in—"

"Where they were produced."

"Precisely. If you could extract spores or pollen grains from them—"

"Yes"—he cut me off again, but it was good to know he was tracking so closely with me—"of course, I might be able to tell the region in which they were produced and perhaps the season of the year—if the pollen of certain flowering plants was present."

Timing and location. It's always about timing and location.

"Right. We're thinking the shipment came from India. If you can narrow down the section of the country, we might be able to find out, at least generally, where the drugs are being produced. Then we can compare that to the facilities PTPharmaceuticals uses to produce Calydrole. We might be able to zero in on their point of origin."

"Hmm . . . I've lectured at a couple of conferences with

two doctors from the Birbal Sahni Institute of Palaeobotany in Lucknow, India. There are more than fifteen thousand different types of flowering plants in India, but if anyone can help identify the flora there, they can. I'll take a look at the pills, see if I can extract spores from them, and contact my cohorts at the institute. I'll call you."

"Great."

After we hung up, I went back to work, but thoughts about the rest of the day distracted me. Tessa was going out tonight with a boy I'd never met, and that always made me uneasy.

A little over a year ago, when we were visiting San Diego, a man in his early twenties tried to sexually assault her, and if it hadn't been for her quick thinking, he would have likely succeeded. Since then, the thought of her being alone with boys I didn't know had made me uneasy.

I recalled my conversation with her a week ago, when she'd asked me, somewhat in good humor, not to do a background check on Aiden.

I didn't know his family, had no idea who he was.

No, don't do this, Pat. If Tessa finds out she'll feel betrayed.

But, truthfully, she didn't need to know it. I could make a few calls, and if nothing came up I wouldn't need to mention it at all. And if anything bad did show up, she might be upset at first, but she would thank me in the end.

Since Aiden was in high school with her, a complete background check seemed too over-the-top even for me, however I did put a call through to the school's safety patrol officer to see if Aiden had ever had any run-ins with the law or if there were any red flags I should know about, but the officer was away from his desk.

After leaving a short message and my cell number, I hung up and worked on the counterfeit drug research and lost track of time until my ringing phone alerted me that Agent Kantsos was at the reception desk, waiting for me to escort him into the Academy's administration building.

59

1:03 p.m.

Jason Kantsos was a weary-looking man whom I guessed to be about my age. He'd put on a little too much weight, the gray hair that he still had left was thinning, and the goatee he'd chosen to grow actually made him look older than he would have without it.

Kantsos had worked undercover for eight years posing as a counterfeiter bringing drugs from Asia into the U.S. He seemed like the perfect guy to talk to.

Rather than return to my office, we went outside to the Academy's 9/11 Memorial Courtyard, situated between the library, the Crossroads Lounge, and the Washington and Madison dorms.

Flower beds surrounded us, as well as a six-foot-tall sculpture of the twin towers in a pentagon enclosure. The towers had an engraved outline of Pennsylvania that overlapped both of them with a star in the lower left-hand corner to indicate where United Flight 93 had gone down.

The 207th National Academy class had raised the money to purchase the memorial in honor of everyone who died when the twin towers fell, including the two National Academy grads who were with the Port Authority.

Agent Kantsos told me that over the last two days he'd studied our case files on Corey Wellington's death, but he had a number of questions that I now did my best to answer. When I was through, I summarized what we knew about Natalie Germaine's suicide in Montana.

"The cable news stations are saying Corey's death was a suicide," he said.

"Yes."

"Are you suggesting his wound might not have been self-inflicted?"

"No, by all indications it was."

"Okay." He sounded confused. "Honestly, from what I've heard so far, I'm not sure I can help you out much here."

"Why is that?"

"Well, first, because I'm no expert on psychotropic drugs. Second, I have a view that's a little more, well, extreme than ICE's official stance about counterfeit pharmaceuticals."

"What view is that?"

He bent and brushed some grass blades off the melon-size piece of the Pentagon that lay in front of the 9/11 memorial.

"In this attack, when the towers fell, how many people died?"

"I'm not sure exactly. I think just under three thousand."

"Do you know how many people die each year of malaria?"

"No, I'm afraid not."

"Over a million, worldwide. And nearly fifty-five percent of the malaria medication used on the African continent is counterfeit. Each year over two hundred thousand people die of malaria that goes untreated because they're taking counterfeit drugs. And that's only a conservative estimate of the death toll of one disease from one category of counterfeit drugs on one continent."

"A quiet, unreported genocide," I said softly.

"That's one way to put it." He stood, then gestured toward the monument. "We remember the three thousand people who died on 9/11. Not many Americans give a second thought to the hundreds of thousands who die each year because they're unknowingly taking counterfeit drugs. Where are the memorials for them?"

I couldn't think of anything to say.

"Agent Bowers, if I knew you were dying of cancer and I purposely substituted your lifesaving medication with one that I knew was inert or dangerous—but in either case, one that I knew full well would not treat your cancer—if I did that to you, fully aware that my action would contribute to your death, isn't that a form of homicide?"

"I would say that it is."

"So would I—but our government does not." He shook his head and we walked to the other side of the courtyard. "Companies and individuals have been prosecuted over wrongful deaths from counterfeit drugs, but no one has been successfully prosecuted for first-degree murder for distributing counterfeit drugs—even though the manufacturers doing so know full well that they're causing thousands or tens of thousands of deaths."

His cynicism seemed well founded. "You might distribute millions of counterfeit drugs and face a sentence of *maybe* five years in prison. Plus, perhaps, some fines for fraud and conspiracy charges, but never homicide or manslaughter. Accidentally start a fire in a national forest that causes a hiker to die and you could spend decades in prison, but knowingly distribute drugs that'll directly defraud people and result in thousands of deaths, you receive a slap on the wrist."

The more he explained the extent of the problem to me, the more I could see why he had such sharp views. His words reminded me of my lecture earlier in the week when I was discussing with my class the three ways criminals have the advantage over those who track them, specifically the third reason: until we catch them they're always one step ahead.

Which means we're always one step behind.

Kantsos went on, "A decade ago it was difficult not only to produce the drugs but to distribute them. Today, the production is easy—just about anyone can do it. And with the Internet and international shipping, the distribution is easy too. No middleman. Apart from a few isolated exceptions, drug dogs can't sniff counterfeit pharmaceuticals out at the airport. And the profit margin is extraordinary. If you produce the drug well enough, no doctor, no pharmacist, not even FDA investigators can identify them using the naked eye."

"Like the people who died in 2008 from the tainted heparin that made it past all those inspections."

"Exactly. Since Americans tend to trust Canadian pharmaceutical firms to sell name-brand drugs at discount prices, counterfeiters know that one of the easiest ways to get the drugs to Americans is to set up Web sites that purport to be from Canada. They simply route the drugs through the Canadian package delivery services. Some counterfeiters will even set up fake call centers."

He reflected on that for a moment. "Of course, you can just ship them into any U.S. ports of entry along with a load of legitimate pharmaceutical products. It's not like the distribution system is secure."

Everything he was saying made me reticent to ever fill a prescription off the Internet again.

We spoke for a few more minutes about the implications of all of this. Then, since I was primarily looking for a connection between Corporal Tyree and a facility that might be producing the lot number of Calydrole under question, I directed the conversation back to the main reason I'd asked to speak with him in the first place. "I told you about Tyree's prints. It looks like there's something more in play here than just counterfeit pharmaceuticals. Are there drugs out there that cause people to commit suicide?"

He wavered his head back and forth slightly, as if he were balancing how to respond to that. "Again, I'm not an expert on that specific topic, but I wouldn't say there are ones that cause you to. However there are certainly drugs that lower your inhibitions, blur your judgment—especially with SSRIs in adolescents."

We entered the classroom building and headed for my office. "SSRIs?"

"Selective serotonin reuptake inhibitors. They're probably the most common kind of antidepressants. They block the reabsorption of serotonin, which helps the brain cells—the neurotransmitters—to communicate with each other, helping the person's mood stabilize. But they cause some people to become more suicidal."

"So, you take an antidepressant to stop from having suicidal thoughts, but it might end up causing more of them?"

"Antidepressants work for most people," he said somewhat resignedly, "but for some people they don't."

In my office, we took seats on each side of my desk.

"Well, that's one more reason we need to track down this production plant as soon as possible. We think this lot might have come from India."

"That would make sense. Taken together, India and China produce nearly ninety percent of all counterfeit drugs."

"Great," I muttered, "that'll really help us narrow things down."

"Well, no one makes one fake pill at a time; you make batches. So every counterfeit drug you discover means there's a batch of thirty to sixty thousand out there. That might help you find some."

"You mean this lot number, this batch, might have tens of thousands of tainted or contaminated products?"

"I'd be surprised if it didn't."

Oh, this was just getting better and better.

He was eyeing the photos on my wall of some of the raft trips I'd led in college.

"Jason, there are a lot of agencies that might have jurisdiction on this, but I'm afraid information will slip through the cracks if too many people stick their fingers in it. Can you see what the FDA finds out about these drugs and then let us head this up? We have a team of people working on the case already. I think it would be best if our agents stayed on task here rather than hand things off."

"I'll see what I can do. In the meantime, we need to stop that lot number from being distributed."

"How do we do that?"

"I can talk to my supervisors, but I'm guessing they'll

say that at this point we don't have enough to approach PTPharmaceuticals about any kind of recall. Right now any decisions like that would probably need to come directly from the pharmaceutical firm. After all, no one at pharmacies or distribution centers really verifies those numbers unless they have to. The only practical way to stave this off would be to stop all Calydrole from being shipped and used."

"I'll see what I can do on that front." My vibrating phone showed a text from Dr. Neubauer that said it looked like he would be done with the analysis of the pills by two thirty, earlier than I'd expected.

"Anything else?" Jason asked me.

"I can't think of anything right now. You've been helpful. Keep me up to speed."

"I will."

"And by the way, all that information about counterfeit drugs—pretty disturbing."

"You're telling me. I've been trying, and failing, to slow down the avalanche for years."

We exchanged cell numbers, he left, and I put a call through to Margaret to see if we had some way to approach PTPharmaceuticals with the request to pull one of its most profitable drugs off the market until we could ascertain if more people were at risk.

While I waited to hear from her, since the cafeteria was closed, I grabbed a quick, albeit late lunch—a turkey sandwich, Snickers, and a Cherry Coke—at the Board Room, the Academy's deli and snack shop across the hall from the dining area, then I returned to my office to record my thoughts from my meeting with Kantsos before heading to the Lab to meet with Dr. Neubauer.

60

1:58 p.m.

The secretary ushered Tessa into Assistant Principal Thacker's office.

"Good afternoon, Tessa."

"Good afternoon."

Even though she wasn't at all excited about the idea, she geared up to tell him her "Death of Everything in the Universe" speech synopsis and hoped maybe he would decide she wasn't the best person to speak at graduation after all. Then she wouldn't be bailing, Aiden would have no reason to think less of her, and she would still get out of it.

Perfect.

Thacker, who was built sort of like a human penguin, laid a stack of papers on his desk. "Mr. Tilson has informed me that you're on your way to an incomplete in his class."

A beat. "Excuse me?"

"It appears you failed to turn in your senior project last week." He consulted the report in front of him. "A paper I see you were writing about Edgar Allan Poe's impact on modern gothic literature."

"No, I handed that in."

But Thacker shook his head. "There's no record of that."

Ah, so this was what she got for standing up to Tilson in class.

What a jerk.

"How can I get this cleared up?"

"You're going to have to work that out with Mr. Tilson on Monday—he's out sick today."

Of course.

"One other thing."

Okay, here it comes.

"I also wanted to check in with you about your graduation talk. How's your progress on that coming along?"

"Yeah, um, okay. I'm . . . what about if I get an incomplete? Do I still get to graduate on time?"

"I'm confident that you and Mr. Tilson can straighten this out. Don't worry, you'll be on that stage come graduation day. So do you need to run any ideas by me?"

"I'm . . . It's coming. I think I'm gonna talk about the meaning of life."

"Sounds ambitious."

"Yeah . . ." She paused. "Listen, here's the thing, though, I—"

The tardy bell rang.

"You should really get to class." Assistant Principal Thacker scribbled his name on a hall pass for her. "We'll talk soon about that speech, okay? I can't wait to hear what the meaning of life is."

"Right," she mumbled. "I'm sure you'll find my thoughts on the matter unforgettable."

+++

Vanessa stared across the table at her new client, Richard Devin Basque.

"The man I represent has an offer," she told him.

Only the two of them were in the detention center's interrogation room deep beneath the Hoover Building. As with all meetings between lawyers and their clients, no agents or other law enforcement officers were allowed to be present. The sessions were videotaped and monitored, of course, in case the prisoner attacked the lawyer, but they were taped in a way that the lips of the two people and any papers the lawyer might have were not visible.

She continued. "He would like to help you."

"How?"

"By getting you out of here."

"That's not going to be easy."

"Trust me. He's a man who does not shy away from a challenge."

Richard eyed her. "What does he want from me in return?"

"He wants you to finish something you started with a certain person who works here at the Bureau."

"And who is that?"

"Special Agent Patrick Bowers."

Silence. "Tell your employer I'm interested."

"I'll do that. In the meantime, I'm going to start reviewing your case files. Is there anything I can get for you?"

"A paper clip."

"A paper clip?"

He held up his shackled hands. "Yes."

She smiled faintly. "I think I can manage that. Are you sure you want to go about things that way?"

"I think it would save us both a lot of time. When do you think you can make it back in?"

"Well, there's no reason to wait. How about this evening? I have some things to take care of this afternoon. Let's say five thirty? I should be able to make it back by then."

"Perfect. I'll see you at five thirty."

61

I stepped through the front door of the Lab and was shocked when Director Wellington met me in the lobby.

"Agent Bowers. I've been waiting for you."

"What are you doing here?"

"This involves my brother. I want to know everything there is to know about how the investigation is going. I want answers, and I want them as soon as possible."

Well, if nothing else, she was direct.

How she'd learned that I'd called on Dr. Neubauer was a mystery to me, but she seemed to have her finger on the pulse of things, and for the time being I didn't ask her how she'd ended up here ahead of me.

There are three sets of elevators in the Lab—one for freight, one for people, and one that's dedicated solely to transporting evidence. It's just one of the precautions to make sure that evidence isn't tainted at all before it's examined here.

As we walked to the personnel elevator, I summarized my meeting with Agent Kantsos.

Margaret listened carefully. "Yes. I received your message about contacting PTPharmaceuticals concerning a recall. However, I agree with Agent Kantsos—there's not nearly enough evidence yet to do that. The Bureau's lawyers would never go for it. We need to at least wait for FDA's analysis of the drug."

Not a big surprise, but catching a break at this point would have been nice.

We left the elevator on the third floor and crossed the hallway toward Dr. Neubauer's lab.

When we arrived, he was bent over a Zeiss microscope studying a slide. The microscope was fitted with a video camera and projection screen so other people could see what was under the lens without having to peer through the scope. Right now a pollen was projected up there for us to see.

A copy of Ronald O. Kapp's book *Pollen and Spores* lay beside the microscope, numerous pages dog-eared and bookmarked.

Peering up from his work, he looked as surprised as I'd been to see Margaret here.

"Director?"

"Yes," she said simply. "What do we have?"

"I . . . Well . . ." Dr. Neubauer was a grizzled, slightly absentminded scientist who'd been working with the Bureau for decades. "I extracted the spores, and the flora of India is really quite unique and, of course, incredibly diverse—but thankfully, in that region of the world, we can look more at species than at the season. That helps us a lot. I didn't expect to see you here."

"I have a personal interest in this case." It was hard to tell if it was urgency or impatience in Margaret's words. "What have you learned?"

"The Birbal Sahni Institute of Palaeobotany is really

the leading research lab on pollen and flora in India. Dr. Bhatnagar was very helpful. We have some pretty conclusive results."

Margaret furrowed her eyebrows. "He was able to identify the pollen already?"

"Yes. When you know what you're looking for it's not that difficult. He named them almost immediately when I sent him the JPEGs of the grains I found."

"What did he say?" I asked.

"We are looking at the state of Andhra Pradesh."

He indicated toward a slew of slides on the countertop. "We find maize and rice, but that's to be expected—common all throughout central and south India. Some bajra, mango, ragi, and red chili, which would lead us to think the Hyderabad area, but also . . ."

Now he pulled up a slide on the microscope projection screen that, quite honestly, looked remarkably similar to the last one. "The *Cycas beddomei* is an endangered plant sometimes used for medicinal purposes. But it isn't found in Hyderabad. The only place in India that it's found is in the hills near Kadapa, northwest of Chennai, about two hundred and fifty miles south of Hyderabad."

He inserted another similar-looking slide. "We also found a rare plant known locally as sariba, the *Decalepis hamiltonii* that is also found in the hills around Kadapa. Also, *Acacia campelli*, and that's a plant that is—"

"Let me guess," Margaret interrupted, "found near Kadapa."

"Not just there, but only there. Yes. At between three hundred and seven hundred meters above sea level."

"So," she concluded, "we're looking for a facility in or near Kadapa, India."

He seemed a little let down that she'd reached his conclusion before he could state it. "It would appear so. Yes."

I already had my phone out. Agent Kantsos picked up on the second ring and I told him what Dr. Neubauer had found.

"Sounds reasonable. I've worked with the police in Andhra Pradesh. Bribes usually do the trick. I'll put some feelers out, see what I can dig up."

His words didn't exactly surprise me—in many countries around the world bribes are the only way to grease the bureaucratic wheels enough to get anything done. I wished it weren't that way, but it was the cost of doing business in the international community. Kantsos was up front and blunt about it and that much I appreciated. And he was experienced at working the system, which could play in our favor.

Margaret said, "I'll contact FDA and PTPharmaceuticals, put some pressure on them to get those results." She tapped the projection screen of Dr. Neubauer's microscope. "You were able to figure this out in just a few hours. They've had plenty of time to identify the chemical composition of those pills. It's time we get some answers."

We all agreed to keep each other updated, then Margaret left for DC and I returned to my office to see if I could dig up anything on Tyree.

I had an idea that just might lead us in the right direction.

Flight manifests.

62

After school Tessa picked up Lien-hua from Ralph and Brineesha's house and drove toward the shop in Alexandria where Lien-hua had seen the dress that she thought would be perfect for Tessa's prom.

+++

Back at her office at the J. Edgar Hoover Building, FBI Director Margaret Wellington hung up her phone a little more authoritatively than necessary.

She wasn't getting anywhere with the FDA analysts.

It was time to move up the food chain.

Her brother's death unnerved her deeply, not just the loss of life, but also the home invasion: by all appearances someone had slipped into his place and contributed in some way to his death.

Thinking about that, she couldn't help but remember what'd happened to her last summer. Her life hadn't been threatened directly, but very likely had been in danger.

And whenever she watched the DVD that a serial killer had left in her car—the footage of her sleeping in her bedroom—she wondered why he'd come into her home. Had he been planning to attack her? Was it all meant just to scare her later? And, of course, how many nights had he been there standing just a few feet away from her, watching her, filming her while she slept?

There was no conclusive proof that the man who'd killed the other women on the video was also the man who'd filmed her sleeping in her bedroom, but Margaret told herself that of course it was the same man. After all, who else could it have been?

But so far she hadn't been able to convince herself.

Not completely.

Ever since she first saw that video, she'd been trying to find some confirmation that the person who'd filmed it was the man she suspected—a serial killer, now dead, who referred to himself as the Illusionist. His partner, known by the name of her online identity, Astrid, was in prison and so far had refused to concede if she was present when the video was taken.

Last year after first seeing the video, Margaret had installed a dead-bolt lock on her bedroom door.

It was tragic: the Director of the FBI was a prisoner in her own home. One of the most powerful women in the worldwide law enforcement and counterterrorism community was afraid to go to sleep.

There are many kinds of prisons and many kinds of doors.

And although she didn't like to admit it to herself, she knew the truth—some of those doors never open. But here, today, with the probe into the suspicious suicide of her brother, was her chance to at last open one. Even if she couldn't solve her mystery, maybe she could solve his.

This man, Corporal Tyree, had left his prints on the medicine cabinet. But was he alone? And why was he in the house in the first place? And how did he know Corey?

So.

Up the food chain.

One more call should do it.

She contacted the FDA commissioner himself and related just how thrilled she was that his people were taking so long analyzing the pills that had been found in Montana.

"I'll be giving a press conference at five o'clock," she told him firmly, "and I'll either announce that our two agencies are working closely together on this, or that the FBI is investigating this case by itself without FDA's co-operation. Your choice."

+++

Since leaving the meeting with Margaret and Dr. Neubauer, I'd been on the Federal Digital Database searching airline flight manifests to and from Hyderabad and Chennai, the nearest international airports to Kadapa, to see if there was any record of Corporal Keith Tyree traveling through there.

So far, nothing.

Finally, figuring that I could work just as easily on my laptop at Ralph and Brineesha's house as I could here at my office desk, I left the Academy. If time and circumstances allowed, I thought I could let Lien-hua cater to her quirks later tonight and we could stream *Sleepless in Seattle*, so I picked up a bag of Fritos for her at a gas station.

A small way to celebrate her continued recovery.

Fortunately, at this time of day, traffic entering DC wasn't nearly as bad as the traffic leaving it, and I merged into the flow toward Ralph's house.

63

Tony answered when I rang the doorbell.

He had his mom's light chocolate skin color and his dad's build. A typical twelve-year-old boy, he was into soccer, skateboarding, and video games and thought that girls were gross—but if you pressed him, he'd admit that he "kind of" liked "some stuff" about them.

"Hello, Mr. Bowers." He was cordial and polite, admittedly more from the influence of his mother than his father.

"Hey, Tony."

He let me in and called over his shoulder, "Mom! It's Mr.—"

"Yes, I heard. I'll be right there." It sounded like she was in the first room off the hallway—what used to be Ralph's study but which was now being transformed into a nursery for their little girl, who was due in July.

I closed the front door. A duffel bag and a rolled-up camouflage sleeping bag sat next to it. "Sleepover tonight?" I asked Tony.

"I'm going over to Eric's."

"Nice."

Ralph's imposing seventy-two-inch wide-screen TV

dominated the west wall of his living room. He and Brineesha often let Tony invite his friends over to play video games on it, so the room was preteen boy–proof, with almost nothing fragile in it. An expansive leather couch and a matching recliner that no longer reclined faced the television.

I said to Tony, "Your dad tells me he's been improving at 'Call of Duty' lately."

Tony shrugged. "Sometimes I let him win. He gets moody when he loses too much."

I smiled. "Your secret's safe with me."

Brineesha rounded the corner. She had on one of Ralph's double-XL T-shirts and a pair of blue jeans overalls with the cuffs rolled up. With a paintbrush and splatters of pink on her cheeks and the backs of her hands, it wasn't hard to guess what she'd been doing.

"Hey, Brin."

"Good to see you, Pat." She held up the paintbrush. "Working on the nursery."

"How's it coming?"

"Good." She patted her tummy. "We should have everything ready in plenty of time." She had a proud mother's smile, and I was glad all over again that she and Ralph were expecting. She was showing, but with the overalls and oversize T-shirt on, it was hard to tell.

She invited me into the kitchen, asked if I wanted anything to eat or drink, and when I declined, told me that Lien-hua and Tessa had gone dress shopping and would hopefully be back within the hour.

"How did Lien-hua look? Was she feeling okay?"

"You need to stop mothering her and trust that she knows what she can handle."

"Just trying to be a good fiancée."

"A slightly overbearing one."

A concerned one, I thought, but said, "Okay, I hear you. By the way, did Tessa mention when Aiden was coming by to pick her up?"

"Six thirty. They're going out for supper with some friends. I don't think the prom officially starts until eight."

I looked unnecessarily at my watch and saw that it was already after four. "That's not going to give her a whole lot of time to get ready. Don't girls usually take—"

"You be careful now. Besides, you know Tessa—it shouldn't take her long at all. Lien-hua and I can help her."

"Do you know anything about this dress that Lien-hua was so keen on having her look at?"

Brin shook her head. "All I know is that it's black and strapless."

"Strapless?"

She looked at me evenly. "I'm sure it'll be fine."

"It's just that, strapless, I mean it's—"

"Really, Pat. You don't need to be so protective of the women in your life. Tessa told me how you like checking up on the boys she dates."

"Did she."

"Mm-hmm." Brin tilted her paintbrush at me scoldingly. "This is her special night. You be nice to that boy. Tessa likes him. Don't go embarrassing her."

"I won't." But I thought again of the call I'd put through to the school's public safety officer. I still hadn't heard back from him. "I want it to be her special night too," I told Brineesha honestly.

"And take lots of pictures. This is her first and only prom."

"Pictures. Got it."

Her gaze shifted to my computer bag. "We moved Ralph's desk to our bedroom, but feel free to go in there if you want to work until he gets here."

"The dining room table will be fine."

"Really, you're welcome to the desk. Our bedroom's not nearly as bad as yours."

"You've been talking to Ralph."

"He may have mentioned something. Is Tessa really afraid to go in there?"

I avoided that question. "The table will be great, Brin. Thanks."

"I need to finish up in the nursery; make yourself at home. You know the Internet code."

Through the doorway I saw Tony had turned on the TV and was pulling up a first-person shooter game I didn't recognize. It appeared to involve taking out some rather impressive-looking aliens.

Brin left for the nursery, and I set up shop at the dining room table to see what I could get done before Tessa and Lien-hua made it back home.

64

Providentially, Tessa found a parking spot just about across the street from the dress store. She helped Lien-hua out of the car and walked cautiously beside her as she crutched through the crosswalk to the store.

Inside, a smiling clerk who didn't look much older than Tessa bopped toward them. "Hello, welcome to Tirabelli's. And can I help you find a dress this afternoon?"

"Yes, thank you." Lien-hua's eyes were on the row of prom dresses along the back wall. "But I think I might already know what we're looking for."

The girl followed Lien-hua's gaze, then assessed Tessa up and looked at her slyly, as if the two of them were privy to some sort of secret. "A prom dress?"

"Yeah. It's tonight."

She blinked. "Your prom is tonight?"

"In like four hours. I figured I didn't want to wait until the last minute." She shared a look with Lien-hua.

"I see." The clerk tried to recover gracefully; obviously she was not used to having girls shop for dresses this close to their proms. "Well, step this way. Let's see what we can find for you."

The lineup of dresses was a little overwhelming to

Tessa, who usually shopped at thrift stores. Some of the skimpy ones reminded her of a pickup line she'd heard once in a movie: "Nice gownless evening strap you have there."

When she saw the price tags on some of the nicer dresses—actually, even the ones that weren't so impressive—she understood why she didn't shop at places like this.

"Um, Lien-hua, we should . . . I mean, these are way too—"

"It's okay." She found a chair and Tessa helped her as she lowered herself onto it.

"So." The girl beamed at Tessa. "What exactly are you looking for?"

Lien-hua pointed to one. "Let's start there. See if it's close to the right size."

Tessa lifted its hanger.

Black. Strapless. Satiny but not too shiny. It had lace that spread over the top of the fabric at the bottom and made Tessa think that it would make her look like she was covered in a smooth, black waterfall.

"I love it."

She held it up in front of her and it looked like it just might fit. She was afraid to look at the price tag.

"Oh, that'll look *just gorgeous* on you," Dress Shop Girl gushed. "With your eye color and your hair. It'll be *perfect*."

Tessa had never in her life consciously chosen something because it matched her eyes or her hair.

Lien-hua indicated toward the fitting rooms. "Try it on."

A few minutes later Tessa emerged wearing the dress. Thankfully, the saleslady had gone to help someone else who'd just walked in and only Lien-hua was there waiting to see her.

"How does it look?" Tessa asked nervously. In the fitting room she'd looked at the price. She couldn't remember ever trying on anything this expensive.

"This boy, Aiden, he's going to be blown away. Do you like it?"

"Yeah, but I'm telling you I can't afford this thing. We should probably—"

Lien-hua held up her hand. "I want to get it for you."

"No, it's too much. I'm serious. Especially for something I'm only going to wear once."

"Well, twice, at least."

"Twice?"

"The wedding."

"Oh, well, yeah. I guess. Sure."

Lien-hua looked satisfied. "Yes, I think this will be the perfect dress for my maid of honor."

A pause as that comment settled in. "Your what?"

"Full disclosure: I had ulterior motives bringing you here. Since last week I've been wanting to ask you to be my maid of honor."

Tessa was quiet. "I don't think I'm really maid-of-honor material."

"Why do you say that?"

"Well, first of all, I have no idea what a maid of honor is even supposed to do. I mean, just help make you look pretty? Believe me, I'm no expert at that." Then she realized how that might have sounded. "Not that you need anyone to . . . I mean—"

"I know what you're saying. But in any case, you do know how to make someone look pretty. Just look at you."

"I'm not pretty."

"You are. Very pretty."

Tessa said nothing.

Sure, Patrick told her she was pretty too, but he had to. He was her dad. The only time boys ever told her she was pretty was when . . . well, when they had ulterior motives of their own.

Lien-hua's just asking you to be the maid of honor because you're Patrick's daughter. She feels obligated to come to you. There's tons of other people she could ask instead.

"Well?" Lien-hua said.

"Um . . . Yeah, I'd be honored. Really, I would."

Lien-hua smiled, and after all she'd been through this week, it was nice to see. "So, what about this dress?"

"I'll pay you back. I promise."

"Let's not worry about that right now. Let's just get you ready for your big night."

65

The public safety officer called me back on my cell.

I stared at the screen for a moment before answering. Although I wanted to find out about Aiden Ryeson, I also knew Tessa might very well resent my checking up on him like this, if she found out.

The phone rang again.

If she found out.

The dad in me took over and I answered the phone.

"Agent Bowers here."

"Sir, this is Officer Ted Young from the school. I'm sorry I wasn't able to return your call earlier."

"That's alright."

"You phoned regarding Aiden Ryeson?"

I took a deep breath.

It's not too late, just tell him you don't need the information after all.

But then the counterargument: *No, Pat, this is about your daughter. She has a history of going out with boys who have a violent streak. Remember San Diego? Remember what happened out there?*

"Yes," I said.

"Well, he's a good kid. Never any problems from my

end. I called his track coach and he hasn't had any issues with him either. Good grades, no detentions." He paused and then added, "Anything I need to know?"

"No," I told him. "I appreciate your time."

We ended the call, and I slowly lowered the phone.

While Officer Young's information reassured me, I seemed to feel worse than I did before I'd spoken with him.

I was sorting through my feelings about the whole thing when an e-mail came in, forwarded to me from Margaret.

The results of the chemical analysis of the pills.

Both FDA and PTPharmaceuticals confirmed it—the pills we'd found in Montana were counterfeit versions of Calydrole.

And they were remarkably good ones—the packaging, the imprinting on the pills, the shape, color, size, everything looked legitimate, and even a cursory chemical analysis established that the active ingredient of Calydrole was present, not in the right dose, but with enough of it present to avoid initial detection that the pills were counterfeits.

But there was something else there too: a neurostimulator most commonly known as Proxictal.

Evidently, it wasn't possible to tell from the analysis they'd done so far, but taken in conjunction with the active ingredient in Calydrole, the Proxictal could very likely contribute to the disorganized cognition and downward-spiraling thought process that led some people to consider taking their own lives.

The FDA proposed that if this pill were taken for seven to ten days the effect could be "exaggerated."

An excipient is the inactive substance in medication that helps deliver the active ingredient, and not only was the active ingredient found in the wrong amount, but the excipient was one that helped deliver the Proxictal rather than Calydrole.

The combination of chemicals that constituted this drug made it appear that it had been designed for one purpose: to make depressed people seriously consider suicide.

However, despite all of that, remarkably, PTPharmaceuticals was holding out on recalling Calydrole or warning consumers about the tainted versions of the drug that were evidently already on the market.

They said that it was because there was no evidence yet that this wasn't just an isolated case, since only one pack had been found to contain the counterfeit drug. But the real reason wasn't all that hard to deduce. Making an announcement like that, recalling their number one pharmaceutical product, would be devastating to their stock prices. Market shares would drop. They could lose millions on Monday alone when the markets opened again.

According to the e-mail, however, Margaret had convinced the FDA to put out a public health warning, and they were going to release the details at a joint five-o'clock press conference.

I'd just gone back to my notes when I got a call from Agent Kantsos.

Things were finally starting to come together.

He found out that two local businessmen in Kadapa had been admitted to the hospital last week with "grievous injuries including amputations of several of their extremities." After quoting the person he'd spoken with, Kantsos added, "One of the men was missing both ears."

"You're kidding."

"No. They're not giving anything up and there's no indication yet who did this to them. According to the local authorities the men were terrified of what would happen to them if they did."

I thought of the amorphous connection to Valkyrie and what they'd already been through. "I can understand why."

Through a couple of factory workers in the area, the police had, however, located a business site in Kadapa where the two men worked.

"The place was cleared out when they inspected it," Kantsos told me, "but there was evidence that pharmaceuticals may have been manufactured there until very recently. That's how they put it, 'may have been.' But they're just hedging their bets. It looks like we found our facility."

I wondered how much this information had cost Kantsos—well, the taxpayers, that is.

He explained that ICE wanted to be involved, and he was trying to navigate through the convoluted maze of overlapping jurisdictions.

"Talk to FBI Director Wellington," I told him. "I have a feeling she'll do everything she can to help move things along."

"Because of Corey."

"Yes."

I remembered the red-haired woman in the photo of Tyree. "Any chance those workers in Kadapa can remember if a couple had visited the plant? I'm guessing that a red-haired Caucasian woman would be memorable."

"I'll see what I can find out."

I gave him Margaret's cell number and a few moments after I ended the call, a car cruised up the driveway and Tony shouted to his mother that Eric and his mom were here.

After Brin had given him a few motherly instructions about how late he was allowed to stay up and how he needed to listen to Eric's mom just like he would listen to her, he grabbed his sleeping bag and duffel bag and was out the door.

He left the video game paused mid-alien-explosion from a rather nice shot across an expansive crater.

Tessa and Lien-hua were a little later getting back from the dress shop than we'd expected and they entered the basement through the lower-level entryway before I could greet them or take a look at their purchase.

Ralph arrived home, and with Tony gone and Lien-hua and Brineesha downstairs helping Tessa get ready for prom, he and I had the living room to ourselves.

He was eyeing the television screen and looked like he was ready to pick up the game where his son had left off.

"That was a good shot," he muttered.

"How's that scratch on your arm?" I asked, pointing to the bandages covering the pit bull bite.

"It's fine. I can hardly feel it."

"You're as bad a liar as I am."

"I'll take that as a compliment. I think."

He bypassed the video game, and at five we watched the press conference with Margaret and the FDA commissioner.

They announced that the two agencies, by working in close conjunction with each other, had identified a potential national health threat and were calling for the recall of Calydrole, after "tainted samples of the drug were found in the national pharmaceutical supply chain."

Ralph shook his head. "PTPharmaceuticals isn't going to be too happy about that."

"Neither is someone else."

"Whoever designed this drug."

"And smuggled it in from India. That's right."

When the press conference was over, Ralph shifted topics. "So that boy is picking Tessa up at six?"

"Six thirty."

"That gives us just about an hour. Let's see if we can dig up anything else on whether or not Valkyrie is behind this by the time that kid arrives."

I took a moment to evaluate things. "Earlier, I was looking into flight manifests, but let's try a different angle and check to see if the airports in Chennai and Hyderabad have any security cameras that might have recorded Tyree checking in or boarding a flight. And also, look more closely at his military record, see if we can find anything that might connect him to Valkyrie."

"Good call. I'll take his military background, you look into the surveillance footage."

We pulled out our computers, but as we got to work I couldn't help but think of Aiden and how Officer Young had nothing but good things to say about him. Calling in for the information still didn't sit right with me. I'd done the very thing Tessa asked me not to do, even though I'd done it because I loved her.

I felt trapped. Had I not made the call to Young, and Aiden had turned out to be a bad kid, I never would have forgiven myself, but now that I'd checked up on him, I felt guilty about it. A catch-22.

I wondered once again if I should say anything to my daughter about it.

And I decided I would not.

+++

As Vanessa brushed her hand across the table, she let the paper clip she'd brought with her slide out from under her fingers. It passed across the table and Richard covered it with his own hand.

"The rest is up to you," she said.

"Yes."

"We're on the level below the FBI Headquarters' underground parking garage. It's not going to be easy getting out of here."

"What can you tell me about the number of agents out there?"

She informed him where agents were stationed, which hallways would take him to the parking garage, and the best route to the elevator.

"That's pretty specific. Are you sure?"

"Yes. I'm a rather observant woman."

"I'm glad to hear that. And you said earlier that your employer would like to meet me?"

"He would."

"How about later tonight? At ten?"

"Will that be enough time?"

"If what you just told me is accurate, I believe it will."

"It was accurate."

"Then tell him I'll see him at ten."

She gave Richard an address and a phone number to call to confirm things if he really was able to get out, then she left him alone with his paper clip.

66

Less than fifteen minutes ago on the television in his hotel suite, Valkyrie had watched the press conference finish up.

Since then he'd been considering his options.

Seventy thousand counterfeit Calydrole pills were about to arrive at the distribution warehouse across town. If the drug was recalled, those pills wouldn't be shipped out from there at all.

The FBI and FDA must have gotten their hands on some of the initial samples, the ones Keith and Vanessa had been using on the test subjects.

How, Valkyrie wasn't sure. But that wasn't what mattered most right now.

Yes, PTPharmaceuticals' stock prices would still drop when the markets opened on Monday, but he wasn't sure if he would be able to sell his options for anywhere near the profit he'd been expecting.

Vanessa and Keith had just become loose ends.

Valkyrie called her and told her that he wanted to chat with the two of them. He caught her right after she'd left her consultation with Basque.

"How did that go?"

"It went well. He's planning on meeting you tonight at ten. I told him where you'd be."

"Tonight? He's that confident?"

"It appears that he is."

Valkyrie explained that he wanted to see her and Keith at the distribution warehouse at eight thirty.

He would take care of them right after connecting with the Chechens at seven thirty on the yacht.

A busy night.

"Is there a problem?" Vanessa asked him.

"There's a state of affairs I would like to discuss with you." He decided that if she hadn't already heard about what was going on with the drug recall, the odds were pretty good she would hear about it by the time of their meeting, so he summarized the press conference to her.

"I'm not sure how that could have happened," she muttered. "How they could have gotten samples, found out about them."

"We'll discuss it at eight thirty. Park behind the warehouse, by the freight loading docks."

"Alright. We'll be there."

+++

When Vanessa informed Keith that Valkyrie was here in the city, and that he wanted to see them tonight, he knew something was wrong, very wrong.

"A state of affairs," Vanessa told him, that's how Valkyrie had put it. She didn't elaborate, but Keith got the sense that she knew more than she was telling him.

His heart squirmed into a tight knot.

Meeting with Valkyrie in person was rare, and there were no guarantees that you wouldn't leave the room in plastic baggies.

"And he didn't specifically say why he wanted to meet?"

"He did not."

Keith had worked with her long enough to know when she was not being completely forthcoming with him. And if she was lying to him right now, that meant the "state of affairs" was probably a worst-case scenario.

If they were supposed to meet Valkyrie at eight thirty, that gave him just over two and a half hours.

There were some things Keith definitely needed to think through.

He could try to run, but Valkyrie would find him.

He could meet with Valkyrie, but if the man was disappointed in Keith and Vanessa, that was not going to turn out well at all.

However.

There was one other option, a way that he might never have to fear—or work for—Valkyrie ever again.

According to what Vanessa had just told him, he knew where their employer was going to be and when he was going to be there.

It was a risk, yes, of course, but what were the options?

Run and die. Meet with Valkyrie and discuss a "state of affairs" and very likely end up dead.

Or . . .

He evaluated everything. The FBI would almost certainly have an anonymous hotline, a way of keeping the identity of the caller secret, but what if they didn't? What if there was a way for them to find out who it really was?

Still, of all the options, that was probably his best bet. Off the top of his head Keith didn't know how much of a reward they would be offering, but it had to be in the millions.

He might make out with the money and with his free-dom, but even if he didn't, he would fare much better falling into the FBI's hands than into Valkyrie's.

Keith decided what he was going to do.

But he would need to be alone—somewhere away from Vanessa—to make the call.

67

Brineesha finished winding the red ribbon into Tessa's hair and carefully tied it off.

They were in the basement bedroom; Tessa stood in front of the dresser mirror with Brineesha beside her. Lien-hua rested on the bed, leaning against a pile of pillows, her crutches angled against the wall. Two elegant flower arrangements sat on a bedside end table.

Since coming back from the dress shop Tessa had been getting more and more anxious that Aiden wouldn't think she was pretty at all, no matter what Brineesha did with her hair.

She was fretting about that when Brin mentioned how impressed she was with Lien-hua's recovery so far.

"I guess God's not done with me yet," Lien-hua said softly.

Brineesha made eye contact with Tessa and winked.

"What is it?" Lien-hua eyed them curiously.

Brineesha answered, "On the night you were attacked, when we were all at the hospital, Tessa mentioned to me that she was praying for you."

"You were praying for me?"

"Yeah." Tessa couldn't help but think of her mom, when she was dying, how prayer hadn't helped at all that time around.

"That means a lot."

Unsure how to respond, she simply said, "Okay."

"Well"—Brineesha fussed with Tessa's hair—"you told me that you didn't know if God was listening to your prayers. Remember?"

Yes, and you told me how Tony was premature and how you'd prayed for him and nothing happened, Tessa thought, but didn't say it; she didn't really want to be talking about any of this at all, it only made her think of losing her mom, and that wasn't what she needed right now. "I remember," she told Brineesha. "What do you think? Is my hair gonna be okay?"

But even though Tessa was trying not to think about the inscrutable nature of prayers—answered or unanswered—she couldn't help but recall her speech ideas, the things she'd been considering saying: If God wasn't there, if there was just a vast, sweeping, empty universe, then prayer wouldn't mean anything at all.

Meaningless, meaningless, all is meaningless.

But if God is there and he really does care about his hurting, questioning race of dreamers and fools, then praying would matter—even if it didn't happen on their time frame or in the ways they expected or wanted.

After all, if we could understand God, then his wisdom would have to be equal to or smaller than ours, and that was logically impossible if he's all-knowing and we aren't. The very definition of God required that people would be unable to understand his ways.

Your mom never gave up on believing, even when it didn't seem to be helping her at all.

"I guess prayer is sort of a rune," Tessa said.

Brineesha finished up with the hairbrush and set it down. "A rune?"

"A mystery."

"I think maybe that's not so bad," Lien-hua reflected.

"No. Maybe it's not."

Brin patted Tessa's shoulder. "You look fantastic, dear."

Tessa stared at herself in the mirror and said nothing, because deep down she was trying to convince herself that what she'd just heard was right.

Then Brineesha gave her a small spray bottle of perfume to take with her and Tessa slipped it into the red clutch purse she was going to use for the night.

+++

We were discovering that the airports in India didn't have the level of video surveillance we needed.

Working with Angela and Lacey, I reviewed the footage, while Ralph compared Tyree's military assignments with the known terrorist activity that Alexei Chekov, now known as Valkyrie, had been involved with at the time of Tyree's service, seeing if there was any overlap.

But so far none of us had made any progress.

While Ralph and I were contemplating what to look into next, Kantsos called me back and told me one of the factory workers in Kadapa remembered seeing a "trim and fit" young man and a red-haired woman at the facility.

I contacted the other two agents whom Margaret had assigned to this case and told them what Kantsos had learned. "We need to identify that woman in the photo with Tyree. Cybercrime came up empty on a facial match, so let's try a different tack. Contact Corey Wellington's and Natalie Germaine's neighbors. See if any of them might have seen this red-haired woman or Tyree in the vicinity in the days leading up to the suicides."

It seemed like a long shot and I knew it would likely keep the agents busy for a while, but I was running out of ideas.

I went back to work, but it wasn't long before Ralph mumbled, "I might have something." He rotated his computer so I could see the photos he'd pulled up of the macabre carnage left in the wake of a suicide bombing in Afghanistan. "There's a covert assignment that Tyree had in Kandahar two months before his contract expired. That same week there was a bombing during a funeral in Kandahar."

I calculated. That would have been after Chekov left the GRU. "Valkyrie."

"It was never verified for certain, but yes, it does look like he was behind it."

I thought things through. "So where does that leave us? Valkyrie connects with Tyree in Kandahar. Maybe Tyree is involved in this bombing, or maybe he isn't, but either way, Valkyrie somehow recruits him and then orchestrates this counterfeit drug operation, using Tyree as his muscle at the facility?"

Ralph was tracking with me. "For whatever reason, Tyree tortures these two guys, puts 'em in the hospital—apparently working with this unknown woman. I don't care if you're into motives or not, Pat, but why would they get this drug to Margaret's brother, to Natalie Germaine, and then try to cover it up?"

I shook my head. "I don't know. But I'll be honest, I can't help but think that Valkyrie might have coordinated it simply because he could, simply to show that he could get to the family members of a congressman and the FBI Director. It fits the profile Lien-hua drew up on him last winter."

"To prove that he's untouchable." Ralph nodded. "To show that he can do what he wants, when he wants, to whoever he wants."

"We should get Lien-hua's take on this." I rose.

"Hang on, buddy." He grabbed my elbow. "I'll go fill her in. You sit down. You're the dad. You're not supposed to see your daughter until she's all ready for her prom."

"How do you know that? You only have a son and he's not even out of middle school yet."

"Brineesha tells me these things. Stay here. I'll be right back."

68

A few minutes later, though, it was Brineesha, not Ralph, who ascended the stairs. "You should go talk with your daughter. Encourage her. She's really nervous. She doesn't think she's pretty."

"She said that?"

"Not in so many words. But there are other ways people communicate. Especially girls."

"And she wants me to talk to her?"

"She needs you to. Lien-hua and I have been telling her that she looks fine, but it might mean more coming from her dad. You know how important this night is to her. Go on. That boy is going to be here in just a couple minutes."

Downstairs, I found Tessa standing on the edge of the living room beside the open bathroom door, eyeing herself uncertainly in the mirror. A clutter of makeup paraphernalia lay spread across the bathroom sink's counter.

Lien-hua and Ralph were in the bedroom, presumably so Tessa wouldn't hear them conferring about the case. Ralph's dumbbells and weight sets had been pushed to the side of the living room to make room for Lien-hua to stay down here.

One glance at Tessa and I knew my daughter had nothing to worry about. She looked amazing. Maybe too good. I remember being a teenage guy. I remember how they think.

"Hey, Tessa."

"Hey."

As it turned out, Lien-hua had great taste and the dress accentuated Tessa's figure without being too tight or seductive. It reached the floor and I wouldn't have seen her red Converse shoes if she hadn't been fluffing the dress to the side, trying to see what it looked like at different angles.

The black raven tattoo curling around her left upper arm served to gently accent the dark allure of the dress.

Her right arm bore the line of straight scars from her cutting days, but she'd become used to them and, for the most part, seemed to accept them as simply another part of her life's story.

She wore her hair pulled back into a loose bun with a single crimson ribbon woven into it, and had on her typical black fingernail polish and dark eyeliner. A leather clutch purse that I hadn't seen before sat on the edge of the couch. It matched the color of the ribbon. I guessed she and Lien-hua must have picked it up while they were dress shopping.

"You look great," I told my daughter. "Really. I'm not just saying that. The other girls at the dance are going to be blown away."

"Huh," she scoffed. "I doubt that."

"Don't."

She was cute, no, way beyond cute.

Elusive, mysterious, gorgeous.

She's beautiful. Your daughter is beautiful.

Man, this guy Aiden better treat her right.

She hesitated, studied her hair in the mirror. "I don't know if I should wear it like this. You think it's okay? Really?"

To put it mildly, Tessa was not one to worry about how she looked, and seeing her so concerned about it right now just underscored to me how much this boy meant to her.

I put my hand lightly on her arm to reassure her. "I know you're going to have a great time. You're very pretty. Your mom would be proud to see you tonight."

At last she turned from the mirror and looked at me directly. "I need to tell you something, Patrick."

"What's that?"

"I know I've always been sort of weird about boys— never really hooking up with, well, the best guys in the universe. You know what I mean."

"There've been a few times, yes."

"Anyway, Aiden's different. I really like him. And I just wanted to say thanks."

"Thanks?"

"For trusting me."

"For trusting you."

"I mean, last week we were talking about guys. Remember? At the picnic? And I told you how I didn't like it when you met them at the door and scared them off or checked up on 'em or intimidated 'em, or anything like that. Thanks for trusting me with Aiden, for not probing or asking me all about him, things like that. It means a lot."

An uncomfortable itch began at the back of my neck and crawled down my back.

She leaned up on her toes and gave me a light kiss on the cheek. "Mom would be proud of you too."

That did it.

"Listen, Tessa, there's something I should probably . . ."

Upstairs, the doorbell rang.

"Oh, that's him." Her eyes grew large. Nervous. Excited. "What is it? What were you gonna say?"

"Hey, listen, I'll tell you later. Why don't you head—"

"No, don't do that. You know I hate it."

"Do what?"

"Bring up something and then tell me we'll talk about it later. Tell me now or else you know how much it'll bug me and I don't want that. Not tonight."

I heard Brineesha answer the door and invite Aiden into the living room. Her words were faint, but I could just make them out: "You must be Aiden. Tessa's been looking forward to seeing you. She'll be right up."

"In this case, Tessa, I think it might be—"

She placed her hands on my shoulders. "What is it, Dad? I need to get up there."

"I did."

"You did what?"

"Check up on him."

She lowered her hands slowly. "What does that mean: you checked up on him?"

"I called the school's safety officer. Just because I love you and I was—"

"You what? You called the cops to check up on Aiden?"

"No, well, I mean . . . the safety officer—"

"Just say what he is. He's a cop."

"Aiden seems like a great kid. I wasn't even going to bring it up but—"

"You knew how I feel about that." Something deeper than disappointment crossed her face. "I told you."

I almost wished she would slap me or sling her hands to her hips and yell at me, anything like that, but she didn't. Instead, the look of affection she'd had for me just moments ago had evaporated, and all I saw on her face was a look of betrayal instead.

"I'm sorry, I wasn't trying to hurt you or anything."

"That's not the point." She shook her head fiercely. "The point is, you didn't trust me."

"No, I do trust you. It's just—"

"Tessa!" Brineesha called cheerily from upstairs. "Aiden's here."

Now my daughter's anger became evident. She snatched up her purse, but the top was open and her lighter and a pack of cigarettes tipped out.

Before I could say anything, she blurted, "Do not even go there. I know how you feel, okay?" She held her hand up, palm toward me. "Just don't."

She retrieved the lighter and the cigarettes, then stood, her eyes showing a mixture of fire and pain. "If you would have asked me I could've told you he was a great kid." Her words bruised the air between us. "You didn't have to call the cops."

"I'm sorry, I—"

She whirled away up the stairs.

As she disappeared, Ralph poked his head out the doorway of the room where he and Lien-hua had been consulting with each other. He rubbed his forehead in empathy.

Lien-hua gently called me over to the door, and when I got there she urged me to go and talk to Tessa.

"I'm pretty sure she doesn't want to talk right now."

"Then just tell her you love her. Don't let her night start out like this. Tell her that much, trust me. She needs to hear it."

I sensed she was right and hurried up the stairs to try to catch Tessa before she met up with her date.

69

I was too slow.

By the time I got upstairs she was standing shyly in front of Aiden. Brineesha had stepped away to give them some space.

This was the first time I'd seen him: Caucasian. Medium build. Tousled blond hair. Athletic. He was wearing a lightly starched tux. He appeared as nervous as my daughter.

Actually, that was a little reassuring. Nervous was good.

He held a red rose corsage for Tessa's wrist. It had black lace and either he'd somehow found out what color ribbon and dress she'd be wearing, or he'd guessed right, because it would match her outfit perfectly.

"Hey," Tessa said to him.

"Hey. You look really great." His eyes glanced across the scars on her forearm, but didn't linger.

She stared demurely at her feet. "Thanks."

"Hello, Aiden." I held out my hand to him. "I'm Tessa's father."

"Hello, Mr. Ellis." It was natural for him to assume I shared Tessa's last name, and I didn't correct him.

He shook my hand. A strong grip.

Tessa was avoiding eye contact with me.

They both stood there awkwardly and I knew it wasn't the right time to pull Tessa aside to talk to her, even if it would be to simply tell her that I loved her. "She needs to be home by midnight, Aiden."

"Yes, sir."

He fumbled with the corsage as she lifted her left wrist. He slid it carefully over her hand, then, like a gentleman, he held out his arm to her and she took it in hers.

"Back by midnight," I reminded them both, at a loss for what else to say.

"Yes, Mr. Ellis."

"Have fun."

Tessa said nothing.

I got the sense that anything else I said right now was only going to embarrass her, especially telling her here in front of Aiden that I loved her. And embarrassing her was the last thing I wanted to do.

As he opened the door, she finally spoke to me and said stiffly, "Good-bye, Dad."

"Good-bye, Tessa," I told her.

Only when she was gone did I realize that I hadn't taken any pictures of my daughter and her date.

70

Aiden started the car and pulled onto the street.

Despite how glad Tessa was to be here and the tinge of electricity that still rippled through her from when Aiden had brushed his hand across hers when he slid the corsage onto her wrist, she couldn't leave the deal with her dad behind.

Even after all this time Patrick didn't trust her judgment.

Of course he doesn't trust you. You told him yourself you don't have a good track record of finding respectable guys.

"I like your tattoo." Aiden drew her out of her thoughts. He was glancing at the raven on her left arm. "It's way cool."

She couldn't help but think back to the trip to San Diego when she got it. The guy who owned the tattoo studio had tried to sexually assault her. "Yeah, it's got quite a story behind it. I'll have to tell you sometime." Now was definitely not the right time.

"Okay. Cool." A pause. "I never saw your scars before."

"I usually wear long sleeves."

"Right." Another pause. "So, did it hurt? I mean when you . . . ?"

"Cut myself."

"Yeah. When you cut yourself."

"Yes. But it hurt worse when I didn't do it. I don't know if that makes any sense." By Aiden's expression Tessa couldn't tell if he understood or not. "I had a lot going on in my life." She wasn't sure she should tell him the rest, but she did anyway. "My mom died."

"Man, I'm sorry."

"It was a couple years ago. I'm doing better."

She thought about how she would have cut tonight, feeling like this, if it was a year ago.

"I'm glad you're feeling better."

"Thanks." She felt like she could really use a smoke but didn't want to light up in Aiden's car.

They drove for a few minutes. She wished he would take her hand, maybe put his hand on her knee, but he didn't.

"Hey, listen, can you check my cell?" He indicated toward his phone, which lay between the seats. "See if Melody texted us yet? If they're at the restaurant?"

"Sure. Yeah."

She checked the texts and saw that the other two couples were already there. "I'll let 'em know we're on our way." Without having to look at the phone she tapped at the buttons to send the text, and her thoughts returned to Patrick and how he'd gone behind her back and checked up on Aiden.

Because he didn't trust her.

He doesn't trust you because you don't deserve it.

It's not Patrick's deal, it's yours.

The words ripped through her, ruined her, crushed her. Because she knew how true they were.

71

Looking concerned, Brineesha joined me by the door. "Something happened downstairs, didn't it?"

"I said something I shouldn't have," I told her simply, then returned to the basement to talk about the case and to try to distract myself from thinking about what had just happened with my daughter.

Lien-hua was on the couch. Ralph loomed near the doorway to the bedroom.

"Let's not talk about it," I said. "I feel bad enough already."

At first neither of them spoke, then Lien-hua tried her hand at reassuring me. "Brin and I got some good pictures of her."

"Good."

"By the way, when we were at the dress store I asked Tessa to be my maid of honor."

"Really? What did she say?"

"She said yes."

"That was sweet of you to ask her."

"It only made sense."

The conversation petered out.

Ralph cleared his throat. "Hey, I was thinking I might

throw in some pizzas for supper. What do you prefer—pepperoni, or pepperoni?"

"Pepperoni," I said.

"I'll take pepperoni," Lien-hua told him.

"Good choice. Let me grab a couple pies. I'll be right back."

When he'd left, Lien-hua said, "Pat, you need to hear this: if I were Tessa I probably would have felt offended too."

"I'm her dad, Lien-hua. It's not easy to know when to pull back."

I really didn't want this to slip into an argument, but thankfully, after a brief pause she said, "She's a resilient girl. Don't worry. I'm sure she's going to have a great time."

"I sure hope so."

When Lien-hua went on, she did what I was hoping and left the topic of my clash with Tessa alone. "So, about the case. Ralph told me what you were thinking, that Valkyrie might have gone after family members of high-profile government officials just to prove he could. I agree, though I think it might also grow from his past involvement in the GRU. Possibly to make a statement to them, to show he's able to do on his own more than they're able to do as a group."

Despite the fact that we were talking about motives, I had to agree that what she was hypothesizing did make sense, especially considering who the victims were.

"Ralph mentioned your search for video footage at the airports in India. It got me thinking. Tyree and this woman were in Atlanta last week when he left his prints at Corey Wellington's apartment. Then he showed up in Kadapa over the weekend to torture those two men."

I could see where she was going with this. "Security cameras at the Atlanta airport. Since Corey's house is in Atlanta, it would make sense that they would've flown out of there."

"It's the world's busiest airport, has the most extensive security presence of any airport on the planet. If anyone had the cameras to catch the two of them on tape, they would."

"Right," I said. "And then we can use facial recognition. Maybe catch the two of them checking in or boarding a flight, figure out what names they're traveling under."

"But," she acknowledged, "even with Lacey working on that, it might take a while."

"Well"—I was already dialing Angela's number—"then let's get things rolling."

72

Overall, supper was a disaster.

Tessa felt so unnatural and gauche in the new dress, and she didn't really know what to say during the meal with the two other couples. Melody's boyfriend kept asking her what she was going to talk about at graduation next month, and she wasn't about to bring up death and oblivion and meaninglessness, not right before prom. So she did her best to change the subject.

Both of the other couples had been together for a while, and since this was the first time she'd ever gone out with Aiden, that just made things even more uncomfortable.

It wasn't her crowd either—admittedly, she didn't really have a crowd, but everyone else at the table wanted to talk about baseball or track and knew all about pop music and the current viral videos on YouTube and what to laugh at and what not to. Tessa appreciated that Melody was trying to reach out to her, trying to include her, but it wasn't really working.

Not to mention how distracted she was—thinking about her argument with Patrick, and how nervous she was about being here with Aiden.

She kept floundering for what to say, and when she did say anything it just seemed to come out wrong or make her seem like a complete idiot.

But the worst thing of all was the server at a nearby table.

Tymber Dotson.

The girl Aiden had been dating until a month ago.

She wore a perky little skirt and moved in a way that showed she knew what guys like.

So why did Aiden choose to come here if he knew Tymber was waiting tables tonight? He had to have known. It didn't sit right with Tessa.

Not at all.

Even though Tymber was supposed to be serving this older couple at the other table, she couldn't seem to keep her eyes off Aiden, and although he was still being polite and nice and everything to Tessa, she saw his eyes wander in Tymber's direction way more often than necessary.

+++

Lacey was able to find Tyree and the unidentified woman on the security footage at Hartsfield-Jackson Atlanta International Airport last Thursday morning boarding a flight to Frankfurt. From there they continued on to Chennai.

By analyzing the names of the other passengers on their flight, we figured out the aliases that our two suspects were flying under: Caleb Hayes and Deborah Moss.

The two names brought up a complete electronic footprint with no hiccups or run-ins with the law.

If they were working with Valkyrie, as it appeared they were, I wasn't surprised at all that he'd set them up with comprehensive false identities.

But now that we had the names they were using, we could track their movements.

When we ran everything through the system, we found out that the two of them had flown from Chennai to Logan International earlier this week, and then flown down here to DC this morning.

Lien-hua and I had finished our pizza but Ralph had thrown in another one and was working his way through the third pie by himself. "Why Logan?" he asked, wiping pizza sauce from his chin.

"Let's take a closer look at the timing and location," I said.

"Timing and location." Now he had his mouth full. "Imagine Pat suggesting something like that."

I found a notepad and drew a timeline as I talked things through. "Last week Thursday, Corey Wellington is killed. As far as we can tell, Tyree removes something from his medicine cabinet."

"Probably Corey's meds," Lien-hua inserted.

"Yes. Then he and this woman we know as Deborah Moss fly to Chennai, travel from there to Kadapa, torture these two men, then return promptly to the States."

"And someone clears out the facility where they were manufacturing the drugs." Ralph finished off his last piece. Chased it down with a long guzzle of Mountain Dew.

"Right. We don't know who that might have been, but we do know something else about these drugs."

"The lot number," Lien-hua said.

"Right. If we can identify the distribution services that PTPharmaceuticals uses to transport their drugs from India to the States to move them into our supply chain, we should be able to find out if any of their planes—"

"Land in Boston," she finished my thought.

"Exactly."

"Or DC," Ralph added.

It was after business hours and we weren't able to reach anyone from the pharmaceutical company, so Lien-hua hopped online to see what she could dig up.

"I'll put an attempt to locate on Caleb Hayes and Deborah Moss," Ralph announced. "They might still be in the DC area."

I had an idea. "Try this: They flew into Dulles; they might have rented a car from there. If they did, we can have Metro start looking for their rental car—or, if it has GPS, locate it through the rental company. Also, have some agents find out if the two of them have checked into any hotels in the DC area."

"I like the way you think," Ralph replied, quoting the words I'd said to him earlier in the week.

I followed suit: "I've been working with you for a decade. 'Bout time you took note of that."

"Funny how it just occurred to me."

"Uh-huh."

We split up the calls between us and got started.

73

Valkyrie stood quietly, hands clasped behind his back, watching Alhazur and his two men board the yacht.

Alhazur's two hulking freedom fighters were wearing jackets that seemed a little too bulky for the cool spring evening. One man's face looked like it was molded out of old clay. The other was an enormous, steel-fisted human wrecking ball. Alhazur himself was a broad-shouldered, densely muscled man with a chiseled jaw and hollow eyes.

Once the three men were on board, they gathered in a small semicircle around Valkyrie. He was on good terms with Alhazur, but there was no doubt that encircling him was an intimidation technique.

Valkyrie was not intimidated.

"I would like you to take off your coats," he instructed the two men who flanked him.

"We're comfortable as is," Clay Face said with more antagonism than necessary.

"I'm afraid that to be comfortable, you have to be alive."

As a flicker of revelation crossed the man's face, Valkyrie made his move.

He was quick and before either man could respond, he'd grabbed the guy's head, snapped his neck, and had his own gun drawn and aimed at Alhazur's forehead before the dead soldier's body even landed on the deck of the boat.

"Kindly remove your jacket," Valkyrie said to the other man. "Do it slowly. I wouldn't want to get anxious with my finger on the trigger here."

"Take it off," Alhazur commanded his man. He was trying to sound unaffected, but Valkyrie heard concern beneath his words. Alhazur may have recruited, trained, and coordinated suicide bombers, but he did not want to make the ultimate sacrifice for his cause—at least not needlessly, at least not tonight.

The man to Valkyrie's right unzipped his jacket. Slipped it off.

Yes, he wore a suicide vest.

Valkyrie knew that style of vest, had organized five attacks with similar ones in the Middle East with suicide bombers of his own. These vests could either be detonated by the suicide bomber himself with a handheld trigger mechanism, or remotely by a cell phone that dialed directly to that vest—and only to that vest.

There was always one dedicated phone for each vest. It wasn't just the number you called, the detonation also depended on the actual phone you used. That was very important. Otherwise, you might have someone else accidentally dialing a wrong number and setting off the bomb prematurely. And that would be inconvenient for everyone involved.

"Hand me the detonator." Valkyrie's voice was soft but firm.

Alhazur nodded for the man to comply and he gave Valkyrie the handheld trigger.

"Before we carry on our discussion any further," Valkyrie said to Alhazur, "there is one thing I am going to require."

"What's that?"

He nodded toward the soldier. "The mobile phones for both vests."

"Why?"

"Call it insurance."

"Do you want me to take my vest off?" the man beside Alhazur asked gruffly.

"No. Keep it on."

He looked suddenly uneasy. "Why?"

"Insurance." Valkyrie tossed the detonator off the side of the boat into the Potomac. "The phones." He leveled the gun at Alhazur's head. "I'm a relatively patient man, but I don't like to repeat myself."

Alhazur reached for the pocket of his windbreaker for the phones. "Slowly," Valkyrie warned. "I'll still make my money if you're dead."

The two cells were nearly identical but each had a unique set of numbers engraved on the back that corresponded to the identification number imprinted on the front of each of the vests.

Valkyrie placed the phones on the console beside him, out of reach of the two men, and carefully noted which phone would set off which vest. He got the keys to the SUV from Alhazur and evaluated how to proceed.

"Alright," Alhazur said, still trying unsuccessfully to sound self-assured. "Let's discuss the next step. I heard the news about the proposed Calydrole recall. Where exactly does that leave us?"

Valkyrie gestured toward some nearby deck chairs. "Let's talk about that."

+++

We were having a hard time finding out which companies PTPharmaceuticals used to ship their drugs in from India.

But we did find out that Avis had rented a Toyota Corolla to Deborah Moss. It was one of their older cars and didn't have GPS, but the manager gave us the plate numbers, and while Ralph was on the phone passing along the info to DC Metro PD, I got word from headquarters that Richard Basque was asking to speak with me.

Most people aren't aware that the FBI has its own police force, but drive past the J. Edgar Hoover Building anytime day or night and you'll see two or three of their cars parked out near the main parking garage entrance on 10th Street. Now the officer on the phone said, "He hasn't been very helpful yet, but he's saying that if you'll talk with him he'll tell you about other crimes that, and I quote, 'you might have an interest in.'"

"Other homicides."

"It would appear so. Yes."

Since Basque wasn't my problem anymore, I'd stayed away from him for the last couple days.

"When?"

"He said it has to happen now. Eight o'clock."

He was being held at Headquarters, which wasn't very far from Ralph and Brin's place, but even if I left right away I wasn't sure I could make it there by eight.

Honestly, I had no desire to talk with Richard Basque. I knew that if I saw him I would be tempted to confront him, to say more than I should—things that I would almost certainly regret.

Or maybe I wouldn't regret them at all.

I knew one thing, though: I wanted to be done with that man, done with all his games and the pain and questions and regrets he'd brought into my life.

"Have someone else talk with him."

"He said this offer only stands for you and only for tonight. If you don't come over, he says he's not going to give up the details about the other homicides."

Of course.

More power plays.

More games.

"He was insistent. It has to be you, Pat."

The family members of other victims deserved to know the truth, and I figured that trumped any reluctance I felt about speaking with him.

"Alright. I'll do it."

While Lien-hua and Ralph continued the search for distribution companies that PTPharmaceuticals used, and waited to hear back from Metro about their search for the Corolla, I took off to meet with Richard Basque, wondering just how many other homicides he was going to admit to.

And what he might ask of me in exchange for the information.

+++

Keith and Vanessa were finishing a late supper at Ravel's Steakhouse when he told her that he needed to use the restroom.

"I'll be right back."

He didn't wait for a reply, but rather picked his way through the restaurant until he found the hallway to the bathrooms at the far end of the bar.

The management had tried too hard to make the

men's room smell nice and it had a faint feminine scent
about it, but beneath that, the smell of stale urine had
refused to go away.

Keith locked himself in one of the stalls, took out his
phone, and surfed to the hotline number for reporting
fugitives and terrorists to the FBI.

He stared at it for a long time.

Five million dollars.

Even more than he'd guessed.

The Web site stated that informants could remain
anonymous, but once again, he wasn't sure if he completely believed that. The FBI and NSA had exhaustive
ways of tracing calls and, though Vanessa had assured him
that this cell was untraceable, he had to wonder if the
government might have some way of zeroing in on anyone reporting a wanted terrorist as high-profile as Valkyrie.

Besides, how would they transfer the funds to him if
he remained completely anonymous?

He told himself there had to be a way. There had to
be, or else they wouldn't have posted the claim so prominently on their site.

And, considering the alternative would mean facing
Valkyrie, Keith slid his reservations aside and tapped in
the number, reached an agent, and told him exactly
where Alexei Chekov, better known as Valkyrie, was going to be at 8:30 p.m.

74

Tessa and Aiden had finally left the restaurant and were on their way to school.

Finally.

Away from Tymber and all her flirty looks.

Aiden tried to engage Tessa in conversation, but whenever he did, she ended up saying something stupid and eventually he was quiet as he drove them to the dance.

During the meal, Melody had invited Tessa to walk to the bathroom with her and, while she was touching up her makeup, had said, "Love the dress."

"Thanks."

"You two make such a cute couple."

"Um, thanks."

"Listen, my parents are gone tonight. I have the house to myself. We're heading back there after prom. If you guys want to come over you're welcome to party with us." Her invitation was so innocent, so natural that Tessa actually believed Melody wanted her to come. A wink. "There are more than enough bedrooms."

"Oh."

"Just saying, he's a nice guy, you know."

"Yeah, okay. We'll see."

Now Aiden swung the car onto the road leading to the high school.

The night was not at all turning out like Tessa had hoped. Here she was, trying to have a good time with Aiden, but all the while she was distracted about not being responsible enough for her dad to trust her judgment, about not looking nice enough, and about what Aiden might really be thinking about Tymber.

Tessa let her gaze drift to the sky. The clouds had gathered and were swallowing the light of the setting sun as day unfurled into night.

And then the sun disappeared.

And darkness began to crawl across Washington, DC.

+++

I was a couple minutes from Headquarters when I heard from Ralph that someone had left an anonymous tip that Valkyrie was in DC and would be at a distribution warehouse near the Potomac at eight thirty.

"Track the firms that ship there," I said. "See if PT-Pharmaceuticals uses—"

"Already did. It's confirmed. They sent a semi full of meds down here from Boston this morning. Tens of thousands of Calydrole pills."

Man, everything was coming together across town and I was going to be stuck in the lower level of Headquarters meeting with Basque.

"I'll turn around," I told Ralph. "I'll come over there."

"It's not our party. HRT is lead on this." The Hostage Rescue Team was the tactical unit of the Bureau's Critical Incident Response Group. They trained year-round with the military's most elite divisions and, despite all the interagency rivalries, were pretty much recognized as being on par with Delta Force and the SEALs.

The HRT's specialty? Rapid deployment, close-quarters combat, and eliminating two-legged threats without civilian casualties. They were called in on any terrorist activity in the States and were eminently more qualified than Ralph, me, or anyone else in the region to face Valkyrie and whoever he might be meeting with tonight.

"They're bringing in the Blue Whale," Ralph told me. The Blue Whale was the Bureau's most advanced, and largest, mobile communication command post. It was the size of a semi. "We'll be three blocks away. You need to meet with Basque, find out about any other victims. Do your job, let the HRT guys handle this."

"I'll call you as soon as I'm done here."

Good timing to end the call, because I lost reception as I passed through security and entered the parking garage.

I found an open space, parked, and stepped onto the elevator to the detention cells deep beneath the J. Edgar Hoover Building.

+++

Keith and Vanessa left Ravel's Steakhouse and walked to the car.

He had done it.

He'd made the call. Now he just needed to make sure that somehow he wasn't there at the warehouse when the FBI surrounded it to capture Valkyrie.

But how he was going slip away from Vanessa was still unclear to him.

She positioned herself in the driver's seat and said to him, "I have something I haven't been completely honest with you about."

"What's that?"

"We won't be meeting Valkyrie at the warehouse."

"We won't?"

She was rooting through her purse. "Plans have changed."

"Where are we meeting him?"

But rather than answer, she drew her hand out of her purse, and only when it was too late did Keith realize what she was holding. She was incredibly quick, and before he could pull away she'd jammed the hypodermic needle into the side of his neck and depressed the plunger.

He gasped and attempted to reach up to get the needle out, but whatever she'd given him was potent, because his arm already felt lead-heavy and his hand never made it to his neck.

"And one other thing," she said. "The cell phone I was letting you use wasn't quite secure. There's one phone that connects to it: I'm able to listen in on your calls."

She removed the needle in her own good time and set it on the dashboard.

Keith felt himself slumping in the seat. "What . . . are you doing? What did you give me?"

"Just something to help you sleep. Until we get there." She drew a pair of handcuffs out of her purse, and he was helpless to resist when she slipped one cuff over his wrist and snapped the other shut around the door handle.

"This isn't . . ." He was having a hard time organizing his thoughts. "You're making a—"

"You called the FBI, Corporal."

Dark dread swept over him. "No, I—"

"Yes," Vanessa said softly. "And now I'm going to take you to the man you tried to turn in to them."

He tried desperately to move his free arm to go for her throat, but it was useless.

She turned his chin so he was looking directly at her. "I've enjoyed working with you, Keith. I'm sorry it has to end like this."

And the last thing he saw before darkness shrouded him was Vanessa pulling the pair of pruning shears out of his jacket pocket and placing them in her purse.

+++

Valkyrie listened as Vanessa told him on the phone what Keith had done.

Well, it looked like a trip over to the distribution warehouse wasn't going to appear on tonight's agenda after all.

He gave her instructions on how to get to the marina. "From where you are it should be twenty to twenty-five minutes. I'm pleased with how you've been monitoring his calls."

"Thank you."

"I'll see you at eight thirty."

Alhazur eyed Valkyrie suspiciously, and when he hung up, he asked him, "Is there a problem?"

"Not at all. Two people will be joining us at half past the hour. One of them will be remaining for the rest of the evening."

Alhazur's gaze drifted toward his dead associate, lying on the deck. "One of them."

"Yes." Valkyrie said to the remaining suicide bomber, "You can remove your vest now. I'd like you to place it in the backseat of the SUV you and Alhazur drove over here."

"For insurance?" the man ventured.

"Let it never be said that you're not a quick study."

As the man left to obey his instructions, Valkyrie found his thoughts drifting from the suicide vests to the discussion with Alhazur about the proposed attacks in Moscow, to the situation with Keith and Vanessa, to Richard Basque.

If Basque really did make it out of FBI Headquarters tonight, he would be heading over to the distribution warehouse expecting to meet there at ten, but now that Keith had made the call, the Feds would undoubtedly be there at eight thirty, and if they waited long enough they might just find Basque instead of the terrorist they were hoping for.

Valkyrie assured himself that Vanessa had left his cell number with Basque. If the famed serial killer did escape, Valkyrie trusted that he would be prudent enough to call before heading to the place where they had been scheduled to meet.

If not, his freedom was going to be short-lived indeed.

75

Still thinking about the team moving in on Valkyrie, I entered the interrogation room and found Richard Basque seated at the steel table, wrists and ankles shackled.

He calmly assessed me. I calmly assessed him. He had a line of dark stitches across his cheek reaching down across his jaw from the knife wound.

"How's your mouth, Richard?"

He peeled back his lips to show me the uneven ridges of splintered and missing teeth. It made him look even more like the cannibal that he was.

It brought to mind my conversation with Tessa about werewolves and vampires and how monsters today look like the rest of us and not what they really are. But maybe in Basque's case, now, tonight, he did look like exactly what he was.

"How do you turn someone into a monster?" Tessa had asked me, then answered the question herself: "Let him be himself without restraint."

That was Richard Basque.

The form of a man but the soul of a beast.

Just like the fable he'd circled in the book at his house.

"It's good to see you, Patrick."

Because of the missing teeth and the stab wound in his jaw I expected his words to be raspy or coarse, but he sounded chillingly normal and for a brief moment I had the sense that he really was some sort of superhuman monster, that he was incapable of feeling pain or letting it affect him.

I took a seat across the table from him and set my phone beside me, making sure there was no way he would be able to reach it. "I'll be recording our conversation." I tapped at the screen to pull up a voice recorder.

"I assumed we were already being recorded." He nodded toward a small hole in the ceiling near the southeast corner of the room where a camera was carefully hidden. But obviously not hidden well enough. "Watched too."

"This is for my own personal use."

"Ah."

"How many?" I trusted he would know what I was referring to.

"Bodies? Victims?"

"That's right."

"I could thank you for not killing me back at the marsh, but from what I've heard, you did."

I chose not to reply.

"But I would like to thank you for not leaving me that way. It would've added too much irony to the scene—the marsh where I disposed of the dead becoming the place where I ended up expiring, myself. Quite poetic. I'm glad it didn't end like that."

"Tell me about them. About the victims."

"I'll tell you everything you want to know if you'll answer two questions."

"I'm not here to make deals, Richard."

"You'll be wanting to hear what I have to say. There

are more bodies than you think." He paused. "Your team is searching the marsh, I assume?"

"They are."

"It's a large area."

"Yes."

"I can help you narrow down your search."

"If I answer your two questions."

A nod.

All of this was a power play, and I didn't like the idea of him feeling any sense of power over me, over the investigation, over anything.

However, I was also aware that it's not uncommon for killers to offer this type of information. Often, recounting their crimes or going to the site of the homicide with authorities to reveal the location of bodies allows murderers to relive the thrill of the kill all over again.

It's not an easy call, trying to figure out what to do in a situation like this.

I decided to just go for it and see where that took the conversation. "What is it you want to know, Richard?"

"Did you ever wonder about the meat hook—why I said it hit me and that's what broke my jaw? Back when you first arrested me?"

"The hook? That's what you want to know?"

"Yes."

"You wanted one thing to hold over me."

A slight grin. "That's so unlike you, Patrick. Delving into motives."

"I'm branching out. What's the second question?"

"I want to know if you've ever thought what it would be like."

"To be like you."

"Yes. I know you try not to enter the minds of the

people you track, but do you find yourself climbing deeper into your own mind as you pursue them? Wondering what it would be like to be them? When you're alone and contemplating the implications of the case, have you ever put yourself in my shoes? Tell me if you have and I'll tell you everything you want to know."

"Why?"

"Why?"

"Why would you tell me about other victims if I answer that question?"

"Because you've already caught me." He sounded so matter-of-fact about it that it unsettled me. "I have nothing to gain by keeping my crimes a secret. And perhaps, by cooperating, I might find some favor with the judge."

I didn't buy it. Basque was too smart for that. He had to know that nothing he said or did at this point would bring him any less than life in prison or the death sentence.

"Yes," I told him. "I've wondered."

"What it would be like? To be like me?"

"Yes."

"And where did that take you?"

To acknowledging that there's a monster inside each of us looking for a way to get out.

It seemed petty to argue with him about the fact that I'd answered his two questions and was now ready for the information about the crimes. It felt almost like if I were to squabble with him, it would prove that he was somehow in control again.

"To the edge of myself," I said. "To the places I refuse to go."

He nodded slowly. "I've seen the look in your eyes, Patrick. Fourteen years ago when you apprehended me in that slaughterhouse, it was there. Then at my trial, at Dr. Werjonic's funeral, just before Renee Lebreau's death when we met at the lawyers' office. It's there. I know it is."

"What's there?"

"The darkness. You try not to feed it, but it's there. I can see it. We're not that different, you and I."

"We are different. Because I fight against it and you don't."

He didn't answer right away. "If you have to fight it, how do you know you're always going to win? One day when you're not so careful, when you're in the wrong state of mind, at the wrong place, at the wrong time, you might lose."

I knew that to a certain extent he was right—just as everyone is capable of fighting against his primal desires, everyone is capable of losing that fight.

From out of nowhere a saying came to me: *There but for the grace of God go I.*

It's more true than we care to admit.

"I told you what you wanted to know. Tell me about the other victims."

He leaned back. "Tomorrow."

More games. More manipulation.

Not a huge surprise.

"I'm not coming back tomorrow, Richard."

"I think you'll want to. You'll finally get the answers you so badly want."

"No." I pocketed my phone. "I'll see you at your trial. We both know you'll never be a free man again. I'm going to be very thorough when I testify."

"I'm counting on it."

Irritated that he'd succeeded in getting me irritated, I returned to my car.

The meeting had been brief, and that was okay by me.

Now I could get over to the Blue Whale.

If the information we had was correct, in less than fifteen minutes the team would be moving in on Valkyrie.

And then neither Basque nor Valkyrie would ever see the light of day again.

I left Headquarters and aimed my car in the direction of the distribution center to join Ralph at the command post.

+++

Even though the dance had started already, there were still a lot of kids outside the school, posing and taking pictures with their dates in the quickly fading light.

Aiden led Tessa toward the front doors. He seemed to know everyone and they all greeted him and gave Tessa mildly intrigued looks. Normally, no one paid her much attention and tonight it kind of got to her. Made her self-conscious.

She wondered what they were thinking, seeing a guy like him—a track star—with a loner girl who argued with their English teacher about the etymology of words.

Despite herself, she placed her left hand over the scars on her arm to hide them from the other kids.

Aiden found some friends, and they all handed phones around, taking each other's picture, and finally Tessa started to calm down, at least a little.

She was here.

She was with the guy she'd liked all semester.

Tymber was nowhere around.

There was no reason to let anything ruin her night.

They went inside the dimly lit gymnasium and stepped

into some kind of boppy song Tessa had never heard before, and she started to dance with her date.

+++

Two male FBI Police officers escorted Richard Basque toward his cell. They were the only two officers in this hallway, the only two he'd encountered all night, so Richard hoped that if something happened to them, it might be a little while before word spread.

Both of them had guns.

Good.

He would be needing a weapon.

Once he had that, it would all be over.

Using the paper clip Vanessa Juliusson had given him, he finished with the lock on his handcuffs when they were halfway to his cell.

76

I was five minutes out from the Blue Whale when Ralph informed me that so far there was no movement at the warehouse.

"No employees. No night watchmen. No lights. Nothing. If Valkyrie was planning to be there tonight, he found a way to shut the place down, keep it cleared out."

If Valkyrie was going to be paying this place a visit it would make sense for him to clear it out so that no employees would be present to identify him. I took what Ralph said as a good sign.

He went on. "HRT is going to monitor the facility for another fifteen minutes or so, see if any cars drive up, then they're planning a full breach. Sweep the whole place. Make sure it's clear."

"You think we were set up here?" I asked him.

"Well, we confirmed that the semi carrying the counterfeit Calydrole arrived here a couple hours ago. That and the fact that the warehouse is shut down—it looks like someone had inside intel."

"Any word on who turned him in?"

"I haven't heard. But if Valkyrie doesn't show up, whoever called it in is out five million dollars."

+++

Keith woke up slowly, blearily. The whole world seemed to be moving around him in a blur of colors and waves of time shifting across themselves. He blinked, tried hard to orient himself.

He was in a small room, he couldn't tell where, but it seemed like it might be in the cabin of a boat. Wherever he was, he was certainly not in a warehouse. He was restrained in a chair.

"Corporal." Valkyrie was standing stoically in front of him. "Good of you to join us."

He was still working hard to clear his head. "This is all a mistake, you don't—"

"You called the Bureau, Keith. That was not a wise move."

Finally, his vision came into focus and he saw two other men, as well as Vanessa, in the room.

She removed the pruning shears from her purse and handed them to Valkyrie.

"Thank you, dear."

"Of course."

But rather than start with the shears, Valkyrie started with his fist.

+++

8:33 p.m.

I met Ralph outside the Blue Whale.

The HRT was taking lead on this, but Doehring was at the command post too, and so were Metro's SWAT Commander Shaw and his team.

Ralph was shaking his head in frustration. "Still no

movement. But HRT decided to wait until nine. I'm not sure why. I guess, since they have all the entrances and exits covered, it doesn't hurt to wait and see if anyone shows up. Personally, I'm thinking either we were played or Valkyrie got wind of everything and rabbited."

"So what do you want to do?" I asked. "Wait here or find Corporal Tyree and his lady friend?"

"You got an idea where they might be?"

"I've got an idea of where we could start looking."

+++

Valkyrie watched Keith spit out a glob of blood and wrestle against the ropes to try to find a more comfortable position. But the way he was tied, that wasn't going to be possible.

"There are some techniques I learned in South Africa. I haven't used them in a long time. Tonight, I thought you could help me sharpen my skills."

"Listen, please—"

Valkyrie put his finger up to Keith's lips. "Shh. I'd rather you handled this with honor, as any Marine would."

+++

It didn't take Richard Basque long to find out that Vanessa's instructions had been accurate after all.

He knew that someone entering the Hoover Building would have to pass through any number of security checkpoints, but once you were in, no one would check an ID or make you pass through security to *leave*. Once you were in, they'd assume you were supposed to be here. After all, that was what the security measures at the entrance were for.

And that played to Richard's advantage.

The other day, wearing a police officer's uniform had served him well, and he was not against using a technique that worked.

He slaughtered the two FBI Police officers, careful to keep blood off of one of the uniforms that he then wore, and, following Vanessa's instructions, headed for the parking garage.

He needed to kill only one additional agent on the way there, so that wasn't so bad.

Finding a car he could use wasn't difficult. He chose one of the FBI Police cruisers with a metal mesh cage separating the front seat from the back.

It would make it easier to transport someone.

It wasn't ten o'clock yet, wasn't even nine. He was early. So as soon as he'd left the garage, using the cell phone one of the officers had been carrying, Richard put a call through to the number Vanessa Juliusson had given him to verify the location of where he should go to meet her employer.

77

While he was working on Keith, Valkyrie got word from Richard that he was free.

Valkyrie told him about the change of plans, about meeting on the boat instead of at the warehouse, and then gave his attention once again to the man who'd tried turning him over to the FBI.

+++

Between songs Tessa asked Aiden about the speech.

"So this whole graduation talk deal," she said, "I mean, I wanted to bail on it, I was going to bail on it, but from the start I could tell you wanted me to do it."

"Yeah, I guess that's true."

He got a text and glanced at his phone. He happened to hold it at an angle that didn't allow her to see the screen.

"Why?" Tessa asked. "Why did you want me to?"

"I've been watching you for a while." He was staring at his phone. "I thought it'd be cool to date a girl who was smart, who was the best at something."

"How am I the best at giving a speech?"

He tapped in a response to the text. Only then did he

look up at her. "You're the smartest person in the school, I don't care who the valedictorian is. I like dating people who are the best at whatever it is they do."

"Oh." For a moment Tessa wondered what Tymber was the best at. "I see."

He slipped his phone back into his pocket. "Come on. Let's get some punch. I need something to drink."

+++

Ralph and I had left the warehouse and were in my car on I-395, where I thought we'd be able to get to any quadrant of the city fastest if we needed to. He'd been on the radio with the guys in the Blue Whale and now ended his transmission. "Still nothing at the warehouse. So what are you thinking, Pat?"

"We know one person who could lead us to Alexei."

"Who's that?"

"Nikolai Demidenko, his old contact at the GRU."

"But why would he give up Chekov's location?"

"Bribes are always a good place to start."

"The five-million-dollar reward."

"It would motivate most people. Maybe we could even up it a little if he gives us something that helps us zero in on Alexei tonight."

"Can we locate Demidenko?"

"The CIA can. From the case files we know—"

"Yeah. They keep tabs on him."

He put the call through.

+++

On the deck of the yacht, Richard Basque met the man who'd arranged for his new lawyer.

He could hear wet, strangled sounds coming from belowdeck. There was also the sound of two men talking in another language. It might have been Russian, Richard couldn't be sure.

A body lay on the boat's deck. Male. Broken neck.

Vanessa, the woman who'd met with Richard in the interrogation room at FBI Headquarters, sashayed up the stairs and stood beside the dark-haired man who'd been waiting for Richard when he arrived.

"Thank you for the information about the layout of headquarters," Richard said to Vanessa. "It came in handy."

"You're welcome."

"And for the paper clip."

"Of course."

"So"—now he addressed the man—"who are you?"

"Just call me Valkyrie."

Basque looked at him doubtfully. "Valkyrie?"

Valkyrie didn't answer him and for a moment they simply locked eyes with each other, then he said, "Come on belowdeck. It's better if we talk down there."

"Here is fine."

"There's a lot going on tonight. Being out in the open isn't the best idea."

They descended the stairs and Richard saw two other burly men standing quietly in the corner. He also saw the condition of the man who'd been making the awkward sounds. He was tied to a chair and was still conscious, which Richard found impressive, considering the extent and nature of his wounds.

"You have skills," he told Valkyrie.

"I have experience."

Richard gestured toward Vanessa. "When we met earlier, she told me that you wanted me to finish what I started with Agent Bowers."

"Yes."

"Why?"

"Because he caught me once. He vowed to come after me. And he appears to be a persistent man."

"He is." Richard thought for a moment. "Can you track a cell phone?"

"I can. Who do you want to find?"

"One of Bowers's sheep."

Valkyrie offered a guess: "Agent Jiang or his daughter?"

Richard told him his preference.

"Good choice. Give me three minutes. I'll find her. In the meantime, I've heard about what you do. Feel free to help yourself to the man in the chair." He pointed toward the knives. "His name is Keith. Do whatever you like. He's yours."

"Actually, I think I'm going to save my appetite."

Valkyrie nodded. "I completely understand."

He pulled out his laptop, used the hacked password his GRU contact, Nikolai Demidenko, had provided him with, logged into the Federal Digital Database, and then set to work finding the person Richard had requested.

"You should know that if I can find her," Valkyrie told him, "the Bureau will be able to as well."

"I'll take care of that when I get there. Just get me to her."

"That, I can do."

+++

Ralph and I received a call from the CIA that they were cutting Nikolai Demidenko a deal.

Ten million dollars.

And immunity.

And a new identity if he would move here to the States.

But only if his intel led us to Alexei Chekov tonight.

Otherwise they would leak information to his associates that he was a double agent.

It sounded like a pretty persuasive offer to me.

They expected to get back to us in a couple minutes.

While we were waiting to hear from them, we got word that the HRT had finally breached the warehouse and found that it was clear. They were going to keep searching the area, but if they found nothing, they planned to leave a small contingent of agents at the site for the night and move the rest back to Quantico.

+++

Richard Basque left the marina.

Valkyrie had given him just what he needed.

He had the location, as well as Valkyrie's number so he could confirm that she was still there when he got closer.

He would pick her up and head to the third and final apartment that he had rented earlier and saved for a special occasion, the place in Fort Hunt, south of DC.

+++

Keith wanted nothing more than to die. He would have done anything to make all this end, but he had no way to move, no way to get free, no way to kill himself.

And he knew it was going to go on for a long time before he would finally get what he wanted.

+++

Demidenko informed us that Valkyrie had a boat in the DC area: the *Diversion*. That was all, but it was enough.

Lacey found it for us.

Unless Valkyrie had left the dock, the boat would be at Seaboard Marina.

Ralph and I called it in to get some cars dispatched, but we were close, only a couple of minutes out, and since Valkyrie had apparently gotten wind that we knew about the warehouse meeting, we didn't want to wait at all before checking the marina.

I directed the car toward it.

Game on.

78

I pulled to a stop in the marina's parking lot.

The yacht Demidenko had told us about was there with the name painted distinctively on the prow. The boat's lights were on, no one was on deck.

Guns drawn, Ralph and I edged forward, trying to avoid moving through the pools of murky light cast down by the vapor lights perched high on the weathered telephone poles in the parking lot. Ralph took the lead. I studied the shadows for any movement, but saw nothing.

The night held a slightly fishy odor, that lingering smell of inlets and bays where there isn't quite enough wind or current to ever clear it away.

Only three vehicles sat in the marina parking lot: two cars and a black SUV with diplomatic tags. Ralph checked the cars while I approached the SUV.

It was unlocked. A suicide vest lay in the backseat.

Okay.

So that's where things were going.

"Cars are clear," Ralph said quietly. I pointed out the vest to him and then memorized the identification number on the front of it.

At first, the night held no sound except for the anxious slap of water against the wooden supports holding up the pier, but when we were maybe ten meters from the boat I heard muffled cries coming from somewhere belowdeck.

My heart was beginning to slam hard against the inside of my chest.

We eased closer.

The cries were getting softer and weaker, but also more desperate, and I didn't like that at all.

Then I heard voices on the boat, muffled by the ripple of water against the hull. Male. Impossible to make out the words or tell how many people were there.

No sound yet of sirens or backup.

Ralph and I proceeded, and when we were nearly to the yacht, a man emerged from the stairway to the area belowdeck.

Valkyrie.

"Do not move!" Ralph commanded.

Valkyrie stood motionlessly in the muted light, then slowly lifted his hands to the sides.

Ralph and I both had our guns directed at him. "On your knees."

He knelt and we approached him, accessing the yacht quickly but cautiously.

"Lie down," Ralph told him. "Hands to the side!"

Valkyrie said nothing, but complied, and as he did, the red-haired woman who went by the alias Deborah Moss emerged from belowdeck.

"Federal agents," I yelled. "Hands out!"

She obeyed.

It struck me that they were giving themselves up too easily. Something else was up. There had to be

more people hiding somewhere nearby or waiting belowdeck.

Not good. We needed backup and we needed it now.

Ralph was covering Valkyrie, I had my gun on the
woman.

Two cell phones were on the deck's control console, a
dead man lay nearby. The angle of his neck told me all I
needed to know about his condition. His jacket was un-
tucked enough for me to see that he had a suicide vest on
as well, although this time I couldn't read any identification number.

Two phones, two vests.

As I approached, I could see that each phone had an
ID number on it and one of them matched the number
I'd seen on the vest in the SUV. So if there were only two
phones it might be a good sign. Maybe no one else on
the boat had a vest on.

"Get down," I ordered the woman. "Keep your hands
to the sides. Lie on your stomach."

"Who else is belowdeck?" Ralph asked.

"You'll have to find that out by going down there,"
she replied.

"Glad to." Whoever was down there cried out again,
his voice choked with pain. Ralph said, "Cover 'em, Pat.
I'll be right back."

Before I could suggest a plan B, he disappeared belowdeck. I wanted to pat down Valkyrie and the woman
to make sure they had no weapons, but if I started on one
of them the other could fire at me. It would be best to
wait for Ralph, then cuff these—

A shot rang out.

"Ralph!" I cried.

No reply, just the thick sound of a body slamming to the floor, and while it momentarily distracted me, it was all that Valkyrie needed.

He was on his feet in an instant and as I shot him in the chest, one of the world's top assassins went for my gun.

79

The bullet didn't stop him.

We struggled, and he angled my arm out of the way before I could empty the barrel into him. The woman leapt up to help him, but he didn't need her. He was good at what he did and was able to get the SIG, but he didn't shoot me, instead, once he had it, he just stepped back beside the red-haired woman.

The sound of a fight continued belowdeck.

"Two against one." She nodded toward the stairs. "Not such good odds."

"You don't know who they're fighting against." I had my hands up and was calculating how to get my gun back—or how to stall long enough for Ralph to get up here or for backup to arrive.

I'd never known Ralph to lose a fight, but I remembered how thrashed his forearm was from the pit bull and I wasn't sure if he could take on two guys with only one arm. It would depend on the guys. I had a feeling that, based on the brutish size of the dead man on the deck, whoever the men were who were down there, they were not going to be pushovers.

And if they were anywhere near as good as Valkyrie, Ralph might be in trouble.

Finally, sirens cut through the night from perhaps half a mile away and the look in Valkyrie's eyes changed, not to fear, but to careful prudence. He was forming a plan.

"Come here, darling," he said to the woman. "It's time we moved along." A widening stain of blood spread across the right side of his chest. A little too high, though. He would need treatment, but it didn't look immediately life-threatening.

He picked up the phone from the console, the one that had the identification code that would correspond to the suicide vest on the dead man near my feet.

Oh.

Not good.

He slipped it into his pocket, then said to me, "Sometimes, Agent Bowers—"

"This isn't you, Alexei," I said, "remember what you—"

"I'm not Alexei anymore."

"Yes, you are."

"No. Alexei is dead." He tossed a set of keys to the woman. "Vanessa, we'll take the SUV." Then he addressed me again. "As I was saying, sometimes you have to adapt when things don't go as planned."

She had only taken a couple steps when Alexei called to her, "Actually, my dear, I changed my mind. I have something else I need you to do."

She faced him. "Yes?"

"Die."

Her eyes widened with shock as he raised the gun and shot her in the forehead.

The same shot placement he'd used to kill his wife.

She dropped heavily onto the deck.

He calmly appraised the body, then looked my way. "A loose end. You understand."

I tried to think like him.

Distractions and contingency plans—

The fight continued downstairs. Fierce grunts and heavy pounding.

There was a suicide vest on the dead man nearby me.

Valkyrie's gonna blow that vest. He has the phone. He—

"Toss the key to your handcuffs over the railing," he told me.

I did. Thankfully, my car keys and my lock pick set were on a separate key ring.

"Handcuff yourself to the console."

I pulled out my cuffs and without hesitating at all, slung them violently toward his face. It takes about half a second for a person to respond to physical stimuli, and as he instinctively raised his arm to block the cuffs, I rushed him, brushing my hand across the console. I tackled him, went for the gun with one hand, his pocket with the other, and he wrestled away as we hit the deck, kicked me fiercely in the abdomen, and then grabbed the cuffs and my arm, yanked me toward the console, and before I could stop him, cuffed my wrist to it. Gasping to draw in a breath, I laid my free hand on the console, pulled myself up, and then held my hands off to the sides.

It hadn't been easy, but I'd done what I needed to do. Hopefully, I'd played this right. Hopefully.

"Where do we go from here?" I said.

His gaze flicked toward the dead man on the deck. "We all go home."

He left the boat and strode toward the SUV while I whipped out my lock pick set and went to work on the cuffs.

The sirens were drawing closer but they weren't close enough.

"It's time to go, Ralph!" I hollered. I couldn't be sure things were going to work out in our favor here, not certain at all.

I finished with the cuffs just as Chekov reached the SUV.

Ralph came bounding up the steps, gun in hand, and saw the dead woman. "Where's Chekov?" he shouted. I pointed. We had no clear shot. Together we ran toward the dock, but hadn't even made it to the edge of the boat when Alexei Chekov paused by the driver's door, lifted the phone, tapped in a number, and I hoped he wasn't—

The SUV exploded violently, blowing the doors off, enveloping Chekov in a harsh mushroom of flame and flying debris.

Ralph and I turned and ducked as a rush of consuming heat enveloped us.

After it passed, we both faced the fire and the charred and burning corpse of Alexei Chekov. Ralph said, "I don't understand. Why would he want to kill himself?"

"He didn't."

Ralph looked at me curiously, then at the dead man on the boat's deck. "But how did you switch the vests?"

"I didn't need to." I pointed to the phone I'd gotten from Valkyrie in our scuffle. "I just needed to switch the phones."

"Nice move, bro."

"What about the guys belowdeck?" I asked him.

"Not gonna cause us any trouble."

Metro and FBI Police cars came screaming around the corner and into the marina parking lot.

"So there were two guys down there?" I asked Ralph.

"Three. One was Tyree. He was restrained in a chair.

He was alive, but barely. That dude was not in good shape." Then he added, with the shade of a grin, "The other two are in worse shape now, though."

"You fought off two thugs with only one arm?"

He held up the arm that'd been bitten and the wound must have ripped open, because it was bleeding heavily through his sleeve. "Turns out I had to get both arms involved."

"If the hospital gave out gift cards, I'd buy you one."

"Thanks for that."

I headed for the stairs. "Let's see what we can do to help Tyree before the paramedics get here."

+++

A slow dance.

Tessa rested her head against Aiden's chest and leaned into his arms. It felt so good to press against his strength, to feel his arms encircling her.

The music embraced them, and everything that'd been hammering in on her seemed to fade away. The stress of this week, the worry, the difficulties with Patrick, all of it washing away. But halfway through the song, the moment evaporated when Aiden got another text and stepped away from her to answer it.

That was it. You don't stop slow dancing with your date just because you get a text, it doesn't matter who you are.

When he came back, she said, "Hey, I left my phone at home. Can I use yours for a sec? My dad's way overly protective." She shook her head as if she were exasperated at how overbearing he was. "I'm supposed to call. It's ridiculous."

"Yeah, sure." Aiden handed it to her.

"It's too noisy in here." She nodded toward the hallway to the restrooms. "I'll be right back."

80

The EMTs took over helping Tyree.

We located my SIG near Chekov's body. The gun was charred, but appeared salvageable and I was glad. This baby had been with me a long time. However, I didn't trust it until I could clean it.

Ralph joined one of the paramedics in the ambulance to have him treat his arm. He claimed it wasn't hurting, but I knew he wouldn't have gone over there unless it did. A lot.

Just before they left for the hospital he lent me his gun. "There might be more of a mess to clean up," he said. "I expect that back later tonight."

"No problem. Thanks."

Fire trucks were on the way to take care of the still-flaming SUV. I filled in the Hostage Rescue Team on what had gone down, then took a seat in my car, where it was a little quieter, and phoned Lien-hua. I told her that Valkyrie, his female accomplice, and three conspirators were dead and that Tyree was in custody.

"I wish I could have been there."

"Next time around."

My phone vibrated. I glanced at the screen.

Headquarters.

"Just a sec." I put her on hold and answered the other call. "Pat here."

"Agent Bowers," a female agent said urgently, "it's Basque. He's escaped."

I blinked. "What?"

"Two FBI Police officers and one agent are dead."

I felt a lash of anger whip through me. "Do we have any idea where he might have gone?"

"There's an FBI Police car missing. He got a uniform from one of the officers—"

"The car has GPS, doesn't it?" I said. "Track it through that."

"We tried that right away. He must have disabled it."

I pounded the dashboard.

He might just try to flee—or he might try to visit Lienhua and finish what he started.

I had no idea if Basque might somehow be able to locate my fiancée, but I went back on the line with her and told her to lock down the house, to be ready in case Basque showed up and to call dispatch to get a car over there right away.

Then I phoned Tessa, who was at prom, and not surprisingly, didn't answer.

I left a voicemail, and then texted her as well.

Then I contacted Metro to have an officer meet her at the school.

+++

Tessa checked the text messages on Aiden's phone and saw a message from Tymber: *Sorry I had to work tonite. So, c u after prom? Can't wait! ;)*

A terrible stone settled in Tessa's stomach.

They broke up. They were supposed to have broken up!

She paced back onto the dance floor, navigated her way through the crowd of dancing students, and held up the phone's screen for Aiden to see. "What is *this*?" She didn't care how many other people heard her. "You're meeting Tymber after prom? What does she mean—sorry she had to work?!"

"I—no, no, listen it's not what it . . . Just let me expla—"

"Oh." It hit her. "So that's why you asked me so last-minute. Because she couldn't make it? I'm, what, your backup plan?"

"It's not like that, really." But his expression told her it was. "I like you, Tessa—"

"What would you have replied?"

"Replied?"

By then the other kids nearby had stopped dancing and were watching them to see how this would play out. Four of them were filming it with their phones.

"To her text!" Tessa said. "Replied! If I hadn't read this first, would you have said you're gonna meet her after prom? That you can't wait to see her either?"

"No. I wanted to—"

She got in his face. "I can tell when someone's lying, and you're lying. Why wait? Go see Tymber now. You wanted to be with her anyway, so *be* with her."

Then she spun on her heels and called over her shoulder, "I'll find my own ride home." She lifted both hands and did not give him the peace sign with her fingers. And she didn't care who was filming it and posting it on the Internet.

"Yeah, well, you're right!" he shouted to her. There were barbs in his words. "She couldn't make it so I had to settle for you. So deal with it."

His words shattered her.

She hadn't wanted to be right. She'd wanted him to tell her how much he did want to be with her, how he'd chosen her, how he thought she was pretty and smart and there was no one else he wanted to spend the night dancing with—to say all those things and *mean them*.

Tears formed in her eyes and she did her best to hold them back.

She didn't realize that she still had Aiden's phone until she was outside the school. There were kids all around the front of the building and in cars, talking or making out, so she walked off by herself behind the gym so no one could see her if she cried.

A single light on the side of the school cast down a weary glow across the pavement.

Alone.

With Aiden's phone.

Well, good. She could send a text of her own to Tymber Dotson.

81

After sending the text, Tessa stuck his phone in her purse, then fished out her own phone to delete every text she'd ever gotten from Aiden Ryeson as well as the pictures of them from before they went into the school for prom.

There was a vm from Patrick but she wasn't in the mood to listen to him checking up on her. However, she couldn't help but see his text to her: *Basque is free. I'm sending an officer to pick you up.*

Her heart seemed to stop cold and dead in her chest.

Basque was free? How?

As she was processing that, a cop car pulled up around the corner of the gym. Its headlights were shining right at her and she had to hold up her hand to shield her eyes.

An officer got out and she started toward him. "Just let me text my dad that you're here."

But first, she tapped at the phone to listen to the voicemail: "Tessa, Basque escaped. I need you to—"

The officer approached her, but was backlit by the cruiser's headlights and she couldn't see his face. He was less than ten feet away when the rest of Patrick's message came through: "—be careful. He has an FBI Police car."

By the time the message finished it was too late.

He turned to the side and, though still partly backlit, in the faint light behind the school she saw his face and realized who was coming toward her.

Richard Basque grabbed her arm and when she tried to pull away, he punched her hard in the face, splitting her lip and sending her reeling to the pavement. Her phone went spinning across the asphalt. He brought a heavy booted heel down on it and then he was on her, dragging her toward the car.

"Help!" she cried. But everyone else was inside at the dance or farther around the corner of the building or in their cars in the parking lot.

As she called for help again he punched her in the face once more and she crumpled to the ground, the entire side of her head throbbing in pain.

"Let's not make this any harder than it has to be," he said.

Her face hurt so badly that she was barely able to hold back the tears, but she didn't want Basque to know how much it hurt, so she forced herself to. She still had the purse in her hand and swung it at him, but he easily stopped her arm.

She memorized the license plate number as he yanked her toward the vehicle. She struggled to get away, but he was oppressively strong and tossed her into the back of the squad and slammed the door, almost taking off her foot as he did.

She knew there wouldn't be a door handle on the inside of a police car, but instinctively, she went for one. Of course it wasn't there.

Basque took his place behind the wheel and turned toward her, his shoulder-length hair flipping to the side as he did. "Hello, Tessa."

She spit in his face through the wire mesh cage separating them. One of her eyes was already swelling shut from where he'd punched her. Her face hurt, it really, really hurt, but she willed herself not to cry.

He drew two fingers across the spittle, then brought them to his mouth, closed his eyes, and slowly licked her spit from his fingers. A few of his teeth were visible. His cheek was stitched up from where Patrick had stabbed him. His teeth were shattered and sharp and uneven and it sent a chill coursing through her.

Then he faced the front and leaned his head back against the mesh so that he could see her in the rearview mirror. Strands of his hair wavered back through the metal divider, but unfortunately not long enough ones for her to grab hold of or tug.

"We have a long night ahead of us, Tessa." To her, it seemed as if each word was a worm dropping from his mouth. "I'm feeling a little adventurous. You never know what the next few hours may have in store."

Then the man who'd abducted and killed more than twenty-five women started the car and left the school with his next victim locked up tight in the backseat.

82

Tessa still hadn't answered her text and when I tried to locate her phone's GPS, nothing came up.

I peeled away from the marina, called Ralph, and told him what was going on.

"Where are you heading?"

"Tessa's school. I need to find her."

"I'm gonna have the ambulance driver take me to my house, make sure Brin and Lien-hua are alright. Call me when you find Tessa."

"I will."

+++

This was bad.

Very bad.

She was trapped in the back of a cop car driven by a serial killer who wanted to punish her father. By eating her.

She definitely needed to get out before they got to wherever he was taking her.

But how do you escape from the back of a locked police car?

The doors only open from the outside, there was no

way she could get through the wire cage to the front seat.
The windows were almost certainly reinforced, and what
was she going to do anyway, kick her way out with her
sneakers?

But one thing played to her advantage: Basque had
been in such a hurry to get her in the car that he hadn't
taken her clutch purse from her.

He'd knocked her phone away, yes, but she still had
Aiden's cell in the purse.

Tessa didn't really think of herself as having very many
skills, but she had one: texting without looking down at
a phone.

Fishing Aiden's phone from the purse, she shielded it
with her hand to cut down the brightness, then silenced
the volume. She stared at Basque coldly in the rearview
mirror so he wouldn't suspect her of trying anything.
Then she let her thumbs find their way across the keypad
to contact her dad.

+++

I was about five minutes from the school when I got the
text from an unknown number: *He's got me. Help me,
Patrick! Track this phone.*

Terror shot through me.

A moment later another text came through as she
messaged me that she was in an FBI Police car, and she
sent me the license plate number.

That's my girl.

I put a trace on the phone and almost immediately
found out it belonged to Aiden Ryeson. Though we still
got nothing on the car we were able to get a lock on the
phone's GPS location. They were traveling south along
the GW Parkway paralleling the Potomac River.

I whipped the car around, did a U-turn through a stream of oncoming traffic, and blazed toward them.

+++

Tessa wanted to look down at her phone so badly, but she didn't dare do it for fear that Basque would notice and get suspicious.

It was possible Patrick wasn't checking his texts or that he wouldn't be able to trace the phone.

Texting him might not be enough.

She definitely needed to think of a way to get out of this car.

+++

I tore down the parkway. I hated high-speed chases, but this was one time I wasn't going to back off the gas at all.

I didn't know if Basque might somehow get to the phone that Tessa had, but since she was texting me I had to assume that she was in the back of the FBI Police car, and that, at least for the moment, Basque would almost certainly be driving, so I used my phone's voice-to-text function to get her the message that I was on my way.

If the GPS on Aiden's phone was accurate, I was about a mile behind them.

+++

Tessa emptied her purse on her lap and felt through the items to see if there was anything she could use to get free.

Some lip gloss and makeup, her cigarettes, the spritzer bottle of perfume Brineesha had given her, her driver's license, her lighter, a few crumpled dollar bills.

Not much, but two of the items she could use.

Oh, yes.

Her lighter.

And the perfume.

Earlier in the week she'd promised Patrick that she wouldn't set anyone on fire with coffee creamer.

But she hadn't promised she wouldn't use something else.

83

Tessa finally looked down.

In the dim light she couldn't make out all the words on the tiny label on the back of the perfume bottle, but she could read the first two words, the ones that mattered most: "Caution: Flammable."

+++

According to the GPS location of the phone we were tracking, I was less than a quarter mile back.

I swerved around a minivan. Sped toward her.

My car started to drift but I wrestled it back under control as I edged past a hundred on the speedometer.

+++

This was where it happened or it didn't happen.

The flame might just singe his hair, she wasn't sure, but it was the only thing she could think of doing at the moment.

She leaned close to the cage.

"You told me we have a long night together?"

Just as she'd hoped, he pressed his head back against the wire mesh to get the angle right to look at her in the rearview mirror.

"Yes."

"Well, I think one of us is gonna have a longer night than the other one."

Raising her hands and holding the lighter in front of the perfume bottle, she simultaneously sprayed the perfume as she flicked on the lighter.

It worked even better than she imagined.

Basque's hair went up in flames. The entire back of his head was engulfed and the fire spread quickly to the front. Maybe he had some kind of product in his hair, some sort of gel or spray that was flammable—she had no idea, but whatever the reason, it had worked.

She didn't stop spraying.

Basque was crying out and slapping furiously at his head with one hand while trying to maneuver the car with the other.

She popped off the top of the perfume bottle and flung the remainder of the fluid through the mesh onto the fire and it roared hotter.

The car began to fishtail.

Tessa frantically buckled her seat belt just before Basque lost control of the vehicle and it careened across the median toward the Potomac River.

+++

I saw their car swerve off the road.

It looked like there was a fire in the front seat.

A fire?

The car bounced across the curb, crossed the Mount Vernon bike trail, shot through an opening in the trees along the Potomac, and launched off the bank and into the river.

84

When they hit the water, the impact jarred Tessa violently forward. Even with the seat belt on she still felt whipped around like a rag doll.

Basque managed to get his door open and dive into the river.

She had no idea how deep the river would be here, but five feet would be deep enough to fill the car with water and she would drown.

Out! You have to get out!

+++

I flew toward the spot where they'd left the road, screeched to a stop, leapt out, and bolted across the road toward the river.

+++

The current grabbed the car and began to carry it downstream, a very bad sign, because if it was this strong here it meant the water was probably deep enough to take her under.

She doubted it would work, but she tried kicking at the window.

It did absolutely nothing.

She yanked at the metal mesh, but it wasn't going anywhere.

Chilled water was pouring in from the open door in the front.

The trunk.

Maybe if she could pull the seat forward and get to the trunk she could get out. Or if there was a spare tire she could maybe unscrew the valve, get some air.

The words that'd been rattling around in her head all week came back to her: *Meaningless, meaningless, all is—*

No, no, it's not!

This moment matters.

Every second does!

She didn't have anything with her to try to rip open the fabric of the seat back, but even if she did, she realized she'd never be able to get through it in time—if it even accessed the trunk at all. There was almost certainly some sort of barrier there.

The car tilted farther forward and the cold dark water engulfed her legs.

+++

I sprinted toward the shore, past a cluster of trees, frantically scanning the water with my flashlight.

Nothing.

Then I saw the taillights of the car about fifteen meters downstream, its trunk angled up through the water. It looked like there was still air in the backseat, but there wasn't going to be for long.

Then the electrical system shorted out and the lights blacked out.

+++

Everything went dark.

Water to her chest.

The clutch purse wasn't big, but it was leather. It might hold a pocket of air, at least for a little bit before the water seeped through it. Holding the phone above her head she texted, *I love you, Dad*, then tipped the purse upside down to capture as much air as she could as the water rose to her neck.

Then Tessa Bernice Ellis tilted her head up to the roof of the car and filled her lungs one last time before the rest of the air escaped from inside the vehicle and the water enveloped her completely.

+++

I was at the shoreline when a shadowy figure burst out from behind a grove of trees just to my left.

Basque.

I could see him in the faint light from the city. With his sliced cheek, broken teeth, and burned scalp spotted with stringy, wet clumps of hair and covered with gruesome red blisters, he looked bestial, barely human, like something that had crawled from a nightmare.

I whipped out Ralph's Glock. "Hands up!"

Basque complied and stood watching me. He held a handgun, probably from one of the FBI Police officers he'd killed.

To my right, in the river, only the back bumper of the car was visible.

He spoke calmly. "Looks like you lose, Patrick."

I had the Glock directed at his chest.

"Drop the gun, Richard!"

Fire, Patrick. You need to get to Tessa!

Do it!

"Now!"

He complied, tossing it three meters away from him. The car disappeared underwater.

"I want you to remember this moment," he said. "Remember when you were so close but you couldn't do it, couldn't get to her. You have to take me in, Patrick. That's how you and I are different."

Criminals don't play by the rules. We have to.

I aimed at him.

He held his hands up. "You were too slow, Pat."

Center mass.

I said, "Remember when I told you I was going to do what I could to get you the death penalty?"

"Yes, I—"

I eyed down the barrel. "I meant it."

It would have been perfect if he would've pulled a weapon or made a move at me but he didn't. He just stood there knowing that if I took the time to arrest him Tessa would die.

If I did my duty, I would lose my daughter.

Protocol.

Justice.

The greater good.

Life isn't always perfect.

I fired three quick shots, all center mass, and the impact sent him lurching backward into the river.

I took a running start, grabbed a deep breath, and, flashlight in hand, dove into the Potomac to save my daughter.

85

The cold water shocked me, made me surface almost immediately and gasp for breath.

Tessa, hold on!

The current was swift and I had to fight it to stay on track toward the car. I stroked desperately through the water. Then went under.

Everything was inky black and murky. Even with my Maglite, I could only see a few feet in front of me. The current wanted to take me downstream, but I struggled against it and swept the light back and forth to try to find the car.

But I didn't find it. Though I'm a pretty good swimmer, holding my breath has never been my strength and I felt myself losing air.

Don't surface, Pat! Get to her!

I still didn't see the car and I had to get air or I wasn't going to be able to stay under long enough to locate the squad, let along get Tessa out of it.

But no, I fought the urge to surface and after two more strokes the car appeared, almost out of nowhere. I swam to the backseat door on the driver's side.

Flashlight scanning the backseat, I saw Tessa's body floating in the car. She wasn't moving.

No!

Cranking on the handle, I swung the door open, but it jammed against a rock on the river bottom before it could open wide enough for me to get Tessa out. I yanked at it but it wouldn't budge and I couldn't get to her.

Come on!

I needed more air but I wasn't going to chance waiting any longer to get her out.

She'd been under at least half a minute by now, maybe longer. Every second mattered for eternity and I kicked urgently through the water to the other side of the car.

I swung the door open, dropped the flashlight and took hold of Tessa's ankles with both hands and drew her out of the car.

Her body was limp and passed easily out the door.

No, please don't let this happen. Please!

The discussion I'd had with Lien-hua about the brevity of life raced through my head and I tried to still it, quiet it, deny it as I tucked an arm around Tessa's shoulder and chest and kicked desperately toward the surface.

As I did, time became a blur. Prayers, love, fire flashed through me. A father fighting to save his daughter, fighting to get to shore in time.

Then I was at the surface and swimming toward the bank, stroking as powerfully as I could.

Then I was at the shoreline and stumbling up the bank, pulling her onto the grass and positioning her on her back so I could begin resuscitation breaths.

Come on, Tessa. Please. Breathe.

I started rescue breaths and thought of what I'd done earlier in the week with Basque. Pulling him from the water. Saving his life.

Now I regretted it.

You should have left him dead! You caused this!

She wasn't moving.

Come on, Tessa!

So much death this week, so much suffering, so much pain.

I prayed for her, that this time there would be a happy ending, begged God to save her.

But she didn't move.

I went back and forth from rescue breaths to chest compressions.

"You're gonna be okay, Tessa." I was pressing on her chest and the words became a prayer. "You're gonna be okay."

While we live, let us live.

Let us live.

Let us—

All at once, her body lurched. She coughed and gagged, spit out a mouthful of water. Breathed, breathed, lived.

Turning her on her side to help her clear her mouth of water, I supported her and swept the strands of wet hair from her eyes. She drew in a deep breath. Then another.

"I knew you'd come," she managed to say.

"Shh. You're safe. It's over."

She nodded, kept trying to catch her breath.

I said, "I love you."

"You too."

She leaned heavily against my arms and I lowered her softly back against the ground.

"Is he dead?" she whispered.

"Yes. And I'm proud of you. You lit him on fire?"

"Perfume." She took a moment to breathe. "I was out of coffee creamer."

86

FBI Director Margaret Wellington spread out the papers in front of her and stared at them, thinking about what all this would mean.

They hadn't found Basque's body.

Metro PD was still searching the river.

The dead FBI Police officer whom Basque had stolen the uniform from was also missing his body armor. No one knew if Basque had been wearing it when Agent Bowers shot him, but Margaret wasn't about to label the case closed until they found Richard Basque's body.

As the search went on, they were finally getting some answers about Corey's death.

Corporal Tyree, the man whom Valkyrie had been torturing belowdeck on the yacht, was in intensive care, but he was conscious and told them what they needed to know about the drug production and the suicides he and the red-haired woman, who was really named Vanessa Juliusson, had overseen.

Tyree was facing a long list of felonies and capital murder charges but he almost seemed relieved. Maybe prison for him was a freedom of sorts from the life Valkyrie had entwined him in. He claimed that—apart from the pills on the semi at the distribution warehouse—there were no other tainted drugs in the supply chain.

But Margaret wasn't going to take any chances.

Earlier in the day, PTPharmaceuticals had agreed to the full recall of Calydrole. National health warnings went out over the airwaves, online, through texts and tweets and Facebook, and they were just hoping and praying that no additional tainted versions of Calydrole had made it into the hands of consumers.

Following up on the demolished SUV's diplomatic tags, Angela Knight and Lacey found out who the Chechens were. Margaret contacted the CIA to have their people look into whatever activities the men might have been plotting with Valkyrie, and they found plans on a laptop in Alhazur Daudov's house for a coordinated attack against schools in Moscow. Classes were canceled indefinitely until the authorities could guarantee the children would be safe returning to school.

That afternoon, Margaret had visited prison to speak with the partner of the man she suspected had been the one filming her while she slept last summer.

The visit had been fruitless and she'd decided it was the last time she was going to pursue this matter. There are some questions, after all, that we never get answers to. Some doors remain locked forever, and that's life. If we're ever going to have the courage to face tomorrow, sometimes we have to acknowledge that and it has to be okay.

She was ready to move on. She'd at least gotten the

answers she'd sought about her brother's death. There was some resolution in that, some peace.

The DVD of her asleep in her bedroom sat on her desk next to the framed photo of her and her brother when they were children, and now she picked it up.

She decided two things: (1) she was going to remove the locks on the inside of her bedroom door when she got home and (2) she was going to fill out the papers here on her desk.

Life is for living, for moving on, for letting the past lie behind us.

She put down the picture, smashed the DVD on the edge of her desk, and brushed the shattered pieces into her wastebasket.

Then she filled out the forms that she needed to submit to create an exploratory committee to run for Virginia's soon-to-be-open first-district congressional seat.

+++

We were at the Hawkins house. Tony and Ralph had just finished a game of the latest version of "Call of Duty." Ralph won and was smiling broadly, but Tony winked at me as he walked past and I knew what had gone down.

Brin and Tessa were in the kitchen cleaning up supper. I went to check on Lien-hua in the basement, then we all met outside on the back porch.

Metro PD was still searching the river for Basque, and for now, that was all that could be done. Relief that Tessa was okay and that Lien-hua was recovering was paramount in my mind, not the possibility that Basque was still out there.

If he was, I would deal with it.

I would get back to the chase. Tomorrow.

We would be prudent, yes. We would be careful, yes. We would keep up the search, keep up our guard, but I wasn't going to let the question of whether or not he was alive control my life or destroy my family. If I ever saw him again I would take care of him, I had no doubt about that anymore. No remorse. No regret. No hesitation. I knew what I was capable of, and call it justice or call it revenge, I was ready to enact it as soon as I had the chance.

Life isn't always perfect.

And justice doesn't always have clean hands—sometimes she has to get them dirty to do the right thing.

Now, as the sun began dipping down past the edge of the tree line, we were all quiet. Even Ralph and Tony seemed entranced by the sunset.

"So you really set his hair on fire?" Tony asked Tessa.

"Yup. Burned really good too." She gave me a slightly mischievous look. "Good thing I've been smoking or I wouldn't have had that lighter with me."

"I wouldn't go that far."

She told Tony, "By the way, don't start smoking just so you can make a flamethrower out of a perfume bottle someday."

"What else besides perfume would work?"

"We're not making flamethrowers," Brin told him firmly, "out of anything."

"Okay."

"Promise?"

"I promise."

Ralph winked at him, and I had a feeling they would be spending a little father-son time later discussing alternate techniques.

Lien-hua's eyes were on the striking sunset.

I made an offer to Tessa. "Tell you what, if you make it until graduation without smoking, I'll buy you a cake."

"Chocolate?"

"Yes."

She looked at me curiously. "You're trying to bribe me."

"Oh, I would never do that."

"You are *so* trying to bribe me."

"It's called an incentive. Parents use them all the time. Don't they, Brin?"

"Don't get me in the middle of this."

"An incentive?" Tessa pressed me.

"That's right. An incentive not to smoke."

"Bribery."

I did my best imitation of a Tessa response: "Whatever."

Then we were all quiet and watched the sunlight filter through a pile of soft cumulus clouds. Finally, Lien-hua spoke. "How much would you pay to see this? To see the clouds just this way, to see the sunlight fading like that from orange to gray? How much would you pay if you knew this was the last sunset you'd ever see?"

+++

Everything, Tessa thought. *Everything I have.*

A Latin phrase popped to mind: *Crepusculum vorat diem; aurora evincit noctem:* Dusk swallows the day; dawn conquers the night.

And when she thought of that, she realized, at last, what she was going to do her graduation speech on.

+++

I heard Tessa whisper to herself, "Yes. That's perfect."

"What is?"

"I think I know what I'm going to talk about."

"Talk about?"

"At graduation."

"Sunsets?" Tony asked.

"Sort of." She leaned forward. "Okay, here it is: What would it look like to live in awe of every moment? To really, really see the terrible splendor, the delicate wonder of life? I mean, most people just go through the motions of living: texting, going to the movies, watching TV—it's tragic how many moments go by unnoticed."

"That kind of awareness . . ." Brineesha said thoughtfully, "I think it's just too terrifying. Most people are barely able to live in awe of just one moment out of a thousand. I can't imagine what it would be like to thread them all together, one after the other."

Lien-hua's voice was barely above a whisper. "It would be life-transforming."

"Yeah." Tessa took a small breath. "Listen. In that car last night I really thought I was gonna drown—I guess, officially, I did—anyway, when you really think you're gonna die it changes the way you think about life, about God and hope and eternity, all that stuff. But nobody ever talks about any of that at graduations—the things that really matter. It's always the same clichés about pursuing your dreams and following your heart." She contemplated that. "I was reading Ecclesiastes lately. There's a lot of stuff in there about how meaningless life is."

"Well," Ralph mumbled. "That's encouraging."

"But it doesn't end with everything being meaningless. The king who wrote it ended up saying that finding God brings meaning into every moment—I mean, that's a paraphrase. Anyway, in my speech I think I'm gonna say that as soon as we put religion out of bounds, we put the search for truth and the quest for meaning out of bounds, and that's not education, that's repression. This isn't 1980s Russia. If we're not free to speak about what matters most, we're not free at all."

"I'm not sure that'll fly so well at a public school," I said.

She gave me a small grin. "Neither am I."

"That's part of the reason you want to talk about it."

"You never know. I'll call it 'Wisdom from the King.'" She hesitated. "As long as I don't puke all over the place first."

"Any more ideas on your plans after that?" Lien-hua asked.

"After throwing up?"

"After graduating. You still thinking English or deep ecology?"

"Hmm, well, I've been considering something else, actually, ever since I lit Basque's hair on fire."

"What's that?" I said. "A career in arson?"

"Criminal science."

"Really?"

"Yeah. I like solving stuff. There's no rule you and Lien-hua get to be the only FBI agents in the family."

"It's a long road to getting accepted at the Academy, Raven. It's not just—"

"I can be a determined girl, Dad."

Well, there was no arguing with that.

"Look." Tony pointed. "The sun's gone."

He was right, and then that moment that we'd shared, we'd lived together, was gone as well.

But as it passed, a new one arrived.

87

I stood at the front of the church and watched Tessa, Lien-hua's maid of honor, walk up the aisle toward me. The prom dress hadn't weathered the Potomac very well and she wore a new dress, red and Oriental, and she looked much older than eighteen.

Her graduation speech last weekend had gone reasonably well. She threw up beforehand and that seemed to calm her nerves enough for her to get through it.

The whole speech lasted less than five minutes, but she said all the stuff she'd told us she wanted to say and I was proud of her for sharing what she believed in most, for challenging people to seek the truth and follow it wherever it takes them, even if that's away from where their own hearts want to go.

If all we do is follow our hearts, we will live small lives indeed.

Now, she ascended the steps, smiled, and then stood beside me as we waited for the bridal procession to begin.

Apparently, one of Tessa's teachers had given her a

hard time about some assignment, but when the administration found out the circumstances and that she'd actually turned it in, the guy was put on leave for the last three weeks of the school year. Tessa tried to hide her satisfaction about it from me, but I could tell how she really felt.

There hadn't been any sightings of Basque since I shot him a month and a half ago, and there was no evidence of crimes that he might have committed in the meantime. Some people at the Bureau wanted to consider his case closed, but I wasn't about to go there. If he was out there I would find him.

The hound does not give up until he has the hare.

I'd heard that Saundra Weathers had a contract to write a true crime book about what happened to her and her daughter. She was going to donate the proceeds to a foundation that helped prospective parents adopt children from Africa. To me, it was welcome news that brought a glint of redemption out of the harrowing experience she and her daughter had been through.

One other bit of national news caught my attention last week.

No one has ever escaped from the Supermax prison in Florence, Colorado, but we'd gotten word that Giovanni, a brutal killer I'd tracked down in Denver a year ago, was caught at the perimeter fence. He'd been moved to solitary confinement and would probably be there for at least five years for that escape attempt.

Nice to hear.

It seemed like there was more closure than I'd had in my career in a long time.

Closure is good.

But so is the chase.

And after my honeymoon, I knew I'd be ready to look for more hares that might have wandered into my field.

Lien-hua appeared at the back of the church and waited for the music to begin.

My heart beat faster with the renewed realization of what was about to happen—my union with the woman I loved more than life itself. We had already burned the unity candle so much since mid-April that it was only a nub. When we used this one up, we would just get another. As many as we needed.

Considering the rocky past I'd had with my brother, it wasn't especially easy choosing between him and Ralph for my best man, but in the end I'd gone with Sean—and Ralph had agreed that was the right choice.

Now I stared down the aisle at my friends and family: Lien-hua's two brothers, Nianzu and Huang-fu, were there, as well my mom and Sean's wife, Amber.

Brineesha sat beside Ralph, beaming, and holding his hand. Tony tugged at the tie his mom had made him wear. He looked as uncomfortable in it as his father looked in his.

Margaret had come; Doehring had brought his wife and two daughters; Agents Farraday and Cassidy were here, as well as Metro SWAT Commander Shaw, and any number of other officers and agents Lien-hua and I knew.

Since her father was dead and my dad never had any daughters, she'd asked him to walk her down the aisle.

Honored, he'd accepted.

And now the procession began and they started toward us.

Lien-hua tried to hide her limp, but it was still there, healing, as so many things do, with time.

Traditionally, Chinese brides wear red, and in her crimson dress she looked absolutely resplendent.

I thought back to the toast Tessa had given at the picnic on that traumatic night Lien-hua was abducted: "*Dum vivimus vivamus.*"

While we live, let us live.

Yes. This brief moment that we have, this vaporous gift reaching only the span of a heartbeat. Yes. While we live.

Let us live.

My daughter, the free-flying raven, had asked us what it would look like to live in awe of every moment.

I'm not certain, but I'm going to try to find out.

Epilogue

United States Penitentiary
Administrative Maximum Facility
Florence, Colorado

"So you were caught at the fence."

Giovanni looked across the table at his latest in a long string of lawyers. "Yes. I have a life sentence, what do I have to lose?"

His lawyer was silent. "You were still cuffed and in leg shackles. How did you—"

"We all have our secrets."

"Well, there are some things we're going to have to talk about."

"No doubt."

The gentleman filed through a sheaf of papers but said nothing. Giovanni was as patient as prison teaches you to be if you're going to remain sane, but when his lawyer didn't speak, he finally said, "What is it you'd like to cover first?"

The man pulled the paper clip off the stack of papers and set them aside, then held it up and smiled. "How to use this."

Watch for the final installment of
the Bowers Files

CHECKMATE

Summer 2014

SPECIAL THANKS TO

Matt T., Liesl H., Pam J., Dr. Todd H., Dr. John-Paul A., Kurt C., Shawn S., Darren B., Brent H., Larry K., Lori M., Trinity H., Wayne S., Ariel H., Richard A., Dr. M. Zadapa, Aneesh D., Anthony F., Atiba A., John C., Austin C., Sandra B., Tiffany Y., and Andrew Y.

Because of your insights and time this is a better book. The Bowers family will forever be indebted to you all.

Read on for an excerpt from Steven James's

OPENING MOVES

Available now from Signet Select

1

New Territories Pub
804 South Second Street
Milwaukee, Wisconsin
11:07 p.m.

Vincent Hayes stepped cautiously into the bar, trying un-successfully to still his heart, to quiet his apprehension.

He'd never done this before, never tried to pick up a man.

As he entered, two patrons who were seated at the bar—a Mexican in his mid-twenties and an older Cauca-sian who looked maybe a few years older than Vincent, around forty-five or so—turned to face him. The younger man had his hand resting gently on the middle-aged gen-tleman's knee.

Vincent gave the men a somewhat forced nod, they smiled a bit, then turned to gaze into each other's eyes again and went back to their conversation—perhaps a joke that the Mexican was telling, because Vincent heard the other man chuckle as he passed by and then took in the rest of the bar.

Country music played. Nondescript. Some singer he

didn't recognize. The neon beer signs and dim overheads did little to illuminate the nook and crannied pub. Vincent scanned the tables looking for the right kind of man—young, athletic, but not too muscular. The drugs he was carrying were potent, but muscle mass might diminish their effect. Maybe. He wasn't sure. He'd never used the drugs before, but tonight he couldn't risk taking the chance that the man would awaken before he was done with him.

He was looking for a black man.

All around him in the dim light, men stood talking. Most were gathered in groups of two or three. Very few single guys. Vincent was brawny and cut an impressive figure that turned a few heads, but none that looked promising.

Even though he wanted to be alert so he wouldn't make a mistake, he also needed something strong to take the edge off, to help anesthetize his inhibitions. Vincent took a seat at the bar and ordered a vodka.

Yes, yes, of course he was nervous. But there was also adrenaline there. Anxiety churning around violently beneath the surge of apprehension.

Keep your cool. This is not a time to make some kind of stupid mistake.

So far he hadn't seen anyone who fit the bill. Some were too old. A few younger couples were moving in time to the music on the dance floor on the far side of the bar. No single African-American like he was looking for.

He felt the brush of movement against his arm. A slim white guy who didn't look old enough to be here legally drew up a barstool. "Waiting for someone?" His voice was melodic and inviting. Charming might be a better word for it.

Yes, he was the right age, but he was the wrong race. Vincent gave him only a momentary glance. He didn't want to be rude or draw attention, but he didn't want to lead him on either.

"Um. Yes."

"Shame."

Vincent downed half of his vodka.

"Lucky guy," the man said under his breath, but, almost certainly on purpose, loud enough for Vincent to hear.

Get out of here. Try another bar. Already too many people have seen you in here.

Although it was supposed to happen at this bar, Vincent realized it was more important for it to happen than where it did.

"Sorry," he mumbled. He laid some cash beside his unfinished drink, then stood to leave. He'd taken two steps toward the door when he saw the type of man he was looking for: an athletic African-American, sitting alone in the booth near the narrow hallway to the restrooms.

Just like the young man who'd taken a seat beside Vincent a moment ago, this guy looked on the shy side of twenty-one, but Vincent guessed that carding people wasn't exactly at the top of the management's priority list.

He had a beer bottle in front of him, a Lienenkugel's. Almost empty. Vincent ordered two more from the bartender, excused himself from the guy who'd been coming on to him, and carried the two beers toward the booth.

Just get him to the minivan. You're bigger. You can easily overpower him in there.

As Vincent crossed the room, he surreptitiously

dropped the two pills into one of the bottles and gently swirled them to the bottom.

When he was halfway to the booth, the young black man looked his way.

Vincent smiled, then, nervous, dropped his gaze.

You can do this; come on, you can do this.

He'd already decided he would cuff him as soon as he got him into the van. Hopefully, he'd be too drugged to fight much or call for help, but Vincent had a gag and duct tape waiting just in case. If he wasn't able to get him to take off his clothes before he cuffed him, he would strip the guy, cutting off his shirt and jeans with the fabric shears when he was done.

And then move forward with things from there.

Almost to the booth now, he waited for the man to say something, but when he didn't, Vincent spoke, trying out the same line the guy had used on him a few moments earlier. "Waiting for someone?"

The black man—kid, really—looked his way, wide-eyed. Wet his lips slightly. "I saw Mark with you. That what he asked you?"

Vincent set down the drinks. "Busted."

"He needs to expand his repertoire."

"I guess I do too."

The young man eyed the beers, and said demurely, "One of those for me?"

Vincent slid the drugged beer toward him, smiled again, and took a seat.

The guy offered Vincent a soft nod, accepted the drink, and held out his hand palm down, a diminutive handshake. "I'm Lionel."

"Vincent." He shook Lionel's hand.

"Mmm. Vincent." It almost sounded like Lionel was

purring. "Very European." His eyes gleamed. "A shade mysterious." He took a sip of his beer. "I haven't seen you here before, Vincent."

"I'm . . ." Vincent couldn't think of anything clever or witty to say. "Well, I . . . This is my first time."

"Your first time, what? Here?"

He hesitated. "Yes."

"Or your first time. Period?"

"Yes. My first time. Period."

Lionel looked at him as if he'd just said something humorous. "You haven't done this before. Ever?"

"No." Vincent took a drink as a way of hiding, but also of, hopefully, encouraging the young man to drink his beer as well.

It worked.

When Lionel had finished the swig, his eyes drifted toward Vincent's left hand. Toward his wedding ring.

"You're married."

"Yes."

"Why tonight? Why did you come tonight? Is she out of town?"

The last thing Vincent wanted to do right now was talk about Colleen. "Yes," he said, lying. "Visiting her parents."

"And you decided to try something a little different? For a change?"

"To step out on a limb. Yes." His heart was beating. Thinking about Colleen made all of this harder.

Vincent took another sip from his drink. So did Lionel.

"I don't live far from here," Vincent offered, and then immediately realized that it was much too forward. On the other hand, if his suspicions were right, Lionel was working the place, looking for payment for his companionship, and wasting a lot of time on formalities wouldn't serve either of their interests.

"Really? Where?"

"Not far."

A wink. "Staying mysterious, are we?"

Vincent had no idea how to respond. "I really . . . I'm not sure how to say this. Um, are you, well, are you—"

Lionel laid his hand gently on Vincent's forearm. "I can be whatever you want me to be, Vincent."

It was a long moment before he removed his hand.

"Okay." Vincent said.

Lionel smiled softly. "Okay."

Another swig.

And another.

And although Vincent was anxious to get going, he realized he needed a little time for the drugs to work, so he answered Lionel's questions about where he'd gone to college, UW–La Crosse, and what he did for a living, managed a PR firm. In response, Lionel mentioned that he had a theater degree from DePaul and was an actor "between jobs."

As the minutes passed, the drugs and alcohol started to have the desired effect.

"Lionel?"

"Um-hmm." His voice was wavering, unfocused.

"Do you want to leave?"

"Your place is close?" he mumbled.

"Yes. Let's get you to the car."

No response, just a bleary nod.

So Vincent helped Lionel to his feet and supported him on the way to the door.

2

Apparently, two men leaving this bar—with one of them evidently drunk—was not too out of the ordinary. Nobody paid much attention to them as they left the building.

Vincent could see his breath as he crossed the sidewalk, but the November night felt brisk rather than icy cold and that would be good for Lionel, for what Vincent had in mind for him.

Earlier, Vincent had taken the backseats out of his minivan and it wasn't difficult to help Lionel into the vehicle. Once they were inside, he closed the door and retrieved the handcuffs.

He hoped Lionel wouldn't struggle, but Vincent had been a linebacker in college, still worked out four or five days a week, and was willing to get physical, if that's what it took.

Vincent began to unzip Lionel's jacket.

"What are you . . . ?" Lionel's words were blurred, confused.

"We need to get you out of these clothes."

"I thought we . . . were going . . . to your place."

"Plans have changed." He tugged off Lionel's coat.

Lionel eyed the handcuffs. A look that went past confusion and dipped into fear crossed his face and he tried to wrestle free. He was squirrelly and hard to hold on to, and Vincent was forced to do something he hadn't intended to do—punch him in the face. Lionel crumpled to the floor. "What the—?"

Vincent cuffed his left wrist and when Lionel tried to get up again, Vincent grabbed his head and smacked it hard against the floor of the van. "Don't fight. It'll make it worse."

"No—"

This wasn't going well, not well at all.

Vincent bent over him. "Be quiet, Lionel, or I'll have to do that again. I don't want to, but if I—"

"Help!" Lionel rolled to his side, tried to scramble toward the door, but Vincent snagged his left arm, twisted it behind his back, brought the right arm around as well and cuffed the wrists together. Once he was assured that Lionel wasn't going anywhere, he stuffed a cloth into his mouth and wrapped a few rounds of duct tape around his head to hold it in place. Lionel tried to shake free, to cry out for help, but could hardly make any sound at all.

Vincent hurried to the driver's seat and started the engine.

Get away from the bar. You need to get away from here. Right now.

Sweating, shaking, Vincent turned the key and the engine came to life. He scanned the street, the sidewalks. A couple of men had just left the bar but were headed in the opposite direction and weren't looking at the van. Vincent heard the muffled sound of Lionel trying to call for help, but it wasn't nearly loud enough for the men outside to hear.

The drugs, they should have knocked him out by now.

Vincent lurched the van onto the street too fast, his heart racing, his mouth dry.

Easy, don't get pulled over. Do not get pulled over.

Eight blocks away he paused in a deserted parking lot, turned off the headlights, and let the engine idle; then he returned to the back of the minivan. The drugs were taking their toll on Lionel. He lay on the floor, barely conscious.

Quickly, Vincent removed Lionel's shoes, then his socks, then his pants and underwear. The fight had gone out of him and he didn't resist, just stared vacantly at the roof of the minivan.

Using fabric shears, Vincent cut a long slit up each sleeve of Lionel's sweater. He removed it and then went to work on his undershirt.

A few moments later Lionel lay naked and cuffed in the van.

"I didn't want things to go like this," Vincent told him.

Lionel rolled weakly onto his side, curling himself into a fetal position.

Vincent returned to the driver's seat and guided the van to North Twenty-fifth Street, to the alley that ran between a ramshackle two-story house and an empty lot that was surrounded by a rusted six-foot-high chain-link fence. Two stout, brick apartment buildings lay just to the left of the fenced-in lot. The alley was empty. No one on the sidewalk that led past it. No traffic.

However, half a dozen cars were parked along the alley's side of the street, leaving room for snowplows to drive along the other side if the weather took a turn for the worse. Vincent realized it was good that there was a string of cars already there by the curb. It would make his van less conspicuous.

He parked and crawled into the back. "Okay, I'm taking off the gag. But don't cry out or I'll have to hit you again, and I really don't want to do that."

Lionel, if he understood, did not respond. Just lay still and submissive.

Using the shears again, Vincent cut off the tape, tugged it free, and removed the gag. Then he opened the door to the van. "Go," he commanded Lionel. "Get out."

At last Lionel looked at him.

"Go on." He swung Lionel's feet around so they were sticking out the door. "Get out of the van."

Lionel tried to leave on his own, but collapsed onto the sidewalk with a low moan.

Get away, Vincent. You have to get away. This is close enough.

But then the reality: *No! They need to find him in the alley. Or else—*

He hadn't wanted to do this, but now he got out and, supporting Lionel, led him fifty feet into the alley, left him standing unsteadily, but on his own, then hustled back to the vehicle.

But he didn't leave yet.

Once inside the van, he tried to calm himself. He looked around. Saw nothing suspicious. No pedestrians. No movement on the street. Because of the vacant lot beside the alley, Lionel was still clearly visible from the road.

Nervously gripping the keys that he'd left in the ignition, Vincent took a few seconds to catch his breath.

The brisk air seemed to be bringing Lionel out of the drug-induced stupor. He stumbled across the alley, eventually leaning for support against a telephone pole by the fence encircling the lot.

Vincent was about to pull into the street when he saw a police cruiser round the corner and come prowling toward him. Heart hammering, he glanced toward Lionel one last time and saw him drop heavily to the ground beside the telephone pole.

From there he would be visible to the cops if they looked down the alley.

Vincent ducked his head down and leaned across the front seat so he'd be out of sight. An anonymous, empty minivan on a quiet, anonymous street. Well, maybe not an anonymous street, but—

He didn't think the cops had seen him, but it was possible—

No, no, no. You cannot get caught!

The squad's headlights swept across the road, through the windshield of Vincent's van, then toward the alley, toward Lionel.

They see him. They have to see him by now!

The movement of the headlights stopped and Vincent heard one of the police car doors slam shut. Then the other.

Get out of here. If you're caught, everything will fall apart. You can't let that happen. There's too much—

"Hey!" one of the cops yelled to Lionel. "Are you al-right?"

Vincent's heart slammed, hammered in his chest.

There was no indication yet that they'd taken note of his van.

They're going to check on him. You can get out of here when they do. You need to go.

Drive.

No, they would follow him. He knew they would. At least one of them would.

Run. You need to run.

Maybe. Yes, leave the van here.

His head was still low, but he heard more shouting from the cops and pictured them hurrying toward Lionel. If they hadn't already started to, in a few seconds they would scan the area. Then they would search the nearest vehicles one at a time. They would catch him if he stayed where he was and follow him if he tried to drive away.

Now. It has to be now. On foot.

Slowly, Vincent edged his head up, gazed toward the alley, and saw both cops leaning over Lionel.

This was it. In a moment they would start looking for anything suspicious. Vincent silently opened his door and slipped onto the street, keeping the minivan between him and the cops. Afraid the door might alert them, he didn't click it shut all the way. No noise.

A dog barked in a yard a few houses away, on the other side of the alley. The cops turned their attention to the sound: "Check it out," one of them said to his partner. While the officers were momentarily distracted, Vincent scurried fifteen feet farther down the road and crouched behind another car.

It would be easier from here. The angle was wrong for the cops to see him. The one who knelt beside Lionel was talking into his radio now, calling for backup.

Go.

Swiftly and without a sound, Vincent went for the next car.

Beyond that there weren't any more vehicles close enough to hide behind, and just as he was wondering if he should try waiting it out here for a few minutes, he heard the sirens. More cops were already on the way.

No, if he stayed here, they'd find him. He either

needed to get behind the nearest apartment, which was about twenty-five feet away—but that meant traversing the lawn in plain sight—or make it to the other side of the road and hope the parked cars would block the view as he crossed the street. Then he could disappear into the neighborhood on the next block over.

Which was better?

Hard to say.

Hard to say.

Maybe crossing the road. If he stayed low enough, the cars would at least partially block the view. Less chance of being seen.

Yes, that would work, he could make it. He had to.

The vague sound of distant traffic floated through the chilly night. Nearby, more dogs were joining in barking, but Vincent tried to block all that out.

He took a breath and went for it, dashing across the road as swiftly as he could, but just as he reached the far curb, he heard one of the cops yell, "Stop! Police!"

Go!

As fast as he could, Vincent sprinted into the dark channel between the two houses in front of him.

A quick glance back told him that the cop was in pursuit. Looking forward again, Vincent managed to duck just in time to avoid a clothesline strung up in someone's backyard. He came to a waist-high wooden fence, scrambled over it, and bolted past a driveway and through the night, weaving between the houses to try to lose the cop.

"Stop right there!" the officer yelled. Amazingly, he sounded like he was gaining on him. He wasn't out of breath and it was the voice of a guy who knew he was going to take you down.

But Vincent didn't stop running, there was too much

at stake. He rounded another house. If he could just stay out of sight, just—he dodged an abandoned tricycle and barely missed slamming into a jon boat stationed on its rusted trailer beside the home—just get to the next street—

Though he was already almost two blocks from the alley where he'd left Lionel, he could see the flicker dance of the blue-red-blue lights of more squads driving toward the scene.

Vincent angled left and flew past a tumbledown duplex. He didn't see the cop anymore and figured he must have lost him somewhere between the last two houses. He kept running.

By now, some of the porch lights in the neighborhood were snapping on as more people woke up from the shouting, the yelping dogs, the police sirens.

Vincent whipped around the corner of a house.

And almost ran into the cop, a tall scruffy guy, who stood in front of him with his gun raised. "Do not move."

How did he get—?

"Hands up!"

Vincent raised his hands. He needed to get away, there was no other option. "Officer, I'm not—"

"On your knees. Do it."

The guy looked like an athlete. Vincent calculated whether or not he could take him. It might not be easy.

Go for the gun.

That would be tight too. But he couldn't risk being taken in. "Please, Officer, I need to—"

"Now." The cop leveled the gun at his chest.

Desperation swallowed everything. This was it. He had to go for it, had to risk it, had to act now, before more officers got here. He started to bend down as if he were obeying the officer, but then used his bent knee to propel himself forward and lunge for the gun.

Years of college football and weight lifting had made Vincent quick and tough and not afraid to mix things up. He went hard at the cop, snagging his hand and knocking the gun away. Then he balled up a fist and aimed a blow at the officer's kidney, but the guy blocked it just in time.

He deftly grabbed Vincent's wrist, twisting it to control him.

Countering, Vincent threw a hard hook with his other fist, connected solidly with the guy's jaw, but that didn't stop him—he drove his shoulder into Vincent's chest and slammed him to the ground.

Vincent tried to wrestle free but the cop was wiry and strong, and as he rolled to get away, he felt his arm being wrenched behind him to subdue him. Vincent strained fiercely to get away, but the cop twisted his arm more, toward the breaking point.

"No!" Vincent couldn't help but yell. If he didn't get away—

But then he was cuffed and the officer was pinning him down with his knee, calling for backup. "Do not move," he told Vincent.

"You don't understand—"

"Quiet," the officer said. "This is Detective Bowers." He was talking into his radio. "I'm on the southeast corner of Twenty-sixth and Wells. I have the suspect."

"Please," Vincent gasped. "He has her. If you don't let me go, he's going to kill her. You can't let that maniac kill my wife!"

ALSO AVAILABLE
from

Steven James

OPENING MOVES

Milwaukee, 1997. In a city still reeling from the crimes of Jeffrey Dahmer, a series of gruesome kidnappings and mutilations haunt authorities. Local cops think a Dahmer copycat is on the loose. But Patrick Bowers, working as a homicide detective, sees from the timing and location of the crimes that this is not a copycat at all, but a killer with an entirely different agenda.

"*Opening Moves* is a mesmerizing read."
—Michael Connolly,
New York Times bestselling author of *The Lincoln Lawyer*

Look for
The Bishop
The Knight
The Rook
The Pawn

Available wherever books are sold or at
penguin.com

S0478